Carley's Song

Carley's Song

BOOK II

PATRICIA SPRINKLE

BellaRosaBooks
ROCK HILL, SOUTH CAROLINA

CARLEY'S SONG
ISBN 978-1-933523-10-1
2008 Reprint Edition by Bella Rosa Books

Previously Published in the U.S.A. by Zondervan Publishing House. First paperback edition: October 2001, ISBN: 0-310-22993-6.

Interior design by Todd Sprague

Printed in the United States of America on acid-free paper.

BellaRosaBooks and logo are trademarks of Bella Rosa Books

10 9 8 7 6 5 4 3 2 1

Acknowledgments

Thanks

to Margie Wessels and her fine staff at the Iredell County Public Library for answering all my questions,

to Chester and Maxine Middlesworth for steering me in so many right directions,

to Mac Lackey for help with the history of Iredell County,

to Delaine DeHainaut for information about what it was like to be a Statesville teenager in 1950,

to Elmer and Juanita Lagg for information about former U.S. Army Air Corps bomber squadrons and what happened to them and their families during the Korean conflict,

to Lori German, firefighter, who described fires so vividly, I nearly collapsed from smoke inhalation,

to Doug Hasty at Florida International University, who went an extra mile getting newspapers I needed from Interlibrary Loan,

to Hali Earwood for her map,

and to Ann Bass, who was nice enough not only to read the final version but to act as if it were an honor.

Most of all, thanks to my dear husband, Bob, for hours of listening, for giving good suggestions when I asked for them, and for managing not to give any when I didn't.

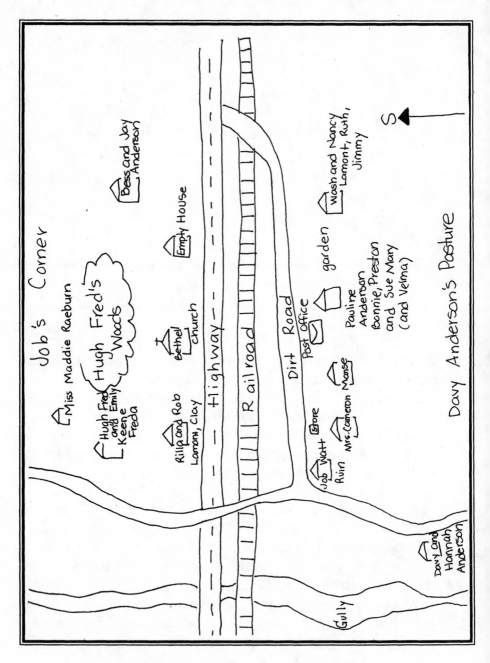

Carley's Map of Job's Corner

BOOK II

Carley's Song

⚜

Prelude

Dear Carley,

Your book about the stuff in Mama's Remember Box[1] brought back lots of memories from Job's Corner. I had forgotten Maggie, and Velma—how could I ever forget Velma?—and all about drawing bunnies and making string houses in Sue Mary's yard. Even knowing now about the bad doesn't take away the good that was there. Last night I laid awake remembering how much I loved my lighthouse room.

But I don't remember some of those people. Did they move away? What else did I miss when I was very small? I think there are things you still haven't told me. Like what you did up in your room all those times you wouldn't let me in.

I remember one funny thing you used to do—walk around pretending you were a television reporter telling them all about our lives. What was it you called it? Something like *Windows without Curtains?*

Write more, Carley Cousin. Nice stories this time. And don't make me talk funny!

Love,
Abby

---

1 *The Remember Box* by Patricia Sprinkle

Dear Abby,

Ungrateful wretch! As if writing a book were something one did between breakfast and lunch, and I could pull up memories at will.

Yet writing that first book did dredge up ghosts long buried of people I had forgotten, whose stories I have not told. Some returned to Job's Corner our second summer's end, that late afternoon hour of the year when all beasts become restless and turn toward home. See, just thinking about them has made me poetic!

Those newcomers had a lot to do with what I was doing up in my room that second year in Job's Corner, after I asked for a key to my door and started locking you out. I was twelve years old, trying my best to understand love. And truth. And grown-ups.

Shall I tell you about that? If I do, you must remember that people act—and talk—the way they choose. All I can do is tell what I saw and heard. Don't blame me if everything I write isn't nice.

Love,
Carley

P.S. It wasn't *Windows without Curtains*; it was *Unshaded Windows* . . .

Part I

All Ye Who Are Weary, Come Home ...

Late Summer 1950

Chapter 1

Maddie Raeburn caused quite a stir when she showed up in Job's Corner in the middle of Hannah Anderson's tray-making party. She approached the Anderson farmhouse just before noon that August Saturday morning, trailing a noble funnel of North Carolina dust—deep iron-red powder with a hint of blue, the aristocracy of red dirt. Maddie was an aristocrat, too—in her own way.

When she arrived, she found a yardful of women almost worn out, having spent the entire morning at long tables under Aunt Hannah's black walnut trees, learning how to make trays from large discs of aluminum. A home demonstration agent named Mrs. Parsons had driven five miles from Statesville to teach the class, and nearly forty women from Bethel Presbyterian Church had come, plus me and Freda Keene. Now we'd finally finished working and were standing in what little shade there was at noon, shooing flies and licking salt from our sweaty upper lips, waiting for Mrs. Parsons to award ribbons so we could set out the food. At age twelve, I was honored to be there and determined to do justice to everything those ladies had brought.

Mrs. Parsons had just put the blue ribbon on Aunt Hannah's tray of roses—which we all agreed was the best by far—and picked up the red ribbon uncertainly. "Our nominations for second place are Kate Whitfield's fruit and Emily Keene's tiger lilies."

Aunt Kate's was better. She'd put little bits of shading on her peach, apple, and grapes to make them look really round, while Miss Emily's stencil had slipped, so her lilies looked more like tulips. But I knew Miss Emily would get more votes. Uncle Stephen might be everybody's preacher, but Hugh Fred Keene owned the Sitwell Chair Factory and was clerk of our church session, which is what Presbyterians call the group of elders who make all the rules. For southern Presbyterians in 1950, clerk of session was right up there next to God.

"First, all votes for—" The home demonstration agent waved the red ribbon over Aunt Kate's tray. Nobody paid her a speck of attention. We'd all turned to stare across Uncle Davy's hayfield at a white car barreling down the Andersons' dirt road, followed by a long red tornado.

Voices rose in question and answer.

"Law, who on earth could that be?"

"Looks like a Cadillac."

"Must be one of Hannah's rich friends."

Nobody we knew drove Cadillacs. Even Mr. Keene just drove a new gray Hudson.

Aunt Hannah (my honorary aunt, not blood kin like Aunt Kate) shaded her eyes with a big, thick hand. "Maybe President Truman coming to dinner."

Everybody laughed. "If it is," somebody joked at a far table, "he'll turn around in your drive." Everybody laughed again, but there was an edge to the laughs.

Seeing Aunt Kate's puzzled look, a woman explained. "He was supposed to come here five years ago but changed his mind at the last minute—after we'd gone to all the trouble of draping bunting from every blessed building in town and hanging flags all over Center Street. Statesville"—she said *Staichville*, like anybody born there—"hasn't quite got over it yet."

They never quite would.

"Maybe he wasn't offered Hannah's ham biscuits back then," someone else suggested. "Could be he's heard about 'em since and decided to come."

I almost believed them. Aunt Hannah wasn't your ordinary farmer's wife. Uncle Stephen claimed she knew and eventually fed everybody in the South. A lot of important people—state senators, company presidents and their wives, even one moderator of the Presbyterian General Assembly—came to eat at her mahogany table and sleep in her four-poster guest bed.

As you may have guessed, her house wasn't a typical farmhouse either; although I'd gotten so used to it, I generally considered it normal and all other farmhouses inferior. Nestled in a grove of tall cedars and wide black walnuts, it was built in the style I'd later learn to call plantation plain, with the living room, hall, and one bedroom across the front, the dining room, kitchen, and storerooms strung along the back to make a T, and five extra bedrooms upstairs, where Uncle Davy and his brothers and sisters used to sleep. But she'd made Uncle Davy paint it shining white with dark green shutters that exactly matched the roof. She'd planted flower beds all over the yard, and she'd filled the house with antiques she claimed to have picked up here and there. All her public rooms gleamed with fine walnut and mahogany, polished silver, and the jewel colors of Oriental rugs. It always smelled of lemon polish, lavender, and Elizabeth Arden bath powder.

The side porch nearest the driveway had six big white rockers and thirty-two African violets in pots. Her front porch had a green swing and a white woven hammock and was hung that summer with basket creations of begonias in outlandish new shades like peach and tangerine. Only the porch on the far side of the kitchen—the one that faced the pasture and was called the back porch—was cluttered with feeding buckets, pasture shoes, and rump-sprung chairs for shucking corn or shelling peas.

On warm weekends people drove forty miles from Charlotte to admire the Andersons' yard, sit on their porch, and drink sweet tea with pineapple and lemon juice served in pastel aluminum glasses so cold they dripped sweat.

Somebody seemed in a powerful hurry to get there that August Saturday morning.

The car turned into the gravel drive too fast and skidded to a stop with a spurt of rocks, its front bumper a few inches short of Uncle Davy's favorite walnut — the one his granddaddy planted when he built the house.

"Is it a party?" a woman called through the open window. "Am I too late?" She pulled off sunglasses as she threw open her door. Nobody said a word as she climbed out, graceful as a panther. If movie stars were real people, she could have been one.

Sunlight streamed through the walnut branches and lit her yellow hair like a candle. It was cut short and waved all over her head. Her black-and-white striped dress wrapped around her neck but left her shoulders and entire back bare. Her full skirt swirled about her knees as she stepped daintily across the gravel driveway in bright red sandals. Her toenails and fingernails were bright red, too, to match her mouth, which curved in a teasing smile. Behind long, black lashes, her eyes danced, pieces of bright sky fallen to earth. "Remember me?"

I'd never seen her before but my stomach quivered. I determined right then to grow up looking exactly like that. At twelve I still believed such things were possible.

Excited voices erupted around me.

"Maddie Lou!"

"Bless your heart, child, nobody told us you were coming home."

"When did you get here?"

"Emily, did you know she was coming?"

Miss Emily pressed one thin hand to her throat. "No, I . . ."

Her daughter Freda—pronounced *Fred-da* because she was named for Mr. Hugh Fred—dashed across the grass and flung her arms around the woman's neck. "Aunt Maddie Lou! I'm so *glad* to see you!"

Women streamed after Freda around the sawhorse tables and across the soft green grass, nearly trampling Aunt Hannah's pink petunias in their eagerness to circle and hug the newcomer.

"What you doin' home?"

"Get tired of the big city?"

"Just look at you, drivin' a Cadillac!"

Their clucking rivaled Aunt Hannah's hens at feeding time.

Seemed to me if that woman was Miss Emily's sister, God had not dealt equally with them. She was curvy and graceful, Miss Emily a skeleton with skin. Both had yellow hair, but Miss Emily's was a brassy yellow that Aunt Kate said she got at the beauty parlor. It was also straight as a stick, a pageboy with not one hair out of place. She always wore so much rouge and lipstick that her face was bright as a flower, but after working all morning in the heat, her petals were blurred around the edges.

The newcomer looked fresh as an early-morning magnolia. She let the crowd of chattering women steer her toward the rest of us over by the tables.

"How long you gonna be in North Carolina, Maddie Lou?" one woman asked.

She held up one hand to stop them. "Just Maddie, please. I've dropped the Lou." Then she flung up her arms and raised her face to the sky. "Beautiful North Carolina! It's so *good* to be home!" I particularly noticed her armpits, since my own were beginning to sprout occasional itchy hairs. Hers were smooth as baby John's.

"Where's that handsome husband of yours?" The booming voice was our jolly next-door neighbor, Pauline Anderson, a heavy, tall woman with a bush of brown hair and a fat, flushed face. A widow, Miss Pauline preferred men to women any day.

The new woman flipped her hand like he didn't matter. "Back in Atlanta, where he belongs." She wrinkled her nose and teased, "What you all been doing? You look just like a bunch of cotton pickers."

The world came to a straggling, embarrassed halt.

❈

Until then we'd had a spectacular morning. For three hours, with coaching from Mrs. Parsons, we had scalloped edges with pliers, painted designs with tar, and etched the untarred parts with acid.

I was honored to be there. Children were not invited. My cousin Abby, five, had watched us leave with her lower lip poked out two inches.

It was hot, of course—what southern summer day is not? But the air was blue and gold and fragrant with new-mown grass, fresh-baled hay, and the earthy must of boxwoods. A steady breeze and puffy white clouds spared us the worst of the heat. And my bare, grubby feet were floating two inches above the grass because I was working beside Freda Keene, one year older and centuries more glamorous than I. Freda had glossy black ringlets instead of thin tan hair, dark brown eyes instead of blue ones hidden by glasses, and fingernails she got to paint a delicate pink. Freda lived not in a church manse, where everybody ran in and out all day, but in a big hilltop mansion with stately white columns out front, where nobody went unless invited.

Freda always dressed like a princess. She'd come to make trays in a blue voile sundress and clean white sandals that showed her toenails, which were painted to match her fingernails.

"I tried to make her wear something old," Miss Emily had said in a plaintive voice when they climbed out of her green Studebaker, "but she always wants to look nice."

Freda huffed impatiently. "I've outgrown this old thing." She thrust out her chest to the other women. "See how tight it's getting?" Sure enough, the dress strained over soft mounds of budding bosoms. She turned to me. "Aren't mothers awful?" Then she pressed three fingers to her mouth. "Oh, Carley, I'm sorry."

"It's okay." It wasn't her fault Mama died in the big polio epidemic the year before. A lot of people died—men, women, and children. That was why I now lived with Aunt Kate and Uncle Stephen. But I had to turn away to hide the quick tears that still filled my eyes at any unexpected mention of Mama.

"Won't you girls come work with me?" Aunt Hannah suggested quickly.

Freda caught my hand and drew me with her. "We'd love to, Aunt Hannah."

Aunt Hannah and Uncle Davy were among those rare saints who genuinely love children. They left behind them generations of unrelated people who still feel kin to one another because we were all their children. When we occasionally meet, even now we laugh at how she talked a blue streak without pausing for breath, how he never hurried for anything, how she terrified us with her driving, how he constantly ate desserts and never gained a pound while she insisted she gained five by smelling a cake. Then we stop and grow silent and our smiles twist, because no matter how long we live, we never get over missing them.

That day, before Aunt Hannah started her own tray, she helped me draw what I wanted on mine: Big Mama's house, where I grew up, complete with the two cedars out front. The roofline was trickier than I expected, but we finally got it right.

Freda was using a stencil of horses, except she didn't want to do them the way Aunt Hannah and the home demonstration agent suggested. "I know what I want," she insisted, painting tar over all the separating lines.

While she painted, she told me not to worry about seventh grade. "It's not hard. I got all A's." She also said she had a new piano piece. "It's called *Für Elise*, with funny little dots over the *u*. It's hard but simply beautiful."

I spoke without thinking. "I learned that piece!" Playing the piano was one of the few things I did fairly well, and Freda and I both had the same teacher, her great-aunt Rilla.

She frowned, puzzled. "You must have had an easier version."

I bobbed my head in humbled agreement. "Of *course*."

"Hey, Carley," Miss Pauline called down the table, "you've got as much tar on your face as on your tray. If you get any on your skirt, get it on the navy, not on the white polka dots. That way it won't show so bad." Her laugh boomed into the open sky.

"Those aren't polka dots," I informed her. "Uncle Stephen threw it in a bleach wash by mistake. If I cover them with tar, maybe I can wear it to school again." I deliberately painted over one white spot.

Everybody laughed, but I could have bitten my tongue when one woman inquired in a scandalized squeak, "Mr. Whitfield does laundry?" and Miss Pauline replied in a hoarse whisper, "It's because she teaches."

"I beat Carley!" Miss Emily exclaimed. She pointed to a wide tar streak on her red gingham chest. "I get the prize for Most Tarred." She drawled it, making it sound like some people said *tired*. Everybody laughed again, but Miss Emily never had to do a lick of work. She had Miranda, a full-time maid.

Of course, Miss Pauline never did any work either, if she could help it, but she just had her stepdaughter Bonnie.

Another woman held up her skirt, full of acid burns. "Do I win the Holiest Award?"

"Zorro was here," joked a third, pointing to a big *Z* of tar on the front of her overalls. "Just don't tell my husband."

Everybody roared except Miss Nancy Lamont, whose long nose was always ready to sniff at something. "My children don't watch those TV westerns." The truth was, her precious Ruthie and Jimmy watched westerns every afternoon with Miss Pauline's son, Preston, but I didn't tell her. Miss Nancy didn't take kindly to criticism of her children.

"I'd give her the Fowlest Award," Freda whispered in my ear. "Doesn't she look just like a hen in that brown shirt?" I stifled a giggle, because Miss Nancy had swiveled her sharp beak and beady black eyes in our direction.

"What'd you say?" she demanded.

Before we could reply, Aunt Hannah wiped perspiration from her plump, flushed face. "I think we need some iced tea. I'm beginning to feel the heat." She was a tall, stout woman who wore hair nets over her grizzled hair, corsets even under her housedresses, and lace-up, square-heeled shoes all her life.

Still talking, she lumbered toward her kitchen, where her cook, Janey Lou, and Miss Emily's Miranda were resting until it was time to carry out the chicken, deviled eggs, ham biscuits, and all those new recipes women had tried.

As Mrs. Parsons cruised up and down the tables, I pointed to two kittens on a small tray Aunt Hannah was making now that she'd finished her big one with roses. "Don't those kittens look real enough to meow?"

Being one of those grown-ups who prefers to talk to adults, she spoke to Aunt Kate instead of me. "Hannah has incredible talent. She won a college scholarship to a New York art school and had her trunk all packed when her daddy fell over with a heart attack. She unpacked that trunk and worked the next ten years putting her younger sister and brother through college, but I hope she gets a chance to study with Leonardo da Vinci in heaven. Nobody deserves it more."

"You think maybe we'll get a chance to continue developing our talents forever?" Aunt Kate sounded like she was rolling the notion around in her mind.

Miss Nancy puffed up like an outraged broody. "That's not what the Bible says. It says if we don't use a talent, we lose it. Isn't that right, Mrs. Whitfield?"

Aunt Kate took a breath like she planned to count to at least fifty before she spoke. "That's right, Nancy, that's what it says. Carley, shall we go help Hannah carry out the tea?" As we reached the porch, though, she muttered softly, "Could I be, just *once*, Kate-Who-Thinks instead of Mrs.-Whitfield-the-Preacher's-Wife? Is that too much to ask?"

It was almost dinnertime before we finished our trays—but of course where we lived, dinnertime was noon.

"Just put your scraps in there." Aunt Hannah pointed to a rusty fifty-gallon oil drum. "Davy will take it to the gully later this afternoon." One of the blessings of the South was that every community had at least one gully, product of erosion and perfect for garbage. Nobody worried about whether it was in their neighborhood. A gully was where God put it. God put ours down behind the back pasture where Uncle Davy kept his dairy cows.

When the tables were clear, Mrs. Parsons rapped on one. "Before we eat, let's vote on the three best trays."

That's what we were doing when Maddie Raeburn arrived, cool and glamorous, to find the women of Job's Corner dressed like hobos, streaked with tar, and wilted by heat.

Chapter 2

A few women brushed themselves like they hoped a fairy godmother would magically change them into decent clothes. Aunt Kate fumbled her grass-stained feet under the table for her old loafers. "I can't meet somebody looking like this!" Aunt Kate wasn't quite as pretty as her sister, my mama, had been, but men often turned to look at her twice. She had deep auburn hair that curled naturally, a lovely nose, green eyes beneath straight dark brows, and curves just like Ava Gardner's. Today, though, her yellow sundress was stained where baby John had thrown up chocolate milk, and her hair was sweaty and pinned behind her ears.

Aunt Hannah and I were the only people there who didn't care how we looked. I figured that glamorous stranger wasn't going to break her neck noticing me, and Aunt Hannah's big heart would never be fazed by tar streaks, acid holes, or a dress so raggedy it would put her hens off their laying. She pushed her way through the flock of women and held out her arms. "Give me a hug, old dear. When did you get back? It's been too long—"

"Aunt Hannah!" The woman disappeared in her large embrace. "It's so good to be home. And your place is gorgeous, as usual. Look at those African violets!" Sure enough, Aunt Hannah's violets on the porch made a spectacular display.

"We're glad to have you back." Aunt Hannah let her go and stepped back. "Prettier than ever." She put one hand at the stranger's waist and turned her our way. "I don't think you've met Mrs. Whitfield, our new preacher's wife. She and her husband just moved here last year."

I stepped behind Aunt Kate in time to see her back stiffen. The other woman pulled away. "I don't want to bother you all when you're so busy. I just wanted to say a quick hello—" She might as well have tried to stop a bulldozer. Aunt Hannah was bound and determined to introduce her to Aunt Kate.

They stood face to face, almost the same height. I knew Aunt Kate was wishing her hair was clean and styled instead of pinned behind her ears with bobby pins, and that she'd not taken Aunt Hannah quite so literally about wearing her oldest dress. But what puzzled me was, the other woman seemed nervous about meeting Aunt Kate.

Nobody said anything. The two women reminded me of wild kittens that often circled Aunt Hannah's big blue hydrangea, each waiting for the other to make a first move.

Aunt Kate finally spoke. "Glad to meet you. I'm Kate."

"I'm Maddie. Maddie Raeburn," the woman said, offering her hand.

"My hand's too dirty to shake," Aunt Kate admitted with an embarrassed smile.

Aunt Hannah rushed in breathlessly. "Maddie Lou is Hugh Fred's little sister."

I peeped around Aunt Kate's shoulder. Mr. Hugh Fred Keene was as handsome as this woman was pretty, but our science book had said a man with dark hair and eyes would have a sister with dark hair and eyes, too. Aunt Kate's voice mirrored my own surprise. "Hugh Fred's? I thought you and Emily—"

"Oh, no," Miss Emily spoke around Aunt Hannah. "Maddie Lou is *Hugh Fred's* sister." She sounded like she wanted to make that very clear.

Miss Maddie wanted to make something clear, too. "I want you all to get used to calling me plain Maddie. It's been years since I've been Maddie Lou."

"How long's it been since you left us?" Without waiting for an answer, Aunt Hannah went right on. "She went to Agnes Scott. How long is it now? Ten years? And she hasn't been back for a proper visit since her mother died six years ago." Aunt Hannah pretended to scold, but she chuckled so everybody knew she was teasing. Aunt Hannah's chuckle was deep and rich, like it came straight up from healthy red clay.

"Well, I'm home now." Miss Maddie lifted her chin and took a deep breath through her nose. "For good."

"Is your husband gonna be a lawyer in Statesville?"As postmistress, Miss Pauline considered she had the right to any news related to what she called "my families." I'd also overheard Aunt Kate tell Uncle Stephen that "Pauline bristles like a porcupine whenever an unattached woman under forty comes around."

I saw Miss Maddie clench her left hand in a fold of her skirt and noticed a light ring in the even tan of her third finger."No, he's still in Atlanta, where he belongs." It was the second time she'd said it, and this time she put an emphasis on the last three words. "We . . ."—she lifted her chin even higher and gave Aunt Kate a quick, defiant look—"we're getting a divorce."

Aunt Kate and I didn't gasp, but the rest of the women did or looked like they wanted to. Nobody in Job's Corner was divorced. That was what city people, heathens, and movie stars did. I was a little more tolerant. My own mama got divorced when I was a baby, and with good cause. I was willing to give Miss Maddie the benefit of the doubt. Maybe she had good cause, too.

If so, she didn't mention it. Instead she turned her head so I could see spots of pink high on her cheekbones. "I'm going to be teaching at Mount Vernon this year. Seventh grade."

Seventh grade? The air went out of my stomach and left me hollow as a sucked chicken bone. Mount Vernon had only one seventh grade, and I was going to be in it.

Stealthily I glided farther behind Aunt Kate, glad she was still taller than me. I didn't want Mrs. Raeburn (no more calling her Miss Maddie) to remember me barefoot and tar-faced, wearing a too-short skirt spotted with bleach.

But I could hardly wait for school to start.

"Mrs. Whitfield, won't you be teaching at Mount Vernon again?" somebody called.

She would, much to my own dismay. It was bad enough at school being the niece of almost everybody's preacher. Being the niece of one of the teachers was twice as bad.

Mrs. Raeburn didn't look any happier about it than I felt. "I'll see you there, then." She turned and started asking one of the other women about her children.

No matter how hard Aunt Hannah begged, she wouldn't stay for lunch. "I just wanted to say hello to everybody. Now I'm fixing to go see Bud and beg him to let me stay in Mama's house until I can get a place of my own. It's empty right now, isn't it, Emily?"

Miss Emily nodded. "But remember not to call him Bud. He goes by Hugh Fred now."

"Would you at least award our prizes?" Mrs. Parsons asked. "We were about to vote on second place when you got here."

Aunt Kate settled that matter right away. "Hannah gave me far too much help. I want to disqualify myself and nominate Emily's tray as the unanimous second-place winner."

Mrs. Raeburn took the red ribbon and held up Miss Emily's tray for everybody to see. "Why, Emily, that's real pretty. I didn't know you could draw."

Miss Emily turned bright pink but acted like it was nothing. "Oh, I used a stencil. But Carley there didn't. Show her your tray, honey. It's her grandmother's house, with the right trees and everything. And aren't you going to be in seventh grade this coming year?"

"Yes, ma'am." I closed my eyes and hoped to die.

Mrs. Parsons beckoned me forward. "Bring it up here, sugar. Let us all see it."

With a face flaming red between streaks of tar, I slunk up to the front table and handed Mrs. Raeburn the tray. "It's very nice," she said, tracing one line with her finger. "And you drew it yourself." She smiled at me, but I could tell her mind was someplace else.

"Miss Hannah helped." Normally I'm a chatterbox, but my tongue had grown thick and my brain had turned to scrambled eggs.

Miss Emily grabbed my tray and asked in that saccharine voice grown-ups use when giving children too much praise, "Don't you all think this deserves third place?"

All the women clapped. Mrs. Raeburn stuck the yellow ribbon onto my tray. "Congratulations." She reached out one soft hand. What could I do but stick out my grubby, tarred paw? If Aunt Hannah's gully had been near enough, I'd have flung myself over the edge.

"Did you make a tray, too?" Mrs. Raeburn asked Freda.

Freda screwed up her face. "Oh *yeah.*" The way she emphasized the second word, she sounded like she hadn't made a tray at all. No wonder. Hers was a disaster. Without shading and spacing from the stencil, the horses looked like ghosts with big, hollow eyes. Freda slid her eyes to Mrs. Parsons. "She didn't tell me right and I messed it up a little."

"Let me see." Mrs. Raeburn held out her hand.

Freda sidled over to get her tray and flung it down on the table. "You should have helped me more, like you did Carley," she stormed at Aunt Hannah right there in front of everybody. "I don't want this stupid old thing." She picked up the tray and hurled it into the oil drum.

"Oh, honey, be sweet," Miss Emily begged.

Freda stuck out her lip and looked ready to cry. "I wish I'd drawn kittens, like Aunt Hannah did on her little tray."

"Take my kittens," Aunt Hannah said hastily. "I don't need two trays."

"Oh, thank you!" Freda went from pout to beam in one second flat. "You are the kindest woman in the whole wide world." She turned to Mrs. Raeburn. "May I drive home with you, Aunt Maddie?" She remembered just in time not to add the *Lou.* "I'm really too hot and filthy to stay for lunch."

"Is that all right with you, Emily?"

Miss Emily looked ready to sink with embarrassment. "Sure. But I don't know what you'll find to eat. Miranda's down here."

"We'll manage." Mrs. Raeburn put an arm around Freda's shoulder and led her toward the Cadillac. Most of the women streamed after them. A few straggled inside to help Janey Lou and Miranda bring food to the tables. Uncle Davy carried out kerosene and rags to clean off the tar and filled a big washtub with cold, soapy water to wash in.

While nobody was looking, I fished Freda's tray out of the trash and hid it in the backseat of Aunt Kate's car. I wanted to put it on my dresser. It wouldn't look too bad when I put my comb and brush on it. And if Freda and I ever got to be friends and she came up to my room, I could hide it in a drawer.

I joined Aunt Kate, who was already rubbing her hands so hard, I was worried she'd take the skin off. I knew exactly what she was thinking. She was thinking that the next time she saw Mrs. Raeburn, she'd be so gorgeous that Maddie Raeburn would see Kate Whitfield wasn't always a frump in a stained dress with stringy hair.

How did I know? Because I was already planning what I'd wear the first day of school and how I'd even endure rolling my hair on socks every night that year. Aunt Kate and I weren't both raised by my Big Mama for nothing.

Mrs. Raeburn sank gracefully into the driver's seat and swung her long legs under the steering wheel. Freda started to get into the other side, then stopped. "What's this?" I could almost see her wrinkling her nose. Something dangled limply from her hand.

Mrs. Raeburn laughed, a trill of silver bells, and reached across the car for it. "Give it here. Aunt Hannah? Remember Suzy?" She held a soft blob out her open door—a shapeless thing that might once have been red. By now it was rosy with age.

"Laws a mercy." Aunt Hannah lumbered across the drive and peered at it. "You still have that old thing? Let me have it. I'll put it in Davy's burning bin."

"No, you don't." Mrs. Raeburn cradled it at her neck. "Aunt Hannah made Suzy and brought her to me the day after we moved out here," she explained to the rest of us, then added to Aunt Hannah, "Remember? Because I'd lost my favorite doll in the move."

"I remember that Suzy doll," said one of the old women. "You brought it to Sunday school every week until you grew out of it."

Mrs. Raeburn shook her head. "I never grew out of Suzy. I just kept her at home for a while. Now she goes with me everywhere."

"Let me burn it and make you another," Aunt Hannah offered.

"Never." Mrs. Raeburn tucked Suzy down beside her and started her engine. A couple of women who were stroking the Cadillac's sleek trunk stepped back hastily. They called and waved until she'd backed, turned, and started back up the road.

But the tornado of dust had barely started to form before one woman called, "Emily, did she leave him or'd he kick her out?"

Miss Emily shook her head. "I have no idea. I had no notion she was coming home. I wonder if Miranda needs help." She hurried toward the house.

As the women drifted toward the washtub, their voices reminded me of Uncle Davy's cows mooing by the fence at dusk.

"Could be either one's fault."

"Atlanta's a long way from Job's Corner."

"Different manners 'n' things."

"Why you reckon they never had a baby?"

"Maybe she couldn't."

"Maybe he couldn't."

They all chuckled at that; then somebody made a quick movement with one hand, and they all remembered I was there.

Miss Nancy heaved a sigh from the depths of her brown biddy breast. "It's a real shame, though, and her so beautiful."

Miss Pauline wiped ham-sized hands down the front of her filthy dress. "Too beautiful to be hanging around here with no husband."

The white car and its red tornado crossed the highway and climbed toward the Keene's mansion on top of the hill.

"Reckon she knows Jerry Donaldson's gonna be principal?" I didn't see who said it, but she had a funny little teasing note in her voice.

A ripple of surprise went around the crowd, and Miss Pauline demanded, "He is? Where'd you hear—"

I was so astonished, I interrupted. "What happened to Mr. White?"

Aunt Kate had her back to me, wiping a table. She turned and I braced myself. Polite children didn't interrupt grown-ups, and Aunt Kate was doing her dead-level best to raise me polite. To my surprise, though, she didn't fuss. Instead she put an arm around my shoulders. "I meant to tell you, honey. His youngest son got killed in Korea last week."

My whole body turned to ice-cold stone. "The one who played cello? The one who was so good?" Even when she nodded, I couldn't believe what she'd said. Aunt Kate played cello, too, and had taken me to hear the high school symphony the previous spring. Mr. White's son Delbert played a cello solo, and the principal had been so proud that his round old face turned pink and shiny with happiness. "When did you find out? Why didn't you tell me?" Tears welled in my eyes and spilled over. For some reason I seemed to cry a lot lately.

She gave my shoulders a repentant little squeeze. "They told us at the teachers' meeting yesterday. Poor Mr. White is so upset, he's decided to take early retirement. I meant to tell you but I forgot."

"You never tell me anything!" I turned and dashed behind the wide trunk of a black walnut so they couldn't see me cry.

"Let her go," I heard Aunt Kate tell somebody.

I leaned my head against the rough, dark bark, and tears of sadness poured down my cheeks. I cried for being so unimportant that nobody told me anything. For Mr. White. For Delbert. "Stop it," I told myself fiercely when I got that far. "Delbert's lucky. He's gone to heaven." But I couldn't stop crying. I kept seeing Mr. White's face, shiny with happiness, and couldn't bear the thought of all the music Delbert would never get to play. "I'll play for you," I promised him.

When I remembered how I'd been joking about a little tar on my clothes while men had been fighting and probably dying for me right that minute, shame stopped my tears. How could I have gone all day without once thinking about the war? It was practically the only thing Uncle Stephen talked about at home. He listened to the radio all summer, so loud the rest of us had to listen, too. And as much as he disliked television, when the United Nations Security Council was on one whole week, he'd gone over to Miss Pauline's and watched her TV every single day. Since I had nothing better to do (and knew Aunt Kate would put me to ironing or mopping if I stayed home), I'd gone with him. Every meal that week, we'd reported at home about what else Mr. Malik from Russia had said to filibuster and keep them from doing a thing to stop the North Koreans. Aunt Kate found a map of Korea in her school stuff and hung it on our kitchen wall. Uncle Stephen stuck in little pins to mark every single battle and said he'd patch the wall later. Men were over there dying for our country. How *could* I have forgotten the war?

I was so lost in disgust at myself, I scarcely noticed when a woman called across the yard, "Did they tell you Jerry Donaldson's gonna be the new principal, Mrs. Whitfield?"

"I didn't catch the name," Aunt Kate admitted.

The woman who'd first started the conversation chimed in again. "Well, my sister works in the school cafeteria, and they got told yesterday Jerry Donaldson's been made principal."

"Oh-h-h." The way several women said that word, it sounded like they'd just learned the beginning of a particularly juicy story.

Curious, I stayed where I was, hoping to hear more. I'd learned a long time ago that the best way to find out anything was to stay still and listen.

What I heard was Miss Nancy Lamont's sniff, and then, from her tone, I knew she was tossing her little bird head. "Unless Maddie Lou's changed her mind about Jerry and that Hart boy, sparks are gonna fly."

Chapter 3

The women kept talking about Mrs. Raeburn and our new principal, but between them, Aunt Hannah and Aunt Kate made sure I didn't hear what they said. Every time somebody brought up the subject, they'd think of something else for me to do. "Carley, would you bring out the salt?" ... "Carley, go 'round with the tea pitcher again." ... "Carley, I think people are about finished; would you go tell Janey Lou to bring out the desserts?" ... "Carley, while Hannah and I help pack up all the art supplies, help Miranda and Janey Lou carry things inside."

You'd have thought I was a maid. And their repeated use of my name kept everybody else reminded I was there, too. If I wanted to find out anything about Mrs. Maddie Raeburn, I'd have to ask another source.

Thank goodness Aunt Hannah finally said, "You've worked hard enough, old dear. Go rest." She tried to shoo Aunt Kate out, too, and send us home, but Aunt Kate and I both knew the women expected the preacher's wife to stay and help until the end—especially women like Miss Pauline, who didn't stay themselves. Uncle Stephen said people's expectations of how Christians *ought* to behave are seldom related to the way they themselves behave.

I went out to one of the side porch rockers to wait. Far to the west, across the dirt road, and beyond Uncle Davy's pasture, rose the Blue Ridge Mountains. I took off my glasses and wiped sweat from the bridge of my nose, then lifted a pretend microphone to my lips.

"This is Carley Marshall, coming to you with *Unshaded Windows* from Job's Corner," I announced softly to an invisible television audience. I'd started the ongoing program right after that weeklong broadcast of the United Nations, quite taken with the newscasters. The fact that all of them were men and I wasn't hadn't yet occurred to me. I'd decided maybe I'd become a famous announcer one day, and had started practicing. "Those mountains to the west are up near my Big Mama's, where I was raised. As some of you know, my daddy left before I was born, so I grew up with Mama and her parents, Big Mama and Pop. Looking at those mountains sure makes me miss Big Mama—and also Mama and Pop, who both died." That wasn't the full story about my daddy, but I figured I would leave it to beauty parlor women's magazines to one day reveal the sordid truth I had learned the past winter, just before he died.

"If you look to the south, you'll see the back of Job's Corner. Everybody's house on this side of the road backs up to Davy Anderson's pasture, full of man-eating cows. In front the houses on this side are blessed with a dirt road, a railroad track, *and* a highway. Our dirt road ends at the dirt road that comes across the track and down to this house. You can see, up at the corner where the buzzards are circling, a patch of trees covering the ruin of Job Watt's house, built in 1750. That's why this is called Job's Corner. Let's hope those buzzards don't see Old Mrs. Cameron in her garden next door. She's an old buzzard herself, close to a hundred. She would be tall if she weren't so stooped, but as it is, she's not much taller than her cane. She keeps our only store, and a sorry place it is, too.

"The cotton field next to Mrs. Cameron's belongs to Davy Anderson and will be ripe come October, if weevils and drought don't get it. We're needin' rain real bad down here." A whistle sounded in the distance. "That's the little train that runs between Statesville and our local chair factory. The train is a constant threat to children and the preacher's black cocker spaniel, Rowdy, who is barking behind the big white house next to the cotton field. That's the manse, where I live with the Reverend Stephen Whitfield, his wife, Kate, and their two children, Abby and John. She's just turned five, and he is one. Poor old Rowdy isn't as perky as he used to be, because he got hit by a car last winter, but he can still bark at trains.

"The person in the next yard is Bonnie Anderson, taking in wash. She is only fourteen but very mature for her age, which means she does all the work while her stepmother, Pauline Anderson—whose dead husband was Davy Anderson's brother—sits on her front porch shooing flies. If she gets hot, Miss Pauline goes in and watches television. The only housework she ever does is shuck corn or shell beans. Both of which, you will note, can be done sitting down."

I stopped long enough to take a long gulp of iced tea from the pink aluminum glass Aunt Hannah had sent out with me. Television announcing was dry work. I wiped sweat from my nose again and crossed my legs gracefully, turning my best side view to the invisible camera.

"You may have heard that Miss Pauline is the Job's Corner postmistress. Every morning she or her son, Preston — a short, fat, obnoxious boy of eleven, with hair like a rusty toilet brush, eyes like a little pig, and about a million freckles — catches the mailbag from the train, and for one hour she puts letters in the right boxes and gives out mail. After that she retires to her porch. If somebody comes late for their mail, she hands them the key and lets them open the post office themselves. Our post office, which you cannot see, is a small, unpainted building in Miss Pauline's front yard. It generally smells of sweat and dirty boy.

"Miss Pauline also has a daughter, Sue Mary. She's five, like Abby, and weird. Her hair is pure white, and her voice sounds like tinkly bells. She moves as slow as molasses on ice and, unless pushed, will still be eating breakfast at dinnertime. She is terrified of everything on God's green earth and has an invisible friend named Velma, who accompanies her everywhere."

I started to move on to the next house, then remembered something. "The Andersons also have a Crosley television. Preston gets to decide what is being watched, all the time. According to *Life* magazine, one point five million American homes now have television sets, but the manse is not one of them. Stephen and Kate Whitfield believe television stunts the imagination, which is why the two manse girls have to grovel before Preston to see their favorite shows.

"Beyond Miss Pauline's is the big garden she shares with the Lamonts next door, except Bonnie does all her gardening. A stand of oaks in the pasture conceals the Lamont's big white house, very like this one except very plain, but if you listen you can hear faint sounds of metal striking metal. Mr. Washington Lamont must be working on his tractor. He works all week with his daddy building houses, but he also grows a little cotton, and he and Miss Nancy have an enormous garden. On weekends he likes to tinker with his tractor while his two children, Ruth the Unlovely and Jimmy the Brat, dig in the dirt or push each other on the swing he hung high from their only tree, a wretched sycamore. The Lamont children are not permitted to play with other Job's Corner children. Miss Nancy, their mother, is a plain woman, as she will tell you herself. Not one bush, not one flower, brightens that stark white house except for a few leggy geraniums in an iron pot. But Miss Nancy's clothes are fancy, because she makes them and can't resist adding a bit of rickrack in a contrasting color to every single garment."

I drank another long gulp of tea. "On the other side of the highway, which you can't see, is Bethel Church. To the west of the church stands an empty house, and behind that is a small white house lived in by Bess Anderson and her son, Jay, but those Andersons are Negroes, possibly descendants of slaves owned by white Andersons. Jay is attending Johnson C. Smith College in Charlotte. He hopes to one day become a doctor."

I paused to let my viewers absorb the idea that a Negro could attend college. Not all of them might be as accepting of that fact as were Uncle Stephen's family.

"To the east of the church live Rob and Rilla Lamont, parents of Mr. Wash. He builds houses and also wonderful little models. His model of the state capitol is currently on loan to the Iredell County Public Library. His wife, Rilla, an accomplished pianist, teaches piano to Freda Keene and myself. Freda lives in that mansion on top of the hill. I have never been inside, but I understand it is lovely. Those houses, one store, and the church, plus this lovely farmhouse at the bottom of the hill, which belongs to Davy and Hannah Anderson, is Job's Corner."

I lowered my voice. "No tour would be complete without the Terror of Job's Corner, the Bethel cemetery. Don't be misled by the respectable brick church with its two white columns and ten prim steps leading to the sanctuary. In that cemetery, spread out behind and along both sides of Bethel Church, ghosts regularly cavort on foggy nights. I have seen them with—"

"Carley?" Uncle Davy's gentle voice swam into my spiel. "I'm goin' up to mow Pauline's grass. You wanna ride up with me or wait for Mrs. Whitfield?"

I sank back into the rocker, face blazing. "I'll just wait."

As he loaded his old red mower into his even older gray truck, I pointed to smoke floating across the pasture from Miss Pauline's. "You'd better tell her Preston's playing with matches again. He sneaks out to their barrel every chance he gets, to burn paper."

As Uncle Davy's ancient truck clattered up the hill in a funnel of dust, I informed my viewers, "It's not tattling to warn people about Preston. It could save somebody's life."

❦

It was after three before we finally drove the half mile home and pulled between two of the five maples in our front yard. As we walked wearily up the cracked front walk, carrying our trays, we saw Uncle Stephen and Abby on the front porch, playing checkers. As he often did, Uncle Stephen had run an extension cord from the living room so he could listen to his little radio while they played. We were greeted by a woof from Rowdy, who left the porch and hobbled down to make sure Aunt Kate hadn't been hurt since he'd seen her last. Rowdy tolerated the rest of us but he was Aunt Kate's dog.

Abby upset the checkerboard in her eagerness to tell us, "We's got a secwet! Guess what we's havin' for supper." She pranced barefoot on the wide floorboards. As her gray eyes danced above her freckled nose and her red curls caught a gleam of sunlight, I had to turn away and swallow hard. How could God make Abby look so much like *my* mama after making me thin and plain with weak eyes, bookworm-rounded shoulders, and Daddy's limp, colorless hair?

"Guess," Abby demanded. "Guess de secwet." A secret to Abby was something you knew just long enough to tell somebody else.

Uncle Stephen picked up his pipe from the ashtray he'd balanced on the porch railing and puffed to get it going again. He was never a handsome man—long and gawky, with straight brown hair parted on one side, which he shoved back with his long fingers whenever he was angry or upset. Horn-rimmed glasses perched on his beaky nose, and his eyes were an indeterminate hazel behind them. But when he smiled the way he was smiling at Aunt Kate right then, you could see why she adored him.

And if you are wondering why a preacher smoked, North Carolina is a big tobacco state, and nobody knew tobacco was dangerous yet. Almost every man we knew smoked. A lot of women did, too—most of them just sneaked.

Aunt Kate set the trays down on the porch table. "Before we guess, can we show you what we made? Carley won a prize."

Abby looked them over, but she wasn't impressed. "If you'da let me go, I'da made a better one. I'da put bunnies and cats on mine." Bunnies and cats were Abby's artistic specialty, thanks to Miss Pauline. When mornings got slow at the post office, she amused Abby and Sue Mary by teaching them to draw, using the backs of letters that hadn't been picked up yet. A lot of Job's Corner mail arrived decorated with lopsided bunnies, cats pictured from behind, or both.

"Now can I tell you?" she begged. "It's hot dogs!" Hot dogs were Abby's favorite food, because we seldom had them. Church members brought us homegrown steaks, roasts, hams, and pork chops, but hot dogs had to be bought. Every family defines "luxury" in its own way.

"And ice cweam," she added with a gurgle. "Can you b'lieve dat? Store-bought ice cweam, not dat hard homemade stuff." She clasped both hands under her chin and shivered, unable to hold so much joy. "And we's gonna cook on our bobby-cue gwill!"

It wasn't really our barbeque grill; it was the church's—like the manse and the telephone. But we were used to thinking of it as ours, since Uncle Stephen had paid for it out of his own pocket and helped build it. In those days if you wanted a grill, you built it from bricks—a little chimney and an open fireplace, with a metal plate fitted over the fireplace to cook on.

This was a chance sent from heaven. "If we're having hot dogs, we'll need ketchup," I told them. "Abby finished the bottle this morning on her scrambled eggs. Shall I get some?"

Uncle Stephen rummaged in his pocket for change. "After you rest."

"I don't need a rest."

"Me *needer*," Abby said firmly. She hated naps.

"Well, I do," her mother said. "I'm plumb exhausted."

Uncle Stephen held out his arms, and she staggered gratefully into them. He nuzzled her neck. "Let's go lie down and let our minions run the errands."

"I have to have a bath first," I told Abby.

She hung over the side of the big claw-foot tub while I washed, pointing out bits of tar I'd missed. Privacy in the bathroom was a concept Abby hadn't yet grasped. Uncle Stephen said she must have Japanese blood, because she considered anybody's bath a social event. And since our bathrooms were

at the end of the big, wide halls on each floor, it was almost
impossible to sneak into one without her seeing you.

I finished washing, wrapped myself in my towel, and hurried down the hall to my room. "You needs to mop again,"
Abby informed me, looking at my wet footprints in the dust.
It was my job to sweep and mop the house. I didn't mind the
rooms so much but greatly resented the time I had to spend on
the room-sized hall on each floor. With the dirt road right outside and church people traipsing in and out to see Uncle
Stephen, those halls took a lot of mopping.

Abby climbed up on my bed and perched like a cheerful
cherub, watching me dress. "Tell de peoples on telebision about
our house, Carley Cousin."

I'd done that at least a hundred times, but Abby enjoyed it
like a favorite book. Obligingly I reached for my pretend microphone and talked into it while I put on fresh shorts and a shirt.
"This is Carley Marshall with *Unshaded Windows*, giving you
a tour of the Job's Corner manse, built in 1890 and scarcely
modernized since. My bedroom occupies one front corner
upstairs. Uncle Stephen's study is behind this room, and we
also have three empty rooms up here, inhabited only by
ghosts."

"Oooh!" Abby squealed and hugged herself. She always did
at that part, but she wasn't the least bit frightened of ghosts.
She didn't have to sleep with them, all by herself upstairs.

"Downstairs are our living room, dining room, kitchen,
and two more bedrooms. The living room is so little and dark,
we use it for a playroom and for our piano. We keep our couch,
Uncle Stephen's chair, and the genuine-walnut cabinet Philco
radio in the dining room, which is big and sunny. Across the
hall at the back is the room shared by Aunt Kate, Uncle
Stephen, and John, which is so huge, Uncle Stephen says if we
ever get real poor, we can rent out the rest of the house and live
in it."

"But we hopes we doesn't has to," Abby interrupted, "'cause
we loves our rooms. Tell 'em about mine, Carley Cousin!"

"Abby's room is under mine, and as you can see," I ges-tured, "these rooms are part of a tower with a curving wall that goes up to a pointed turret on the roof, so Abby and I each have five curved windows. Abby looks out through the front porch, while I look through the tops of our maples."

"An' I gots free doors, too."

"Three," I corrected automatically, scrubbing at a bit of tar I'd left on one leg.

"Free," Abby repeated. "One to Mama's room, one to de front hall, and one to de porch. Nobody else has free doors in their room, not eben Carley." She wriggled off the bed. "Dat's enuf. Let's go to de store."

❀

Even after a bath it wouldn't occur to me to put on shoes between Memorial Day and Labor Day, so we picked our way gingerly down the dusty road, trying to avoid sharp granite chips that could bruise our arches.

"We's celebwating," Abby informed me importantly, tip-toeing through a bad patch of gravel, "'cause we's been in Job's Corner one year dis month."

I heaved a sigh of impatience. "*This* month, Abby. Say it right. You're five already." None of us could figure out why she still spoke baby talk. Her parents never used it with her, and I constantly corrected her, but Abby clung to "dis" and "we's" in spite of all our efforts.

"I can't," she whined.

"Sure you can. Say Bethel."

"Bethel." It came out clear as a bell.

"Now say *beth-this*."

"Beth-this month," she repeated, hissing the *th* like a snake. "One year beth-this month."

Had it really been a year since Big Mama sent me up to West Virginia to help Uncle Stephen and Aunt Kate move to Job's Corner? That was soon after Mama died, when *polio* was still a word we were terrified to even say. At the time I'd thought I was going for a visit. When I found out Big Mama meant me to stay, each day seemed a year long. Now, looking back, I felt like I'd been in Job's Corner just a little while but like I'd been living with the Whitfields almost forever. As we walked to the little store, I pictured time like a great big snake, changing its shape depending on what it ate and when you looked at it.

Mrs. Cameron's store was there before Moses saw the burning bush. No bigger than any decent tractor barn, it squatted on short brick pillars in her yard, its front porch sagging like her lower lip and its two wooden doors spread back against the front like grimy wings. Bugs were kept out in summer by rusty screened doors practically held up by old metal signs advertising Cheerwine, a cherry-cinnamon soft drink bottled thirty-five miles away in Salisbury.

Mrs. Cameron was the orneriest old woman God ever made. Still, I had to respect the way she sat on that porch day after day in a succession of black skirts and cardigans, shoving long gray hairpins back into her skimpy white bun and waiting for three or four customers to come her way. She reminded me of Pop staying in his store late Christmas Eve after the rest of the clerks had gone, in case somebody came by wanting one more present. Big Mama always used to say he had merchant blood. Now I knew what she meant.

As we turned onto the path that crossed her yard like the crooked part in a child's hair, she wasn't there. We found her inside with a black crayon, remarking sugar bags from fifty cents to a dollar. "Why you doin' that?" I demanded. "That's not the way you hold a sale."

"It's not a sale. With this war, things're goin' up."

"Nobody's going to pay a dollar for five pounds of sugar. Especially since you paid the same for those bags as for the ones you already sold this week."

"Folks'll pay what they have to, to get what they need. Now, what were you wantin'?"

"Ketchup," Abby informed her. "We's havin' hot dogs. We's celebwating, 'cause we's been here one whole year."

Mrs. Cameron regarded her sourly. "Seems longer'n that." She jerked her head toward the deep wooden shelves behind the counter. "You know where things are. Get it yourselves. Don't touch anything else, mind." She rescued a slipping hairpin and reseated it.

The store was sweet with a blend of fresh bread, tobacco, and a mustiness that rose from the dust beneath wide cracks in the floorboards. It was also dim, for Mrs. Cameron never turned on the single swinging bulb before dark. Abby went straight to a shelf that held two bottles of ketchup and one jar of mayonnaise beside a box of tenpenny nails, another of combs, and a stack of dusty dishtowels. It was all dusty. Mrs. Cameron never cleaned, so anything that didn't get bought gradually accumulated a soft red blanket.

Mrs. Cameron had no refrigerator except a red box with a heavy lid where she kept bottles of RC Cola and Cheerwine floating in cold water. We who lived in Job's Corner grew our own perishables—vegetables, fruit, meats, and milk. Some still made butter. And we bought most groceries in town. Mrs. Cameron's was just for things we ran out of.

I sidestepped to avoid sticky flypaper hanging from the ceiling and sidled over to candy jars on the oak counter that was smooth from years of palms. Dusting the wooden top of one jar with my fingers, I wiped my hand on the seat of my shorts, then took out ten Mary Janes. "My treat," I said airily, handing Abby half the peanut butter taffy and fishing in my pocket for a dime. Her eyes widened but she took the candy.

We handed Mrs. Cameron Uncle Stephen's money for the ketchup and mine for the candy, then followed her as she hobbled out to the cigar box on the porch where she kept her money. The old screened door closed with a tired *whoosh* behind us.

"That store is filthy," I muttered while she made change. "My granddaddy used to keep a store, and he'd have been ashamed to let his look like that. You could at least dust."

"Folks know what to expect," she said. "They get what they pay for."

I wasn't about to leave without getting some information. Mrs. Cameron generally knew anything there was to know about Job's Corner, and she'd tell you if she didn't think you cared too much about knowing. "Uncle Stephen and Aunt Kate are napping, so we aren't in any hurry," I explained elaborately, sitting on the silvery old porch floor with my feet on the top step and the ketchup beside me. The boards beneath me were silky with age and warm from the sun. I unwrapped a Mary Jane.

Abby plopped down beside me and added treacherously around a wad of taffy, "'Sides, we's not 'posed to eat candy afore supper."

"You're just followin' where you been led," the crone assured her. She lowered herself into her sagging chair and turned her bright black eyes on me. "Who was in that fancy car went down Hannah's road this mornin'?"

I tossed my head, delighted to have news she didn't. "Mr. Hugh Fred's sister, Mrs. Maddie Raeburn."

"Maddie Lou?" All the wrinkles in her thin, old freckled face rose in surprise.

"Yes, ma'am. She's moved back and is going to be my teacher next year at Mount Vernon. But she wants to be called just plain Maddie now."

"What about that husband of hern?"

I shrugged. "She said they're getting a divorce." I tried to make it sound like it was something everybody I knew did at one time or another, but couldn't help dropping my voice on the last syllable. Even if my own mama had one, divorce still wasn't respectable to talk about.

"What's a tufforce?" Abby demanded, immediately alert.

I didn't answer but Mrs. Cameron did. "When two people can't make up their minds to live together."

Abby chewed slower while she considered that. "Then me 'n' Preston got a tufforce. I could never make up my mind to live with *him*. He stinks!" She wrinkled her freckled nose.

"Preston just considers extry baths a waste of time," Mrs. Cameron told her tartly.

I didn't want to talk about Preston; I wanted to talk about Mrs. Raeburn. "Did you know Mrs. Raeburn when she was growing up? She's mighty pretty."

"Always was." Mrs. Cameron waved her cane toward the Keene's big, white-columned house on the hill across the road. "Lived right up there most of her life, and I been livin' on this property nigh on sixty-four years. Come as a bride of nineteen. So I know everybody. They all come into the store one time or another."

I saved the figures in my head. When I got home, I'd find paper and add nineteen and sixty-four, but I had something else to ask right then. "Did you ever know a Hart boy?"

"Four generations of 'em lived in that big house on the hill. I knowed 'em all."

"I thought you said Mrs. Raeburn lived there."

She cackled like I'd said something hilarious. "Not *there*, Missy. Her folks were dirt poor. Stella and Hugh Keene, they were. His business failed, 'nd they had to come live with Stella's mama, Mildred, in the *second* house up that road. A little green one it is now. Stella was Rilla Lamont's sister, and Rob built that house for her folks soon after he and Rilla married."

I traced the connections in my head. Miss Rilla and Mr. Rob were the parents of Mr. Wash, who was married to Miss Nancy, to whom Freda would have given the Fowlest Award. I'd forgotten until that second that Miss Nancy and Freda were cousins by marriage. But then, most people in Job's Corner—except the manse family—were related.

Mrs. Cameron was still droning on. "... five of 'em crowded into that little biddy house. 'Course, Maddie Lou was real little, maybe four, but Bud—Hugh Fred—was ten years older and 'most grown. Mildred died a couple of winters later, then Hugh the next year. Poor Stella had a job keeping body and soul together 'til Hugh Fred quit school and went to work."

I couldn't picture elegant Mr. Hugh Fred or his beautiful sister living in a "little biddy house," but if Mrs. Cameron said it was small, it must be. Her own didn't have but three rooms.

"So when did Mr. Hugh Fred buy the house he has now?" I popped another Mary Jane into my mouth and busied myself chewing like I was just making conversation.

"The Hart Place? That's what we used to call it. Was in the Hart family for nigh on a hundred years before Hugh Fred bought it. Built in 1850 and wasn't even damaged in the War."

She didn't need to explain to a southern child which war she meant.

She rubbed her whiskery old chin and thought so long, I worried she'd forgotten my question. Then she said suddenly, "Six years back, I guess it'd be. He and Emily stayed with Stella until she died."

Freda and Miss Emily had lived in that "little biddy house" as well? I'd never tell Freda I knew, but somehow she seemed different in my mind. Not so superior. What dark corner in all of us rejoices to learn something embarrassing about those we most admire?

Once you got Mrs. Cameron started on something, she was almost impossible to stop. I contentedly chewed Mary Janes and listened. ". . . rented out Stella's and bought the Hart Place. It'd been empty three years by then. Most folks who can afford a house that big don't want to live so far out of town."

"Why did the Harts move?"

"Didn't stay but a year after Taylor up 'n' left. Moved up near Charlotte, I heard."

Abby asked the next question before I could. "Where did Taylor go?"

"Joined the army. Leastways, that's what folks figured. We weren't in the war yet, but some boys couldn't wait. Maddie Lou was right cut up about it, I remember. They wuz sweethearts, and he never even bothered to say good-bye. Didn't write his mother, neither. Looks like he coulda done that. But maybe he got kilt. I don't know. Never heard one way or t'other."

I knew from the way her voice trailed off that she'd said what she had to say on that subject. I tried another. "Did you know a Mr. Donaldson? He's going to be our new principal."

"Pwincipals doesn't let you eat ice cweam," Abby warned darkly.

"Huh?" I asked.

She shook her curls solemnly. "Dat's what Daddy said dis mornin'. He said I couldn't have ice cweam afore dinner, and when I said how come, he said, 'It is a good principle.'" I had begun to notice that when Abby was quoting somebody else, her pronunciation was perfect. Oblivious, she unwrapped another candy and filled her mouth. "But we got ice cweam for supper," she informed Mrs. Cameron sunnily. "Pink and bwown and banilla in one box. If you comes to my house, you can eat some. It's store bought."

"Waste of good money when you can make your own." The old grumbler shifted in her chair, and I smelled the Duz she washed her clothes in. "No, I didn't know him." She stamped her cane twice on her worn old porch. "You got what you came for. Now go on home."

"Carleee? Abbeee?" Uncle Stephen's voice rose with wisps of smoke over the cotton.

Abby jumped up and shouted indignantly, "Don't you cook wifout me!" She bustled across the yard.

I stood and brushed the seat of my shorts. "Well, we gotta go. See you later."

I was all the way to the road before I heard a croak from the porch. "Come back here."

When I got back, Mrs. Cameron said, as if she begrudged me the information, "About that Donaldson feller. If it's the one I'm thinking on, I never met him, but best as I remember, he was mixed up with Taylor Hart somehow. For a while they thought he'd killed him." She cackled. "Surprised you, didn't I? Now pick up that ketchup over yonder. You paid for it. Might as well take it on home."

❧

Uncle Stephen and Abby insisted that they would not only cook, they would wash dishes. I went out to the swing while

Aunt Kate went to give John a bath, but when I heard her singing, I wandered back to the bathroom and peeked inside. She was gently washing John's upturned face and singing one of Pop's favorite hymns. Rowdy lay on the gray linoleum at her feet, thumping time with his stubby tail. Aunt Kate swore that dog had perfect rhythm.

I propped myself against the door frame and added alto to the third verse:

> *O for the wonderful love He has promised,*
> *Promised for you and for me;*
> *Tho' we have sinned, He has mercy and pardon,*
> *Pardon for you and for me.*
> *Come home, come home,*
> *Ye who are weary, come home;*
> *Earnestly, tenderly, Jesus is calling,*
> *Calling, O sinner, come home.*

When we finished singing, I had to blink back tears. Aunt Kate dabbed her own eyes with the washrag and gave a watery laugh. "Pop would be proud. You sing real well."

"He taught me. We sang duets all the time."

She blinked back more tears. "We sang duets all the time, too."

She held out her arms and I went into them. We had a good cry until little John looked up and asked in a puzzled voice, "Mommy cwy? Lee-lee cwy?"

Aunt Kate sniffed and tugged off some toilet paper for us each to blow our noses. "I reckon I'd better dry this boy and get him to bed."

As she reached for a towel, I remembered something I'd forgotten to do. I went to the living room and played Beethoven's *Für Elise*. But this time it was *Für Delbert*, to say how sorry I was he'd died. I played it real slow on the sweet parts and loud and angry on the chords and runs, to show how mad I was that Mr. White had lost his boy.

"Very nice," Aunt Kate called as she carried John toward bed. "Good expression."

"Freda's got a harder version," I called back.

"Oh? I never knew there was another version. You'd better get your bath now. Church tomorrow." Aunt Kate knew a lot about music. It was funny she didn't know there were two versions of that piece. Since it was short, I played it one more time before going upstairs. As the last notes died away, I felt I gently laid Delbert to rest.

Chapter 4

Sunday morning I dressed with special care in my favorite pink organdy dress. I polished my white shoes. I even wore gloves, which were optional for girls. I hoped Mrs. Raeburn would think I looked nice. Aunt Kate must have been thinking about Mrs. Raeburn, too, for she wore her best brown two-piece dress with a big white collar and white cuffs on the short sleeves. Her thick auburn curls shone, her white gloves gleamed, and she'd even put on a pearl choker and a little straw hat with yellow flowers. She didn't usually wear a hat on Sunday because of choir.

After Sunday school I hurried to the creamy sanctuary and took Abby's and my usual pew, second from the front, where Aunt Kate could keep an eye on us from the choir, which was over to the right of the pulpit. Nobody was there yet except a few old people who didn't like to rush. A breeze circled the big room, which still had the holy smell of an empty church. Families straggled in to their usual places and teens ambled up to the balcony, where, Uncle Stephen said, slaves used to sit when the church was built. He said maybe teenagers felt the same freedom up there the slaves used to: for one hour nobody could see them except the preacher and the choir.

I turned around to look several times, but Mrs. Raeburn never came.

Abby did, sliding in breathless with her face pink and red curls damp with sweat. She barely made it before Uncle

Stephen and the choir came in. I was so busy fussing at her for going outside to play between Sunday school and church, I didn't notice the choir until Uncle Stephen finished the invocation. A new man sat behind Aunt Kate, next to Mr. Hugh Fred. He was tall and thin, with a fox's face: wide at the eyes, pointed at the chin. His nose was long and pointed, and he even had fox-red hair and red-brown eyes. He wore a blue and white seersucker suit with a white shirt and a bright red tie, and kept running one finger down between his tie and his big Adam's apple. I felt sorry for him. Even with all the windows open, we sweltered in August. Only Uncle Davy wore a suit. Most men settled for shirts and slacks. I don't know how Uncle Stephen stood his long black robe, but I do know he took his coat off before he put it on, and still came home drenched with sweat.

While I tried not to stare, I couldn't help peeking at that poor hot man now and then. He grinned at me and his eyes twinkled. My face flamed and I forced my eyes back to Uncle Stephen, who was announcing the first hymn.

Freda always played for church. She would have missed fewer notes if she had practiced more, but she never seemed to notice—just skipped nimbly from wrong notes to right ones as if inventing new harmonies.

When it was time for the offertory anthem, Mr. Hugh Fred stepped to the pulpit. I thought he'd sing a solo—he did that sometimes when the choir hadn't practiced enough. Instead he gave us a big smile and announced, "We've got a special treat today. Clay Lamont's home and will sing for us. His mama has even consented to play. Aunt Rilla?" He motioned for her to come up.

I darted a look from Uncle Stephen in the pulpit chair to Aunt Kate, who was directing the choir until we could get somebody else. I wondered how they'd react to this takeover of the service. But they both had on polite "Let's give him a chance" smiles, so they'd known all along. Just one more thing they hadn't bothered to tell me.

A lot of people made happy little rustling sounds as Miss Rilla came down the side aisle like a tall gray dove. She had to come from the very back, because she and Mr. Rob sat where she could get out quick after the benediction. Until the past winter, he was the Job's Corner drunk, and she'd stayed in her house all the time. She still wasn't used to being around people. But she was one of my very favorite people as well as my piano teacher, and I never tired of hearing her play. While she was getting to the piano, the new man came from his seat, clapped Mr. Hugh Fred's shoulder, and spread music on the pulpit.

Miss Rilla's big, strong hands began the opening notes of "The Holy City." The new man looked at the far ceiling, like he was saying a quick prayer. I figured we'd better all be praying. Pop used to sing "The Holy City" in our Baptist church back home, but it took a very good tenor to soar on the high notes of the final measures. I prepared for an ordeal.

Then the man began to sing. On the verses he barely whispered but we heard every word. On the chorus Miss Rilla's fingers flew and his voice rose so true, I held my breath. He was better than Pop. When he was done, we didn't clap of course—Presbyterians would die rather than clap in church. But he gave Miss Rilla a triumphant smile, and she turned pink right to the end of her long, thin nose. Then he looked down at me and winked. I got hot all the way down.

After church I usually joined other kids under the magnolia tree, but that Sunday I went to stand behind Uncle Stephen while he shook hands. Aunt Kate was still taking off her choir robe, but Abby always stood beside him shaking hands like we had one big preacher and one little one. As people passed Uncle Stephen, they'd often say something about the sermon: "Good message" or "Mite long but real good" or "You want to hear a real good sermon, you need to hear that fellow Billy Graham." When they reached Abby, the men grinned and the women smiled, but they every one shook her hand. If they didn't, she'd call after them, "You forgot to shake me."

I didn't want to shake anybody's hand, but the front door was the best place I knew to find out more about Miss Rilla's son.

He came with Hugh Fred and sure didn't look like his cousin. Mr. Hugh Fred was the handsomest man we knew. With wavy black hair and broad shoulders, he looked a lot like Rock Hudson, except Rock Hudson probably didn't give a Tootsie Roll to every child he met. "Here's Clay," he greeted Uncle Stephen. "Sorry he didn't get to church in time for me to properly introduce you before we all went in. The old lazy-bones slept so long, he almost had to put his choir robe on over his pajamas."

"Been keeping Air Force hours too long," Clay said with a little laugh. "Need my sleep."

"Got out just in time, didn't you?" Uncle Stephen stuck out his hand.

Clay shook it and nodded. "Thought about staying in for one more hitch, with this new conflict 'n' all, but I've done my bit and am ready to wear comfortable clothes for a while." He ran a finger around the front of his collar to ease it away from his Adam's apple. "Speaking of which, this is the last time you're gonna see me in a coat and tie this summer."

Uncle Stephen grinned. "That's fine with me. I've been duly impressed."

"Good." He beamed down at Abby and me, which made the hair on my neck rise with unexpected happiness. "And are these two young ladies part of your family?"

"I am Abby." She stuck out her hand.

He squatted and shook it gravely. "Glad to meet you, Miss Abby. You're mighty pretty."

"Yes, I am." She'd heard it so often, she took it for granted. "Dis is Carley."

I wished he'd stand up and say, "You are beautiful," but what he said was almost as good. "You're the kid Mama talks about all the time, the one she says can really play the piano."

"She talks about you all the time, too." I spoke without thinking, then blushed. I hadn't blushed so much in one day in my whole life. Maybe I was getting sick. I hoped he wouldn't want to know what his mama talked about. Mostly it was, "I wish we'd get a letter from Clay. He's so awful about writing."

Mr. Hugh Fred saved me. "Any chance Wash will get called up? They've begun to activate reserve troops."

Clay shook his head. "Little to none. When he took the option of getting out of the Army Air Corps early back in forty-five, he was told he'd be on reserve just five years. That'll be up the first of December, and with two kids and all—"

He stopped politely as Aunt Kate joined us. She told Uncle Stephen, "I already asked Clay if he'll take over as choir director, and he said yes."

Uncle Stephen nodded, like that was one more thing that didn't surprise him. "Hugh Fred said you might be willing, once you got settled."

"I'll be tickled to. Just give me a week or so. By the way, I want to thank you folks for what you've done for Mama and Daddy. Got her to goin' out now and then, got him off the sauce. Now that I'm back, if you need anything—anything at all—just give me a call. You hear me?" With another grin for Aunt Kate and me, he left.

I hoped he couldn't hear my heart pounding.

❦

That afternoon I took the funny papers to the porch swing, but I couldn't settle down to read them. Instead I sat pushing with one foot to keep the swing gently moving and watched the big white house across the highway. Cardinals squabbled in one of the maples. Abby chattered to Sue Mary in our side yard. Finally, to my delight a motor started behind Lamonts', and Mr. Rob's old gray truck pulled into the highway. It turned up the road, and Clay waved one hand over the cab as he passed. My day was complete.

"Need something cold to drink?" Aunt Kate carried out two glasses of cherry Kool-Aid. With soft drinks a nickel each and Kool-Aid a nickel for half a gallon, we drank a lot of Kool-Aid.

She pressed her glass to her cheek before taking a long swallow. My first gulp went down my throat like a ball of ice, making my head ache for a second. Aunt Kate sank into one of the porch rockers. "It's too hot to stay inside. I don't know how Stephen and John can sleep." She waved away a fly. "Where's Abby?"

"In the playhouse." Mr. Rob had built Abby a playhouse the Christmas before, complete with wallpaper left over from Aunt Hannah's bedroom and a scrap of linoleum left from our new kitchen floor. Uncle Stephen had built a little table, two stools, a doll's bed and dresser, a stove, and a sink.

Aunt Kate leaned over the porch bannister and peered past the house. "Sue Mary's sitting on the front step dressing her dolls, but I don't see Abby."

"That's all Sue Mary ever does when they play house—dresses and undresses her dolls. She doesn't cook, sweep, nothing."

"Being dressed is probably the only mothering she ever gets, poor thing." Aunt Kate rocked gently and waved at the persistent fly.

The next second we heard Abby bellow, "I's home from wuk. Where's my supper?" She ran past the porch, her face brick red.

"Do you all want some Kool-Aid?" Aunt Kate called.

"No, ma'am. I gotta go home from wuk. Gimme my supper, Sue Mary, or I'll bash you."

Aunt Kate gasped. "Where did she learn that? People will think Stephen beats me."

"Or that you beat him," I pointed out. "You're the one who goes to work."

❋

Sunday evenings we all gathered in the dining room around the Philco console radio to listen to *The Greatest Story Ever Told*. I particularly liked that show, because every time Jesus was about to speak, beautiful music played. I'd always wondered how people could recognize who he was. It was good to finally know.

After that, as a welcome break from the week's war news, we laughed ourselves silly at *Our Miss Brooks, Jack Benny, Amos and Andy, Charlie McCarthy and Edgar Bergen, Red Skelton,* and *Corliss Archer.* Even Abby could stay up as long as she could stay awake, because neither Aunt Kate nor Uncle Stephen wanted to leave the radio long enough to put her to bed. Uncle Stephen always said the same thing every Sunday night, though. "It's no wonder nobody wants to go to Sunday night church anymore, with all this going on."

That evening I sort of wished we did have Sunday night church, so I could see Clay. The shows weren't as funny as usual. Finally I excused myself and went up to my room. I leaned on the sill of my open window and stared over the tracks, wondering which of the lighted upstairs rooms was his, and if he was there looking across at our house.

Then I went to pirouette in front of the mirror, wondering if I should become a famous dancer instead of a television announcer. I removed my glasses and leaned close to the mirror to examine my face. It wasn't a bad face, just plain—ordinary features arranged in an ordinary way. Why hadn't Mama given me her pretty red curls, cute little nose, big gray eyes? Would Clay think me even a little pretty? I closed my eyes, stretched far over my dresser, and kissed the mirror. The lips that met mine were cool and flat.

"What you doin'?" Abby demanded from the door, hands on her hips like her mother did when disgusted. "You's crazy, Carley Cousin. Come make me some brown sugar toast."

Thus does ordinary life get in the way of romance.

While Abby and I were eating brown sugar toast with milk, Uncle Stephen came into the kitchen singing a hymn we used to sing back home in the Baptist church. We'd never sung it at Bethel, though, so I wondered where he'd learned it. I joined in on the chorus.

Let the lower lights be burning! Send a gleam across the wave!
Some poor fainting, struggling seaman you may rescue, you may save.

Abby stopped eating and looked up. "What's a lower light?"

Uncle Stephen was getting himself an ice cream bowl, so he answered with his head in the cupboard. "I think it's a light at the bottom of a lighthouse, a light people can see from a long way off, to keep them out of danger."

"Dat's nice. Sing it again."

We taught her the chorus before she finished her toast. Later when Aunt Kate put her to bed, she refused to have her shades down or her light out. "I has to keep my lower lights bunnin. Somebody might need to see dem."

"They'll see you, too." Aunt Kate jerked down one shade. Abby kicked her heels and roared.

Abby's roar was a phenomenon. It involved no tears. She merely opened her mouth and made an enormous racket. Gradually she outgrew it. But when we met for lunch her last year of college, a small boy tyrannized the entire restaurant by running around yelling. When the child came near us and deliberately knocked her elbow, Abby looked him straight in the eye, opened her mouth, and roared. Terrified, he backed silently to his mother. Abby picked up her roll with a smug smile. "I thought I'd forgotten how."

When she roared that Sunday night, Uncle Stephen hurried in. "What's going on?"

"I gotta leab my lower lights bunnin," Abby explained, indignant. "Mama's pulling de shades."

He looked at Aunt Kate and shrugged. "Her theology is sound. Besides, who can see in?"

"Just God," said Abby. "And he's prob'ly asleep alweady."

I didn't bother to tell her that Preston Anderson still peered in windows. Preston wouldn't see anything in Abby's room he hadn't already seen at home.

❦

I was getting sleepy, too, but our maid, Grace, had been to visit her sister for a week, and Uncle Stephen and I had to pick her up at the downtown bus station at ten-thirty. Grace helped keep the house and took care of Abby and John while Aunt Kate taught, and if you are wondering how a preacher could afford a full-time maid, Uncle Stephen said it was the least he could do after taking a gently reared southern woman away from her roots. Aunt Kate said she paid Grace most of what she made but it was worth it to be teaching again. And they both said that giving Grace money toward her college education was the best investment they could make with what money they had.

I was real eager to see Grace. Not only because her sister, Pearl, lived behind Big Mama and Pearl's daughter, Geena, was one of my best friends but because Big Mama—who was also Mrs. Henry Marshall and now owned Henry Marshall's Department Store in Shelby—was sending my school clothes with Grace.

After Abby and John were in bed, I went out on the porch. Humming to myself, I was perched on the top step watching the Lamont house when Uncle Stephen poked his head out the door. "It's too hot in there. You find a breeze?"

"Not much of one."

"More than we've got in here." He called softly to the dining room, "Come sit with me, Kate. If Carley doesn't watch, we can smooch." He took one corner of the swing, and she chuckled happily as she sat and rested her head on his shoulder. Rowdy stretched out on the floor and beat his tail in time to the swing's squeaking chain. I stayed on the top step watching fireflies and enjoying a whiff of honeysuckle from Uncle Davy's pasture.

"Listen!" Aunt Kate suddenly lifted her head. "What's that?" Through the dusk we heard soft, plunky music coming from somewhere not too far away.

Uncle Stephen went out to the road to listen, then started across the tracks. Next thing we knew, he'd brought back Clay with a mandolin.

"Bring out your guitar," Uncle Stephen told Aunt Kate, "and let's all sing." I haven't mentioned that Aunt Kate started college as a music major. Big Mama convinced her to become a teacher, but she still played both cello and guitar and had a beautiful soprano voice.

We sat on the steps and sang four-part harmony while the air grew soft and dark and lightning bugs twinkled bright as stars. We started with songs older than Big Mama—"Down by the Old Mill Stream," "Let Me Call You Sweetheart," "I Love You Truly, Truly, Dear." Aunt Kate's voice and Clay's blended like honey. If Uncle Stephen was a bit off-key at times, he was too happy to care. I carried the alto and Rowdy kept time with his tail. "We don't just have a dog, we have a metronome," Uncle Stephen boasted, rubbing his curly black head.

I knew how happy Rowdy felt when, after one song, Clay strummed a couple of chords and said, "Carley, you're a danged good singer." I could have sung all night after that.

We switched from old songs to new ones from the radio— "If I'd Known You Were Coming, I'd Have Baked a Cake" and "Good Night, Irene." When we sang "I Love You a Bushel and a Peck," Clay leaned over real close and rubbed his cheek on the top of my head. I thought I'd died and gone to heaven. Finally Aunt Kate started strumming "Now the Day Is Over." As we sang, tears of pure happiness stung my eyes.

We all hated to stop.

Singing on our porch steps became a late Sunday tradition as long as evenings stayed warm. When autumn came and the air grew nippy, none of us wanted to move our singing indoors. As Clay said, "It just wouldn't sound the same with lights on." He was right. All my life when a summer evening gets up a little breeze and night begins to fall, I hear echoes of that golden quartet and remember the dreams I spun.

Chapter 5

When Uncle Stephen and I got ready to go pick Grace up, Aunt Kate handed me Rowdy's leash. "I don't want you all driving up to Pleasantdale that late without him."

Uncle Stephen gave an impatient huff. He always got mad if anybody acted like Negroes were more dangerous than white people. He also made us say "Negroes," not "colored people" like I'd been raised. He said it showed more respect. But he and I knew it wasn't Negroes Aunt Kate was worried about; it was Pleasantdale, a circle of unpainted shacks back in piney woods at the end of a dirt road, a short path away from the chair factory, where most of the men worked.

I hated that Grace had to live there. Its houses reminded me of a story I'd read about a witch whose house sat on high chicken legs. In Pleasantdale chickens ran underneath the high houses and out again. It was noisy, too. The houses were built close together, and everybody seemed to keep a radio in the window playing loud. Children yelled. Grown-ups shouted. Dogs barked. Roosters crowed at all times of day. I'd heard that sometimes men fought with knives.

None of the Negroes we knew lived there except Miranda, with whom Grace boarded. Janey Lou, who worked for Aunt Hannah, lived on the highway with her husband, Meek, who worked with Mr. Rob and kept their yellow house neat and trim. Jay Anderson and his mother, Bess, lived in a tidy house down behind the church, and she kept their bare yard swept and their windows polished. Jay's sister, Cecile, lived next to Janey Lou, who was their aunt, with her husband and her little girl, Maggie. But only Miranda, up in Pleasantdale, had a spare room—tacked onto the back of her house so recently that the boards were still yellow. As Mr. Hugh Fred's maid, she also had glass in her windows, all the boards on her house, an oil stove for winter, a fan for summer, and linoleum on her floor. Hers was the nicest house in Pleasantdale, which wasn't saying a lot.

I had wondered what I was supposed to do if somebody pulled a knife, so I was glad to have Rowdy along. "Grace will be glad to see Rowdy, anyway." I shoved his wide black rump into the backseat. But thank goodness we could ride with the windows down. Dog smell always made me sick in a closed car.

Grace was tall and slender, a cinnamon young woman with a soft, deep laugh. Her gold tooth flashed as she got off the bus and found us waiting for her. "I've got your school clothes," she announced, pointing to a big box. I sure hoped Big Mama had outdone herself this year.

Grace helped Uncle Stephen stow her cardboard case and Big Mama's box in the trunk, then got in the car and wrapped her arms around Rowdy's thick neck. "I missed you, dog." She wasn't just a maid; she was part of our family. Uncle Stephen called her "the grace of God in our midst." And she was saving her money to go to college like Jay and become a teacher. Uncle Stephen was tutoring her for the entrance exams.

As we drove down the dirt road through the warm evening darkness, walls of pines cooled us. Deep molasses voices called to one another with sudden bursts of laughter in between. As if the dark muted its exuberance, Pleasantdale wasn't as noisy by night and looked a lot friendlier than Job's Corner after dark. Late as it was, we found people sitting on porches on straight chairs or steps, looking for a breeze like we had earlier. The men wore undershirts or no shirts, the women cotton dresses. Everybody was barefoot like me. Moths hovered around porch lights while mothlike children played in the hard-packed yard in the middle of the houses. Girls jumped rope; the boys played a rough game of tag. Nobody fussed that they weren't in bed. Maybe Pleasantdale wouldn't be so bad to live in—in summertime.

But then Rowdy caught a scent of dog and started barking out the back window, and soon our car was surrounded by a pack of fierce, snarling dogs. "Hush, Rowdy," Grace commanded, but he was determined to protect us.

The dogs were the only noise when we drove up. All the people had hushed. Then one of the bigger boys recognized our black Chevy coupe. "It's the white preacher, with Grace. Hiya, Grace!" He tore across the yard on tough-soled feet. A pack of screaming children followed him. "Hiya, Grace! Hiya!" Uncle Stephen ordered Rowdy to hush, which he finally did. The bigger children smacked the other dogs, who slunk back under their own porches.

Grace was scarcely out of the car before a tiny boy was lifting his arms to be picked up and a slightly larger girl was hanging on to one of her legs. She picked up the baby and let him squeeze her around the neck. Around him she waved and called greetings to everybody by name. "Hiya, Seth. What's happening, Masie? I made your new dress."

"'Bout time you got here!" Miranda loomed large and very black on her porch. Her teeth shone in the dim light, and her eyes were big and white. She wore shoes, as befitted her position as cook for the wealthiest people in town, but she had cut the outer edges to give her corns room. She'd taken off her uniform and put on a loose wrapper that tied around her waist. It was the first time I'd ever seen her without an apron and white shoes.

"I got a surprise for you," she went on as soon as she'd swallowed Grace in her big arms. "My boy Ronnie's home on leave from the army. Thirty days. But don't you worry none. I've put him in the living room. You still have your own place."

I followed Grace and Miranda inside while Uncle Stephen got Grace's suitcase. The room was dim, lit only by one naked bulb dangling by a long cord from the ceiling, but I could see that a pillow and rumpled blanket covered the living room sofa, and a man's clothes were littered all over the floor. As Uncle Stephen carried Grace's suitcase in, a tall, chunky man with skin the color of shiny fudge came from the kitchen. He wore gray pants with dangling red suspenders and a ribbed undershirt. His shoulders and upper arms bulged with muscles.

He pulled up his suspenders and popped one against his chest as he stared down at Grace. "Well, what we got here? Mama never told me you was little and pretty."

Grace laughed nervously and looked at her shoes.

Uncle Stephen's glasses reflected the light bulb as he turned to Miranda and shoved his hand through his hair—a sure sign he was upset. "You still got room for Grace, Miranda? We can take her back with us tonight and look for another place tomorrow."

"'Corse I got space!" She stood with arms akimbo and spoke fiercely. "I told you, Ronnie's sleepin' out here. It's just temporary, anyhow. He'll be goin' back next month."

Uncle Stephen shoved his hair back again, hesitated, then turned to leave. "You take care of Grace, now."

Miranda folded her arms over her huge chest and frowned. "I'll take care of her," she assured him. "I surely will."

But as he climbed into the car, Uncle Stephen shook his head and muttered under his breath, "I just don't like it. I don't like it one bit."

Chapter 6

Janey Lou always brought Grace to work on her way to Aunt Hannah's, because they came at breakfast time and Miranda didn't go to the Keenes' until nine-thirty. In the evening Miranda stayed to wash their supper dishes. I had to wash ours and Aunt Hannah did her own.

When Janey Lou dropped Grace off the next morning, she came up the porch steps humming as usual. But as Uncle Stephen scrambled our breakfast eggs—he never let anybody else cook breakfast if he was there—he had a pucker between his eyes. "You going to be all right at Miranda's this month?"

Sunlight streamed through the kitchen window and glinted off Grace's gold tooth as she looked up from pouring steaming coffee for the grown-ups. "You don't need to worry. Miranda sleeps light, and she keeps her door open all night."

"How come you worryin'?" Abby wrinkled her own forehead as she started to climb into her chair.

"I'm not worrying, Abby. I'm cooking eggs. Have you fed Rowdy?"

"I forgot." She got out the dog food and poured it as importantly as if she was fixing to feed five thousand.

Over at the counter pouring milk, I, too, wondered why Miranda keeping her door open would keep Uncle Stephen from worrying, but I figured I'd ask Grace when Abby wasn't around. The only thing bigger than Abby's ears was Abby's mouth.

I didn't get a chance to talk to Grace that morning. At breakfast Aunt Kate announced she was going to school to fix up her classroom. No wonder she had put on a fresh-ironed green-and-white checked dress and tied her auburn curls at her neck with a big green velveteen bow.

"You don't fool us," Uncle Stephen teased. "You just want to drive your spiffy new car." We all laughed, because Aunt Kate's "spiffy new car" was a beat-up 1938 DeSoto she'd bought secondhand so she'd have something to drive back and forth to school. It was nearly as big as a boat, the body was so dented that Abby called it the Dimples Car, and we'd had to lay old quilts over the seats because the seat covers were so split. But Mr. Wash and Uncle Stephen had spent several evenings checking out the engine and assured everybody it would run.

"Don't insult my car." Aunt Kate spoke in her most severe schoolteacher's voice, but her eyes twinkled. "Anybody want to come along?"

"Me! Me!" Abby bounced like a sunbeam in her yellow sunsuit. She'd been begging to go to school practically since she could talk.

I'll come, too," I offered, holding my breath and eyeing a bushel of tomatoes a farmer had dropped off the day before after church. Since July the grown-ups and I had spent part of almost every day canning produce not only from Uncle Stephen's garden but also from all the church gardeners who regularly brought bags, baskets, and boxes to the manse. Canning involved peeling, chopping, and blanching the food, washing and sterilizing jars in boiling water, boiling the jars of food in a large speckled pot, then setting them on the counter to cool before storing them in the pantry. Staying in a kitchen full of boiling-hot steam wasn't my idea of fun, but with Aunt Kate at school, I suspected I'd be wanted at home to help Grace.

I saw Aunt Kate and Uncle Stephen look toward the tomatoes, too, but Grace said softly, "You go ahead. I'll get those done in no time."

I gave her a happy grin of thanks and swiped up the last bite of egg with my last bite of toast, trying to remember if my red and white dress with strawberry appliqués on the pockets was clean. My hair looked pretty good, but I'd need to wash my feet before I put on my white sandals ... I was picturing myself running into Mrs. Raeburn when I noticed Uncle Stephen looking at me curiously.

"Have you had a conversion? I never noticed any marked enthusiasm on your part last year to go to school."

"Last year was different. I didn't know anybody except Freda and Bonnie, and they never talked to me or let me sit with them on the bus."

"You could have ridden with me," Aunt Kate reminded me.

"Oh *yeah.*" I tried saying it the way Freda had Saturday. Uncle Stephen raised his eyebrows and Aunt Kate frowned, but Abby got her outrage in first.

"You tole a *story*, Carley." She put one hand on her hip and glowered. "You knew Preston and Ruthie. You better be careful, or Daddy'll wash your mouf out wif soap."

Before I could give my opinion of how much good it did anybody to know Preston or Ruthie, Uncle Stephen pushed back his chair. "This year Carley will know more people, so maybe school will improve." He hauled John from the highchair onto his shoulders. "How about if we men take a load to the gully while the women go to school?" John shrieked with delight and grabbed a fistful of his daddy's hair, as dark and straight as his own.

"Don't let him fall in," Aunt Kate said automatically.

Abby poised on her chair, one finger in her mouth, quivering with indecision. Going to the gully to hurl tin cans was one of her favorite things. Everybody in Job's Corner burned what would burn in fifty-gallon drums, and most, like Uncle Stephen, had a compost pile building fertilizer for the garden, but we took everything else—and I do mean everything—to the gully. Tin cans. Furniture broken beyond repair. Old appliances. Bottles. Wooden boxes. Every southern gully holds several hundred years of history. The only problem is, it's not in layers, for the smaller falls between the larger and the heavier outsinks the lighter. I would love to read how archaeologists will reconstruct our history from what they find there.

Finally Abby took her finger from her mouth with a pop. "I can go to de gully anytime, but school's dist for today."

Uncle Stephen gave her a pat of approval. "If everybody could learn to do the things that are just for today and postpone the ones they can do anytime, we'd have a wiser world."

As Abby and I headed to the car, Preston called from their porch, "Where you all goin'?"

"To school," I yelled back. "We gotta help Aunt Kate get ready."

"Maybe I oughta go help Uncle Gil. Let me go ask Mama if I can." Before I could point out he wasn't invited, he'd slammed the screened door behind him.

Preston's Uncle Gil was Mr. Gilbert Mayhew, our music teacher. He had also been the Bethel choir director and my Sunday school teacher until he'd had a falling out the previous winter with Uncle Stephen. They just couldn't agree about communism. Mr. Mayhew thought we ought to be digging nuclear shelters and was in charge of bomb drills at school, while Uncle Stephen maintained that most Russian people weren't dangerous and that both sides' leaders were just trying to scare us all to death. Mr. Mayhew finally got so mad, he left the church.

In just a second Preston bustled out the door and called breathlessly, "Mama says we can go if you get us home for dinner." Sue Mary ambled behind him, one hand held out for her invisible friend, Velma.

"Miss Pauline runs everybody's life but her own," I muttered as I climbed in front.

Abby scrambled into the backseat. "I gets a window. I doesn't want to ride the hump."

Aunt Kate arrived at the car with an armload of supplies and found her car full of children. She opened her mouth like she was going to protest, then huffed a little sigh and got in.

All the way to school Abby prattled importantly to Sue Mary about "decowating" bulletin boards, and Aunt Kate answered Preston's chatter like she wasn't really listening. I tried to picture what it would be like to go to school this coming year.

It had to be better than last year, which got off to a dreadful start and never improved. I always carried a book to recess in case I wasn't chosen for a team or invited to swing. Almost nobody talked to me as we waited our turn in the big gray bathroom or lined up at the long, white drinking trough with four spigots. Even at lunch people seldom spoke.

But then, I didn't try to make friends, either. Back home I was Carley Marshall of the department store Marshalls. I knew everybody and everybody knew me. I never had to make new friends, so I never learned how. And my first year in Job's Corner I'd been dealing with so much else, school seemed pretty unimportant. Climbing onto the yellow school bus in front of Miss Pauline's post office each morning divided my body from my spirit. My body, with part of my mind, went to school and performed adequately, if not brilliantly. My spirit and the best part of my mind hovered at the bus stop, awaiting my return. When I climbed down off the last high step, I'd inhale my waiting spirit and become whole again.

So it was not friends but Mrs. Raeburn I looked forward to. Always able to create whole cloth out of a few threads, I was well into a daydream in which she was confiding, "You have suffered so much, you truly understand me. I am so glad you are in my class" when gravel crunched beneath our tires as Aunt Kate turned into the school's wide circular drive.

"There's Uncle Gil!" Preston waved one warty hand out his window. "Hey, Uncle Gil. I came to help you get ready for school." As soon as Aunt Kate stopped, he roughly pushed out from behind my seat—our car had only two doors—and lumbered across the parking lot as fast as his thick body could go, toward Mr. Mayhew's shiny Ford. Driving a new green Ford instead of an old Chevy and an older DeSoto was another way Mr. Mayhew was different from us.

" ... haven't had my growth spurt yet," we heard Preston say as we got out of the car, "but it's comin' soon."

Mr. Mayhew gave us each a chilly nod. "Good morning, Mrs. Whitfield, Carley."

I wasn't feeling exactly friendly toward Mr. Mayhew. The last time I'd seen him was at a church trial where he'd told the world that I'd said things about Uncle Stephen I'd never said. On the other hand, I'd have to sit through his music class all year. Since I knew more music than most kids, last year he'd made me his assistant and let me play piano for our class while he conducted. If I didn't want to go back to writing pages of whole notes and half notes, I'd better be nice.

All those thoughts went through my head in a second. Aunt Kate must have been thinking something similar, because at exactly the same moment we put on the false smiles we'd learned at Big Mama's knee and said in unison, "Good morning, Mr. Mayhew."

Like we'd hoped, the smiles disconcerted him. Coals of fire on his head.

Preston waved one arm imperiously. "Come on, Sue Mary."

Mr. Mayhew looked like he didn't know what he'd do with a five-year-old all morning, but Sue Mary had other plans anyway. "I'm going to help Abby decowate the bulletin boards."

As Mr. Mayhew and Preston headed toward the school, I informed her, "It's not decowate, it's deco*rate*. Abby just won't say it right."

Abby ignored me. She was looking up at the school with satisfaction. "We's here. Isn't it a bee-*you*-tee-ful school?"

"Nobody but you ever thought so," Aunt Kate replied.

She had that right. Mount Vernon Elementary, grades one to eight, was a two-story brick cube any child could have designed. Offices were to the left of the front foyer, the library to the right. Double doors led to a huge, two-story auditorium with a high stage in front, six classrooms along its left side, and tall windows in its right-hand wall. Seventh and eighth grades were off an upstairs balcony, above the other classrooms, along with Mr. Mayhew's music room, the large art classroom, and a storage room. Bathrooms were behind the stage, and across from the girls' bathroom was a small school store. The cafeteria, like an afterthought, had been built in the backyard. We got wet going to lunch when it rained. The only earthly resemblance the school bore to George Washington's graceful home was eight white columns that held up a porch roof too high to provide shelter when we had to wait for buses in blowing rain. Unlike the other Mount Vernon, this one's porch was fifteen steep concrete steps above the ground, a real menace on icy days.

Abby, however, skipped like a ray of sunshine in her yellow sunsuit up the steps, copper curls bouncing in delight to be there. Sue Mary and Velma climbed timidly behind. Sue Mary wore red shorts and a red-and-white checkered shirt. I wasn't sure about Velma.

As soon as Abby tugged open one of the double white front doors, she shouted, "It still smells like school! And dere's de liberry still on dat side, and de office on de udder—"

"Imagine that," I told Aunt Kate as we struggled up the steps with boxes of supplies in our arms. "Nobody moved them all summer."

She chuckled and stopped halfway up to adjust her load and rest. "I just hope school lives up to Abby's expectations when she finally gets here."

We heard her announcing as we entered, "Dis big room after de office and de liberry is de awbitorium where Carley played de piano last year. It's got de tallest windows in de world on dat side, an' a stage behind dose curtains. Do you know de curtains got a cute little picture on dem?"

Expecting to hear Sue Mary, we were surprised to hear a man's clipped voice. "Yes, I do. I went to this school when I was a boy. I practically memorized that seal during chapel."

"What's chapel?" Abby asked.

"It's when you sit on a hard seat and listen to other boys and girls sing off-key, forget their lines in a play, or miss notes on the piano."

"Carley nebber misses," Abby said loyally. She turned and saw us coming. "Does you?"

But he didn't wait for my answer. By the time we got to her, all we saw was a brief glimpse of a tall rigid back disappearing around the stage.

"Mr. Pleasant," Aunt Kate murmured.

"Dere's your room, Mama!" Abby threw the words over her shoulder as she darted accurately toward the fourth-grade room. "Where's your room, Carley?"

"Big kids are upstairs with music." The seventh-grade door was closed. My stomach quivered. Would I get to see Mrs. Raeburn today? Would we speak?

Abby stopped and peered up. "How come de big kids gets to go upstairs?"

I'd never wondered, but Aunt Kate answered absently, "They're afraid smaller children might fall over the railings. Don't you and Sue Mary go up there, you hear me?"

"Okay." Abby skipped toward the classroom, Sue Mary behind her. I stood looking worriedly at the railings. Seemed a lot more likely big boys would push big girls over.

"Where's de bafroom?" Sue Mary asked at the door. "I gotta go."

"I'll show you." Abby turned, full of importance. They hurried past us and we heard her voice getting fainter and fainter. "Dat's de store where you can buy fings durin' wecess if you bwing a nickel. Carley likes pwetzels and Moon Pies, but I'm gonna buy ice cweam ebery day."

Aunt Kate hurried to open her classroom windows. "The first thing I want you to do is take Stephen's train to our car. I set it up for a unit on transportation last spring, and things were so confused at the end of last year, I just walked out and forgot it." She started taking apart the little oval track. "I want it in our car before somebody thinks it belongs to the school. He bought this train with his very first paycheck, and heaven help me if I don't get it home safely."

We couldn't find a box, so she piled my arms high with track, transformer, cars, a locomotive, and a caboose. As I headed for the front door, I could hardly see over my load. Before I was halfway down the auditorium, my glasses started slipping. I wiggled my nose to work them up, but they wouldn't budge. Exasperated, I rubbed my nose against the locomotive and finally got the glasses where they were supposed to be, but something fell to the floor.

A man came from behind and bent to retrieve it. "You dropped your coal tender." It was the man Abby had been talking to earlier. His voice was not mean, just remote and clipped, like he didn't want to talk very long.

"Is it dented?" I asked anxiously.

"No." He perched it on top of my pile. "May I ask where you got those and where you are taking them?" With black eyes, dark bristly hair, and a pointed nose, he looked like the porcupine in one of Abby's books.

"My Aunt Kate teaches fourth grade, and she forgot to take them home last spring, so she told me to take them to the car so nobody would think they belonged to the school." I finished a bit defiantly, because it dawned on me that was exactly what he was thinking. I adjusted the load to balance it better. He didn't deserve to know more, after suspecting me of stealing them.

He must be a teacher's husband, hanging around to drive her home when she finished with her room. But then I had a charitable thought. Maybe he was lonely for somebody to talk to. I was a real good talker.

"Uncle Stephen hasn't had them long, because he bought them secondhand with his first paycheck, since he never had a train as a little boy. He keeps saying he's going to build a shelf in his office for it to run on, but he hasn't had time. Maybe he will once Abby starts to school. Baby John isn't half as much trouble."

A muscle twitched in his cheek like he wanted to smile but had forgotten how. "Do you need help getting them to the car?"

"I'll be okay as soon as I get outside."

"I'll get the front door for you." His legs were long, so he reached the door before I did. As he reached out with his left arm to open the door, I saw that the right sleeve of his brown jacket was empty, pinned up at the elbow.

When he saw me noticing it, I blushed.

"Lost an arm in the war." It was the kind of tone that didn't welcome questions.

"Oh." I didn't know what else to say.

Still looking at him instead of where I was going, I stepped out the door and ran smack into Mrs. Raeburn.

She took several steps backward on high-heel shoes and teetered at the top of the concrete steps.

"Maddie!" The man rushed past me, caught her arm with his good one, and steadied her. "Are you okay?" He looked real glad to see her. His whole face was wrinkled in a smile.

For an instant her face brightened, too. But that changed so swiftly, I would wonder later if I'd imagined it. Anybody who didn't know better would think she was looking at a dog who'd just crawled out of a septic tank. When he saw that look, he dropped her arm like it had suddenly burned him.

She took a couple of steps along the porch and shivered all over in spite of the heat. "*You!* What are you doing here?" Even glaring, she was beautiful, her blue eyes flashing today more like steel than sky, and her cheeks bright pink. She wore a short-sleeved shirtwaist dress in black-and-white checks, with little red buttons down the front and a red belt. The dress curved where she did and had a wide flared skirt. Peering around my armful of train cars and tracks, I could see that her shoes were also red, with small white squares on the toes.

He flushed and turned so she couldn't see his empty sleeve. When he spoke, he didn't move his lips any more than if he'd been carved out of wood. "I'm the new principal. What are *you* doing here?"

So this was Mr. Donaldson. Who might be a murderer. He didn't look any older than Uncle Stephen or any more danger-ous. I ought to move a few steps, just in case, but I might have to protect Mrs. Raeburn. Bravely I stood my ground. Nobody noticed.

Her face was white and still angry. "I'm supposed to be teaching seventh grade. But when I applied for the job, they said Mr. White was still principal."

"He took early retirement last week. I was just assigned."

For one exciting second I thought she was going to faint.

He must have, too, because he stepped quickly toward her and took her elbow. "I didn't—your name wasn't—"

She pulled away. "It's Raeburn now. Maddie Raeburn."

"Raeburn." He spoke the word like it was the end of some world.

She turned to leave. "I'll go downtown and see if I can get a transfer."

"You can't. They've filled all positions as of today. I've had two teachers call already to see if we had a vacancy."

"Well, now you do. Seventh grade." She marched down the first few steps like she was going off to war. My heart fell the rest of the way. So much for this being a better year.

Halfway down she stopped.

He looked as upset as I felt. "You don't have to go," he called after her.

Her back stiffened and she spoke without turning around. "I ought to. But frankly, I can't afford it. I need this job. And I need to teach, to take my mind off—things. Just don't talk to me, you hear me?"

"I won't speak to you unless I have to. You just do a good job for the children. That's all I ask."

She turned, eyes flashing and fists clenched. "You're a fine one to talk about being good to children!"

He opened his mouth, then changed his mind. We all stood still for so long, I thought we'd probably die from old age on those steps. Obviously, neither of them remembered I was there. I didn't know whether to back into the building, cough, or what. The delicate way the coal tender was still sitting on top of my load, I was scared to move lest I topple it.

Finally he turned and reached with his left hand for the door. For the first time she could see his empty sleeve.

She gasped. "What happened to your arm?"

It was his turn to speak without turning around. "Well-aimed enemy fire."

"Your pitching arm?" The words were more cried than spoken.

His hand clenched the door handle. "My ex-pitching arm. Excuse me, I've got work to do. You know where your room is?"

"I know."

I wished he would turn around and look at her now. She was biting her lip, and her eyes were full of tears. She even made a little motion with one hand, like she wanted to draw him back. But he didn't see. He spoke over his shoulder. "We'll have a brief teachers' meeting just before noon."

"I'll be there." Her voice was very small.

He strode past me into the hall like I was part of the door.

I cleared my throat and tried to think of something—anything—to say.

She looked at me in surprise and wiped tears off her cheeks. "Have I seen you before?"

"Yes, ma'am. Down at Aunt Hannah's on Saturday. I'm Carley Marshall—" I stuck out one hand from beneath the load and dropped the dratted coal tender.

She picked it up and put it back on my stack. "Hello, Carley," she said absently, then walked quickly inside. For all she had noticed, I could have had two heads and seven eyes. I'd sure wasted time putting on my red and white dress with strawberry appliqués. And now I'd have to iron it all over again before I could wear it to school.

Chapter 7

School began on the last day of August. I went to breakfast hoping nobody would pay me any attention, but Abby immediately spoke around a mouthful of scrambled eggs. "What's de matter wif your socks?"

I ducked my head. "Nothing. I just hitched them up, that's all."

She craned her neck and peered at my face. "An' you got on lipstick!" It was just Tangee natural—hardly any color at all.

Uncle Stephen's hand pulled my chin reluctantly upward, then he and Aunt Kate shook their heads in unison. "Not yet, honey," Aunt Kate said, almost apologizing.

"But the socks pass," he added. "Flags flying high into adulthood. Next thing we know, you'll have children of your own." He grinned as he handed me the milk.

Rather than ride with Aunt Kate, I climbed on the bus that crossed our far-flung community collecting children for both Mount Vernon and Statesville High in town.

Seventh grade failed to live up to any of my dreams. Same old desks and splintery floors. Same smell of pine cleaner, chalk, and ghosts of sweaty children. Mr. Donaldson made a change from our old principal at morning chapel but talked like the tin woodman of Oz, hardly moving his mouth. He never even cracked a smile to welcome us. Mr. Mayhew made the same speech he'd made the year before, telling us Russia could bomb us any minute and we'd be having our first bomb drill later that day. He did his best to pretend I wasn't there during music class. Since we weren't singing yet, I didn't know if I'd get to play or not. And Mrs. Raeburn treated me like I was a stranger, not somebody who had witnessed a wrenching episode in her life.

"She acts like she's never seen me before," I told Uncle Stephen indignantly that evening. "And she's seen me twice!" At my feet Rowdy gave a sharp woof. We could always count on him to support us in indignation.

Uncle Stephen and I were rocking companionably after supper while Aunt Kate put John to bed. It was Abby's first night to help Grace with dishes, which she took very seriously. Halfway through the meal she'd started ordering us, "Eat fast. I gotta wash all dese dishes."

Before Uncle Stephen came out, I'd been poring over an ad for deodorant in the newest *Life*. I wasn't certain what deodorant was for, but the ad challenged, "Are you always lovely to love? Suddenly, breathtakingly, you'll be embraced, held, kissed. Perhaps tonight." I looked longingly across the road, willing it to happen, but saw no sign of Clay. Maybe if I got some...

At that point Uncle Stephen wandered out, so I knew the evening news report was over.

"Do you think I ought to get deodorant?" I blurted before I thought. My cheeks flamed, but he just settled himself in his chair and slid down on his long spine.

"I haven't noticed you needing it. Have you?"

"Not yet. . . ." I looked across the road again, wishing Clay would appear.

He reached for his pipe and tobacco. "Ask Kate. She's more likely to know about that than I am. How do you like your new teacher?"

That's when I told him indignantly, "She acts like she's never seen me before."

He sucked the pipe to clear it and filled it with fresh, sweet tobacco. "Maybe she's got a bad memory. What can you say good about her?"

"She wears gorgeous clothes. Every time I've seen her, she's had on black and white, and she looks truly elegant in it. Today she had on a black circular skirt with one little yellow stripe at the bottom, a white linen blouse, and a yellow scarf at her neck. And her shoes had daisies on them. . . ." I trailed off. He was more interested in filling his pipe and getting it going. "So now I've said something nice. Are you satisfied?" I sounded sassy but didn't care. She was so beautiful. I was certain we could be best friends if she'd just get to know me better.

"It's a beginning." Uncle Stephen puffed away.

"You know what's weird, though? She's got this old doll. It's nothing but red flannel cut out, sewed, and stuffed. The face is a circle with the eyes, nose, and mouth embroidered. And it's so old, it's not even red anymore, more like dark pink. The face is so old, it's gray." I wrinkled my nose in distaste. "It's really dreadful! But she had it in her car down at Aunt Hannah's, and today she brought it in and propped it up right on her desk. Then this afternoon when she got ready to leave, she put it with her pocketbook to take with her. Isn't that funny?"

"Maybe somebody special gave it to her."

"Just Aunt Hannah. And Aunt Hannah said to burn it and she'd make her a new one, but Mrs. Raeburn wouldn't." I sneaked another peek across the road, hoping Clay would come out on his porch, see us, and come over.

Uncle Stephen raised his arms high over his head in a big stretch. "I gave up trying to understand women a long time ago. How are you doing with the other students?"

I tried to think of something that would make him happy. "Freda and Bonnie would have let me sit with them on the bus today, but Freda had on a full skirt and didn't want to mash it. She said they would've liked to have me otherwise."

Abby came through the screened door rubbing a dollop of lotion into her hands. Climbing onto her daddy's lap, she burrowed her head under his chin and wiped extra lotion across the front of her blue shirt. After that none of us said a word. It was the kind of late summer evening that deserves silence. Cicadas were buzzing their little hearts out in all the trees. The air was sweet with pine trees and cotton dust, with whiffs now and then from Uncle Davy's pasture behind the house. Cows smell pretty sweet when they aren't too close. The last of the lightning bugs winked just above our grass as the sky turned slowly gray.

Then I smelled something else. "Preston's burning trash again. You don't reckon Miss Pauline lets him burn our mail, do you? I haven't heard from Big Mama all week."

"Co'rse not!" Scandalized, Abby defended Miss Pauline, her second-best friend.

"I'm sure she doesn't," Uncle Stephen agreed. "And if it makes Preston feel like a man to burn a few papers each evening, let him burn them."

"He'll burn us all down one day," I warned.

"Maybe you and Preston will fall in lub when he's a man," Abby suggested. "Den you can stop him burnin' stuff."

"Never," I told her. "I can hardly stand going to school with him."

"Me'n Sue Mary's goin' to school." She rubbed her head against her daddy's chin. "Did you know dat, Carley? Grace is gonna teach us eb'ry mornin', an' we's gonna color and wead and wite. Just like you." She sounded like she'd been awarded a prize by President Truman.

"Miss Pauline will have a fit," I warned. "She won't let Sue Mary be taught by a Negro." I tried not to remember I'd felt the same way myself only a few months ago.

"Grace must be part white," Abby informed us. "She's too smart to be all colored."

Uncle Stephen's rocker stopped.

"Negro, not colored." I spoke quickly before he could. "And where did you hear that nonsense?"

"Miss Pauline says."

"You know better than that. Lots of Negroes are smart as white people. Look at Jay. Right, Uncle Stephen?"

If I expected praise, I had another think coming. Instead he asked in a mild tone, "What do you mean, lots of Negroes are as smart as white people? Are all white people smart?"

"Well, no, some of them aren't. . . ."

Abby was smart. She figured out what he wanted before I did. "Some white peoples are smart and some Negroes are smart. Grace 'n' Jay are real smart."

"That's right, Abbikins!" He sounded like she was the smartest one of all.

"Smart people don't say *peoples*," I told her tartly.

"Dey does if dey isn't allowed to go to school." She slewed her eyes at me. "I still bet you 'n' Preston will fall in lub."

I didn't deign to answer. I was hugging the knowledge that I didn't have to fall in love. I was already in love. Every song I ever practiced those days I dedicated to Clay, and I preferred those that were soft and sweet. In a flat stationery box between my mattress and my springs I had three gum wrappers Clay had thrown away at various times and Sunday bulletins with a circle around "Choir Director, Clay Lamont." I figured they'd be the beginning of the scrapbook I'd keep when we got married. He'd be real pleased, when we got married, to know I'd kept them.

I was getting ready for Clay almost every day. When Aunt Kate took me to Newberry's Dime Store for school supplies, I bought pillowcases to embroider for my hope chest. I practiced kissing my pillow every single night. And I persuaded Aunt Kate to buy me some Listerine. I didn't think I had halitosis, but the ad said, "It could be absent one day and present the next, without your realizing you have it." I'd looked *halitosis* up in my dictionary and been appalled. When Clay and I finally kissed, I didn't want to have bad breath.

I remembered something I wanted to ask Uncle Stephen. "Do you think I could get a key to my bedroom door? I'm a little scared up there at night, and if I could lock myself in, I'd feel a whole lot safer." I'd practiced saying that several times to get it sounding right.

He shrugged. "I can't imagine what could get upstairs without me hearing it, but there's probably a key around somewhere. Look in the junk drawer in the kitchen."

The first key I tested fit the lock in my bedroom door. It didn't occur to me to check and see if they all did. I was delighted to finally be able to lock out Abby's prying eyes when I needed to practice kissing Clay in the mirror. That night I felt very grown-up as I locked my door for the first time. As I sat by my window yearning for just one sight of him, I counted. It would be five years until we could get married. I doubted my family would let me marry before seventeen.

Considering that nobody had even hinted at the facts of life in my presence, that was a pretty good assumption. The very next Saturday, however, my education began.

One reason Uncle Stephen was popular with the men in his church was, he grew up on a farm and knew how to do things most preachers didn't. That particular Saturday afternoon he went up to help Mr. Wash Lamont fix his hay baler. He always said it was a shame men couldn't find the same harmony in religion and politics they achieved tearing down a piece of machinery. Abby and I didn't find harmony, though. "You girls come play with Jimmy and Ruth," Uncle Stephen suggested as he got ready to leave. "They don't play with other children much."

"I doesn't like Jimmy," Abby objected. "He's mean. 'Sides, he looks funny." Both Lamont children had large nostrils and dark eyebrows that nearly met across their foreheads.

"He doesn't look funny; he just looks like his daddy," Aunt Kate corrected her. "And if you stay home, you'll have to nap. I'm canning applesauce this afternoon." Abby immediately started for the door. But right off the bat Jimmy sprayed her with the hose and she stomped home, dripping and furious. Ruth took me inside, despite my suggestion that we stay and play in the hose, hot as it was.

"I don't want to stay out," she whined through her nose. Ruthie always talked through her nose, to make up for breathing through her mouth. "Let's play in my room." Trying to be nice, I agreed, even though what she offered was silly coloring books of animals and flowers.

"Don't you have any paper dolls? I've got Debbie Reynolds."

She tossed her stubby dark braids. "Movie stars are evil."

"Not all of them. Debbie Reynolds is real sweet, so her paper dolls are okay. My Big Mama says so, and she's a strict Baptist."

"Well, my mama says they aren't, and she's a Presbyterian." She thrust a babyish coloring book at me. "Pick a page to color. But tear it out carefully and don't rip my book."

I was coloring a dumb brown bunny in some grass when Ruthie's green crayon snapped. "Peanuts and pickles!" She hurled it to the floor. "Now I can't color trees or grass or anything!"

"Make the trees orange and brown, like they've already changed color."

"Don't want to." She ripped up the page and threw the pieces in her wastebasket. Suddenly her voice dropped to a hiss. "Wanna see me draw?" She ran to her school notebook, tore out a page, and quickly drew a woman with no clothes and huge bosoms.

I was horrified. I'd never even seen a naked woman except once when I walked in on Mama in the bathtub. She'd squeaked and grabbed a towel, and I hadn't been able to look her in the eye the rest of the day.

"I don't like that kind of drawing," I informed Ruthie. But I couldn't help looking.

Miss Nancy came to the door. "You girls are mighty quiet. What's going on up here?"

Ruthie thrust the page at her. "Carley's drawing me pictures."

Miss Nancy snatched that picture and tore it into little bitty pieces; then she hurried down the hall. I heard the toilet flush, and she stomped back sounding like five women instead of one. "Don't you come back up here to play again," she told me, black eyes snapping.

"Don't worry," I told her, scrambling to my feet, "I won't." I rushed downstairs.

Uncle Stephen was coming toward the porch. "I was about to call you. Ready to go?"

I stiffened my shoulders, waiting for Miss Nancy to tattle, but she just pinched her lips and shook her head at me. As far as she was concerned, I was a sinner beyond the pale.

Chapter 8

At Sunday school assembly the next morning, Mr. Hugh Fred and Miss Emily came in beaming. She was carrying a cake covered with pink icing. He announced, "Today is Freda's fourteenth birthday. Miss Emily and I thought you might like a little birthday cake and punch before you start your lesson. Come here, Freda, honey, and let us all sing to you."

As Freda rose from the piano bench, one of the high school boys called from the back, "It's Charles's birthday, too, isn't it Charles? He's *sixteen*." All the big boys sniggered.

Charles Beal turned bright red as we all turned to look at him. Charles was a sophomore on the Statesville High football team, and his parents had a farm up the road. The second of their eight children, he looked just like the rest: blue eyes, blond hair that curled if he didn't keep it short, and cheeks that always looked chapped by an icy wind. His cheeks grew even redder if he had to talk to a girl, even a little girl. We went to Sunday dinner at their house once, and he never spoke one word to Abby, Aunt Kate, or me. The only thing he discussed with Uncle Stephen was football. As soon as dinner was over, he ducked his head and excused himself.

"That right, Charles?" Mr. Hugh Fred called. Poor Charles nodded like he was confessing to murder. "Come on up here, boy. We'll sing to you both."

Charles stumbled to the front and stood waiting for us to shoot him. Freda stood on tiptoe and kissed his cheek. "Happy Birthday, Charles. I didn't know we were twins."

"Happy birthday," he mumbled, eyes on his worn brown shoes.

"Well," said Miss Emily brightly, "shall we sing? I guess we can do without the piano."

"Carley can play," Preston called. "She practices every day on the Anderson piano." He still resented Aunt Hannah giving our family her sister's piano.

"Can you play 'Happy Birthday'?" Mr. Hugh Fred sounded like he suspected I couldn't, but thought he ought to ask to be polite.

"Yes, sir. It's not hard." I went to the piano and did so. I even threw in a few flourishes Pop had taught me.

"That was fine!" He beamed. But Freda gave me a look like I'd missed a hundred notes and should never be allowed to play in public.

She laughed, though, and tossed her curls as she passed out the cake. Both the cake and its pink icing tasted of strawberries. I had two pieces. Freda even persuaded Charles to hand out little paper cups of drink. Being rich, the Keenes had brought big cans of Hi-C with real juice in it. We went into church feeling truly blessed.

The next morning Bonnie and I climbed on the school bus to find Freda already sharing her seat with Charles. "We don't have any more room," she said with a helpless little shrug. Obviously, they couldn't share with Bonnie—Charles's shoulders took up half a seat.

His sister Mary was in twelfth grade and drove our bus, a job allotted to responsible and mature seniors. It wasn't as dangerous as later generations might think, because putting children from six to eighteen on the same bus curbed rowdy behavior. It's hard to be too bad when all your siblings and half your cousins are there to carry news back home. Uncle Stephen said Mary was exceptionally bright and he wanted her to apply for a scholarship at Duke. Aunt Kate always added, "Poor thing." I think that was because Mary was nearly as big as Charles, a lumpy girl with frizzy blond hair and glasses thicker than mine. And while she didn't blush like Charles, she was equally silent. She never greeted us as we climbed on the bus, just closed the door like a robot.

That morning as I took the end of a seat beside two second-graders near the back, I saw Mary watching Freda and Charles in her rearview mirror. His head was bent toward her, and she was talking almost as fast as Aunt Hannah could. She was also smiling, tossing her ringlets, blinking her stubby eyelashes, and twinkling her hands. I couldn't tell if Charles was fascinated or numb. I also could not see what Freda saw in him. Sure, he was a good player for the Statesville Greyhounds. Uncle Stephen saw him play when he was just a ninth-grader, and he said Charles got tackled by three boys at once and never fell down. The other Greyhounds called him Old Unstoppable. But compared with my slender, sweet Clay, he was a mound of boy almost as wide as he was tall, with huge red hands.

Freda sat with Bonnie going home, because football players had to stay at school to practice, but after that she sat with Charles every morning. Bonnie, like me, now had to find a seat where she could.

The next Sunday, after Freda played for the children's Sunday school assembly, she left as if she were going to the bathroom. I wandered down the hall later and saw her in the high school class, sitting between Charles and Mary. After church she went to stand with the two of them in a group of high schoolers under the big magnolia in the middle of the churchyard. As Miss Emily and Mr. Hugh Fred came out of church, they glanced that way. Miss Emily exclaimed, "Mary Beal seems to be taking a great interest in Freda."

Mr. Hugh Fred puffed up a little with pride. "Freda's getting too mature for children her own age. Oh, not you, Carley," he added when he noticed me standing there.

The Beals had so many children, Mary and Charles usually drove the pickup to church. Freda came running to her parents and begged, "Can I go home with Mary this afternoon? She'll bring me back, and she can help me with arithmetic." Her parents never saw how much closer she sat to Charles than to Mary.

At dinner—which we ate at home for a change—Uncle Stephen told us, "I've had an idea, Kate. A lot of our kids don't drive. How about if we ask their parents to drop them off here on the nights Statesville plays a home game, and I'll get a couple of other men to help me drive them down to watch, then bring them back here for popcorn or something after the game?" Aunt Kate agreed, but I knew it wasn't Uncle Stephen's idea. I'd seen Freda talking to him right after church.

She must have talked to her daddy too, because he was one of the men who drove. How she persuaded either of those two men to include herself, Bonnie, and me in with the high school crowd, I will never know. Bonnie and I didn't care a thing about football. But I was glad to go. Clay drove the third car.

Mrs. Raeburn came to all the games, too. It mortified me to see my teacher acting like a regular woman, but she never noticed me, even when she came to sit with Mr. Hugh Fred. One night she brought another woman with her, and he said proudly, "Maddie and Cassie used to be cheerleaders back in high school." I could have guessed. Every time somebody from Statesville caught a ball, they jumped up yelling and waving their pom-poms. It like to embarrassed me to death to be sitting where people could see me when they stared at *them*.

Mr. Donaldson came to most games, too, but he sat by himself down at the other end of the bleachers. He must like football. Whenever Statesville carried the ball, he actually got excited.

Until then I'd felt well dressed if I had on clothes I liked. Now I discovered that well dressed had nothing to do with what I liked but everything to do with what other girls liked. By the second week Freda had persuaded her mother to buy her V-necked sweaters and white blouses to go under them, wide circular skirts, and even some fake pearls. She looked just like the high school girls from town. And whenever Charles carried the ball, she jumped up and down and screamed just like them—as if he were about to save the world. I was surprised her daddy didn't fuss at her. Instead he seemed real pleased. "Freda really loves football," he told Uncle Stephen. "She even understands the game."

Chapter 9

One afternoon after I'd practiced the piano for an hour, I decided to go to the store for a Mary Jane. I gargled with Listerine real good, in case Clay came along, then wandered down the road with Rowdy lumbering slowly along, sniffing weeds at my heels.

Though the wind was brisk and the air smelled of fall, the sun lay in great golden bands on the worn floorboards of the store's front porch. I found Mrs. Cameron inside waving a white rag over the dusty counter like a witch casting spells. Motes whirled in the autumn sunlight, then settled right back.

"What you doing?" I plopped my penny on the counter and fumbled in the jar for candy.

"Dusting. Needed it, you said."

"What you really need in here is a jukebox. Liven the place up a bit." I snapped my fingers, hoping she'd notice I could snap my left hand as well as my right. I'd been practicing.

She didn't notice squat. "Lively enough to suit me. But I thought a little dustin' might not hurt." She darted the cloth toward the counter and back without removing hardly a thing.

I popped the Mary Jane in my mouth and chewed until the sweet taffy began to soften, then spoke thickly through it. "Needs more than dabs here and there."

"Well, if you're so smart, do it, then." She handed me the cloth and hobbled toward a rush-bottomed chair near the cold black stove in the middle of the store.

Me and my big mouth. I ran the dust cloth over the counter and lower shelves and promptly sneezed. Pretty soon the cloth was pink rather than white. But finally the oak counter gleamed where one ray of sun hit it. "There. That looks better. But a little polish wouldn't hurt." I bustled out the front door and shook the cloth, hoping somebody would see me doing a good deed. I knew the Bible said to do them in secret, but I liked for somebody to *know* I was doing them in secret. Unfortunately, nobody was out to notice.

I went back in and found Mrs. Cameron considering the shelves rising from the floor to far above both our heads behind the counter. "Maybe we ought to do them shelves next."

I wasn't about to dust all those shelves. I offered as much charity as I felt. "I'll do the top two. You can reach the rest."

Her hooded eyes considered me as she weighed the offer. "What'll you take?"

Four sections times two shelves—about a half hour's work. I was about to say, "A Hershey bar" when my eyes lit on two small, square boxes on a lower shelf. "A box of deodorant?"

Her eyes narrowed. "What you needin' that for?"

"You never know when you'll need it. It's good to be prepared," I said recklessly.

She nodded. "Better'n candy, anyway. Your teeth are gonna rot."

"If they do, they're my teeth." Big Mama would have skinned me alive, talking that way to a grown-up, but the old witch had been rude first. I climbed onto a box, then onto the counter itself. In order to reach the shelves, I had to lean across the space between the counter and the shelves and brace myself with one elbow. I hoped to goodness I wouldn't fall.

I pulled out some old cans, wiped their furry tops, then opened them and wrinkled my nose. "This snuff's been here a hundred years. The cans have rusted! You can't sell them."

"Leave 'em be, girl. I never throw anything out. Like you said a minute ago, can't ever tell when somebody'll need it. Best to be prepared. That snuff, now. Might not be good for dipping, but it'll kill bugs. You just get on with your work and don't worry about what's there. Some of them things been on the shelf since old Mr. Cameron died."

I was in the mood for a good love story. "How did you all meet?"

"He owned this store. Saw him most every week all my life."

"Was he young and handsome?" I stretched to reach the far back corner. A spider scuttled out, and I nearly lost my balance getting out of its way.

She snorted. "More'n twenty years older'n me and had a game leg. But his wife had died that winter, and my mama and daddy, too. It was a bad winter, that one. I'd moved in with my brother, but it warn't a good place to be. Too many children to look after, and me 'n' his wife didn't suit. So when I come for shoe polish one day, Mr. Cameron reached out and caught me by the wrist. 'Marry me?' he said, just like that. I was fair surprised, it being so sudden, but I said yes. Wasn't nobody else I liked, and marrying him was better than raising my brother's brats."

Didn't sound very romantic to me. "Did you have children?" Big Mama said some women didn't like to be asked that, because they had sorrows too great to bear. Mrs. Cameron didn't strike me as likely to be one of them.

"Never had and never wanted 'em. Mr. Cameron had a girl by his first marriage might near as old as me, but we never got along. Ain't seen hide nor hair of her since her daddy got kilt and left me the store." She gave a raspy little cackle.

I remembered something Miss Nancy said a year before. "Didn't he get hit by the train?"

She shifted in her chair. "Sure did. Died on that track right out there." She pointed with her cane. "Was staking his cow and didn't hear the train coming. He was deaf as a post by then."

I shuddered and frowned down at her in disbelief. Twice I'd been too close to trains for comfort. "He staked his cow on the railroad tracks?"

"Yup. Hated seeing all that good, sweet grass beside the tracks go to waste, so he'd stake her out there on a long rope. No need to worry; she'd get out of the way when the train come by. But that day he had his back to the train and didn't feel it coming, I guess. He was dragged a hundred feet, but they said he never knew what hit him."

"Were you heartbroken?" I still hoped for a good romantic story.

She considered. "Nope. But I was saddened some. He was a good man. The edge has gone off it by now, of course. It's been nigh on thirty-five years."

I was so astonished I nearly fell off my counter. "Thirty-five *years?* From the way Miss Nancy told it, I thought it happened a year or two back."

"Nancy always could milk a story for the last drop of death and disaster."

I nodded, feeling grown up and wise. "That's what I've noticed, too. Seems like anything that happens to anybody, she can think of somebody else it happened to who died."

She cackled. "That's Nancy to a tee. Up to her gizzard in anticipated disaster."

I held up a box of the funniest little round buttons I'd ever seen. "What are these for?"

"Shoe buttons. Bet you never saw a shoe that needed buttons, did you? All our shoes had buttons when I was a girl. Used to buy mine in this very store. You can't tell to look at me now, but I was a pretty little thing back then. Red hair I could sit on, and a seventeen-inch waist. Tiny little feet, too. I bought lots of shoe buttons. I keep 'em because they may come back in style."

I sincerely doubted it but didn't argue. I was getting tired of leaning over that wide space. I'd struck a bad bargain. One little box of anything wasn't enough for dusting two shelves covered with years of filth. Old witch, she'd known that when she made her bargain. But if she was waiting for me to complain or quit, she could wait until kingdom come.

To pass the time, I said, "If you'd had children, you'd have needed a bigger house." The Cameron house was odd in Job's Corner. All the others were made of wood, but hers had white asbestos shingles instead of boards, and a couple of little stoops, in front and at the side, instead of a proper porch. Inside, the whole thing didn't have but three rooms and a little bathroom.

Her answer surprised me. "Had a bigger house. Big as the manse. Burned down four years after Mr. Cameron died."

"Oh, I'm sorry."

I could have saved my breath. "Best thing ever happened to me. Cold, drafty place, impossible to clean and more impossible to heat. Built what I wanted, a snug little place just my size. Every woman ought to have a house her own size once in her lifetime. Now you get on with your work and let me rest a bit. All this chatter wears a body out."

When I looked down a few minutes later, she was dozing, one cheek resting on the back of the hand that held her cane before her. I could practically count the soft white hairs that crossed her pink scalp to meet in a white bun at the nape of her neck. I finished the shelf and slid off the counter as silently as I could.

Feeling very righteous and a bit martyred, I tiptoed out to the porch to shake out the filthy rag for the final time. All that hard work—and I'd really just shifted a little dust. My skirt and blouse were so filthy, they'd both have to be washed and ironed before I could wear them again.

When I got back, Mrs. Cameron was sitting erect, slewing her snake eyes at me and daring me to say she'd been asleep. She jerked her head toward the counter. A box of deodorant sat by five Mary Janes. I left the Mary Janes, although it nearly killed me to do it. "My granddaddy always said a bargain's a bargain; make it and stick to it," I informed her haughtily.

Her black eyes snapped. "My granddaddy said pay your workers fair, and he was older than your granddaddy, Miss Smartypants. If you don't think you earned that candy, give it to Abby. She knows how to be grateful for what she gets. Take it and go, before I change my mind."

I took it and got out. As I headed across her yard, I found myself thinking, *What we need in there is a stiff broom and buckets of soapy water.*

"What you need," I told myself sternly, "is a man in a white suit and a little wagon to carry you away for even *thinking* such a thing!"

I hurried up to my room and opened the box that would prepare me for Clay's sudden passion. Inside was a tiny white jar filled with cream. The directions said, "Apply daily to prevent odor." It didn't say where. Since I was preparing to be kissed, and since Listerine already took care of my breath, I gingerly put a small circle of cream around my mouth. After that I went out each morning ready for anything.

Part 2

Nobody Knows
the Trouble I've Seen ...

Autumn 1950

Chapter 10

Janey Lou's car stopped out front, like it did almost every morning, to let Grace out. Since it was Saturday, I was reading on the porch and Aunt Kate and Abby were fast asleep. As Grace came up the steps, I saw she had a scrape on her cheek and one eye swelled shut.

"What on earth happened to you?"

"I ran into a door." Her voice trembled. "Is Mr. Stephen here?"

"No, he's still out on his walk. Are you all right?"

Grace began to tremble all over like a little bird. Next thing I knew, she'd flung herself into a rocker, dropped her head into her lap, and started to bawl.

"What's the matter? What's the matter?" But no matter how often I asked, she just shook her head and sobbed, rocking back and forth. Aunt Kate liked to sleep late on Saturdays, but this was too much for me to handle. I ran to get her.

Aunt Kate was burrowed down with the covers pulled up over her ear. I shook her shoulder, but she burrowed deeper, like waking up was the last thing in the world she wanted to do. At seven-thirty on a Saturday morning, it practically was. "Whassamatter?"

"Grace is having a fit on the porch. I can't make her stop crying."

Aunt Kate groaned. As she hauled herself out of bed, I could tell that if Grace wasn't crying when Aunt Kate got

there, I was going to be in big trouble. I eased toward the door
to be sure I could still hear her. "Listen." I held the door wide.
"She's sobbing like her heart will break." I'd read that somewhere and it seemed to fit.

Aunt Kate ran her fingers through her hair, reached for her
old green chenille robe, and padded toward the porch. I hoped
Miss Pauline wasn't looking. She'd tell everybody in Job's Corner Mrs. Whitfield went out on her porch in nothing but her
nightclothes, and the way she'd tell it, people would think
Aunt Kate had been parading out there practically naked, when
the truth was, that old robe covered her more than most of her
clothes. Miss Pauline had what Uncle Stephen called "a real
knack for embellishing the truth."

"Grace?" Aunt Kate asked sleepily from the screened door.
But as soon as she opened it, she hurried over, bent down, and
wrapped Grace in her arms like she was Abby or me. "Honey,
what on earth's the matter?"

Grace rocked back and forth and shook her head.

Aunt Kate lifted her from the chair. "Come to my room."

Grace stood up as bent over as Mrs. Cameron and looking
almost that old. Aunt Kate put an arm around her and helped
her across the hall. Grace hugged her stomach like it might fall
apart if she let go. When I started to follow, Aunt Kate shook
her head. "Stay out here and help Stephen fix breakfast when
he comes."

I waited until she'd closed her door, then tiptoed swiftly
around the porch and into Abby's room by the side porch door.
Until a few months ago I'd gotten most of my information by
listening at doors. Then Uncle Stephen and Aunt Kate declared
a new policy in the family of telling children about important
things that happened. I suspected they wouldn't tell me the
whole truth about this, though. So to justify being there, I told
myself that good reporters had to know what was going on at
all times. I was just practicing being a reporter.

Abby, as usual, was sleeping humped on top of her covers.
I eased her back under the blanket, then crept to pull the door

between her room and Aunt Kate's open just the teeniest crack. I could see Grace sitting on the edge of Aunt Kate's bed with Aunt Kate's arm around her. She was crying so hard, I could hear just a few words and had to piece them together like a quilt. Even then I didn't understand everything she meant.

"... up to Keenes' ... overnight with Freda ... a concert."

Mr. Hugh Fred loved classical music and always bought tickets when a concert came to Charlotte. Because they were so late getting home, they generally arranged for Miranda to spend the night with Freda. She must have done that last night.

"... went on to sleep ... came in ... held me down ..."

I didn't understand the question Aunt Kate gasped, but it sounded like "Taped?" Grace nodded and looked at the floor like she was ashamed of something. I could picture Ronnie, Miranda's son, going into Grace's room but couldn't figure out why he should have taped her, or with what. Most of all, I couldn't figure why Grace was ashamed.

Aunt Kate murmured something else, and Grace raised brimming but indignant eyes. "I did try to fight him!" She gingerly touched one cheek, then bent her head and mumbled again. I only got a few words. "... threatened ... knife." Again she clutched her middle, and rocked on the bed crying like a woman I saw once after her baby died. "I feel so dirty. I'll never get clean again." I didn't understand that part either, because her gold dress and olive green sweater were spick and span, and so was she—except for the bruise and swollen eye.

Aunt Kate held her, crooning like she was Abby or John. When she grew still, Aunt Kate spoke too low for me to hear. Grace shook her head and cried loudly, "Never had and never want to again. I want to die! Put me on a bus for home, please. Please let me go home."

"You need to see a doctor first." Aunt Kate got up and went to her dresser for a Kleenex.

My eyes met hers in the mirror, but before she turned, I had shut Abby's door and fled to the porch. Uncle Stephen sat peacefully in one of the rockers, scraping out the inside of his pipe with a little metal tool he carried in his pocket. Aunt Kate always said that cleaning and refilling pipes took up as much time for men as cleaning whole houses did for women. Rowdy sprawled beside him, cooling his stomach on the wide floor-boards, recovering from their walk. A year before, he went walking with Uncle Stephen every morning, walked at least twice as far by the time he'd chased all the fascinating odors and rustlings on their way, and still came back with pep. Now he didn't even go walking every morning, and when he did it wore him out.

"Everybody else still asleep?" Uncle Stephen asked softly. "Grace doesn't seem to have arrived, either."

I sat in the swing and pushed off with one toe. "Aunt Kate's talking to Grace. She's been beat up. I think Miranda's son went in last night and taped her while Miranda was up at Freda's."

"Jumpin' Jehoshaphat!" Uncle Stephen's pipe and the little metal tool clattered onto the gray porch floor, and he hurried inside without noticing he'd dropped them. I picked up the pipe and the tool and tried reaming it out, but it stunk so much, I gagged. Pipe tobacco smells wonderful burning but pipes are nasty things.

In a few minutes I heard Aunt Kate in the hall dialing the phone. "Hannah, this is Kate. We've got a bit of a mess up here. Could the girls come down to you for the morning?" Next thing I knew, she'd hung up and was calling Abby to wake her. "Aunt Hannah needs you girls to help her clean out her lower kitchen cabinets today. Get up; she's coming to get you."

"Oh boy!" I heard Abby's feet hit the floor and knew she was flinging off her gown. Abby slept hard but woke like she'd missed too much of the day already and had to hustle to make up for lost time. Her words grew muffled as Aunt Kate pulled a shirt over her head. "I's a good cab'net cleaner. Better'n Carley, 'cause she's too big to crawl in de bottom cab'nets, and too short to reach de top ones. Only giants and Aunt Hannah can reach de top."

"I don't want to go," I objected. I didn't want to miss whatever was going on.

"You're going." Aunt Kate spoke grimly and turned away before I could argue.

We had barely finished our Cheerios when Aunt Hannah came up in her green Oldsmobile. "Hello, old dears. I sure am glad you could come help me today."

After a hair-raising ride, she set Abby crawling around pulling things out of her bottom cabinets while she pulled stuff from the top ones. I had to wash anything that was dusty, but Aunt Hannah made even washing dishes fun. When we finished, we all took a picnic to her side porch, even Uncle Davy. It was an exceptionally good Saturday for us.

When we got home, though, Uncle Stephen put Abby down for her nap and Aunt Kate followed me up to my room. Quietly she closed the door. "Honey, I need to tell you something." She sat on my bed, plucking the chenille spread like she was plucking up her courage.

"What is it?" I'd gotten pretty grubby and wanted to change my clothes, but I didn't want Aunt Kate to see me topless. I didn't have bumps on my chest yet, but I was growing increasingly shy. Abby had complained because I'd put her out of the bathroom the last time I bathed.

"It's Grace." She stopped again, took a deep breath, and said quickly, "She's napping on the guest room bed. She's not feeling very well, and the doctor gave her something to help her sleep all day. When she wakes up, Uncle Stephen wants to invite her to stay with us a few nights until we can find her another place."

"Are we gonna get in trouble again?" The past year some members in the congregation had not been happy when we moved Raifa, our first maid, into our house.

"I hope not. We aren't telling anybody, because it's just going to be for a few days. But we can't send her back to Miranda's."

"Why?"

"We just can't. It's ... it's not healthy. But don't tell *any-body* she's staying here, okay?"

We exchanged a long, wordless look. Uncle Stephen had been raised on a farm and didn't always pay attention to what other people thought. But Aunt Kate and I had been raised by Big Mama. We knew that what other people thought was important.

I shrugged. "I won't say anything, but you know how Abby loves to tell secrets."

"I'm not telling her. She'll go to bed before Grace, and Grace will be up first, so Abby won't know. It's just for a little while," she repeated, as if trying to convince herself.

"She'll see Grace's things in the bedroom."

"If she asks, we'll tell her Grace is leaving some things here for a while. It's the truth, just not the whole truth." Big Mama always said you should never tell a lie except a socially accept-able one, but you didn't always have to tell the whole truth. That wasn't the same as lying.

I headed to the closet for clean clothes and asked casually, as if I hadn't heard a thing, "What isn't healthy at Miranda's?"

In my mirror I saw Aunt Kate give me a quick look, prob-ably wondering how much I already knew. "She and Miranda's son had a disagreement. We don't want her staying up there."

Thus did the women in my family deal with truth. Chil-dren were told stories that curled our hair and ruined our sleep about what *could* happen if we didn't obey, or what *had* hap-pened to people in the distant past. Big Mama must have told me a hundred stories about people gored by cows, run over by cars, expired from not drinking milk, or slit in the throat by angry field hands. But when it came to actual unpleasantness in the present, she and Aunt Kate both tended to feed us pallid platitudes that ill prepared us to become either compassionate or wise.

If the weight of all the painful secrets adults have tried to keep from children was put in one box, the earth would plum-met through space like lead.

❋

I'd barely gotten dressed when I heard Aunt Kate say sharply in the downstairs hall, "Then at least take Carley. I don't want you going up there by yourself on a Saturday. It's payday."

Uncle Stephen made a huffing sound that meant he wasn't happy but he'd oblige her anyway. I hurried down. "Where are we going?"

"Up to fetch Grace's things from Miranda's. She's going to be staying here awhile."

"Shhh!" Aunt Kate pointed to Abby's door.

Uncle Stephen shoved back his hair. "I'm not going to lie to the children, Kate."

He hadn't been raised by Big Mama, so on our way to Pleasantdale I tried to explain the difference between telling a lie and not telling the whole truth.

He slid his eyes my way without turning his head from the road. "Aren't you the person who objects to the way Miss Pauline tells the truth?"

Miss Pauline detested Aunt Kate, for no good reason I could see. She was nice as pie to Abby, me, and Uncle Stephen, but she scarcely spoke to Aunt Kate and was always hinting things that weren't true. Like when Aunt Kate stayed after school for a teachers' meeting, she would say to me in front of anybody else who happened to be around, "Oh dear, I see Mrs. Whitfield is late coming home *again*." The way she said it made it sound like Aunt Kate was deserting us.

I glared at Uncle Stephen for daring to compare what I was trying to teach him with Miss Pauline. "There's a difference between not telling the whole truth and telling the truth in a way that makes it sound like a lie."

"What's the difference?"

I struggled to figure it out. "One person is trying to be kind to somebody, and the other is trying to be mean."

"Not bad," he murmured. "Might make a Jesuit out of you." I had no idea what he meant, but at least he didn't disagree. If Aunt Kate and I lived with him long enough, he might actually get some common sense.

I settled back into my seat and enjoyed the September air blowing through the open windows: a hint of cotton dust, a tinge of cool, the smell of a year just beginning to wind down. As we turned onto the Pleasantdale road—now carpeted with soft pine needles—I thought that the nicest thing about Pleasantdale was the smell before you got there.

Children jumped rope or played tag in the middle of the yard, just like the night Grace arrived. One baby, wearing only a diaper and a shirt, sat in the dirt, crying. Women rested on some of the front steps talking porch to porch. The same cur dogs came out snapping and barking. Only difference from before was, I didn't see a single man. I felt like we'd taken a tuck in time. Grace probably wished we could.

Miranda came to her door barefoot, wrapped in an enormous robe. "I was fixin' to stretch out a little while."

"We won't stay long," Uncle Stephen promised. "We just came to fetch Grace's things."

"Her things? What happened to her?" When Uncle Stephen didn't answer right away, Miranda gripped the porch railing so hard, it wiggled. "She ain't dead, is she?"

"No, she's just decided she needs to find another place to live."

"What 'nother place? Ain't no better place anywhere about here." She stopped and glared at him, but something in his face made her take a step back and ask in a frightened voice, "Did Ronnie try to mess with her?"

Uncle Stephen shoved back his hair but he didn't say a word.

She pressed one hand to her huge bosom and carried on like I wasn't there. "My lawd, he coulda stood it one more day. I tole him and tole him to leave her alone. 'That's the preacher's girl what's goin' to college,' I tole him at least a hunderd times. 'And she's walking out with Jay Anderson. You leave her alone.' Oh, lawdy, why didn't that boy listen to his mama?"

"Boys seldom do. Is he here?"

"No." She sounded relieved. "He run over to the fac'try to get my money from Mr. Hugh Fred. Left a good while ago and he ain't come back. Gen'ly I gets it Sunday, but Ronnie ran a little short and needed somethin' for his trip back—you heard his leave is up? I don't know how I can stan' having him go to Kree-a. But I tole him to go on down and tell Mr. Hugh Fred I sent him for my pay. Maybe he went out with some of his frien's, it bein' his las' day. Oh, Mr. Whitfield, I just hate this. Grace is the nicest girl anybody could meet. I just plumb hate it."

"Well, we want to pick up her things. Carley, fetch the cases from the car."

"He's leavin' tomorrer," Miranda pleaded. "He won't bother her none tonight. I'll see to that. Tell her to come on back, now." She stood in the doorway, arms crossed.

"I'm afraid not. Carley, get the cases."

I went to the car and dragged two empty suitcases from the backseat. I don't know what he said to Miranda while I was gone, but she went over and sat in a chair and just stared at air while we went in and packed up Grace's things. "Are those her sheets and blanket?" I asked when we'd filled the suitcases with clothes and stuff from the top of her dresser.

He took off his glasses and polished a spot on the front of his shirt. "I don't know. Run ask Miranda."

She was staring out at the dirt circle in front of the houses like she was seeing things that weren't really there. Her voice sounded like a dead person's. "They's hers." She nodded. "Pillow's mine, though."

I folded the blanket neatly and dragged off the top sheet, then gasped. "There's blood on the bottom sheet!"

Uncle Stephen turned to look. He didn't move for a minute, just stood looking down at that blood. Suddenly he grabbed the sheet and ripped it off the bed. He shoved it down in the pillowcase and flung it to the floor. "Look under the bed," he called harshly over his shoulder as he picked up both suitcases and marched out. "See if there's anything we missed."

I knelt and found Grace's slippers. With them dangling from one hand and the pillowcase hanging over my shoulder like a beggar's pack, I followed him. "We'll be goin' now," I told Miranda politely. Uncle Stephen hadn't said a word to her as he marched past.

Her eyes slewed my way but she didn't even nod. Looked like both grown-ups had lost their manners.

Uncle Stephen didn't say a word as I threw the pillowcase and slippers into the backseat, got in, and closed my door. "Why're you mad at me?" I demanded.

"I'm not mad at you. I just want to get out of here."

Somehow the pine trees didn't smell so good on the way out. The turpentine had a whiff of blood.

Chapter 11

When we got to the road, Uncle Stephen turned right instead of left.

"Home's the other way," I reminded him.

"Thought I'd run up and see Hugh Fred a minute."

"What about?"

"This time I can't tell you. I want you to wait in the car."

"It smells like blood in here." I didn't want to stay in the car with those sheets.

He darted me a look, gave a short nod. "Okay. You can come in. But you'll have to wait by the door." That was fine by me. I just wished I'd brought a book.

I'd never been to the chair factory, so I had no idea what to expect. But given the house the Keenes lived in, I certainly didn't expect a big tin building sitting in a dirt parking lot. Tin everywhere. Tin walls, tin roof, long blotches of rust running down the outside like it cried for its own ugliness. Weeds and high grass growing up around the parking lot, which was dotted with broken wooden boxes and half full of Negro men. Some of them stood near the door. They were mostly older and looked beaten down and tired. Another group stood under a big hickory tree at the far side of the lot. They were much younger and looked rough and disgruntled. The only cars except ours were a Chevy that was newer than ours, and Mr. Hugh Fred's Hudson, parked near the corner with its sleek nose pointed out, eager to head to the big white mansion on the hill.

I pointed to a loading platform running alongside one wall full of high, closed doors. "The tracks are so close, looks like the train would knock that platform off."

"The good thing about trains is, they stay on their tracks." Uncle Stephen spoke like his mind was on something else. But even when he wasn't thinking, he could be counted on to use a simple statement to teach some lesson. "So they can build the dock right up to the boxcars and roll chairs straight on. Every minute saved is pennies earned. That's a basic law of economics." He looked out his window at the crowd. I didn't recognize a single person except Ronnie, who was with the group under the hickory. When he noticed who we were, he turned his back slowly like he hadn't really seen us. He had, though.

We crossed the parking lot under the hazy blue sky. Seemed hotter than September ought to be—or maybe that was because my face was flaming. All the men were staring at us, wondering what we were doing there. Just like me.

I didn't like the way Uncle Stephen's jaw was set, either. He'd been clenching it off and on since he saw that blood.

The factory was just one high room, warm as a sick dog's nose and sweet with fresh sawdust. Machines—saws and things I could not name—towered over me and marched in rows toward dim far corners. Huge fans were set high up in the walls, but they, like the machines, were still. The whole place was hushed, like a church in the middle of the week.

Shoving back his hair, Uncle Stephen headed down an aisle between machines straight to a room built in one corner of the factory. I stayed right behind him but he didn't seem to mind. Through a big glass pane in the door we could see Mr. Hugh Fred sitting behind a desk with narrow stacks of paper in front of him. He was putting smaller stacks into envelopes. A man in uniform with a gun at his belt sat on a wooden chair just outside the door.

"Why's the policeman here?" I asked softly.

"He's a guard. Hugh Fred feels like he needs him, with all that cash."

I gasped. "Those stacks of paper are money? I bet even a bank wouldn't have that much!"

As Uncle Stephen approached the door, the guard put one hand on the butt of his gun. Uncle Stephen nodded toward Mr. Hugh Fred. "Ask him if I can talk to him a minute."

While the guard rapped on the door, I peered into the office. Big Mama always said rich people stay rich because they don't waste money on nonessentials. Mr. Hugh Fred's office must be a nonessential. It was just a poky little walled-off square with charts hanging on the walls, and papers spilling off gray filing cabinets. It didn't even have a rug.

Mr. Hugh Fred looked up. When he saw who it was, his face lit into a smile of welcome. He was already fumbling for a Tootsie Roll when he got to us. "Let 'em in, Wally. They're pretty honest. This is my preacher and one of his girls. Come on in." He handed me two candies.

"Thank you, sir." I stuck one in my shorts pocket and unwrapped the other. While I chewed the chocolate to get it soft, he went right on talking.

"I'm a little behind today finishing up the pay packets. Emily and I went down to Charlotte last night for a real fine concert, but we were late gettin' home, and I decided to sleep in a little this morning." By then he had herded us inside the office and pointed us to kitchen chairs right in front of all that money. It was all I could do not to reach out and touch it.

He saw me looking and grinned. "Lots of money, isn't it? Think what you and I could buy with all that. But the men there"—he jerked his head—"to a lot of them it's just so many Saturday night drinks and a little food on the table." He held up one hand like he was stopping Uncle Stephen from saying something. "And I know what you're thinking. I ought to give the money to the women so it doesn't get wasted. But I don't like to take away my men's dignity."

Maybe I'd been living with Uncle Stephen too long, but it did seem to me that men's dignity shouldn't matter as much as women and children's food. Besides, I hadn't seen a lot of dignity to lose among those men outside. They'd shuffled their feet and looked at the ground when I looked at them. Maybe, I decided, they were ashamed in advance, knowing how they were going to spend most of their pay.

But if Mr. Hugh Fred expected Uncle Stephen to worry about his factory workers that particular afternoon, he had another think coming. Uncle Stephen sat clenching and unclenching his fists and didn't say a word.

"What brings you way up here?" Mr. Hugh Fred asked helpfully, leaning back in his chair like he had nothing he'd rather do than talk to us. He was charming, Mr. Hugh Fred Keene.

Uncle Stephen looked at me. "Wait outside a minute while we talk."

"Look around." Mr. Hugh Fred waved his hands toward the machines. "Just don't push any red buttons."

"Sure." I knew what Uncle Stephen was going to say. He was going to tell Mr. Hugh Fred that Grace wasn't staying with Miranda anymore and ask if he knew of someplace else for her.

I cruised around looking at those enormous machines, and my fingers started itching to try some of the red buttons to see what they'd do. I was just examining a pile of different kinds of chair legs when Mr. Hugh Fred hurried outside. In a minute he came back with Ronnie. They both went in the office and Mr. Hugh Fred shut the door. Next I heard somebody shouting. It sounded like Uncle Stephen but it couldn't be. A preacher would never say those things!

"... ought to take you outside and beat the tar out of you! ... no better than an animal! ... ruined that girl's life ..."

I crept around the stack of chair legs and peered down the aisle. Uncle Stephen was standing up and leaning toward Ronnie, who was backed into one corner. Mr. Hugh Fred was leaning on his hands over his desk. His mouth was moving but I couldn't hear a word he said. Neither could Uncle Stephen, making all that racket. The guard had gotten up and moved over next to a stack of chair bottoms. He was cleaning his fingernails with a pocketknife.

Finally Uncle Stephen ran out of breath, and I heard Mr. Hugh Fred, his voice sounding little and far away. "Let me handle this, Stephen. Let me handle it."

Uncle Stephen nodded and leaned against the wall of the office, breathing hard. His shirt was soaking wet and his hair fell in his face. I crept closer so I could hear better.

Mr. Hugh Fred looked at Ronnie. "This was a terrible thing you did, boy. We don't put up with that kind of behavior around here, you understand me?" Ronnie hung his head and nodded. "Now you apologize to Mr. Whitfield here and send your apology home to that poor little girl."

"I'm sorry," Ronnie said, deep in his throat. "Tell her I said I'm sorry, sir."

"That's better. Now get back to your mama and don't you cause any more trouble while you're home." Mr. Hugh Fred handed him an envelope. Ronnie started to the door. "And boy?" Ronnie turned with the door half open, which made Mr. Hugh Fred's voice sound louder. "Good luck in Korea."

"Thank you, sir. Thank you, sir."

Ronnie more shuffled than walked, keeping his head down, until he was past the guard. Then he lifted his head. From where I was standing I could see his face. He was grinning.

"Hey, boss, pay ready yet?" Several other men crowded the factory door, calling to the guard.

"Not yet, boys. In a little while." He moved toward the open door and lounged against one of the machines, with one hand resting lightly on the butt of his gun. He was grinning, too. The men backed away and stood looking hungrily in.

I crept almost up to Mr. Hugh Fred's door. The stack of chair bottoms nearby let me hide so I could both see inside the office and hear what Uncle Stephen was saying. He was talking so loud, he wasn't hard to hear. "A talking to isn't going to make one speck of difference to him. I want him locked up!" He pounded the desk. "I want people to know our community won't tolerate this sort of thing."

Mr. Hugh Fred shook his head. "Let's don't be too hard on him, Stephen. He's heading to Korea, you know. Like a lot of soldiers, he was just seeking a little solace before battle."

"Solace nothing." Uncle Stephen now rested his hands on the desk and met Mr. Hugh Fred nose to nose. "It was rape, pure and simple. That girl was torn and bleeding."

"You see her?"

Uncle Stephen took one step back and glared at him. "Of course not. Kate took her straight to a doctor while I called the sheriff."

"I wish you hadn't done that. I don't want any trouble for my people."

Uncle Stephen wiped his mouth with the back of his hand. "You won't get any. The sheriff laughed and told me Negro girls expect that kind of thing. But he's wrong. Grace may never trust a man again."

"You want him to marry her before he goes? If you do—"

"We aren't talking about animals here—your bull to my cow. These are human beings. What if it was Freda he'd raped?"

Mr. Hugh Fred put out one hand. "Now, Stephen, that was uncalled for. Ronnie did a terrible thing, and I know Grace means a lot to you and Kate. She means a lot to our little children in the church nursery, too. But she'll get over this if we just give her time. Don't get yourself so worked up, you lose your perspective." He came around the desk and put his arm around Uncle Stephen's shoulders to turn him toward the door. "I tell you what. If Grace's daddy wants to come down here and deal with Ronnie when he gets back from the war—if he does get back—I won't stand in his way. But for now, like I said, Grace will get over it if you just give her time."

Uncle Stephen flung open the door. He strode across the wide floorboards and out into the sunlight. I hurried after him. It was evident to anybody with eyes in their head that he had plumb forgotten I was there.

❧

He trembled all the way home. He didn't even acknowledge my presence for most of the way. Once he clenched his fist, knocked the steering wheel with it, and spoke angrily under his breath. "That's the closest I ever came to knocking somebody down since I became a preacher."

I didn't know if he was talking to himself, to me, or to God, but it seemed like somebody ought to answer. I figured I was elected. "Would you even know how to knock anybody down, Uncle Stephen?"

He looked at me like I came from some other planet. "Of course I would. You don't grow up with six brothers without learning to fight. I was the littlest, and the littlest learns to fight best. Everybody else is always bigger, so you learn to fight harder, meaner, and smarter."

"But you're a preacher!"

"You don't get born a preacher. As John Calvin would say, you get born a bundle of original sin."

"But weren't you always gooder—I mean better . . ."

"Nope, and I'm still not. It was only by the grace of God that I didn't knock him down back there."

"Why didn't you? He deserved it. What could Mr. Hugh Fred have done?"

He gave a little grunt of a laugh. "It was Hugh Fred I wanted to knock down."

Chapter 12

While Uncle Stephen and Aunt Kate talked with Grace in the dining room, I went to practice the piano in the living room next door. Miss Rilla had given me a Chopin prelude, the happy little seventh one every student learns first. But that afternoon I worked out the huge, crashing chords of the twentieth, even though my fingers ached with stretching those octaves. When I had mastered the chords, I played all three lines very, very loud.

Finally, when I finished, I sat in silence and heard Grace through the open windows. "Well, I like working for you, and I do want to save money for college—" I heard her draw a deep, ragged breath. "Okay, I'll stay if I can sleep here."

After I heard her go upstairs, Aunt Kate opened the living room door. "That's not how that prelude is supposed to be played. The first line's supposed to be *fortissimo*, the second *piano*, and the third *pianissimo*."

"Not today." I shook my head. "It's not a *pianissimo* kind of day."

She waited a minute to nod. "You're right. Play it again. Real loud."

The next week Grace cried a lot, but she did it in private. When Abby asked, "You got pinkeye? Your eyes are red as Sue Mary's," Uncle Stephen took her out for ice cream and explained that Grace had had some trouble, so we should be very kind to her. But when Abby and I caught her crying in the kitchen one afternoon, Abby's patience was exhausted and our subterfuges were proven useless. "Doesn't you *like* libbing wif us?"

Grace wiped her eyes with the corner of her apron and managed a watery smile. "I like it a lot. Shall we make fudge?" I excused myself, saying I had homework to do. To hear Abby tell it, she made the fudge and Grace "he'ped a little."

I never saw her cry again, but I heard soft crying if I got up in the night. One evening Rowdy—who slept in a basket near Aunt Kate's bed since he'd been hit by that car—laboriously climbed the stairs. When Aunt Kate got ready for bed, she gave the little whistle that called him, and he padded to the top of the stairs. They exchanged a look—green eyes at the bottom, big brown ones at the top—then he turned and padded back to Grace's room.

Aunt Kate and I went up after him and found him plopped down beside Grace's bed, nose on paws. "Do you mind if Rowdy sleeps in with you?" Aunt Kate called down to Grace.

"I'd be glad of the company," Grace replied from where she was bathing Abby.

"He's a mighty present help in trouble," Abby yelled. I expected Uncle Stephen to fuss at her for using a psalm to describe a dog, but I heard him give a surprised, pleased chuckle.

Aunt Kate carried Rowdy's basket upstairs, and he slept there for two weeks.

Grace didn't go out much, either, not even to run down to Mrs. Cameron's store. Worse, she stopped writing Jay. Generally she got a letter every Monday and Wednesday and mailed him one the next day, but the Thursday after Grace's trouble, Abby met me at the school bus with a frown.

"Grace didn't gib me a letter for Jay dis whole week. Tell her to write, Carley Cousin. I need my moneyfunt sum." Abby was the official mail carrier in our household, for what Uncle Stephen called the munificent sum of five pennies a week to fetch the mail plus a penny per piece to deliver letters to the post office on extra trips. Grace usually paid her two cents a week.

I sought out Grace, who was ironing in the kitchen. She used to hum happy hymns while she worked. Now she was softly crooning an old spiritual.

Nobody knows the trouble I've seen,
Nobody knows but Jesus.

She kept time with the thump of her iron on the board.

"Why aren't you writing Jay?" I asked without preamble.

The iron wobbled in her hand. "People grow apart when they don't see each other." I saw her blink a couple of times like she had something in her eye, but she didn't fool me one bit.

"You don't grow apart from people you like. He's going to wonder what happened."

She tried to laugh—a pitiful attempt. "He'll find somebody else down there at college. You wait and see."

She also grew apart from her church. She used to go every Sunday afternoon to Rock of Hope, the Negro Presbyterian church up near Pleasantdale. In those days Negro churches had services in the afternoon so cooks could go after they finished Sunday dinner dishes. But Grace stopped going. After two weeks I moseyed into the kitchen and asked her why.

"Oh,"—she waved one hand like it didn't matter—"I don't need to go way up there on Sundays. I get enough church keeping the Bethel nursery in the morning and reading Mr. Stephen's sermons."

That very evening, though, Janey Lou and her husband Meek stopped by after dark. Meek was clerk of session at Rock of Hope. Uncle Stephen invited them in, of course, but Grace went out on the porch to talk instead. I could hear every word from the open windows of my bedroom.

"Folks miss you," Janey Lou told her. "'Specially the children. Several of them told me they wish you'd come see them."

Grace's voice was soft. "I miss them, too, but I've been real busy lately with everything down here. We still got some late canning to do, and this is a big house to clean."

"You don't clean and can on Sundays," Meek said bluntly but gently. "I know the Whitfields wouldn't permit that."

"Well, no," Grace admitted. "But I been kinda tired."

"Honey, is there something you want to tell us, something we could pray about together?" Janey Lou sounded anxious, and I could almost see her thin hands reaching out for Grace's.

"No, ma'am. I just been tired. But I'll come one of these days. You tell them that."

"We sure will." Meek sounded puzzled and sad.

I was sad, too, about Grace not writing Jay, going to church, or visiting the children, but I discovered I liked having her upstairs. She was just enough older than me to be endlessly fascinating. I admired her cinnamon brownness and her smell of Swan soap and rose powder. I liked to sit on her bed and watch her put Vaseline on her eyebrows to make them shiny, comb it through her hair to keep her pageboy straight, rub cream into her arms and legs to take away the ash, and put on rouge and lipstick.

"I didn't know Negroes wore rouge and lipstick," I told her. "Aunt Sukie never did." Aunt Sukie had been Big Mama's cook since before Mama was born, and practically raised me.

Grace laughed. "Aunt Sukie's *old*. I'm modern."

Grace also solved one mystery for me. One morning I barged into her room and found her rubbing cream under her arm. "What's that?" I asked.

"Deodorant. It keeps me from stinking."

I sniffed under my arm. "I don't stink."

"You'll start before you know it."

I crept back to my room and, shamefaced, rubbed a little under each arm.

Raised until I was eleven in a strictly segregated household where Aunt Sukie had her own dishes and kitchen hand towel, I'd been a little apprehensive about sharing a bathtub with Grace. But Grace left the bathroom so spotless, I had to work hard to leave it that clean myself. I didn't want her to think I was white trash. I began to think that separate drinking fountains and bathrooms were silly for Negroes as clean as Grace.

After using one of the public bathrooms at the Iredell County Fair, I decided that rather than segregating people by colored and white, somebody ought to segregate us by clean and nasty.

I found the fair segregated in another sense, too. "City children got to go Monday, when they judged quilts and jams," I complained at supper, "but county schools had to go today to watch them judge cows and pigs. Who cares about cows and pigs?"

"Future farmers?" Uncle Stephen was more interested in buttering his biscuit.

"Well, I don't. Looks like they could have given us a choice."

"Choice is always good," he agreed. "Wasn't there anything else to do?"

"Yeah. We got to look for a two-year-old boy who got lost from his mother and like to worried us all to death until a patrolman found him."

The way Uncle Stephen was eating that biscuit, I could tell he wasn't paying much attention. But I knew something that would make him listen. "Next week we're going to start having three bomb drills a week. Mr. Mayhew says the Russians may come any day now, while our attention's focused on Korea. So he's going to make us practice until we can get under our desks faster than greased pigs."

If I was trying to goad him, I almost succeeded. But Aunt Kate gave him a look, and he asked instead, "How fast can a greased pig get under a desk?"

"I don't know, but you'd better start practicing around here. You'll be sorry if a bomb drops and you can't get to cover fast enough."

From the look he gave me, obviously our family's safety depended on me.

The next afternoon I made a reconnaissance tour of our property. I decided our old barn, built for former preachers who had up to ten children and needed a lot of milk, would make the best bomb shelter. I dragged boards over four rotting bales of hay in the far corner and covered the boards with more hay.

Then I took Abby and Sue Mary to show them where to go when a bomb dropped. "It might have mice," I warned, "but at least you'll be safe."

"So will de mice," Abby agreed with satisfaction.

I'd stocked it with a quart of water and a box of saltines. "It won't feed you long," I apologized, "but it will do for the first day or two, until the radiation goes down."

"Can we see it go down, like de sun?"

I had no idea, but Abby would pester the living daylights out of me if I admitted that. "You can just see little shimmers in the air," I told her. "Like those over there." I pointed to the barbeque grill, where heat was shimmering up from the metal plate.

"Oooh! Radiation! Get in de bomb shelter, Sue Mary. Come on, Carley."

It was a tight fit, but we crouched under the boards a few minutes, then crawled back out. "We's safe now," Abby announced. "No more shimmers." She looked up at me, gray eyes shining. "Fank you, Carley Cousin, for making us safe. I doesn't have to be 'fraid anymore." I suspected safety wasn't really that simple, but I honestly didn't know.

Abby wasn't the only one in our family who was afraid. The times I was gladdest Grace was living with us were moon-less nights when I woke up hearing noises. Our old house was full of creaks, and before Grace came, I would lie there in the pitch-black dark picturing ghosts, fire, and Russians right out-side my locked door. Russians scared me most. I could just see them creeping into homes at night to spy on us. With the rest of the family sleeping downstairs in that enormous old manse, spies could creep upstairs and kill me without anybody hear-ing a thing. It never occurred to me to wonder why spies would want to. I just pressed myself against the mattress, pulled the covers all over my head, and hoped ghosts and spies couldn't see the hump in my bed.

Now when I woke afraid, I'd remember Grace was closer to the stairs than me. They'd find her first. I was ready of course to go to her immediate aid, but it was comforting to know I was second in line.

Chapter 13

October drifted in so subtly, I scarcely noticed the leaves were changing, although I spent a lot of time at my windows watching Clay's for occasional glimpses of him. I always hoped he might be at his house when I went for music lessons, but he never was. Miss Rilla said he was building houses with his daddy.

One afternoon, though, something happened that was almost as exciting as seeing Clay. Miss Rilla handed me a piece of paper. "This is about a music camp next summer up in Brevard. I want you to ask your aunt and uncle if you can go." I dashed home waving the brochure.

Aunt Kate scanned it for one line. "It costs a lot. We'd never be able to afford it."

"Maybe Big Mama ..."

She shook her head. "Mama's saving for your college education, and people aren't shopping like they did before this war. You can ask, but I doubt she'll have it. Of course, you can save your allowance ..."

"My allowance is one quarter a week, and I put a nickel in the offering. Even if I gave up Mary Janes and didn't buy Christmas presents, it wouldn't ever be enough. Maybe I could help people like Aunt Hannah and they could pay me."

"You couldn't take money from Hannah after all she's done for us."

There was only one solution. Resolutely I dug out the past month's issues of *Life*. Almost every week there was a new contest. "Win $60,000!" "Win a new Mercury convertible!" I didn't have much use for a convertible, but I entered every contest that whole winter, hoping to win just one. My prayers at night expanded to include "Please, God, let me win enough for music camp. I'll gladly give you all the rest."

Freda now sat with Charles in the back of the bus. All the way to school she talked and bounced her curls while Charles held her hand and smiled at her like she was choice pigskin. Gradually they grew bolder. She put her head on his shoulder and he put his arm around her. They'd have had plenty of room for a third person on the seat, but nobody sat there. Whenever I looked around, I could see the side of his thick finger stroking her cheek as she talked and he listened. Mary watched them in her mirror so much, I wondered when she looked at the road.

Freda was also wearing his football jacket on the way to school—a blue jacket with a greyhound on the back. She took it off before we got to Mount Vernon, though.

I stomped into school each morning feeling ornery as a disturbed wasp. "Freda already has everything a girl ever wanted," I fumed to myself one Thursday morning. "Why should she have Charles, too?" My friendship with Mrs. Raeburn wasn't developing, either. Any hopes I'd had that she would recognize in me a fascinating student and kindred spirit were fast evaporating before the reality of homework. I had good intentions, but she assigned twenty-five spelling words every night and made us write the questions as well as answers for science and history. I'd far rather be reading Nancy Drew or playing the piano, so I started writing my homework as fast as I could. I was getting a lot of red comments on it like "Cannot read this word" and "Write neater, please."

One weekend Aunt Hannah brought up a bucket of black walnuts, and Aunt Kate and I made fudge. The next Monday I proudly wrapped four pieces in waxed paper, put them in a small brown bag, and carried them to Mrs. Raeburn. Now she would see there was more to me than an average student and a sloppy writer.

She looked so pretty that day. Her golden hair lay in short shining waves, and her black corduroy suit was slim and smart with a white blouse. My heart thumped as I approached her desk. She smelled good, too. I vowed that when I grew up I'd always wear that very same perfume. By then of course we would be friends and she would tell me what it was.

When she opened the bag and smelled what was inside, however, she shook her head. "Thanks, Carley, but I'm allergic to nuts." She must have noticed my disappointment, because she added, "Why don't you take it down to Mr. Donaldson? He loves black walnut fudge."

"Now?" I dared to ask, even though the bell had already rung. When she nodded, I hurried down the stairs, blinking back my tears.

The secretary told me to go on in. When I pushed opened the principal's door, I thought he had on a radio until I realized he was singing softly while he wrote at his desk. "You sing good!" I said without thinking, then turned bright pink.

He looked up, startled, and his expression—which had been almost pleasant—went back to normal, which meant it looked like somebody had carved him out of wood and painted him to look human. "Can I help you?"

Quickly I thrust the bag at him. "Aunt Kate and I made fudge with black walnuts. I brought you some."

He looked for a second like he didn't believe me, and I hoped he never found out I'd brought it for Mrs. Raeburn first. "Why, thanks. I love black walnuts." I set the bag on his desk, wondering if I ought to open it for him. He picked it up and anchored it with his chin while he opened it, pulled out a chunk of fudge, and took a test nibble. "Wonderful! I used to eat black walnut fudge down at my cousin's when I was little."

As he took a larger bite, I tried to picture him as a boy. I couldn't. Still, since he seemed more friendly than usual, I said impulsively, "You really do have a lovely voice. Do you sing in your church choir?"

His mouth was full of fudge, so he shook his head. After he swallowed, he said, "I don't go to church. I'm an unregenerate heathen."

I took an involuntary step back. I hadn't known we had any of those in America.

"Don't worry, I don't bite. And I won't try to convert you to my views if you don't try to convert me to yours." He rummaged in the bag for another piece of candy. "This is perfectly wonderful. Thanks again."

Before I could stop it, my tongue blurted out, "Well, that sure is a waste of a lovely voice." I was so embarrassed, I turned and ran, face flaming, all the way to the stairs.

❃

After school I took my books up to my room and started writing those dratted spelling words. Uncle Stephen's radio was playing next door in his study as usual. In a few minutes he came to my door and announced, "I just heard that a little plane may have crashed near Stony Point. I'm going up there in case I'm needed."

"You think they'll need you to pray?"

"No, but they may want me to help tell a family if somebody has been hurt or killed."

"Do you want me to come with you? In case they have children or something and I need to be with them?"

He knew I was just trying to postpone spelling. As he shoved his hand through his hair, I braced myself for "No," but instead he nodded. "If you promise to do exactly what I tell you. And bring a book. You'll probably have to wait a long time in the car."

"Okay." I grabbed up two Nancy Drew mysteries in case it was a very long time.

In the ten miles to Stony Point we were passed by another ambulance and two police cars, but when we finally found the crowd, we learned that nobody had found any trace of a plane. We hung around for two hours, until we finally needed to go home for supper. They hadn't found a thing.

"I want to stop by Rob's for a minute," Uncle Stephen said as we approached Job's Corner. I spent the rest of the trip in a happy daydream about Clay taking me out for a walk in the backyard to confess he loved me, while Uncle Stephen transacted his business with Mr. Rob. I hoped the deodorant I put on that morning was still working.

But when we stopped and Uncle Stephen asked, "Want to come in?" I was almost too paralyzed by self-consciousness to walk.

"Does my hair look all right? Is my face clean?"

"You'll past muster for a kitchen visit." A most uncomforting reply.

The Lamonts ate early, so they were almost finished when we got there. "Howdy, Rob, Miss Rilla, Clay," Uncle Stephen greeted them.

Miss Rilla jumped up to offer us plates, which we refused, and iced tea, which we accepted. Mr. Rob wiped a last bit of gravy with his biscuit and fed it to his bulldog under the table while she wasn't looking. We stood propped against the counter, and Uncle Stephen told them, "We've just come back from Stony Point. They thought a little plane went down up there, but they can't find a thing." I hoped Clay thought we'd been searching, too.

Miss Rilla gasped and clasped her chest, and Mr. Rob said, "That's bad," but Clay just sat there eating like he couldn't care less that somebody might have died. I didn't understand that at all.

Uncle Stephen took a long swig of tea. "I hear they're gonna dedicate the new Statesville airport Sunday."

Mr. Rob's head bobbed like a toy. "Clay here's been asked to participate, being just back from the Air Force and all."

Uncle Stephen drained his glass and set it on the counter. "Done any flying since you got back, Clay?"

Clay still hunched over his plate without looking at us. Miss Rilla reached out and touched him gently. "Son, Mr. Whitfield is speaking to you."

He nodded, not looking up. "Yeah, I've taken a little plane up once or twice."

"Those little planes can be dangerous. Like I said, we've just come from Stony Point. Lots of folks up at the Blacks' farm, looking for that crashed plane."

"Blacks' place?" Mr. Rob was looking at Clay now, too. Miss Rilla looked worried.

"Yeah." Uncle Stephen took off his glasses and polished them on his handkerchief.

"Anybody get the registration number?" Clay reached for butter for his biscuit. He still hadn't looked straight at either of us.

"Nope. They just saw it fly real low over the Blacks' farm; then it vanished. Scared a lot of cows, though, and a few people. They've combed every inch of the farm, including the gully."

Mr. Rob leaned forward on both forearms. "Son, you know anything about that?"

Clay bent back to his plate and ate like Miss Rilla was fixing to cut off his supplies. "I don't know a thing about cows and gullies, Daddy."

Uncle Stephen put his glasses back on and pocketed his handkerchief. "Just thought you'd like to know, being interested in planes and all. They were calling off the search when we left. I figure maybe somebody buzzed the farm, pulled up, and headed west."

Clay nodded several times. "Probably somebody out for a joyride having a little fun."

"It wasn't much fun for people looking for a body. Pretty grim, in fact. Well, I don't want to keep you all from your dessert. Good to see you, Miss Rilla, Mr. Rob. See you later, Clay."

For the life of me, I couldn't figure out why we had bothered to stop.

❋

Sunday was finally chilly, but we still went to the new airport dedication. All of us except Abby, who wanted to stay home "and do homework" with Grace. Aunt Kate wanted to leave John as well, but "John will love it," Uncle Stephen assured us.

John clapped and waved every time a plane flew over, calling, "Pane! Pane!" and pointing. And when Uncle Stephen put him down on the grass, he surprised us all by taking his first steps—toward an airplane. "See?" Uncle Stephen boasted. "Gonna be a pilot one day."

Aunt Kate and I were so chilly, we didn't enjoy it at all. I hadn't worn my coat because I wanted Clay to see my new green sweater and plaid skirt. She didn't wear hers because "it's so big since I lost weight, it makes me look like a frump." We shivered in the wind and promised each other hot chocolate as soon as Uncle Stephen took us home.

Clay didn't fly, to my disappointment, but he did come over in a brown suit and green tie to shake our hands. I nearly burst my buttons with pride when I saw people looking our way.

"Grounded today," he told Uncle Stephen when he thought nobody was listening.

Uncle Stephen grinned. "A little late, isn't it?" They both laughed.

Aunt Kate saw my puzzled look and bent to murmur, "Don't even try, Carley. You'll never understand men."

❋

We got home to find Abby napping and Grace poring over dresses in the *Ladies' Home Journal*. "If I had material, I could make that in no time." She pointed to a yellow long-sleeved shirtwaist.

None of us really believed her, but Aunt Kate said with a sigh, "I wish you could remake my coat. I bought it when I was pregnant with Abby and it's way too big now, but I can't afford a new one this year."

Grace stood up. "Let me look at it." Aunt Kate fetched it, and Grace turned it inside out to peer at all its seams. "It's got a lot of wear left in it, and I could take it in real easy. But I'd need to use your machine." That was the first time her voice had shown any life since her trouble.

Uncle Stephen stood in the doorway, and his voice sounded just like it did when Abby counted correctly to twenty. "Voilà, a new coat! That's great, Grace!"

"She may ruin it," Aunt Kate worried that night when Grace had gone upstairs. "And I don't like her working in our bedroom, especially if I'm not here. What will people say?"

"I'll move the machine from our room into the living room," Uncle Stephen said. "And you won't wear the coat like it is. Why not let her see what she can do with it?"

In a day the living room became the playroom/piano room/sewing room. While Abby and John crawled around on the floor and I practiced, Grace whirred away on the sewing machine. She finished the coat in two days and instead of ruining it, did such a good job that Aunt Kate bragged, "I feel like I have a new one. Where'd you learn to sew so well?"

Grace's gold tooth gleamed in her first smile in ages. "My sewing teacher was the best one I ever had in school. I took home economics three times. If you'll get me some material, I'll make Abby a dress."

Aunt Kate rummaged in her cedar chest and brought out green and navy plaid flannel she'd bought a couple of years before and never used. Grace sewed late after the children were in bed, changing the pattern to give the dress a white piped collar and ruffled hem, and finished it the next afternoon. Uncle Stephen said she was like the princess in *Rumpelstiltskin*, spinning straw into gold.

When Aunt Hannah came up the next afternoon to bring us a roast from the calf they'd just slaughtered, she told Abby, "I'm real jealous of your new dress. It's prettier than any of mine." She asked Aunt Kate, "Would you mind if I paid Grace to make me a winter dress?"

Aunt Kate confided at suppertime, "After everything Aunt Hannah has done for us, I couldn't say no, but I'm afraid the children will get sticky fingers on her material."

"Why don't we set up a sewing-and-ironing room upstairs?" Uncle Stephen suggested.

Saturday morning I took my television audience on a tour. "This is Carley Marshall with *Unshaded Windows*, in the new Grace's Sewing Center. Notice that the cutting table is economically built from two sawhorses and an old door Mr. Whitfield found in his barn and covered with leftover linoleum from when they remodeled the manse kitchen last year. Grace has been informed she can put sewing money she earns in her college fund."

"So long as she doesn't 'glect the children," Abby added at my heels.

"It was very cold when we woke this morning," I continued, "and the price of coal being what it is, the Whitfields can only afford to heat their dining room, the kitchen, and Mr. Whitfield's study. But Mr. Whitfield has driven to the Farmers' Cooperative Exchange today to purchase a new electric heater for the Sewing Center, saying Grace can take it to her room at night. Note that her room will therefore be warmer than that of Carley Marshall, who has only a smelly kerosene heater and three hot water bottles between herself and nightly freezation."

"You can sleep wif me." Abby circled my waist with her arms. "My bed is weal warm."

It was, heated by a small red-headed furnace.

Chapter 14

Aunt Kate often said we got through one crisis just in time to face the next. Our next one started the morning Uncle Stephen went to town to buy Grace's heater. I'd run over to mail a letter to Big Mama (saving myself a penny and making Abby furious) and on my way home I noticed Mrs. Cameron in her yard, bundled up in her black coat, raking. "Good morning," I called. "Cold today, isn't it?"

"Workin' too hard to notice," she called back. "All these leaves blew down the road from your maples. My trees don't put out like this."

It wasn't true, of course. Our maples were barely turning red. She was mostly raking up leaves from her own poplars. But I asked, "Want me to get a rake and come help?" Any minute now Clay might drive by on his way home for dinner. He was helping his daddy and Mr. Wash build a house up the road, but he always quit at noon on Saturday to go get a haircut in town, and he often came by the store about then. By that time I had his weekly schedule in my diary and arranged my own around it. I hurried to grab a rake and arrived at her yard breathless.

"I ain't paying you to rake your own leaves," warned the old skinflint.

"That's okay. I need the exercise. Of course, I could use some money, too."

"What's a girl need money for? You don't need to be eatin' any more Mary Janes."

"I'm saving for music camp up in Brevard next summer."

She jutted her head out like a turtle, acting like she wasn't the least bit interested. "What's music camp? Never heard of sich a thing."

"Miss Rilla told me about it. You go and practice with other kids all summer, then you give concerts and things. She says she thinks I can get in, but it costs a lot of money. You don't know how I could earn some, do you? Maybe helping you in the store?"

"Been runnin' this store on my own longer'n you've been born, 'n' the little bit I make wouldn't stretch for two. Shame you can't make a livin' talkin'. That's what you're best at. Now wield that rake and give your jaws a rest."

We raked together for nearly an hour—except she did more bossing and I did more raking. Uncle Stephen once said, "Nobody ever beat Nora Cameron at bossing people around." He was pure-tee right. The only work she did was pull weeds from the side of her yard and pile them in her burn barrel out back.

But I had ample reward for my work. Not only did Clay come home, he ambled over the tracks to buy a pack of gum and an RC Cola. "I see you got a helper. She worth her hire?"

"Worth 'bout what I'm paying her," said that treacherous old woman. "Said she needs the exercise, so that's what she's gettin'."

He gave me a grin and raised a foot toward my pile of leaves. "Want I should kick these around so you can get even more exercise?"

"Don't you dare!" I shook my rake at him and felt very bold.

"Have some gum." He held out the pack. My hand trembled at being that close to his, especially when he held out his palm for my wrapper. He put it in his pocket, and I wondered if he had a box of souvenirs from me. He stayed and talked with us while he drank his RC and I finished the front strip of the yard. I didn't mind that Mrs. Cameron didn't even offer me a Mary Jane. I'd already been paid.

That afternoon I went back to the store for bread. The day had grown steadily colder, but Mrs. Cameron's big black wood-stove in the middle of the store was cold as death. In addition to her usual black sweater, she wore an old black jacket with one big silver button. I shivered in my new gray windbreaker.

"You ought to fire up your stove," I greeted her, rubbing my bare hands together and blowing on them. "You want me to tote in some wood?"

"I don't fire that stove," said the obstreperous crone. "Don't want everybody in creation comin' here to sit, wastin' my wood. Besides, I'm goin' out to do some burnin' soon as you get your stuff and get out of here."

I blew on my hands again. It was frigid in the store. "Don't you ever light the stove?"

"Nope. Don't need heat this far south. When I was your age, the only heat in our house was the kitchen stove. Never heated a bedroom. People 're getting too soft. Oughta wear more clothes." She held out her coat, and I saw she had not one but two black sweaters beneath it.

"Do you wear black all the time because you're still mourning Mr. Cameron?"

"Mr. Cameron is perfectly happy frolicking in heaven, Missy. I wear black because it doesn't show dirt."

I was too cold to stand there talking, but as I left, I made one parting remark. "People aren't soft because they don't want to be miserable. They're smart." I ran all the way home and practically hugged the dining room stove, I was so glad to see it.

Mrs. Cameron wasn't at church the next day, and Uncle Stephen asked me to run the bulletin down to her. I found her huddled by her kitchen table, her face so swollen, I almost couldn't recognize her.

"What's the matter with you?"

"Poison ivy. Found a lot of it at the side of my yard yestiddy and pulled it out. Didn't want you girls gettin' in it. I wore gloves when I was pulling, but old fool that I am, I burnt it yesterday evenin' and stood in the smoke." She made a motion like she was waving away smoke, and I saw her hands. They looked like somebody had put a tire pump to them and blown them up.

"You got it on your hands too?"

"All over me, itchin' me plumb to death." She stuck out a thick, swollen ankle.

I ran straight for Uncle Stephen. As soon as he saw her, he went for his car and rushed her to the hospital so fast, she didn't even lock her door. When he got back, he said I might have saved her life. The doctors had never seen a worse case of poison ivy.

He also said it would be an extra good deed if I'd keep the store open for her that next week after school. "It's the start of cotton picking, and she's worried sick she'll lose all that trade. If you can be here in the afternoons, I'll see who I can get to cover the late mornings and lunch hour. Think you can handle it?"

"Sure." I was already thinking what might happen when Clay came and found me alone. I wasn't precisely sure but hoped it would involve a lot of kissing. I was getting tired of kissing my pillow and mirror.

Aunt Kate, however, only agreed to let me go if I took Rowdy and if Uncle Stephen promised to come help me close up once it started getting dark. Abby begged to go, too, so we took Rowdy over Monday around three-thirty to open up. She paused on the doorsill and took a deep breath. "Yumm! It smells good wif Daddy's tobacco." I agreed. Since Mrs. Cameron had started carrying pipe tobacco, it masked the musty earth smell seeping between the cracks in the floorboards.

That day the weather had warmed up considerably. Rowdy found a handy sunny spot on the porch and settled down for a nap. Abby played store, rearranging lower shelves. She got bored, though, after five minutes and skipped up the road to play with Sue Mary.

That first day we had a lot more customers than usual—all of them wanting to know how Mrs. Cameron was. I'd taken a book for slack times, but I hardly had time to sit down. I also had to watch Uncle Stephen closely when he came. He was bad about leaving the cigar cash box on the counter instead of putting it out of sight. Far too trusting. However, he accepted correction so meekly that I reassured him, "There's no reason you ought to know. Your granddaddy didn't own a store."

When we closed, we'd sold so much stuff that he took five dollars from the box and said he'd go to Fraley's Food Fair the next morning to replenish our stock on his way back from visiting Mrs. Cameron. And Miss Nancy would keep the store from ten until two.

That night at supper I told Aunt Kate, "I can't stand selling food in all that filth. Can I take over some stuff to clean with?"

She grinned. "There's more of Pop in you than I knew." But she gave me rags, a broom, and a mop. "Use pine cleaner from her shelves," she told me. "I buy it from her anyway."

Every day that week, as soon as I got home, I put on my old clothes and headed to the store. I'd washed down two shelves Tuesday by the time Uncle Stephen came just past five for the evening onslaught of cotton pickers. By Friday afternoon I'd used all Mrs. Cameron's pine cleaner and most of her furniture polish, but I'd washed down and polished every shelf and cleaned every item except those hanging from the ceiling. I'd swept sudsy water over the floorboards and through the cracks. The only thing left to do was the window. I was standing on a chair washing the inside when Clay came in.

"Smells like a forest in here. Needing more exercise?"

"Doing good deeds," I told him, my mouth primmed with virtue and my heart pounding so hard I could scarcely breathe.

"How about if I fetch a ladder and do the outside?"

It wasn't at all like I'd imagined, but washing that window with Clay Lamont, laughing at the silly faces he made through the glass, I could have died happy.

"This old store is as pretty as a picture now, and that's the truth," he told me when we finished. He plunked a dime on the counter. "Open us both a cold RC. We earned it."

That was the first soft drink a man ever bought me. I saved the bottle three years.

❀

Saturday Uncle Stephen fetched Mrs. Cameron home. She insisted on coming straight to the store. I was polishing the countertop when they arrived. She stomped up the steps, pounding her cane, and pulled open the door. Then she stood, a tiny silhouette against the sunlight, and glared. Sunbeams reflected from polished wares and lay on the old oak counter like a yellow blanket. "I swan." She craned her neck looking up and down the shelves and at the shining window. "Who done all this?"

"Miss Nancy and Carley kept the store open for you, and Carley cleaned." Uncle Stephen ushered her toward the chair by the stove.

"D'you fire that stove?" she demanded.

"It's been too hot for a stove," I informed her, "but I polished and cleaned it so you can fire it later if you want."

"I don't light that stove. Don't want people hangin' 'round in here."

"They don't hang around. They've got better things to do. Now, here's the tally of what we sold, what we've had to buy, and how much profit we made." I held out my notebook but she waved it away. I was glad to see her hands were skinny claws again.

"I need to rest a mite before I do any lookin'. Did you put everything back where you found it, girl?"

"Yessum. Abby rearranged a few things, but you'll be able to find them."

"Good. I don't want to have to look for stuff. Now you both clear out and let me catch my breath." She waved us out. "Come back later, Mr. Whitfield. I have something to say to you."

"Probably going to fuss about all our good work," I grumbled as we walked home.

Later that day Uncle Stephen went down for pipe tobacco. When he got back, he handed me a five-dollar bill. "Mrs. Cameron said to give you this and tell you your granddaddy would be proud of you. That's probably the closest Nora ever came to saying thank you. She also said you used all her pine cleaner, and next time go easier on the wax."

Chapter 15

I didn't mention report cards until bedtime Sunday night. We'd gotten them Friday, in thick paper cases the color of raw liver, but mine was nothing to brag about. Since little John had a cold, Aunt Kate had been too busy to notice I hadn't said anything, but they had to be signed and returned Monday. Reluctantly I took it to the table, where the family was gathered eating what Abby called "a bed-night snack." "What's dat?" she demanded.

"My report card from school showing my grades."

Her lower lip went out past her nose and she glared at Grace. "Me'n Sue Mary didn't get 'port cards, and we worked hard as Carley."

Grace hurried for a piece of paper and made her one. Abby showed it to me with a flourish. "Now show me yours." She looked from mine to her own, then at mine again. Her lower lip went out even farther, and she thrust hers back at Grace. "I doesn't want just A's. I wants B's and C's, too. Like Carley."

I glared at her, but Uncle Stephen raised his eyebrows and put out his hand. Unwillingly I handed it over. "B in arithmetic and history and B minus in science? You can do better than that."

"I got an A in reading." I reached for the card, hoping he wouldn't see the worst, but his eyebrows were already half an inch higher. He'd reached my C in penmanship and Mrs. Raeburn's neatly scripted note: "Carley's handwriting needs improvement."

"You try writing twenty-five spelling words five times each and every single night," I defended myself before he could speak. "Your hand gets so cramped, it nearly falls off. And we have to write the questions as well as the answers in science and history."

When he pulled a pen from his pocket, I expected him to merely sign the report card and hand it back. Instead he wrote in the "Parents' Reply" box, "Carley seems to have too much writing to do. Please set a time to discuss." I carried that card back the next day with the delight of a prisoner delivering her own death warrant.

Mrs. Raeburn sent home a sealed note. Wednesday afternoon when the last bell rang, I hurried into the bedlam of home-going children in time to hear Preston shout above the din, "Look! It's my preacher! Hey, Preacher!" He waved his fat arm in the air.

I looked over the balcony rail to see Uncle Stephen towering above the lankiest boys. He wore his usual suit, white shirt, and tie and had put enough tonic on his hair to make it lie flat and smooth. Normally I'd have been proud to claim him. Today I backed against the doorjamb and wondered if I could reach the bus before he saw me.

"Hello, Preston!" He waved over the crowd. Preston flushed to the roots of his red hair and pushed his way upstream to stand importantly at Uncle Stephen's elbow. Bonnie, Ruth, and even Freda followed with a lot of other kids, until Uncle Stephen stood elbow-deep in students basking in the notoriety of having their preacher at school. It was fine for them. He hadn't come to discuss their report cards. My heart thudded like an approaching train.

I sidled down the stairs and tried to slink along the wall toward the bus, but Uncle Stephen called over the throng, "Don't catch the bus, Carley. I'll drive you home. I already told Kate, out on bus duty. I want you to introduce me to Mrs. Raeburn." Great. Now everybody in the school knew he'd come to talk with my teacher. They probably thought I was failing.

He nudged the others off to their buses, then crossed the auditorium to drape an arm around my shoulders, and bent to shout in my ear. "How does a pipsqueak like you manage to survive this every day? Looks like you'd come home plumb worn out!"

I nodded. The noise was too deafening to talk even if I'd had anything to say.

"Where's your room?"

I pointed upward. He held my shoulder all the way up the stairs, along the balcony, and through Mrs. Raeburn's door. What could I do but introduce them?

They shook hands; then he turned to me. "Wait for me downstairs. You have a book?"

"Carley always has a book," Mrs. Raeburn said in the friendliest tone. Nobody would have guessed they were about to dissect me together. "It's one of the endearing things about her."

Down in the auditorium I plopped into a seat but had no intention of reading. I was trying to think of what to say for a brand-new contest: "I like a brightly lighted home because . . ." If I won, Westinghouse would pay for my summer music camp.

However . . . I looked up at that shut door and wondered what was going on up there.

Teachers were back in their rooms finishing up their day, so as soon as the janitor carried his supplies into the boys' bathroom, I tiptoed back upstairs to right outside our classroom door. I could hear every word. But I was too late. By now they'd finished talking about me and were talking about her.

Uncle Stephen could always get people to talk. I found it highly embarrassing. We'd stop for gas and the next thing you knew, the filling station man was telling Uncle Stephen all about his fight last night with his wife. Or we'd be at the grocery store and the checkout clerk would start telling him about her sick children. It wasn't that Uncle Stephen was nosy; he just cared. Some men have a passion for cars or boats. Uncle Stephen had a passion for people. By the time I had reached the door, Mrs. Raeburn was telling him the story of her life.

"I grew up in Job's Corner, near where my brother lives. Hugh Fred Keene."

"Carley told us you're Hugh Fred's sister." My cheeks grew hot. I didn't want her knowing I talked about her at home. "Did you all grow up in the house he owns now?"

She laughed but it wasn't funny. "Not hardly. We grew up poor, wishing for things we couldn't have. I wasn't more than six when we started hitching rides into town so we could walk up Center Street looking in store windows and picking out things we'd buy one day. I'd pick diamonds, and Bud—Hugh Fred—would pick out fine dark suits and real silk ties. And all the time we were shivering in the wind because we didn't either one have a decent coat after we outgrew the ones we took to Job's Corner."

"Was your daddy dead?"

"Pretty soon he was. First he was just a dead failure at farming. He was a pharmacist who couldn't turn away anybody with a pitiful story. Mama always said Daddy thought a promise was as good as cash, until he found promises didn't pay the mortgage. He lost the store when I was four, so we moved out to help look after Grandmama. Granddaddy had died that fall and she couldn't run the place by herself. But Daddy wasn't much help. He didn't know a thing about farming. Within three years he'd caught pneumonia and died. Mama planted a garden to feed us, and Bud quit school and went to work with Uncle Rob building houses. But he hated that and said it would never pay enough. So when a job came up at the chair factory, he applied for it. He came home that first day and told me, 'Maddie Lou, I'm gonna own that place. We're gonna make the world's best kitchen chairs for the lowest price, and I'm gonna get me a house like the Hart place up the hill.'" Her laugh was low and proud. "He did, too."

"What about you? What did you want?"

"Me?" She sounded surprised, like she hadn't thought about that for a long time. Now her laugh was small and unhappy. "I haven't done much better with my life than Daddy did with his. For a little while I dreamed it would be me, not Bud, living in the Hart house. I dated Taylor Hart my senior year of high school and thought he was crazy about me. But right before we graduated, he . . . left. And never came back." Her voice went down a drain.

"So you went to college?"

That was a dumb question. She must have, if she was a teacher. It took me a minute to realize Uncle Stephen was just encouraging her to keep talking.

"I'd already received a scholarship to Agnes Scott. My history teacher made me apply there, even though I thought I wanted to go to Mitchell, where Taylor was going. But after Taylor left, nothing could hold me here. I went to Atlanta and never came back. I got a good teaching job there and finally married an Atlanta boy. If anybody'd told me I'd wind up back here, I'd have said they were crazy."

"The war left a good many of us in places we didn't expect. I found myself in the coal fields of West Virginia."

"The war didn't have anything to do with my coming home. I came home because I didn't know where else to go. I'm in the process of getting a divorce." She brought out the last word like it was too big for her mouth and she needed to get rid of it.

I fully expected Uncle Stephen to tell her that divorce was wrong. But he just asked, "You didn't think you could stay in Atlanta and make a go of it on your own?"

"No. All our friends were his friends first, and none of them would have been sympathetic. You see, Marcus didn't leave me; I left him. There came a day when I would rather face eternity in hell than spend another day with that man. Do I shock you?"

She had certainly shocked me. I took a step back, nearly lost my balance, and was so busy trying not to fall that I almost didn't hear Uncle Stephen say, "I'm hard to shock." He went on, his voice as gentle as when he picked Abby up after she'd skinned her knee. "Sounds like you've had a rough time and still have a lot of pain. If you want to talk about it, you know where to find me."

She didn't say anything for what seemed like five minutes. Then she gasped, "I'm sorry. I'm sorry." I could tell she was crying. He murmured something and she flung out in anger, "Don't be nice to me. I can stand anything but that."

He was quiet for so long, I poised on my tiptoes in case he started out; then I heard her blow her nose just as he asked, "Where'd you get the doll?"

She gave a damp, sniffy laugh. "Hannah Anderson made it for me when I was four. We'd just moved and I'd lost my favorite one. On top of moving and leaving my best climbing tree—well, it was all too much. I cried and cried all day—must have driven my mother crazy. Then Aunt Hannah came back with Suzy." Her voice softened. "She said she'd made her especially for me because she loved me. For the rest of my life, no matter how bad things have gotten, I've had Suzy."

He chuckled. "And you've still got Hannah too—the most lovingest, talkingest woman I ever met."

She gave a little hiccup of a laugh. "You've got that right."

Sounded like their talk was dwindling down, so I quickly tiptoed back downstairs and called up, "Are you almost done, Uncle Stephen, or should I go get another book from the library?" My voice echoed in that cavernous, empty auditorium.

He came out onto the balcony. "We're done." He turned back. "So any child who makes an A in spelling one week will be excused from copying spelling words the following week? Carley will be glad to hear that. And we'll work on her penmanship. I think she'll work for you. She admires you so."

There he went, embarrassing me again. And you'd have thought they'd been talking about me the whole blessed time. He loped downstairs whistling.

"You've got a real nice teacher," he said at the bottom.

Mrs. Raeburn leaned over the balcony, hugging that ugly doll to her chest, and gave us the smile of a teacher ending a plain old parent conference. Only if you looked carefully could you see that her nose was red and her eyes watery. "Carley's a good student, Mr. Whitfield. She just needs to take her nose out of the reading book during science."

"We'll work on that too. Thanks for meeting with me. And we'll hope to see you at church some Sunday."

She laughed like she usually did, bells ringing through the musty auditorium. "You want your roof to fall in, Preacher?" She inclined her head with the teasing smile she'd worn that day down at Aunt Hannah's, so beautiful she made my chest tight.

He chuckled. "We've got strong rafters. And when you shake my hand at the door, do me a favor."

"Yes?" She sounded a bit anxious.

"Call me Stephen. Come on, Carley. Time to get home."

Neither of their faces looked like they'd just been talking about sin and using bad words. Would I ever understand grown-ups?

Chapter 16

The following Thursday just at dusk I sat in my locked room watching for Clay to come home from work. One solitary star glittered in the gray sky.

Star light, star bright,
first star I see tonight,
I wish I may, I wish I might,
have the wish I wish tonight.

It was warm enough for an open window, so I whispered my wish—and prayer—to the breeze: "Please let Clay like me soon."

Then I cleared my throat and began televising a special edition of *Unshaded Windows*. Sometimes talking to an invisible audience was almost like having a best friend.

"This past week we have talked of nothing except war, weather, and seats for the new Statesville High Stadium. News from Korea is that the war could be over any day. Men have gone around slapping each another on the back and saying things like 'Those communists can't beat free people' and 'We all knew it would just be a matter of weeks.'

"Tuesday was the United Nations Day of Freedom, so Uncle Stephen preached about that last Sunday. Some people said it was a fine sermon, but Mr. Wash Lamont was incensed. 'That United Nations is nothing but a bunch of communists, and you know it,' he insisted at the church door. 'It's well enough to talk about loving everybody, but you don't know some of those people like I do. I flew with a bomber squadron in the last war—'

"Clay gave him a playful shove from behind. 'You've been out of the army air corps so long, it's become the Air Force. You're a relic. Now get the starch out of your shorts and move along so others can greet these charming Whitfields.' Clay Lamont," I reminded my viewers, "is the future husband of Carley Marshall.

"On Tuesday Mount Vernon Elementary had a special chapel program. Mr. Donaldson told us how important it is for all nations to work together for peace and talked about what a fine model Mrs. Eleanor Roosevelt is for girls. Then Mr. Mayhew got up and said he had a better model for girls: a young Polish girl who resisted communism and declared, 'I do not like the stamp of boots on my soul.' By the time he finished his speech, he'd almost managed to convince us the United States ought to declare war on the United Nations once we finish in Korea.

"It's been so hot this week that women have gone around saying things like 'Can you believe it? Forty-two degrees last weekend and nearly eighty today' or 'I'd just gotten all our summer clothes put away, and now I've had to pull them out again.'

"Even in the heat, Hannah Anderson wore her new navy wool crepe dress to church and bragged to anybody who'd listen, 'I declare, Grace made this and it looks exactly like one I saw at Efrid's for sixty dollars.' Several women asked Aunt Kate if Grace could make dresses for them. Miss Emily wants two for Freda.

"Tuesday evening Bonnie Anderson showed up at the manse with green corduroy purchased by Hannah Anderson, her aunt. Apparently, Bonnie mentioned in the nursery that she was taking sewing in home economics, and Grace invited her to come sew some evening. Miss Pauline, needless to say, thinks Bonnie is sewing with me, which is sort of true. As they were going upstairs, Grace said, 'You can come, too, Carley, if you like. You can help press seams and pin.' Wasn't it nice of her to invite me upstairs in my own house? But I was so bored, I figured I might as well join them. Grace half finished a bathrobe for herself, Bonnie got her skirt cut out, and we had so much fun, we agreed we'd sew again next week. Aunt Kate even promised to get me some flannel to make a nightgown. She calls us the Job's Corner Sewing Circle.

"Poor Bonnie can use some nice clothes. Miss Pauline still buys hers big enough to grow into, but Bonnie has stopped growing. Everything she owns hangs on her. She really likes pretty things, too. Grace thinks they can alter some of her dresses so she'll have a smarter wardrobe.

"But by far the biggest news this week in Statesville was Stadium Week. The Lion's Club asked everybody to pay five dollars for one new seat for the new high school stadium. Mr. Hugh Fred got up in church and announced he'd bought twenty, which gives him twenty seats in a special section of the old stadium for Statesville High's homecoming game tomorrow night. He offered seats to anyone who couldn't buy seats of their own. Uncle Stephen had already bought two, so he and I will go. Aunt Kate says she is not particularly enamored of football.

"Freda certainly is—or, rather, enamored of a football player. She hasn't mentioned the U.N. or the weather this week. All she has talked about is the Statesville High homecoming game and dance. Even though she is only in eighth grade, Charles has asked her to go.

"'Mama bought me a pink angora sweater,' she told us at recess yesterday. 'Charles adores me in pink. He says it makes me look like a princess.' Then she leaned over and whispered like we were in a crowd instead of at the far edge of the playground, 'I'm getting to wear Mama's best perfume!'

"Bonnie told her she was surprised Mr. Hugh Fred was letting her go to the dance, and Freda giggled. 'He doesn't know. He gets livid if I even mention Charles. Says I'm too young for all that nonsense. But Mary Beal has invited me to spend the night. I'll leave the game with her and we'll meet Charles at the dance.' Freda squeezed her arms around her chest, which made her bosoms rise. Bonnie and I tried not to be jealous, but neither of us had anything rising yet. Nor would either of us be permitted to stay up late enough to go to a dance after a football game. As if any boy would ever ask us.

"Today Freda was so silly, we could hardly stand her. She kept whirling around and around at recess, chanting, 'We'll dance and dance and dance.' I got so jealous, I stopped by the bathroom on my way to class to be sure my face hadn't turned green.

"Have you noticed that football does funny things to people? Mr. Wash came by last night to say he'd bought a ticket for the homecoming game and to ask Uncle Stephen if we'd like to ride with him in his Chrysler. Uncle Stephen said, 'Sure. That'd be fun.' They disagree about a lot of things, but I'll bet if Mr. Stalin and President Truman got together for a summit and somebody had football tickets, they'd stop fighting long enough to go together.

"Speaking of fighting, I have a puzzle for you. Everybody at church seems to know Grace is sewing nights at our house. How do they think she does that if she doesn't live here? The only answer I can give is, there aren't really any secrets in Job's Corner, just things people are too polite to talk about. Oh! Special bulletin! Mr. Clay Lamont just turned in his drive.

"This is Carley Marshall for *Unshaded Windows*. Good night."

I never imagined that one very real Job's Corner secret was slowly worming its way up from the bowels of the gully.

Chapter 17

When we got to the homecoming game, Freda not only had on a pink angora sweater, she wore a new poodle skirt. She even had a hair band with *Freda* written on it in silver sequins, like all the popular high school girls wore. She was so beautiful, Bonnie and I scarcely watched the game for admiring her. Mr. Hugh Fred was proud of her, too. You could tell from the way he kept introducing her to men in the crowd. "This is my little girl, Freda."

Just after the kickoff my heart stopped. Clay had come in! He was with a crowd of people who all had dark curly hair, blue eyes, and plump figures. His hair glowed like a live coal among cinders as he gave us a wave and settled onto a bleacher. I wondered why he hadn't taken Mr. Hugh Fred up on his offer of a special-section seat. Especially since one of the girls, with dark hair curling almost to her waist, kept leaning all over him and worrying him to death.

I watched him a lot more than I did the game. I kept thinking about Freda dancing with Charles and tried to picture myself dancing with Clay. It wouldn't matter a bit that he was over six feet tall and I barely four foot eleven, or that I didn't have the vaguest notion how to dance. He'd just pick me up and turn us both around and around like Freda twirled on the playground.

Once, just when I was picturing him leaning down to give me a long movie kiss, he looked our way. I was so embarrassed, I grabbed Bonnie and dragged her to the bathroom.

Charles hardly got to play that night at all, since he was just a sophomore, but the one time he got the ball, Freda jumped up and down and screamed so loud that you'd have thought a touchdown depended on her yelling. Maybe it did. He made one.

Just before the game was over, Mary lumbered up to the reserved seats. Freda bent down and picked up a suitcase as big as the one I took to Big Mama's for a whole week. "There's Mary, Daddy. I need to go."

He leaned over and kissed her. "Okay, honey. You be good, now."

"I will." She practically skipped down the steps. He turned to Uncle Stephen and said, "Freda really likes Mary. I hope Mary will have a good influence on her study habits."

"Maybe so." Uncle Stephen didn't sound convinced.

❧

I didn't think I could sleep when we got home, but I did. Yet when I opened my eyes, it was still night. Job's Corner had no streetlights, so the world was very dark except for a little glow from Abby's "lower lights." Rowdy was raising sand in Aunt Kate's room, and someone was gasping, crying, and pounding on our front door. "Stephen? Kate? Let me in. Oh, please let me in!" It was a woman's voice but I couldn't recognize it.

I heard Uncle Stephen tell Rowdy to hush, and then his slippered footsteps hurried down the hall. A flash in the yard meant he'd punched on the downstairs hall light. The voice cried out in alarm and the light went out. I heard Uncle Stephen speak a few urgent words; then somebody stumbled in downstairs, making high, frightened sounds.

I crept out of bed, thrust my feet into slippers, and pulled on my robe. The upstairs hall was faintly lit by a small bulb in the bathroom. I met Grace in the hall, a shadow in her new blue flannel robe. She hugged it around her and moved hesitantly toward the stairs. Quickly I caught her arm to hold her back and pointed to the upstairs rail. She hung back. I leaned over.

"We can't stand here in the dark," Uncle Stephen said softly. "Go into the dining room. I'll call Kate." I heard him pad back down the hall and saw the dining room light go on. I drew back as he moved toward their bedroom door; then I peered over again.

Miss Emily Keene staggered to the dining room door, weeping. She wore her camel's hair coat, but the hem of a white nightgown poked out, bedraggled and full of grass burrs. Her usually sleek hair snarled down over her face. Her hands twisted before her like she was wringing clothes. I saw all that before I saw her face. There my eyes stopped. Years later when I saw how Hurricane Andrew bludgeoned once-beautiful parts of Miami, I thought of Miss Emily's face.

Her lips, instead of bright and pink with lipstick, were cut and bleeding. Her normally rouged cheek was savagely red and swelling. One eye was shut with a gash beneath it. And her face was crooked somehow. She cradled her jaw as she more fell than walked through the door, and then the dining room light went out.

I heard Aunt Kate come out and glide across the hall. I slipped silently away from the banister and motioned Grace to be quiet. Grace motioned me fiercely to head back to bed. She backed quietly into her own room and shut the door without a sound.

I wasn't leaving. Not with Miss Emily sobbing below. "Carley Marshall of *Unshaded Windows*," I whispered to justify being there.

Aunt Kate's voice, drowsy and uncertain in the dark: "Emily?" I heard the click of the dining room light again, then Aunt Kate's cry of dismay. "Oh, honey! Honey!"

"Don't turn on the light! He'll see it!"

"I'll pull the curtains. They're thick. Bless your heart, what happened?"

"Oh, Kate. Oh, Kate!" Miss Emily sounded like she had marbles in her mouth. She broke off and whimpered, then spoke again, more breath than words. "I am so ashamed"—she

gasped—"but I didn't know what to do"—she gasped again—
"where to go . . ." She started making little noises like a hurt
cat.

I heard Uncle Stephen walk out their door in shoes instead
of slippers and leaned just far enough over to see that he was
fully dressed. He paused uncertainly at the dining room door,
then squared his shoulders, took two deep breaths, and turned
the knob like a circus lion tamer about to enter the cage.

I heard Aunt Kate say sharply, "Fetch the medicine kit, a
towel, and a bowl of warm water." He rummaged for a time
in the bathroom, then went to the kitchen for a bowl. In a
minute I heard Aunt Kate say, "You are shivering. Let me light
the fire. Stephen, light the stove, please."

He also shut the door. I could only hear muffled sobs and
mumbled voices. My own teeth were beginning to chatter.
Even with the recent heat wave, the house got cold after dark.

I knew I ought to go back to bed. But if I was going to be a
television reporter, hadn't I better practice listening in on private conversations? Besides, maybe I'd learn something so I
could know how to pray. I tried to figure out how I could hear
better. The kitchen wouldn't work—Aunt Kate was sure to go
make hot chocolate. I remembered that the living room had a
closet beside the fireplace and that its back wall was the dining room wall. I had a similar closet in my bedroom, where I
often crouched to hear what went on in Uncle Stephen's study.

So, armed with rationalization and the quilt from my bed,
I crept down toward the living room closet, hoping it, like
mine, had a crack under the baseboard. As I passed the dining
room door, I heard Miss Emily yelp and Aunt Kate exclaim,
"That jaw must be broken! Stephen, we have to get a doctor—"

"No!" Miss Emily cried.

One step at a time I laboriously crossed the hall and let
myself into the living room. There I almost gave up. The room
was cold as a tomb—we hadn't had a fire there yet—and
equally dark. I was deathly afraid of the dark. One reason I
always slept with my shades up was to let in the faintest light
from stars.

Even at the door, though, I could hear their voices better: Uncle Stephen's rumble, Aunt Kate's soft comfort. Miss Emily's contribution was mostly sobs and whimpers.

Resolutely I hugged my quilt to me and felt my way past the toys. The closet smelled of mice and damp, but I wrapped myself in the quilt and sank to the floor. A sliver of light gleaming on the floorboards rewarded me. I could even feel occasional pulses of warm air on the hand I pressed to the floor to steady myself, but they weren't going to be enough to keep me from freezing. Hoping this wouldn't take long, I pressed my ear to the wall. All I could hear were voices but I could identify them.

Aunt Kate, mid-sentence: " . . . did he find out?"

Miss Emily, in quick, jerky phrases as if trying not to move her mouth: " . . . found her jacket . . . in the car . . . thought she might need it . . . called the Beals to say he'd run it up . . ."

My toes were becoming ice cubes. I eased them out of my slippers and rubbed them hard, then tucked the quilt carefully around them. I tried to fold myself into the tiniest ball I could within the quilt and breathed down my front to conserve body heat.

Miss Emily took a couple of ragged breaths and started speaking in whole sentences. "I didn't know he was calling. One of the younger children answered and said Freda wasn't there yet; she was at the homecoming dance—with Charles. Hugh Fred . . . Hugh Fred . . . " She broke down and sobbed. I would never have imagined that a skinny woman could have so many tears in her. Finally she grew calmer and daintily blew her nose. "He doesn't understand that girls grow up."

"So when did he do . . . this?" Uncle Stephen had only sounded that angry once since I knew him, the day of Grace's trouble. Sounded like he wanted to knock Mr. Hugh Fred down again.

Miss Emily must have thought the same thing, because she started right in defending him. "He went crazy, Stephen. He didn't mean to do it. I was getting ready for bed, and he stormed upstairs yelling that Freda had tricked us both. When he found out I already knew . . ." If she kept crying like that, we could all drown.

"Let me make some hot chocolate," Aunt Kate suggested, like I'd known she would.

"How'd you get away?" Uncle Stephen asked.

"He left. Grabbed his keys and yelled, 'I'll find them if it's the last thing I do.' He went simply tearing down the drive. I'm terrified he'll wreck his car, even before he finds them." She sobbed again for a long time and Uncle Stephen didn't say a word. I wondered if he knew what to say. I sure wouldn't.

Finally Miss Emily sniffed several times and blew her nose again. "Thanks. It's my own fault. I shouldn't have let Freda deceive him. He's right to be mad." Her words were still warped from trying not to move her mouth as she shaped them.

"He wasn't right to hit you!" That was Aunt Kate's voice, indignant. I got a whiff of hot chocolate from the crack at the floor and wished I was an adult and could sit in a warm room drinking hot chocolate with marshmallow while Miss Emily poured out her heart, instead of crouching in a freezing closet. Full of indignant self-pity on behalf of all children, I drew my toes farther under the quilt and breathed harder down my front.

"If he finds them," Uncle Stephen asked tensely, "will he hit Freda?"

"Oh no! He never hits Freda. She's his princess."

"Has he hit you before?" He sounded almost as miserable as Miss Emily. After all, Mr. Hugh Fred was clerk of his session.

She waited so long to answer, I had time to thrust my hands under my armpits to warm them. "Hugh Fred grew up hard. He was a fighter when I married him. He used to hit me a little when we were first married, but he stopped years ago. But tonight . . . he scared me. I couldn't stay there. I was afraid he'd kill me when he came back!"

"I think I'd better go looking for him."

"Stephen—" Aunt Kate's voice had a sharp edge of fear.

"I'll be fine," he assured her. I heard him take his hat, coat, and keys from beside the front door. In a minute I heard the old Chevy stutter and start like it always did when cold.

"Why don't you lie down on the couch and try to get some sleep?" Aunt Kate suggested. "We'll wake you if anything happens."

As it turned out, she didn't need to.

I heard her going to her room and started to my own, but she must have heard me, because she opened her door. "You heard?"

"Some of it."

"Run up to the study and get Stephen's softball bat. I don't think we'll need it, but . . ."

I fetched it and she took it in with her. Then I scurried as fast as I could to my room. My bed was like ice. I lay there wondering if I ought to get up and refill my hot water bottle, trying to convince myself I wasn't really miserable enough to have to get up, then trying to convince myself I was. Before I'd made up my mind, Rowdy barked in Aunt Kate's room again, and tires skidded to a stop in front of the house.

I flew to my windows as one door slammed, then another. I could just make out a truck parked by the road. Another car squealed around the corner up by the crossing.

Before I reached the stairs, somebody was ringing our bell and pounding on the door. "Mr. Whitfield! Oh, Mr. Whitfield! Let us in! He's right behind us. Let us in!"

I slid down the banister and reached the front door before Aunt Kate did. She carried the bat. Freda, Mary, and Charles stood on the porch, their faces white and their eyes terrified. I jerked open the door just as Mr. Keene's Hudson slid to a stop inches from Charles's bumper.

"Quick, come in," Aunt Kate urged. Mary hurried past her.

Freda stood frozen on the porch.

Charles hesitated, too well mannered to go ahead of her.

Mr. Hugh Fred jumped out of his car yelling at the top of his voice. "Charles Beal? Don't you go in that house. You hear me? I got something to say to you." He started running up the walk.

Those next few seconds seemed to last a lifetime. In Aunt Kate's bedroom Rowdy hurled himself against the closed door again and again, barking fierce warnings of what he'd do once he arrived. Little John woke and started to wail. Grace came running down the stairs to get him, but Aunt Kate warned, "Don't let the dog out," so Grace stood at the bedroom door, not moving.

From behind me Miss Emily grabbed Freda's arm and jerked her in, but by then Mr. Hugh Fred had made it up the walk and onto the porch. He clutched Charles's sleeve, jerked him around, and before we saw it coming, he punched Charles in the face with one fist and in the gut with the other.

Aunt Kate slammed and bolted the door, leaving Charles to protect himself. I flipped on the porch light so we could see. Old Unstoppable knew how to respond to another football player, but nobody ever taught him how to hit his girlfriend's daddy. Charles just put up his arms to shield his face and stood there like a block of granite while Mr. Keene hit him with fists like a Dutch windmill, hitting, hitting, hitting.

"Daddy!" screamed Freda, shaking the doorknob. "Don't, Daddy!" Miss Emily held her back as she twisted and writhed. Miss Emily's face was whiter than any ghost, and she was shaking from head to toe. Freda started beating her fists against the glass pane in the door.

Aunt Kate reached past Miss Emily and grabbed Freda's fists. "You don't want to do that," she said softly. "If the glass broke, you could get cut."

"But Charles!" she shrieked. "Daddy—"

Rowdy flung himself at the bedroom door more desperately.

Charles stepped back, landed on a truck John had left on the porch. With a look of utter surprise he fell backward.

Mr. Hugh Fred went very still. Then he started to tremble. I don't think he'd have hit Charles again, but as Charles struggled to sit up, his huge foot kicked Mr. Hugh Fred in the shin. He fell across Charles and started beating on Charles's chest like a madman.

I pressed my face to the glass pane beside the door, sick that after all my dreams of heroism, in real life I was neither brave enough nor smart enough to do a thing. Freda huddled beside me, sobbing as she watched. She wasn't so pretty with both her eyes and her nose running. Mary slumped on the telephone chair, saying nothing. I took Aunt Kate's bat uncertainly. "Should I go out and hit him?"

"No—" Aunt Kate looked over her shoulder toward Grace, as if asking what she should do. They both looked as uncertain and worried as I.

Suddenly a black streak dashed across the porch, followed by a little white figure yelling, "Get him, Rowdy! Get him!"

Rowdy threw himself on Mr. Hugh Fred's back, barking fit to wake the dead across the highway. Mr. Hugh Fred reached back to push the dog aside and stuck his fingers in Abby's mouth. Abby chomped down for all she was worth.

Finally Aunt Kate grabbed back the bat and unbolted the door.

Mr. Hugh Fred turned to free his fingers from Abby's teeth and saw his preacher's wife standing over him with a bat while the preacher's dog hunched, ready to bite. His face grew red and embarrassed. He reached his other hand and touched Abby's jaw to make her let go. Then he stood up awkwardly, shaking his head like he was trying to remember who he was.

"Hush, Rowdy. Sorry, Kate, I . . . I got carried away. Is Stephen here?"

Aunt Kate shoved Abby behind her and still clutched the bat like she'd hit a home run with his head if he so much as moved one inch. "He's gone looking for you."

Charles grunted and got up, shaking his head like a battered bull.

"Charles?" Freda cried from the doorway.

Mr. Hugh Fred jerked his head toward the house. "You women go back in the house. I won't touch him again, I promise. But I got something to say." Aunt Kate hesitated, then backed in, bringing Abby with her and calling Rowdy to follow. He did but sat right at her feet.

"Don't you hit him again," Abby warned as the door shut. Aunt Kate gripped her shoulder hard to shush her. But she didn't lock the door this time, I noticed, and she gripped the bat like she would use it if she needed to. Freda pressed her face so close to the window that tears ran down the pane. When she moved, she left a smear of snot and another of lipstick on the glass. I knew who'd have to clean that glass tomorrow.

Mr. Hugh Fred reached down and helped Charles up, and we could hear him through the closed door. "Sorry I hit you, Son. Didn't mean to do that. I apologize. Will you forgive me?" He stuck out a hand. Charles rubbed his right hand on the back of his neck, then reluctantly put it out and shook.

Mr. Hugh Fred gave his shoulder a friendly little shake. "Did I hurt you any?"

"Not much." Charles kicked at the little truck that had felled him, sent it scudding across the porch.

"Didn't think so. You're tough, boy. Real tough. And I didn't want to hurt you. I just got carried away. But I want you to understand something. I don't want you messing with my little girl, or even talkin' to her. She's not old enough for all this nonsense. You go right on playing football and have a good time in high school. Just leave her alone. You understand?"

"No! No!" Freda whispered fiercely.

Charles had already nodded. "Yessir."

"Honey, it's for your own good." That was the first time Miss Emily had spoken. She still sounded like she had marbles in her mouth.

Freda looked over her shoulder, and her own face turned white. "Mama! What happened?"

Miss Emily turned her face away. "I . . . I ran into a door."

Mr. Hugh Fred came to the door and saw them together. "You here, Emily? Good. Take Freda home, will you? I want to follow Charles and Mary up the road to be sure they get home all right. It's not safe for kids to be out this late alone. Mary, you ready to go?"

Mary lumbered out to the truck without having said one word to anybody. Charles followed her and climbed into the passenger seat. Mr. Keene went to his Hudson and waited for them to start. Then he pulled out behind them.

"Emily?" Aunt Kate sounded like she was asking a whole question with that one word.

Miss Emily smoothed her hair back with one hand, then swiped her mouth with one long motion. "We'll be all right. Thank you. Come along, Freda. It's time you were in bed." She looked tired and old.

Freda turned at the top of the porch steps and hissed, "You told him, didn't you Carley? He would never have known if you hadn't."

She stormed down those steps without giving me a chance to say a word.

Chapter 18

I crept to my bed and couldn't get warm. In a few minutes I heard little feet pattering across my floor. "Carley Cousin, can I sleep wif you? It's lonesome in my bed."

I was glad to have her, and not only for the company. Abby was warm as a puppy.

"Is Mr. Hugh Fred a bad man?" she whispered, curled up against me.

"I don't know. He did some bad things tonight but he's not usually bad."

"Eberbody does a few bad t'ings," she said philosophically. She yawned. "But if he comes back here hittin' again, I'm gonna bite him harder."

Biting people who attacked her was a habit with Abby. Most children in the nursery had gone home at least once with her tooth marks in their arm. She wasn't vicious about it—rather matter-of-fact. But anybody who put their hands near her face got bitten.

"Whatever stopped you from biting so much?" I once asked her as an adult.

She grimaced. "In first grade I bit a boy who tasted like dirt. After that every time I started to bite somebody, I found myself wondering what they would taste like. I guess thinking about it beforehand was enough to make me stop." Not permanently, though. Not long ago she was able to identify a would-be mugger for the police by her bite prints on his hand.

The next morning we got up and started working. In later years a family might have spent hours discussing what had happened, even gone to therapy to be sure nobody had lasting trauma. We simply did not have time. Uncle Stephen had invited the whole congregation to the second annual Manse Weenie Roast that next night, and we had to get ready. I often wonder how much counseling could be avoided if people had enough worthwhile and physically hard work to do.

Aunt Kate, Grace, and we girls finished cleaning the house while Mr. Wash and Uncle Davy helped Uncle Stephen put planks over sawhorses for long tables in our big side yard, out near the barbeque pit. After a while Clay and his daddy came to help, too, so I abandoned my mop to join the outdoor crew. Preston, still short, fat, and bragging about his upcoming growth spurt, saw me working and came to help.

"You're going to be five feet tall forever," I told him when nobody was listening. Then I ran to help Clay carry planks for two sawhorses he'd just set up. My heart nearly pounded itself out of my chest when he said, "Hey, Carley, why don't you come with me over to the church to get chairs?" I was halfway to his daddy's truck before he'd finished the sentence.

"Carley?" Aunt Kate stood on the back porch, shading her eyes from the sun. "I need you in here to help Grace and me in the kitchen."

"I'll go with Clay." Preston was already climbing into the back of the truck.

"Me, too." Mr. Wash headed toward the cab. "I need to show you how to work, little brother."

As they drove away, I stomped to the porch. If looks could kill, Aunt Kate would have lain pulverized. "You didn't have to do that," I snarled. "He wanted *me* to help." I couldn't help it that tears were rough in the back of my voice. I turned so she couldn't see my eyes.

She spoke to the back of my head. "It's not right for you to go over there by yourself with a man. You're growing up. It's time you realized there are things you can't do anymore."

I swiped away one tear that had crept down my cheek. "It's time *you* realized I'm growing up. Maybe he *wanted* me to go over there alone with him. Had you ever thought of that?"

She didn't answer for a very long minute. Was she about to throw her arms around me and exclaim, "Oh, honey, I am so sorry! I didn't realize that's how it is between you and Clay"?

She started out all right. "Honey—" Then she stopped. "There's something—" She stopped again. Finally she heaved a big sigh. "Let's go make tea. We're going to need gallons tonight."

Mr. Hugh Fred showed up at the party like nothing had happened, laughing and joking and apologizing for Miss Emily with a laugh. "She ran smack into a door and busted her jaw. Doctor says it'll be all right in a week or two." I noticed he kept one hand out of sight, though—the one with Abby's tooth prints.

Most of the people had arrived when Abby came running from the front porch to the kitchen to announce, "Clay's here. And he's got a wummin wif him!"

I didn't believe it but hung around the kitchen, not wanting to go out and see. Finally, though, Aunt Kate sent me to the yard with a tray of mayonnaise, mustard, and ketchup.

Clay saw me before I saw him. "Hey, Little Buddy, get over here. I got somebody I want you to meet." He waved a bottle of Cheerwine. His other arm was draped around a woman's neck. "This is Laura Black. Laura, this is my little singing buddy, Carley Marshall."

It was the woman who had been hanging on his arm at the game. Some people might have thought her pretty. I heard later she'd fooled enough of them to get chosen Miss Statesville back when she was younger. But I thought her long, curly hair about as attractive as a dusty crow, her blue eyes no better than squashed blueberries, and as for that little mole on the top of her nose—I would have yanked it off in a minute. In a black straight skirt and black twinset that hugged her curves, all she needed was a pointed hat to look like the witch she was.

She put out one claw. "I'm so glad to meet you. I hope we'll be friends, too."

I never could understand what people liked about Laura's voice. Uncle Stephen called it "husky and enchanting." Aunt

Kate said it gurgled like water over pebbles. I just wished she'd go find some water and drown.

I could hardly bear to shake her hand. "I've got to go help Aunt Kate some more right now." I wheeled and fled inside, but her face went before me all the way to the upstairs bathroom, where I could cry in private.

After that I spent most of the party inside. I overheard Aunt Kate telling somebody, "Carley's as much help as a grown-up tonight."

A lot of people seemed to know Laura, and none seemed surprised to see her with Clay. I found it disgusting the way the two of them grinned at each other, and other people grinned at them, all night. I also found it disgusting that even though most women went inside to look at the manse and talk women stuff, she stuck with Clay like a burr on his socks. Worst of all, Rowdy curled up at her feet and went to sleep with his nose on her toe.

Uncle Stephen said after everybody had gone, "Delightful girl. I'm glad Clay's found one."

"Found her under a rock, most likely," I muttered.

"Oho!" he crowed. "Not running for president of the Laura Black Fan Club?"

"Only if we were fanning her out of town."

But I didn't have time to grieve right then. As soon as the last guest left, we had to clean house again. Missionaries were coming to church the next day and spending Sunday night with us. As Aunt Kate muttered, "There's no rest for the wicked and preachers' families." When I went to bed at nearly midnight, she was still wiping countertops and Uncle Stephen was mopping the hall. When I got up early enough to change my sheets—the missionaries would sleep in my room and I'd sleep with Abby—Aunt Kate was already preparing the roast for Sunday dinner.

I'd fallen asleep consoling myself that Laura was just somebody Clay felt sorry for. He ruined that notion by bringing her to church.

"There's Laura!" Bonnie exclaimed when they came in.

"You know Clay's girlfriend?" Just saying the word nearly cut my tongue in two.

"Sure. She's a beautician and cuts all our hair. Miss Emily's and Freda's, too. She and Clay went steady in high school, and she used to come to Bethel a lot. Then they had some sort of fight before he left for the air corps, and broke up. Mama says he's real serious about her now."

Thus do worlds fall apart.

❄

Lest you think I am exaggerating about how many things happened that same weekend, I offer this letter, which I found among Aunt Kate's things after her death.

Dear Mama,

Thank you for the children's costumes. As you well know, it was the hottest Halloween on record, so they didn't even need coats. Carley made a cute gypsy, Abby loved being a ballerina, and John was an adorable cat. Stephen took them around trick-or-treating to the few houses on our road. I was too tired.

I love that man, Mama, but when I die, please put on my tombstone, "I Have Endured." This one weekend we have been up all night with a family having a major fight, had a party for well over a hundred people, and entertained missionaries from China overnight. They spoke at the morning service and showed slides Sunday night about their work and what they fear will happen to Chinese Christians now that missionaries have been expelled. Hearing them shows me how small my problems are. But I wish Stephen hadn't scheduled their visit the same weekend as the party. I was almost too tired to crawl back to school the morning they left.

The only good part about the weekend was that none of the Keene family was at church Sunday except Hugh Fred, so Rilla Lamont played for the service. I would give anything to have her every Sunday, but I don't think her nerves could stand it, and it's not easy to unseat a princess.

I don't mean to complain too much, for we really are fine, just a bit tired. But it's a good thing you didn't know to warn me about everything that's involved in marrying a preacher. I might have become the first Baptist nun.

Your loving daughter,
Kate

Those missionaries from China made more difference in the lives of Job's Corner children than they ever knew. Years later Bonnie wrote Aunt Kate,

Until that Sunday it never occurred to me that I could do anything with my life except cook, sew, and clean. That Sunday a fire began to glow in my heart that has never gone out.

We children didn't know about Bonnie's fire, but after the missionaries left, she started gathering us one afternoon a week in her living room to teach us hymns, Bible stories, and short Bible verses. "You never know when you'll need to know them. What if you are put in jail for your faith without a Bible or hymnbook?"

Preparing for that unlikely eventuality in central North Carolina, we caroled at the top of our lungs while I banged out the tunes on Miss Pauline's ancient piano. Even Ruth and Jimmy were allowed to come to Bonnie's Bible Class if they went straight home afterward and didn't stay to watch TV.

They generally stayed for *Western Theater* and told their mama we ran late.

To this day certain hymns and Scripture carry me back to that tiny, stuffy room with green linoleum, a big piano with cracked black varnish, and the smell of an oil heater.

Bonnie was more prophetic than she knew. She died in prison during one of Africa's recent revolutions. I hope in her last weeks she was comforted by the treasure of verses and hymns she laid up in the ungrateful, squirming hearts of the children of Job's Corner.

Chapter 19

November slid in as an already unsettled month, and unsettling things kept happening. Freda didn't show up at school for two days. Charles sat alone in the back of the bus, morose and silent, his face to the window. When I came down the aisle and said, "Hey, Charles!" he turned slightly, and I saw that his face was purple, green, and blue.

"Where's your girlfriend?" his football buddies kept teasing. "She look as bad as you do?"

"Don't be prehistoric," Charles growled. "I told you, I ran into a door. She must have a cold or something." He turned his back and stared out, hogging a whole seat to himself.

At Wednesday morning recess I spent a nickel for a Moon Pie and went out to the playground to meet Bonnie. It was so warm and dry, we sat on our favorite bank of grass over beyond the ball field. Up came Freda—pretty as ever in a red plaid jumper and red socks.

"Did you miss the bus?" Bonnie nibbled her ice cream bar before it melted.

Freda unwrapped a box of pretzels and plopped onto the grass beside us with a huge sigh. "No, Daddy insisted on driving me to school. He found out about me going to the dance, so he says he wants to keep an eye on me for a while. Can you imagine anybody being that prehistoric?" She had to have picked that word up from Charles. Nobody in our school said *prehistoric*.

164

"Was it fun?" I asked. "The dance, I mean."

She hugged herself, making her bosoms rise. "It was wonderful. We danced and danced."

We waited. Finally Bonnie asked, "Was that all?"

"At the dance. Afterward we went out for a hamburger."

I was jealous enough to kick her. I'd never been, but I knew where all the high school kids went and got hamburgers on a little tray that hung in the car window. "Then what?"

"Then we drove around and around their parking lot to see who else was there, and that's when"—she paused and shot me a look that warned me that if I said a word about what had happened, she'd never speak to me again—"that's when we came home."

"Was your daddy *real* mad when he found out?" Bonnie asked innocently. As hard as it is to believe, her family slept through the entire ruckus.

Freda darted me another glance, then looked across the playground. "Daddy wasn't mad with me. He fussed some at Mama, but then she got upset and ran into a door and broke her jaw, and we both felt so bad, we've taken turns nursing her."

Bonnie and I were too polite to tell her we knew good and well Miranda did all the work there was to be done in that house. If I'd had to bet what Freda had been doing, I'd have bet she was watching her daddy's new television. But I felt wicked for even thinking such a thing when she said, "Say, Carley, do you want to play a duet in the Christmas concert? Our class is doing a talent show and our teacher asked me to play, but Aunt Rilla said she has some nice Christmas duets if you'll play with me."

I could hardly breathe. "I . . . I'd love to." Was it a bribe to keep their secret? If so, I was willing to be bribed. And as soon as we got the music, I'd practice half an hour extra every day so I wouldn't make her ashamed of me.

I didn't get a chance to tell Aunt Kate and Uncle Stephen about the duet that afternoon, though. When I got home after school, I found out somebody had tried to shoot President Truman! Mr. Truman wasn't in any danger—he was in taking a nap, and the man shot somebody else instead—but that's all everybody wanted to talk about. I went out to the swing and felt real sick to my stomach. How could something that enormous happen without a single ripple in the air to let us know it was happening?

Friday night it was still unseasonably warm. Uncle Stephen said as he rose to get more tea, "I see *Cinderella* is at the drive-in for the very last night. Wanna go smooch, Kate?"

She looked at the rest of us around the table and gave him a wry smile. "It's not like it used to be, is it?"

"I wanna go smooch," Abby told him. "Can I go smooch?"

He picked her up and swung her high. "No, that's just what grown-ups do at drive-ins. But how about if we all go and just watch the movie?"

Grace said she'd rather stay home and sew, so we left John with her. John was walking everywhere now and apt to get noisy if he wasn't allowed down on the ground. As Abby said, "Can't you imagine de fuss he'd make 'bout stayin' in de car two hours?"

When we got there, we rolled down all the windows and hooked the sound box to Aunt Kate's window.

"You girls want to go perch on the fenders?" Uncle Stephen suggested. When we climbed up there, we had the best of both worlds—the freedom to be outdoors and the sound of the movie. It was glorious—until Abby had to go to the bathroom.

"It's just down there at the projection booth." Aunt Kate pointed to a short tower with a triangle of light beaming toward the screen. "Count the cars so you don't get lost."

I carefully counted. We were the ninth car in the second row. But when we came out of the restroom, no matter how many rows we went down and counted nine cars, we couldn't find ours. The first two times Abby was patient, but at my third failure she opened her mouth and yelled, "I wants my daddy. I wants my daddy!"

We heard a car door slam; then Clay hurried between cars toward us. He knelt so he wasn't blocking anybody's view. "What's the matter, little Abby? You get lost?"

Before I could inform him we were just looking for our car, Abby burst into tears and flung her arms around his neck. "Daddy's gone an' lef us," she sobbed. Fat tears rolled down her cheeks. "He was de ninfh car but now he's gone."

"You've just gotten turned around." Clay put one hand on each of our shoulders like we were both in kindergarten and steered us back to the little building. "Got two lost kids here," he told the girl selling popcorn behind a short little counter. "Can you announce for Reverend Stephen Whitfield to come get his children?" She picked up a phone.

The next thing I knew, a man's voice was booming all over the entire movie lot: "REVEREND STEPHEN WHITFIELD, PLEASE COME TO THE PROJECTION BOOTH TO GET YOUR CHILDREN." He repeated it twice. I would have gladly thrown myself off the projection booth, but it wasn't high enough to positively kill me.

Clay felt in his pocket and brought out a quarter. "Give them some popcorn and an orange drink to share until he gets here." She handed him a box of popcorn and a drink with two straws. Clay handed them to me and said the first words he'd spoken to me all night. "I'm real surprised at you, Carley, letting Abby get scared like that."

"If she'd waited a few minutes, I'd have found the car," I replied crossly. I wasn't about to tell him how worried I'd been myself.

"You wouldn't," Abby said pitifully, sniffing to make him feel even sorrier for her. "Daddy's gone an' lef us."

"No, I haven't." Uncle Stephen came through the door and reached down for her. She jumped into his arms with a squeal. He reached out an arm to me and smiled at Clay. "Glad you were here. Thanks for rescuing the bairns."

"Glad to be of service, sir." Clay gave him a salute. "But I'd better get back to the movie."

"Watching it, were you?" Uncle Stephen teased.

"Well, some." Clay turned light pink and grinned.

As we left, I saw Mr. Rob's gray truck just ahead of us. Clay and Laura were sitting so close, they looked like a two-headed driver. I'd never seen anything so disgusting in my life.

❧

Autumn weather in North Carolina is like a southern belle, changing its mind every minute. Friday was balmy enough to sit outside and watch a movie, but by Sunday we had frost. Uncle Stephen went over early to fire up the furnace, but the church was chilly. I huddled in my coat and glared at Laura across the aisle. Yes, she was there again, and since she couldn't carry a tune in a poke and couldn't join the choir, I'd have to endure watching her moon at Clay.

What happened was even worse.

Just before church Clay came from the choir room and straight to me. I was thrilled until he whispered, "Okay if Laura sits with you, Little Buddy? I hate for her to have to sit all alone."

I would have liked for her to sit alone—in a dark cell with rats and scorpions playing about her feet, tarantulas swinging about her face, and bats swooping overhead. But Big Mama didn't raise me to air my deepest feelings to everybody, so I put on my friendliest smile and said, "Of course. That would be nice." The reason so many southern women become great actresses is, we practice from our cradles.

Laura just assumed I'd move over and give her the aisle edge of the pew, where the view of Clay was better. Then Abby, sitting on my left, turned and called to Sue Mary, "We's got a bee-you-tee-ful wummin sittin' wif us. You wanna come?" Sue Mary (and Velma) bravely left Miss Pauline and wandered down to join us.

Freda had barely started plonking out the unrecognizable opening measures of the first hymn when Preston sauntered up and pushed his way past Laura and me. "Mama said I might as well sit up here on the children's row." Trust Miss Pauline to get rid of her children whenever she could. And trust Abby and Sue Mary to move down to give him room beside me. He'd had his Saturday bath, so he didn't stink, but when we all stood, he reached out one stubby hand to share my bulletin. His nails were dirty and his fingers covered with warts. We had to use the bulletin because we were singing one of Uncle Stephen's favorite hymns, which wasn't in our book. Since I'd heard it often enough from Uncle Stephen to know it by heart, I shoved the whole bulletin at Preston. Then I looked up and caught Uncle Stephen's eye. He grinned at me as we reached the chorus of the first verse.

Grant us wisdom, grant us courage, for the facing of this hour.

When we'd finished singing, Uncle Stephen looked down from the pulpit at our row, then out to the congregation. "Why don't all the children come up front this morning and sit with Carley and Abby?" Children streamed up to fill our pew and the one behind us—every child in the church except Ruthie and Jimmy Lamont. So instead of worshiping God in the beauty of holiness, I sat and steamed in the chilly air. Laura grinned at Clay on my right. Preston rubbed warty hands down his corduroy thighs on my left. Two rows of squirming little kids colored Sunday school papers beyond Preston and behind us. When Uncle Stephen prayed before his sermon, "May the words of my mouth and the meditations of all our hearts be acceptable to you, O Lord," I hoped God wasn't paying attention to mine.

Some of the kids got pretty noisy up there with no grown-ups. I frowned at them but they didn't pay me a speck of attention. Laura was no use at all; she just sat and smirked at Clay. Uncle Stephen finally leaned over right in the middle of his sermon and said, "We'll wait for the children to get quiet before we go on." Everybody froze, and I turned bright pink to think anybody thought he was talking about me.

A few minutes later Preston cracked his credit right out loud. He snickered. Abby fanned the air in front of her nose and glared at him. All the other kids started giggling. Laura wrinkled her moley little nose in a gentle sniff and glanced quickly at me as if she thought *I'd* done it.

At dinner Aunt Kate said, "I think children ought to sit with their parents from now on."

Uncle Stephen nodded. "Let's consider that an experiment that failed."

I wished Clay would hurry up and recognize Laura as an experiment that failed, too.

I huddled in the swing that afternoon watching the trees give up and die, and that's just how I felt. Being cold on the porch was a miserable pleasure. The weatherman was concerned because we hadn't had enough rain in October. I figured I could cry enough tears to satisfy him.

❀

The second Tuesday in November was election day, so Aunt Kate and Uncle Stephen had to go vote right after school. "Not that it makes much difference," he said glumly. "We don't have but one party in this state. It calls itself Democrat and acts Republican."

While they were gone, I moseyed over to Mrs. Cameron's. Abby was running most of our errands those days, and I was saving for music camp, so I hadn't been to the store for nearly a week. But she'd missed church Sunday with a cold, and I wanted to see her reaction to Mr. Hugh Fred raising Cain in the neighborhood.

Our weather still hadn't warmed up much, and since she wouldn't light the stove, she huddled in a black sweater, black coat, and long skirt, with a black shawl wrapped around her head. "They's a box of paper and pencils over there to put up." She nodded her head toward a cardboard box on the oak counter. "I'm a mite stiff this afternoon."

"You're just frozen," I informed her. "If you'd fire that stove, you wouldn't have to freeze. Uncle Davy will bring you all the wood you want for free, and Uncle Stephen will come over here and light it for you every morning." I moved boxes of nails and combs to a higher shelf and arranged the pencils, paper, and ink down where schoolchildren and their mamas could see them. By now I felt that store was half mine.

"Mind your own business, Missy," she snapped. "I know how to light a stove if I want one. I just don't want folks hangin' round here using up my good heat. Besides, I don't feel the cold much. You young'uns these days are too soft."

"I'm not soft; I'm just smart enough not to be miserable if I can help it."

"You can help it right now." She tapped her heavy cane on the floor. "You can go home where it's warm and leave me in peace."

"I haven't finished putting up these things. And don't you have a shipment of bread?"

"I can put up my own shipments." She rapped her cane on the floor one more time, then raised it to point. "It's down on the floor at the back."

I opened the box, taking deep white-bread breaths. "I've been meaning to ask you. Over in the cemetery there's a tombstone that says, 'Cameron' on top and 'Thomas' and 'Alvina' underneath. At the bottom it says, 'Awaiting your coming.' Was Thomas your husband?"

"Yep. 'Cept most folks called him Tom. I allus called him Mr. Cameron."

"Was it you who carved that message on his tombstone? It sounds pretty morbid."

She cackled. "I didn't pick the text; he chose it when his first wife died. But I 'speck they're both awaitin' my coming by now. She'll have right smart to say to me about marryin' her man." She cackled again in anticipation.

"Did you all—you and Mr. Cameron, I mean—ever fight?"

"'Course we fought. What married couple doesn't? He was an ornery old cuss, and while I'm easy to get along with, he sometimes pushed me too far."

She was about as easy to get along with as a copperhead in a bucket, but I didn't say so. Instead I asked, "Did he ever hit you?"

She peered at me through white caterpillar eyebrows. "The preacher been hittin' his wife?"

I drew back, shocked. "Heaven's no! He can't hardly bear to switch Abby when she needs it. I just wondered."

"I don't hold with hittin' women." Mrs. Cameron rested her chin on her cane and pursed her lips. "There was trouble along those lines some years back—one of our boys had a real hot temper. He cooled down nicely, though. Became a pillar of the community. Of course, pillars can topple." She cackled and nodded to herself. "They surely can."

I didn't wonder anymore if she'd heard what went on Friday night. There was seldom anything in Job's Corner that Mrs. Cameron didn't know. But what could we do with what we knew?

❄

After Freda's daddy drove her to school for a couple of weeks, Bonnie and I got on the bus one day to find her sitting with Charles in the back like nothing ever happened. She chattered and bounced her curls, and he looked at her like she was a bowl of sweet whipped cream.

At recess she joined us in the auditorium. After all that dry weather, we were having a deluge almost every other day. Because our playground was too wet and slick to play on, we stayed inside for recess. Bonnie and I had started bringing embroidery. I was working on my hope chest pillowcases, telling myself Clay would come to his senses any day now.

Freda asked me first thing, "Does the session meet tonight?"

I placed my finger and wound thread around twice for a purple French knot before I answered. "It's the right night, so I guess so."

"And they're coming to your house?"

I finished a second knot before I replied. My French knots had a tendency to pull through to the back, so I had to make them very carefully. "Must be. Aunt Kate told Grace this morning to make a yellow cake with chocolate icing."

Freda looked around to make sure nobody was listening, then leaned so close, one curl brushed my cheek. "Good. Would you do me a real big favor? Would you call me the *second* Daddy leaves to come home?"

I had never in my life called a friend before, and didn't know how I'd explain it to Uncle Stephen, especially so late. Even he and Aunt Kate never called anybody after nine unless it was an emergency. When I didn't answer, she begged, "Please. It's real important and nobody can do it but you. Please?"

What can be sweeter than to be begged by a princess to do her a favor nobody else can do? Of course I agreed. But being practical, I insisted, "We'd better think of a real good reason why I'm calling. Uncle Stephen might be in the hall still saying good night to the other men."

Thinking—and worrying—weren't Freda's strong suit. "Like what?"

"You're going to Miss Rilla's for piano today, aren't you?"

She nodded.

"And she's going to tell you when we can both come over to practice our duet for the school program, right?"

She nodded again.

"Then why don't I call to see when that is. If anybody asks why I didn't wait to ask you tomorrow, I'll tell them I was worrying and couldn't sleep."

"Why are you worrying about that dumb duet?"

"I'm not. But when I call and ask about the practice, you'll know your daddy's left. I won't have to say a thing about that. You'll *know*. See?"

"But you won't call before he leaves, will you?"

I sighed. "Of course not. That's the point in my calling."

"Oh." I wasn't sure she understood, but a private little smile turned up both corners of her mouth. "How late do you think they'll be?"

"Usually they finish around nine; then Aunt Kate brings out cake and coffee. If your daddy stays for that, he might not go until ten."

"Could you tell him it's real good cake?"

"I guess so. Grace's cakes always are."

She gave me a blinding smile. "You are absolutely marvelous!"

I opened my mouth to ask why she wanted me to do her this favor, but the bell rang and she pranced back to her room.

About eight that evening I realized there was one serious hitch in our plan. My bedtime was nine, and I couldn't think of any good reason to stay downstairs long enough to know when Mr. Hugh Fred left. I'd have to watch from my window and hope I recognized his back.

I went upstairs at eight-thirty as usual and read in bed with my door cracked, waiting to hear sounds that meant they were through meeting and ready to eat. They must have had more business than usual, because Aunt Kate didn't take the cake in until quarter past nine. By then I was nodding over my book, but I wrapped myself in my quilt and crouched by my window. A cold drizzly rain rolled down my long curved panes.

Across the highway there was a light in Clay's room. Even if he was temporarily unfaithful, I still wished for him on every first star and kept tabs on his window. I knew which was his room, because I'd asked casually one day at piano lesson, "Is that your bright light I see some nights?"

Miss Rilla murmured absently, "No, dear, that's Clay's room. We sleep at the back." I felt terrible for using her that way but consoled myself it was for a good reason. She'd forgive me when I married Clay and moved in with her.

I sat there hoping for a glimpse of him and wondering if he knew which was my window and ever looked my way. Getting sleepier and sleepier, I rested my head against the cold pane and pinched one cheek. Finally I heard sounds downstairs that meant men were putting on their coats. In the glow from the front porch light I saw a dark shape hurry down our walk and get into Mr. Hugh Fred's car. Feeling like a spy about to attempt a dangerous mission, I tightened the belt of my robe and eased down the steps, embarrassed to be seen in my robe and slippers. Pushing past two or three elders standing around like they had no homes to go to, I checked the number I'd written down, and dialed. The only calls I'd ever dialed before were to Aunt Hannah, sometimes if Aunt Kate said, "Carley, call so-and-so and tell them such-and-such," and once in desperation to Big Mama. I trembled to think I could dial a wrong number at that hour of the night.

Just as I'd expected, Uncle Stephen came over to see what on earth I was doing. I put my hand over the mouthpiece. "Have to ask Freda something." She answered after the first ring. "Hey, Freda? Did you find out when we're going to practice?"

"Has he gone?" she asked breathlessly.

"Okay," I said, pretending she'd answered me. "I can do that."

"Do what?" she asked blankly.

"Okay, good night." I hung up and turned toward the stairs before Uncle Stephen could stop me. "I wanted to know when we're going to practice our duet," I called over one shoulder.

Thank goodness somebody else spoke to him right then. I could tell he thought that was a dumb reason to call anybody an hour past bedtime. He was right, too. I just hoped Freda wasn't too dumb to figure out her daddy was coming home.

I crept gratefully to bed and was almost asleep when I heard Clay's voice in the hall. I imagined for one foolish second he was coming to see me. Then I heard Uncle Stephen. "Come on into the study. It's still a bit warm."

As soon as they shut the door, I tugged the quilt off my bed, wrapped up in it, and slid to the floor of my closet.

"But who could have expected the Chinese to come in?" Clay's voice was high and anguished. "Our boys are dyin' over there, Preacher! Seems like I ought to go back in. But it would like to kill Mama if I did. And Laura—what should I do?"

I shivered in spite of my quilt. Clay going to war? What if he got shot? Killed? I held my breath. What would Uncle Stephen say?

I was relieved when he counseled, "Why don't you wait and see what happens? We don't know for sure the Chinese are in, and the way things have been going, up and down from one week to the next, it could well be over before you got your name signed and your uniform on. Then you'd be stuck. I hear MacArthur still expects the boys home by Christmas."

"That's true." Clay sounded like that was exactly what he'd wanted to hear. "Thanks. I sure do appreciate havin' you all here. You and Miss Kate both. She's a fine musician."

"That she is," Uncle Stephen agreed. "And so are you."

They headed downstairs and I went back to bed. "The reason Clay didn't say I am a fine musician, too," I consoled myself, "is that he's too shy to say my name to Uncle Stephen."

The next day at recess I asked, "What was that about? My calling, I mean."

Freda giggled. "Charles came over and we talked. But he had to leave before Daddy got home, or Daddy would've been furious."

Bonnie frowned. "How did you keep your mama from finding out?"

Freda tossed her curls. "She knew. She even brought us Cokes and cookies. She says Daddy's old-fashioned, so we have to work around him if I'm to lead a normal life. Charles and I needed to talk about—" She stopped, then changed what she meant to say. "We just needed to talk. So he came over at eight after Daddy went to the meeting, and he left the second Carley called. He went home the back way so he didn't even have to pass Daddy on the road."

I couldn't help admiring her, Miss Emily, and Charles. Where did they get the courage to walk that close to Mr. Hugh Fred's angry fists?

Chapter 20

One evening Uncle Stephen took two carloads of our men to a Presbytery-wide men's meeting at Barium Springs, and Aunt Kate planned to go to the church women's circle meeting down at Aunt Hannah's. Aunt Kate claimed circle was for fellowship and Bible study, but when it met at our house, it involved a lot of good dessert and conversation.

At the last minute Aunt Hannah called. "Janey Lou is feeling poorly and I'm taking her home. Could Carley come with you to pass the cake?"

I was glad to. Aunt Hannah's pineapple upside-down cake not only had cherries in every pineapple slice, she put pineapple juice in the cake and fresh whipped cream from Uncle Davy's cows on top. I did homework in the kitchen while they had their lesson and business, but once the silver and napkins were distributed and cake and coffee were passed, I perched on a chair in the corner of the living room with the other ladies.

I loved that room. It had slate blue wallpaper, a maroon velvet sofa with mahogany trim, long blue drapes to match the paper, and an oriental rug in soft cream, blue, and rose. Because it was still very cold, Uncle Davy had built a fire that crackled happily and made the room glow. So did the rose silk shades on her lamps. One sat under my favorite oil painting, of the sun rising over a snowy pasture that looked just like the pasture across the road. In one corner the artist had signed her name in spiky letters: *Hannah Anderson*.

"Did you paint that picture?" I blurted out in astonishment. "It's great!"

"Oh, pshaw." Aunt Hannah's glasses glinted in the rosy light and her face grew rosier still. "Hardest part of that was getting up early every morning. Anybody here learned to play that new game, canasta? I've been wanting to give it a try."

Several women said they hadn't but had thought about learning it.

Miss Nancy lifted her sharp nose. "Wash and I don't play cards except Rook."

Uncle Stephen and Aunt Kate played Rook, too, which bothered me. Big Mama had certainly taught Aunt Kate that cards were a tool of the Devil, and as far as I could see, Rook cards weren't different from the other kind except they had big numbers in four colors instead of little numbers along with red hearts and diamonds and black spears and clovers. (I'd never played cards but had taken a quick look at a deck Miss Pauline used for solitaire.)

I was as shocked as the rest of them when Aunt Kate admitted, "Stephen and I've talked about learning canasta, too, but we haven't yet."

A woman across the room arched her brows. "You play cards, Mrs. Whitfield?"

"Just since I was married." Aunt Kate took a bite of cake and added, "I didn't grow up playing cards, of course. I was raised a Baptist."

"*Baptist?*" several women chirped at once. From their tone you'd have thought Aunt Kate had said, "I was raised a thief." One of the puzzling things to me—raised Baptist and now living with Presbyterians—was how those two denominations could sing in each other's choirs, go to each other's revivals, and still mistrust each other's religion. I'd heard Big Mama say "*Presbyterian?*" in just that tone of voice.

"Well," somebody else said with a nervous little laugh, "we're real glad you converted."

Aunt Kate turned so red, I hoped she'd count to a hundred before she spoke.

Aunt Hannah spoke first. "Mrs. Whitfield will be thinking the rest of us ought to convert. Has anybody heard whether Lenora had her baby yet?"

"Oh, my yes. She was in labor nearly nineteen hours, and said she thought she'd die, but finally . . ." They sheered off happily into a discussion of that labor and delivery, followed by comparisons of their own, until they remembered I was there and changed the subject to recipes.

As we were leaving, Aunt Hannah leaned over to Aunt Kate and whispered, "Davy and I will come up and learn canasta with you. Just say when."

"Friday night?"

"We'll be there."

When we all got home, Aunt Kate told Uncle Stephen they were coming, and I finally got to say what I'd been thinking.

"Card playing is a sin. Big Mama taught you that."

"She taught me lots of things, honey. When you grow up, you sort out any that aren't explicitly in the Bible and decide what's right for you."

I couldn't believe what I was hearing. "Then what's the point of learning right from wrong in the first place? That's dumb!"

Rowdy gave me a sharp bark of reproof for sassing Aunt Kate, but Uncle Stephen, refilling the coal bucket, laughed so hard that he knocked off the top three chunks. "She's got a point, Kate. How are you going to wiggle out of that one?"

Aunt Kate gave me a look we both knew very well. "I'm not going to wiggle out of it. Carley knows better than to disrespect her elders. In fact, Carley, I'll need you to serve dessert. Grace asked to go up to Janey Lou's that evening, and I've already said yes."

I was delighted Grace was finally going out but wrestled with what I ought to do. If they were bound and determined to sin, should I shun them and lock myself upstairs? Or was it my Christian duty to show them love and mercy by serving dessert? I finally decided I'd serve dessert, setting such a good example that maybe they'd throw down their cards and repent.

Uncle Stephen felt they ought to build a fire and play in the living room, which we seldom used. "That way Carley and Abby can listen to *Ozzie and Harriet* in the dining room, and after Abby goes to bed, Carley can read in there until we need her."

Aunt Kate, dubious, went with him to consider the possibilities. I stood in the doorway behind them and didn't see many. The room was dismal, its only furniture the piano and a battered steamer trunk holding Abby's least favorite toys. Even she preferred the sunny dining room now that the days were short and cold.

"It has a beautiful mantlepiece if it was polished, and that's a working fireplace," he coaxed. "We can set a table in the middle of the room and bring in a couple of floor lamps."

Aunt Kate cocked her head and sighed. "It will be tacky but I guess it'll do."

When we got home the next afternoon, Uncle Stephen was grinning from ear to ear. He wouldn't let us open the living room door, and he'd pulled down the shade to the porch.

I went to look for Abby. "What's going on in the living room?"

She gave an elaborate shrug she'd learned from Sue Mary. "Daddy won't tell me. He eben locked de door!"

We stared at one another. Doors weren't locked in the manse, except mine when I didn't want Abby coming in.

Uncle Stephen was mysterious again when we got home Thursday, but on Friday he flung open the door as we walked into the hall. "Voilà!"

Abby jigged beside him as Rowdy barked to contribute to the general excitement. "Me'n Sue Mary he'pped wax de floor. We put wags on our feets and skated all ober it."

I scarcely recognized that drab old living room. The walls had been painted a soft cream. The newly waxed floor was covered by an Oriental rug in browns and blues. At the window hung a pair of blue drapes. In each corner stood a lovely brass floor lamp. Next to the door stood a low table, covered with Big Mama's ecru tatted tablecloth over a soft brown cloth.

A vase of bare branches and a pretty brass bell decorated the table. On one wall hung a watercolor of mountains. In the fireplace, logs sent up a soft glow that chased away the chill. And in the center of the room stood a card table and four chairs.

Aunt Kate gasped. "What ... where ... how on earth could we afford all this?"

He beamed in delight. "We didn't. Hannah brought up damson pies Wednesday morning and caught me painting the walls. I figured that would help a little. She said she had a card table, rug, drapes, and lamps in her storeroom she wasn't using. She even lent me one of her paintings, and we can keep it all as long as we want."

"You begged?" Aunt Kate was aghast. "How could you? Take them right back!"

"I never begged!" Uncle Stephen flung back his head and glared at her. "Hannah offered them. She even sent Davy up today to hang the drapes. I thought of using the branches in your vase, though. I thought you'd be pleased." His mouth looked as balky as Abby's could.

Aunt Kate sighed. "It's beautiful, but I never took somebody else's things in my life."

"We aren't taking them; we are borrowing them until we can replace them with things of our own. Come on, you know how much Hannah likes to do for people. And all these things were in a storeroom. She'd be hurt if I took them back. Let's just enjoy them awhile."

Aunt Kate softened and leaned against him. "For a while, Stephen. But once Christmas is paid for, let's buy some nice things ourselves. What did you do with Abby's toys?"

Abby ran to the table covered with Big Mama's tablecloth. "Boilà!" She lifted a corner. The table was the toy trunk.

"You're crazy," Aunt Kate said, nuzzling Uncle Stephen's chin, "but I love you."

❦

Friday night when the doorbell rang, I hurried to answer it. Aunt Kate was still dressing and Uncle Stephen was making coffee. There stood Miss Hannah with Mr. Donaldson.

I was too shocked to say a word, but fortunately she was already talking. "Davy pulled his back throwing our old washer into the gully this afternoon," she said in her fast, breathless way. "We now have a splendid new one that spins the clothes almost dry—I just love it. I told him to get somebody to help him throw that heavy old thing over, but you know men—they always think they can do everything by themselves. So he's had me rub him with linament, and he's lying on a heating pad—"

"Will he get all right?" I interrupted, anxiety overcoming my shock at seeing the principal on my own porch. Uncle Davy was never sick.

"Oh yes, old dear, by tomorrow he'll be fine. But I roped in my cousin Jerry, since he already knows how to play and can teach us." She led Mr. Donaldson inside.

Aunt Kate came out from putting John to bed and looked as disconcerted as I felt to find the principal in our front hall.

"Hey, Mrs. Whitfield," Mr. Donaldson greeted her.

When Aunt Hannah explained what he was doing there, Aunt Kate smiled. "If I'm going to beat you at cards, you'd better call me Kate."

He nodded formally. "I'm Jerry."

I went to the dining room rejoicing. "We've got a chance to witness to an unrepentant heathen," I informed Abby, who was industriously braiding poor Rowdy's thick black hair. "If Jesus could convert prostitutes and tax collectors by eating with them, maybe Uncle Stephen can convert Mr. Donaldson by playing canasta."

"What's convert?" Abby frowned at the coarse hair that refused to stay braided.

"Make a Christian out of him. He told me he isn't a Christian."

"Co'se he is, Carley Cousin. He dist doesn't know it yet. Daddy'll tell him." Rowdy thumped his tail in approval.

I guess the cards went well. Maybe they even played some. But mostly they talked and laughed. Nobody could be with Aunt Hannah long and not laugh. The first time I heard Mr.

Donaldson laugh, though, I didn't know who it was. He had a really nice laugh when he used it.

Abby flat out refused to go to bed. "I wants to see Daddy convert him." So I let her pick out four of Aunt Kate's prettiest cloth napkins while I got out the best dishes instead of the plates Aunt Kate left out. I even ironed those napkins. Big Mama always said guests deserve our best.

About nine I took in the chocolate cake, then went back for ice cream and coffee. Abby handed around the forks and napkins with a face so solemn, you'd have thought she was passing the offering plate. When Aunt Kate saw the plates and cloth napkins, her eyes widened and she squeezed my arm. "Thanks!" she whispered.

I scarcely noticed. I was admiring a wire-and-wooden stand Mr. Donaldson used to hold his cards instead of a second hand. I'd been wondering how he could hold cards and play too.

Abby had only given the wooden stand one brief look. Instead she kept looking from her daddy to Mr. Donaldson with wide, waiting eyes.

"What's the matter, Abbikins?" Uncle Stephen finally asked.

"Nussing." She plopped to the floor cross-legged, propped her elbows on her knees, and cradled her chin in her hands. "I's ready."

"Ready for what?" Aunt Kate asked.

I grabbed her by the arm. "Ready for bed. She wouldn't go until she got to help serve dessert." Abby opened her mouth but I jerked her toward the door. "We're going to read both her new library books."

Promising to read a book was the only way to swerve Abby from a chosen path, and it almost didn't work. As soon as we got to the hall, she jerked away. "Fust I wants to see—" I clapped one hand over her mouth and dragged her down the hall. I should have known better. My fingers would carry her tooth marks the next two days.

"Well?" I asked Aunt Kate and Uncle Stephen when they'd gone. "Is he a Christian?"

"We didn't bring that up." Uncle Stephen carefully slid wedding china into hot soapy water. "Let's let Mr. Donaldson get to know us as people first."

I was horrified. "What if he dies tonight and goes to hell? You'll feel awful!"

"If he dies tonight and goes to hell, I sure will feel awful," Uncle Stephen agreed, "but I'd also feel awful if I rammed religion down his throat and he choked on it."

I stomped to bed informing my disappointed viewers, "I used those good dishes and ironed those napkins for nothing."

❋

Mr. Donaldson got in the habit of dropping by to bring books for Uncle Stephen. They both liked to read, and since Mr. Donaldson reviewed books for the Statesville paper, he got a lot of new ones. He'd sit down in the dining room, they'd bring out pipes, slide down in their chairs, and they'd talk. They'd also light and relight those pipes—neither one could talk and smoke at the same time—and fling matches toward the wastebasket. Since they missed more than they hit, our floor looked like a matchstick factory by the time he left. Uncle Stephen picked them up. He said men didn't learn that skill until they got married. After those evenings the dining room smelled like pipe tobacco for a whole day.

I was puzzled that Uncle Stephen seemed to enjoy Mr. Donaldson more than any other man in Job's Corner, when Mr. Donaldson never came to church. A lot of evenings I'd stay in the corner, doing homework or reading, and I think they forgot I was there. Their conversation, like the matches, covered a lot of territory. I was baffled, though. The two of them talked about the same things Mr. Wash and Uncle Stephen did—communism, the economy, Negroes, the war in Korea—but while Uncle Stephen and Mr. Wash disagreed about all those issues, Uncle Stephen stayed polite and never showed he was mad until Mr. Wash went home. He and Mr. Donaldson agreed on the issues, but when they got to talking about solutions, they'd get mad and yell at each other at the top of their lungs—then laugh. Our house was the only place I heard Mr. Donaldson laugh.

One evening, though, he came in with a bleak face. "I wish you were a drinking man. I've just heard Al Jolson died and I'd like to drink a toast."

"We've got coffee." Uncle Stephen headed to the kitchen. "And for this we must bring in Kate." The three of them sat around the kitchen table listening to phonograph records and talking about music well past my bedtime. I got up to go to the bathroom and they were still down there.

Another evening Mr. Donaldson told Uncle Stephen and me to give him a hand bringing in something he had in the car. It was long boards and a box of nails. "I thought we could build those railroad tracks you keep talking about up in your study." He surprised us by being able to hammer with just one arm. Abby was so entranced, she spent two evenings handing him nails.

While they worked, they still discussed the news. They were both riled up, I remember, about South Africa's new rules to keep Negroes and white folks separated. "If they get acceptance for that over there, somebody's gonna want to try it here," Mr. Donaldson fumed, pounding a nail into a track support.

"As if they hadn't already. That's not quite level," Uncle Stephen replied. "It's Jim Crow laws all over again on a national scale. But surely they won't last. People won't stand for it."

"I'm not optimistic about people's intolerance for injustice." Mr. Donaldson stood back and looked at his work. "And it is level; you're standing crooked."

Years later I took fencing in college. As I parried with friends, I realized why those two men enjoyed one another. Steel sharpening steel. And I think both, in their own ways, were lonely. Uncle Stephen missed having his brothers to talk with, and Mr. Donaldson had isolated himself from friends he grew up with. With everybody but Uncle Stephen, he carried bitterness around to replace the arm he'd lost.

Aunt Kate said one night after he left, "Stephen, tell Jerry it wouldn't hurt him to smile at his teachers once in a while."

"You know, it just might," Uncle Stephen said thoughtfully. "Jerry's a lot easier to hurt than you might imagine."

I thought of that one Friday afternoon when Mrs. Raeburn took five of us who had made one hundred on our last three history tests to see *Treasure Island*. As we were coming out, Mr. Donaldson was buying a ticket for the next show.

"Hey, Mr. Donaldson," I called, wanting to impress him that I was out with my glamorous teacher, and equally wanting to impress my fellow students that I knew him well enough to speak to away from school. "It's a great movie."

Instead of me it was Mrs. Raeburn he was looking at. She was certainly worth a long look that afternoon. Since we weren't in school, she wore black slacks with a white angora sweater and a red wool jacket. Her shoes had high heels and were red and black.

He didn't say a word. He seemed to be waiting for her to speak first.

"Extracurricular history," she told him, tossing her head like a horse scenting the air. "The kind you used to be so fond of."

"I'm still fond of it."

The woman behind the ticket window said something sharply. He bent to hand her some money and get his ticket, then turned, leaned on his elbow, and asked, "Is it as good as I've heard?"

"Wonderful," she told him. She looked like she'd like to say something else, but didn't.

An angry, stout woman poked him from behind. "Move along so other folks can get tickets, too."

He flushed and stepped toward us, but Mrs. Raeburn put out a hand to gather us up. "We need to get ice cream, then get you all home." She sounded almost cross.

She didn't turn at the corner to look back, but I did. He was still looking our way and he looked sad. I wished we had invited him to go with us for ice cream.

❧

One evening at our house he tapped his pipe into the big metal wastebasket and stood up. "Guess I ought to be getting up the road. Some of us have to work in the morning. By the way, did you see the results of that *Life* magazine poll last month, 'How Good Is Your School'? They rated schools on things like fire-resistant buildings and whether we have a dental hygienist and full-time clerical help. Dental hygienist? Heck, I'd settle for enough fire extinguishers. That old place is a firetrap. Scares me to death to think what would happen if anybody lit a match."

Uncle Stephen stood to fetch Mr. Donaldson's overcoat from the rack in the hall. "Maybe we ought to start a community outcry for a new one," he said over his shoulder.

Mr. Donaldson made a short, rude noise. "As if any of the fine Christians in this community would ever get that involved in politics."

Uncle Stephen handed him the coat and helped him into it. "What makes you so prejudiced?"

"Prejudiced? I'm the least prejudiced man in North Carolina! Anybody'll tell you that."

"You're not prejudiced against Negroes, Jews, or communists, just Christians. You think we're all either hypocrites masquerading as good people or simplistic do-gooders without a lick of sense."

Mr. Donaldson raised his hand in protest. "I never said that about you!"

Uncle Stephen laughed. "Some of my best friends are preachers! You're as prejudiced as Wash Lamont."

Mr. Donaldson grew rosy with anger. "Never!"

"Sure you are. He believes Negroes are utterly inferior— you should have seen him last week when I told him a Negro scientist invented peanut butter."

Mr. Donaldson's black eyes sparkled as he buttoned his coat. "I'd like to have been a fly on the wall. Think he'll ever eat it again?"

Uncle Stephen chuckled. "I thought he'd choke on the bite he had in his mouth. But he finally washed it down with a swallow of RC and said, 'It just goes to show that some of them are practically white.' That's how you treat me, Donaldson— like a Christian who's miraculously escaped being a Simon Legree, Ebenezer Scrooge, monster of immorality, or simpering idiot without an ounce of gumption. Prejudice, pure and simple."

Mr. Donaldson growled. "Cut out the preaching. I'm not prejudiced; I just know what I've seen."

Uncle Stephen blew out a quick, impatient breath. "Then you've been looking in the wrong places. Look at your cousin Hannah—"

"Hannah's a saint," he conceded, "but she's different."

"Not different, just part of the committed minority. There's a book I want you to read—letters by a man named Dietrich Bonhoeffer, a German preacher who was executed in a Nazi prison for trying to help stop Hitler. I dare you to give it a fair review. Some of your readers might find him a welcome relief from all those so-called Christians you attack."

Mr. Donaldson reached for the dining room door. "Hogwash."

Uncle Stephen chuckled and opened it for him. He left the door open, so I could hear them as they went down the hall. "What does Jerry stand for—Gerald?"

Mr. Donaldson gave a short bark of a laugh. "No, Jeremiah. I was named for my grandfather. Isn't that a whale of a name for an agnostic like me?"

"It's a lot to live up to. Have you ever read Jeremiah five?" Uncle Stephen went into what Abby called his preaching voice. "'Run ye to and fro through the streets of Jerusalem, and see now, and know, and seek in the broad places thereof, if ye can find a man, if there be any that executeth judgment, that seeketh the truth; and I will pardon it.'" His voice dropped back to normal and I heard someone open a door. "Imagine, Jer—if God can find one just, true man, he will pardon a whole city. Why do I suspect you've been trying to live up to that—and wanting others to live up to it—all your life?"

I won't repeat what Mr. Donaldson said but I was shocked. I was even more shocked when Uncle Stephen laughed. "You know what's the matter with you, Jeremiah Donaldson? Deep inside, you know there really is a God who truly wants people to live up to all we were made to be. Your problem is not that you *don't* believe in God. You're one of those rare men who believes utterly—and can't forgive the rest of us for not being quite so pure."

Mr. Donaldson didn't say anything for a minute. When he did, his voice was gruff. "You've quit preaching and gone to meddling." But he didn't sound mad. He left whistling, banging the door behind him.

I was utterly confused. When Uncle Stephen came back to the dining room, I asked, "Why do you like him so much, Uncle Stephen? He just likes to argue."

Uncle Stephen put one hand on top of my head and shook it gently. "I feel for old Donaldson what God must have felt about Saul of Tarsus. If he ever changes his mind—what a giant to have on your side!"

Chapter 21

Miss Emily got a lot of attention at church the Sunday she finally came back. Her bruises had faded but her jaw was still wired. Whenever somebody asked about it, she and Mr. Hugh Fred joked about her running into a door. Everyone was a lot more interested in how she looked than in Uncle Stephen's invitation for people to come to the manse the next night to consider how to get the county to replace Mount Vernon School before it burned down around the children's ears. One farmer going out the door expressed what Aunt Kate claimed was the prevalent opinion. "That school was around before my daddy was, and it'll be there when my grandchildren come along. You don't have to worry about Mount Vernon. It's built to last."

Only four people came to the meeting, including Aunt Hannah and Miss Nancy Lamont. She came in the door explaining, "Wash says we aren't supposed to mix religion and politics, but I am scared to death for my children in that school." She marched into the living room, head high. "So I don't care if I'm mixing religion and politics; I just want a new school to replace that firetrap."

"Will we get a new school?" I asked when they left.

Uncle Stephen scratched his left ear. "God only knows, literally. We look like a bunch of lambs heading for the lions."

"Don't worry," I told him confidently, setting a bowl of ice cream before him. "There are more with you than with them."

Seeing his puzzled stare, I added, "That's what Elisha told his servant when enemies were coming. It was just two of them, but when Elisha opened the eyes of his servant, he saw God's chariots all around." I'd studied Elisha a lot the previous spring, hoping to become a prophet of the Lord. I'd given up that calling but still remembered the stories.

"I'll keep an eye out for chariots. We're going to need them," Uncle Stephen said. Then he rumpled my hair. "But thanks for reminding me we've got power behind us in this. Start praying, okay?"

The next afternoon Miss Rilla gave me the duet Freda and I were to play for the Christmas program. To my surprise she suggested I play the top.

"Isn't that part harder?"

She fluttered her hands. "I think the top is more suited to your style than Freda's."

I practiced extra long every day because I'd lose time when Big Mama came for Thanksgiving. That was the Big Event in our family that month. We had figured we'd all go see her like we did the year before, but Uncle Stephen wanted to have a Thanksgiving service at church. When Aunt Kate told Big Mama we might not come until Thursday afternoon, she wrote right back to say,

> I haven't left this blessed store for months. If you have a bed, I'll come to you. If they can't manage the Thanksgiving sale without me, Pop and I haven't trained them right.

You'd have thought the king of England was coming, the way Aunt Kate made us all clean. Abby grumbled one day while she was on her knees scrubbing baseboards, "Big Mama doesn't see good 'nough to look way down here."

Aunt Kate decreed Big Mama was to sleep in my double bed and I would share Abby's, so I cleaned every inch of my room. We even washed my bedspread and curtains. But Abby felt slighted, and Abby was never one to suffer slight gladly. She pouted, she sulked, she glowered, and she roared.

"Carley got de mushnaries from China. I oughta get Big Mama. She's my Big Mama, too. She oughta sleep in my bed and let me sleep wif Carley." Finally she came up with an argument that convinced us all. "Big Mama's too old and fat to haf to climb all dose stairs."

We changed direction and started supercleaning Abby's room.

The day before she was to come, Big Mama called long distance at suppertime. When I answered and heard her voice, my heart nearly stopped. "Who died?"

"Nobody, honey. But Sukie's niece's baby has whooping cough, so she can't go there. I want to ask Kate if I can bring her with me. I don't dare leave her alone. She's so forgetful."

I went to call Aunt Kate, who was cutting up John's meat. "Just tell Mama to bring her," she instructed me. But when I hung up and rejoined the others at the supper table, Aunt Kate said, "I just don't know where we'll put her."

"Put her in my bed, and I'll sleep on a pallet on the sewing room floor," Grace suggested. Instead Uncle Stephen called Aunt Hannah, and she had Uncle Davy bring up one of the extra beds in her bulging storeroom. She also sent up an extra kerosene heater—which, as it turned out, was a real blessing.

That weekend—Friday evening, to be exact—the United States had what *Life* magazine would call "the worst blizzard of modern times." Snow covered the entire eastern United States and was so deep up north that New York City was paralyzed. A lot of people died. We didn't have that much snow in North Carolina, but in Statesville the temperature went down to twelve degrees on Saturday and eleven on Sunday. We kept our pipes dripping to prevent them from freezing. Roads were so iced up, we had to keep Big Mama and Sukie until Tuesday.

Our dining room was big but not big enough for that many people to stay in all day every day. "I think this is a time to splurge and heat more of the house," I heard Uncle Stephen tell Aunt Kate. "I'll call Davy and see if he can sell me some firewood." The rest of the United States was already heating homes with coal- or oil-burning furnaces, but our big manse still only had one big coal-burning stove. It kept the dining room toasty but didn't heat any other rooms.

Uncle Davy brought up a truckful of wood, and Uncle Stephen and I spent half our time carrying in buckets of coal for the dining room and armloads of wood for the living room, but I felt downright rich having more than one heated room. We moved happily between the living and dining rooms, playing and singing together and assembling a big jigsaw puzzle in the living room or sitting at the dining room table listening to the radio and drinking hot chocolate with as many marshmallows as we wanted.

Poor Rowdy absolutely hated having to go outside to do his business, so Uncle Stephen and Aunt Kate took turns carrying him out to a place Uncle Stephen had shoveled near the barn and standing with him to make sure he did what he was supposed to. John's diapers had to be washed, and Grace strung a clothesline across the kitchen and turned on the oven to help dry them. Aunt Sukie wouldn't join us. She claimed she was warmer than anybody, sitting by the open oven door. At night we filled hot water bottles and used electric and kerosene heaters to take the chill off the air, but I was glad Abby was sleeping with me. It was like having a small furnace of my very own.

Our biggest problem was, while we had a pantry full of canned fruit and vegetables, all our meat except the turkey was in a freezer locker downtown, and the highway was too icy to drive on. Aunt Kate kept reminding us to be glad we'd had such a big turkey, but Abby spoke for us all Monday night when she looked at her casserole and heaved a huge sigh. "I'm powerful tired of turkey."

"I know what I want for Christmas," Aunt Kate told Uncle Stephen as they were putting the food away.

"I know what you're getting. A chest freezer."

She pulled off his glasses and kissed him right between the eyes. "Those are the three most romantic words you've said all day."

❀

Sunday afternoon Uncle Stephen surprised us by climbing up to the barn loft and bringing down a sled. "I never thought we'd need this. The Grants left it when they cleaned out the place, but it still looks serviceable." Aunt Kate made him dust it good and made Abby and me wrap up like cocoons, but she did let us go out to try it.

As I pulled Abby up and down the snow-covered road, Sue Mary heard her happy shrieks and came to join us, bundled in coat, hat, and leggings. She enjoyed the sled, but we were gravely told, "Velma likes it most." Finally even Preston wandered out. "Want me to pull you, Carley?"

"Sure." I was tired of doing all the pulling.

I'd no more than sat on the sled, though, when he yelled, "Hi-ho, Silver!" pranced like a horse, and took off at a run. In less than a minute he'd overturned me in the ditch, and I got snow all down my neck. Disgusted, I stomped back into the house. "Sleds are for children!" I yelled back at them.

I figured I'd go into the living room and read. Aunt Kate and Uncle Stephen were napping and Big Mama probably was, too.

I was wrong about the last part. Big Mama heard me come in and decided it was time for a little chat.

She followed me into the living room and lowered her bulk into one of the armchairs Aunt Hannah had loaned us for the room. Bending to throw another stick on the fire, she said, "I've been wanting to talk to you. You know, don't you, that your mother and Aunt Kate were born in our house?"

Of course I did. For most of my life that had been a source of pride and mystery to me, a talisman that in our family things went on and on and never changed. One of my first memories is of giving a new friend the honor of inspecting Big Mama's Jenny Lind bed, both of us so small that our eyes were level with the white chenille spread. "My mama got born here," I told her in a reverent whisper, poking one of the spread's fuzzy white worms. "Right here, in this very bed."

When I was little, some afternoons Big Mama let me nap in her bed. The mattress had a hollow in the middle, like a saucer, where I'd curl myself like a black-eyed pea and pretend I cradled a tiny baby Mama in my arms.

That all changed, of course, when Mama died in 1949 and I went to live with Aunt Kate. Big Mama moved the Jenny Lind bed to my room and took my single bed for herself. When I went back for visits, the Jenny Lind's saucer mirrored a concavity in my own center that nothing seemed to fill.

As Big Mama spoke, I closed my eyes and tried to picture an infant Mama in my arms, or even Mama just before she died, but I could no longer truly see her face. The soft living flesh had diffused and reduced itself to the flat smiling image in my locket or the ethereal studio portrait on my dresser.

Losing my mental picture of Mama was bad enough. But the reason Big Mama had brought her up was worse. "It's high time you learned how babies get born."

Her voice was so grim, I shivered in spite of two sweaters. She reached up and adjusted the combs in her hair, which was white at the wings now and only auburn when she let it ripple down her back at bedtime. Then she smoothed her warm wool dress over her corset. Some snowbound women might get up from their Sunday naps and neglect to put on their corsets for the rest of the day, but not Mrs. Henry Marshall.

Finally she took a deep breath and began.

No woman in our family ever passed up an opportunity to teach a child about the terrors of daily living. Big Mama pulled out all the stops in describing what she called "God's curse on women." She wasn't explicit enough for me to actually learn how women got pregnant, just said that when people got married (she repeated *married* in almost every sentence), the man put a seed in the woman. "It will hurt at first but you'll get used to it," she promised. "And someday the seed will grow to a baby. When the baby is being born, you will hurt so bad, you will wish you could die, but you probably won't." But then, being Big Mama, she also threw in a few stories about women she had personally known who died in childbirth, and others who were bedridden for months afterward. By the time she finished, I was willing to bring human procreation to a grinding halt.

She must have realized she'd scared me to death, because then she started talking about rosy, sweet-smelling babies and how getting one is worth all the pain. Having just lived through my cousin John's first year—which had *not* been all sweet-smelling and gurgles—I remained unconvinced. When I grew up and Clay and I got married, we wouldn't bother with any of what she was talking about. Kissing would be good enough for us.

Finally Big Mama felt in her pocket and laid something on her big hand. A small circle of gold. "This was your mama's wedding ring. I've put it on a chain for you to wear now, and when you get married, you may want to use it for your own." When I slipped that chain around my neck and stuck my finger through that golden ring, I felt Mama very near.

What Big Mama had said raised one big question, though, and I knew better than to ask her. When I heard Aunt Kate in the hall, I said, "Excuse me" and hurried to the kitchen, where Aunt Sukie was dozing by the stove. As my sock feet slid to a stop on the linoleum, I demanded without preamble, "When Mama got born, was there a real mess on the bed? The bed I have to sleep in when I come to your house?"

Aunt Sukie was light brown, stooped, and so crippled with arthritis that her fingers looked like twisted branches on the stumps of deformed trees. But she'd lived with me all my life and was accustomed to my dashing in with unexpected questions. She roused herself in the chair where she'd been resting after helping Grace with the dinner dishes, and didn't even take time to think. Just nodded the starched white cap pinned to the front of her grizzled hair. "Some mess, right 'nough. Heapsa laundry."

I stuck out my tongue and made a retching noise. "Did they throw away the mattress? It's not the same one, is it?"

She cocked back her head and puckered her forehead. "What you talkin' 'bout, t'row away a good mattress? Washed the sheets. That wuz enough. Used lots of newspapers to protect that mattress. Miz Marshall saved papers for weeks."

"I'm not sleeping on that mattress ever again. You tell her to get rid of it." I plopped into a chair and faced her defiantly.

Aunt Sukie closed her eyes. "You kin fix a pallet on de floor, den. We ain't gonna buy no new mattresses or put you in de best guest bed just 'cause you got crocheties."

I sat on the hard kitchen chair and sulked. Outside the window, trees blew and bowed in the wind, branches black and weighted with snow. Aunt Sukie sank into another doze. Lately she fell asleep in mere specks of quiet.

Gradually it began to occur to me that the real reason I was sulking was, I didn't want them to leave. Part of me wanted to go with them, and part of me couldn't bear the thought of going. Seemed like I didn't want to be *anywhere* lately. I just wanted to seize time and hold it steady until I could decide what I did want. My back teeth ached with a yearning I could not name.

Aunt Sukie started to hum two descending notes. Her purple-blue lips worked in and out; then she spoke softly, from inside a dream. "Dat Lila. Prettiest baby you eber did *see*. Beautiful right from de start. Sweet-natured too. Nebber gabe a specka trouble." She added softly, "Nebber libbed to make thirty, neither." Her voice faded like Mama's memory.

We sat silent for several minutes, missing the pretty, vague girl who had died with no more effort than she'd put into living— catching polio while sitting down cradling a feverish little boy.

Aunt Sukie gave three descending grunts and went right on talking like she'd been awake all the time. "Miss Kate, now— smart as a whip. But nebber satisfied. Always wantin' a change of scenery, from de day she 'uz born. Miss Lila? She jist lay dere and looked at her fingers like dey was the greatest t'ing in de world." Aunt Sukie opened her eyes, held up her gnarled tan hands, and wiggled her poor fingers in the sunlight.

Not until I grew old would I come to appreciate the loveliness of Aunt Sukie's linked language, a holdover from the music of African speech. In those days it was a trait mistresses tried to overcome, a dialect white children had to lose before we started school.

"What did I do?" I rested my chin on my hands, distracted. "Was I smart, sweet, or ... what?"

"A peck o' trouble. Trouble den, trouble now. Look at you botherin' me when I got your dinner to think about." She moved as if to rise.

I wanted to shake her. "We already had dinner, Aunt Sukie. And Grace'll fix supper."

She looked uncertain, then nodded furtively. "I 'member. We had poke chops."

"No, we had turkey again. We've had turkey every day you've been here. You've gotta try harder to remember things, Aunt Sukie. You just gotta!"

She looked down and traced one bent finger on the table's green linoleum top. "T'ings seem to leak t'rough my brain lately, like water in a colander."

An icy shawl of fear settled on my shoulders. I wanted to fly back to a time when Aunt Sukie knew everything and answered all my questions. I wanted to be the child again, and she the grown-up. I refused to believe those days were gone.

"You've just got too much *in* your brain, that's all," I hurried to reassure her. But under the table my fists pounded my lap. "Look how well you remembered Mama gettin' born. You didn't have any trouble with that."

She grunted. "Coulda been yestiddy. 'Cept it's yestiddy I mostly forget. Maybe Miss Lila was lucky. Nebber got old." She braced her hands on her thighs and pulled herself painfully to her feet. "But my eyes still work and I see some cake on dat Kelvinator. Mought as well finish it up while we're sittin'." She brought the cake down from the top of the refrigerator and looked around helplessly for a knife. I got up and found her one. She asked, "You gonna cut or choose?"

"Choose." I knew she'd cut unequal pieces and expect me to take the big one, just like I knew she expected me to use a good plate and give her a cracked one with mismatched silverware. A year ago that wouldn't have bothered me. Now, after living with Uncle Stephen, I couldn't do anything of the sort. I waved her back to her chair, got down two of Aunt Kate's next-to-best rosebud plates, and set one before her. "Here." I pulled two matching forks from the silver drawer and put them at our places, with a white paper napkin each.

Aunt Sukie gave me a sideways look through milky eyes that had aged from gray to a light lavender, but she didn't say a word. Just ate that first bite of cake like a queen.

Part 3

The Hopes and Fears of
All the Years ...

December 1950

upstairs yelling that he'd had tucked us both. When he found her [parents] there... in the front of the FBI, that we could talk down.

"Let me make some hot chocolate," Aunt [Bett] announced like I'd known she would.

"How'd you get away?" Uncle [Stephen] asked.

"He left. Grabbed his keys and yelled, 'I'll find them if it's the last thing I do.' He went simply tearing down the drive. I'm terrified he'll wreck his car even before he finds them." She sobbed again for a long time and Uncle Stephen didn't say a word. I wondered if he knew what to say. I sure wouldn't.

Finally Miss Emily sniffled several times and blew her nose again. "Thank. It's not my fault," I shouldn't have let...

Chapter 22

The Statesville Christmas parade was held the last day of November. Temperatures were only a little warmer than the weekend before, so Uncle Stephen and Aunt Kate bundled us all up like Eskimos to stand on Center Street and watch the floats, bands, and Santa pass by. I overcame the cold by softly describing to my viewers every float and band. Abby, on her daddy's shoulders, bounced up and down and squealed at the floats but tugged his poor hair every five minutes to beg, "Is it time for Santa yet?"

John, in Aunt Kate's arms, loved the bands, particularly the shining, blaring brasses. Uncle Stephen always claimed it was that parade that made a trombonist out of John.

Aunt Kate worried the whole time about how cold the girls looked on the floats. "They'll all get pneumonia," she muttered again and again. "They'll catch their death of cold."

When the Sitwell Chair float rolled slowly by, Freda, in a gorgeous pink evening dress and gloves to her armpits, waved and smiled down from a huge kitchen chair with nine other beautiful girls. I would have gladly died of pneumonia for a chance to be one of them. When she saw us, she blew us a kiss and smiled as if her teeth weren't chattering at all.

We got home to find a new black Mercury convertible in front of our walk.

I caught my breath. God must have forgotten that was the one contest I didn't really want to win. But it was so gorgeous, I decided I'd give it to Uncle Stephen for Christmas.

Both Abby and John had fallen asleep in the car, so Aunt Kate said, "Run in and see who it is until we can each get a child to bed." I skipped eagerly up the steps to accept my prize.

Clay sat in the dining room grinning from ear to ear.

"Whose car is that?" I demanded.

His grin told me before he answered. "Mine." That was all right with me. One day whatever was his would be mine. He kept grinning. "You like it?"

"Yeah! Can we go for a—" I stopped. I'd just noticed Laura sitting beside him, holding his hand like it belonged to her. "Hey, Laura," I added, wishing I could add a bit more: "Go jump in a lake, swallow a snake, and swell up and die from a bellyache."

"Hey, Carley." She beamed like we were the best friends in the whole wide world.

"Is your uncle home?" Clay asked.

"Yeah, but we just got back from the Christmas parade and he has to put Abby to bed. He'll be here in a minute." I perched on Uncle Stephen's big chair. "You missed a great parade."

"We'll have to go next year." Laura gave a throaty laugh. He squeezed her hand.

Aunt Kate came in and looked from me to them. "Would you all like some hot chocolate? We're nearly frozen."

"No, thank you." Laura said at the exact same time Clay said, "That would be great." They laughed.

Aunt Kate looked back at me. "Why don't you go fix it, Carley? And I think Grace made cookies. Look in the jar."

In those days we had to simmer powdered cocoa, sugar, and a little water in a saucepan to make syrup before we added milk. I was busy trying to dissolve the sugar when I heard Uncle Stephen come in and ask cheerfully, "What have we here, refugees from the cold?"

"Something like that." Clay sounded even happier than before.

"Is that your car?"

"Sure is. Just got it today. What do you think of her?"

"I'm wrestling with envy and covetousness but they're winning. What can I do for you?"

"Laura and I want to ask you to marry us on the sixteenth."

The kitchen floor tilted so badly all of a sudden that the saucepan just slid off the stove and crashed to the floor. I held on to the oven door handle for dear life to keep from sliding off the earth. Aunt Kate hurried in and clicked her tongue against her teeth at the mess, then handed me a rag. I was glad to kneel. At least I was nearer to the floor in case I swooned. As I swiped at the sticky brown mess, they went on talking in the next room.

"The sixteenth of what?"

"December. Two weeks from now."

I stood to rinse the rag but the room whirled. Aunt Kate put a hand on my shoulder and led me to a chair, pushed me to sit, shoved my head into my lap, and finished cleaning up the mess. I had nothing to do but manage not to fall off that chair and keep listening.

Uncle Stephen whistled. "That's pretty soon, isn't it?"

"Yessir, but I don't wanna give her time to change her mind."

"You sure about this, Laura?" Uncle Stephen sounded happy and serious at the same time.

"I sure am, sir. I've been in love with Clay since high school, but he had a wild streak back then that I wasn't sure I could live with. Now that he's settled down some, I'm ready to take a chance."

"It's not a chance; it's a lifetime commitment," Uncle Stephen warned. "And he's still got a wild streak. Ask him about a plane over Stony Point last month."

Laura gurgled. "He did that to surprise me for my birthday, but he like to scared Daddy's cows to death." She got serious. "I know marriage is a lifetime commitment, sir, and it's one I'm prepared to make."

"You don't want to get married in your own church?"

"No sir. I came to Bethel with Clay all the time we were in school, and now that I'm coming back, it feels more like my church than the one I grew up in. Besides, our preacher just moved to Alabama. So we'd rather get married where we plan to go afterward."

"How about you, Clay? You willing to settle down forever with this woman?"

"Thinking about her's the only thing got me through the past six years, Mr. Whitfield. I will strive to be worthy of her."

"Then you may kiss the bride. Hey, Carley," he called loudly, "hurry up that hot chocolate. We've got some celebrating to do."

Aunt Kate shook her head and put a finger to her lips. She stirred the steaming pot on the table and set out her wedding china. "You want to join us?" she whispered.

I nodded unhappily. Being in the room with Clay was worth the pain of sharing him with Laura. Before I carried her cocoa in, I thought about adding salt to it to make her sick, but I didn't bother. That witch probably had insides of cast iron.

I sat by my window for hours that night, watching Clay's house and wondering why he preferred Laura to me. He didn't come home until after two.

When the last light went out in his house, I climbed into bed. I didn't even refill my water bottles. I might as well prepare for my cold, lonely grave.

I closed my eyes and murmured a farewell message to my television viewers. "This is Carley Marshall of *Unshaded Windows*. I will probably not be with you tomorrow. I will have died for love."

The next morning I woke to a bright winter morning. For a moment my heart leapt to meet the sunny sky. Then I remembered and it plummeted like a fishing weight back to my chest. I sighed deeply and hauled myself out of bed, feeling two hundred years old. "Here I am after all," I told my relieved but sympathetic fans. "I woke up, so I guess you do not die of sorrow."

❀

All Job's Corner was absorbed by that wedding. Nobody talked about anything else at church Sunday, and in the afternoon when Aunt Hannah came to talk with Aunt Kate about the Circle, she said as if I weren't there, "Clay's a dreamer, but I don't think there's a woman in the world better than Laura to keep his feet on the ground. She seems like a fine girl." That was the only time in her life that Aunt Hannah hurt me.

When I went in the kitchen Monday afternoon to help with pre-Christmas baking, Grace asked, "How're those lovebirds doing? Still twittering away?"

When I went to Miss Pauline's post office Tuesday to mail in an entry for a General Electric contest, she wanted to know, "What are the bridesmaids wearing?"

Freda, who *was* a bridesmaid, worried Wednesday at recess, "I hope Aunt Rilla doesn't mess up the music." That was silly but I did worry she would get one of her panic attacks. She had stayed inside for so many years, it was still hard for her to come out in crowds.

Abby, who was going to be a flower girl, did all her walking in tiny mincing steps. "Is dis little enough?" She worried Rowdy to death. He kept nudging her heels with his nose to hurry her up. The only bright spot in my whole picture was the conviction that it would take Abby so long to get down the aisle, everybody would get bored and go home. Clay would never get married.

At first I thought everybody in Job's Corner was talking to me about Clay because they knew how I felt and wanted to make me feel worse. It took a while to realize that most of them just assumed I had inside information as part of the preacher's family.

I had more than I ever let on.

Uncle Stephen never married anybody without several sessions of premarital counseling, and since their wedding was so close, they came almost every night. Years later when my own groom and I went for sessions, I knew exactly what Uncle Stephen was going to ask and say. I'd heard it all before.

When it sounded like they were about to leave, I'd hurry downstairs so I could at least see Clay on his way out. Friday evening he grabbed me around the neck in a hug. "Hey, Little Buddy, we've got so many nieces and cousins, we couldn't ask you to be a bridesmaid, but we wondered if you and your aunt would sing a duet at the wedding, in memory of our Sunday night sing-alongs. We'd be real honored."

"We sure would," Laura agreed with a smile of pure sugar.

Aunt Kate wasn't home to accept, so I shook my head. "I don't think we could."

"It sure would mean a lot to both of us," Clay begged with that grin that still turned my heart over in my chest.

"It's a song from the hymnbook," Laura added. "It's not real hard."

I wanted to kick her. Aunt Kate and I could learn harder music than any the Bethel Church ever sang. However, Big Mama didn't raise me to be rude to people in my own home. I just stretched my lips out in a smile and said, "If we can learn it in time, I guess we'll be honored to sing." It's no wonder southern women live so long. We swallow enough anger to petrify our vital organs.

But after they'd gone, I went to the piano and opened a songbook Aunt Kate had asked Big Mama to bring with her, one full of the songs we used to sing on the porch on Sunday nights. I played them over one by one, tears running down my cheeks. Finally, when I got to "I Love You Truly, Truly Dear," I reached up, grabbed that page, and ripped it straight out of the book. I wadded it up and flung it across the room. Then I laid my head down on the keys and sobbed.

❧

That next weekend was gorgeous. The newspaper called it "an apology from Mother Nature" for the dreadful cold spell we'd had. Since the sucking mud had finally dried enough to walk on, I took Rowdy for a long walk down to Aunt Hannah's on Saturday and found Uncle Davy loading his truck with trash for the gully. "Want to ride along?" He motioned both me and Rowdy to the cab.

His truck was older than God's grandfather, with seats so torn that he covered them with old quilts, and springs that stuck up in unexpected places. It had no shock absorbers left to speak of, and he drove it through those pastures like they were flat and smooth. But I loved bouncing beside him, teeth jarring in my head and trees swishing the top of the cab.

When we got to the gully, though, he scared me to death. He backed right up to the edge, where that truck could slide off any second. "My Big Mama knows lots of people whose cars jumped into gear and went over cliffs," I cautioned. "How deep is that gully?"

"More'n thirty feet, I expect, but we're all right." He climbed down so casually, you'd never have known we were poised on the brink of eternity. "The brake's set. It's not going anywhere."

I scrambled down before I fell in when it did. Rowdy climbed awkwardly after me and began investigating the edge of the gully in a doggy way. Uncle Davy reached over the back and hauled out a roll of rusty baling wire. "Get up and pitch over those oil cans." He tossed that roll of wire like it was shredded wheat. "My truck's been using a powerful lot of oil lately."

I gingerly climbed on the running board and tried to reach the cans, but my arms weren't long enough. "Get right on in," he suggested, heaving another bale of wire. "You'll weight it down some."

Convinced that my eighty pounds would be enough to steady a pickup, I threw one leg over the edge and gracelessly climbed in. I had never felt so daring in my life as when I stood erect and pitched my first can. I truly did expect the whole truck might slide in.

After that each can was an adventure. I stood high enough to watch them fall among glittering bottles and jars, decaying cardboard boxes, rags, a rusting washing machine with its legs in the air, and—

"Somebody else's truck already went over!" I yelled in panic. "Are you sure your brake is set?"

"That old truck didn't fall; it was pushed, " Uncle Davy told me in his deliberate way. "It was my daddy's Model A. It finally gave out, so I pulled it down here with a tractor and pushed it over." He reached for the last roll of baling wire. "Reckon Laura'll be able to talk Clay out of that airplane notion?"

I was startled, hearing him say Clay's name like that. "What airplane notion?"

Uncle Davy tossed a boxful of garbage with the same ease with which I'd thrown one measly can. "He's been goin' on about building him a little plane in his daddy's old barn. Even asked if he could buy a strip of pasture yonder behind the houses for a runway. But I don't think my cows would like all that racket, so I told him I'd have to think about it." He turned back to the truck for the last box of trash. "Clay's always had a wild streak in him. But I reckon Laura will settle him. She's got a good head on her shoulders."

"I guess so." I peered glumly into the earth's crease at the colorful jumble of Job's Corner residue. Laura was certainly going to settle *me*. I threw an oil can at the old washing machine and hit it with a satisfying *thunk*. I wished it could have hit her square between the eyes.

"What's that?" I pointed to a big sheet of galvanized tin just a few feet below us, caught by boxes, little scrub bushes, and the branches of trees growing out of the side of the gully. "I never saw that down here before."

He peered down over the edge. "Looks like a piece of old Tom Cameron's roof before he had shingles put on. Must have been in the gully might nigh on forty years." He pointed south with one work-roughened finger. "We used to dump up yonder a ways, between here and the highway, but the road to the gully washed out one spring, so we started coming on down here. Lots of things from the old dump got washed down here by those recent rains, I reckon, but I sure didn't know the water got that high."

I leaned over as far as I dared. "Do you ever go down in there?"

"Not if I can help it. Don't you be going down there, either. Mighty lot of snakes, and yon rusted cans will cut you bad if you're not careful." He turned back to the truck, a long-limbed man with soft white hair who would look at ninety much as he did at fifty-five. "Now let's get that mattress and we're done. Hannah finally talked me into gettin' a new one. Can you give me a hand?"

Every day of his life Uncle Davy did harder things than throw a double bed mattress down a gully, but one of the lovable things about him was the way he always made children feel needed. He climbed up into the truck beside me, and together we wrestled the lumpy felt mattress up on edge. "We'll give it a solid push with our shoulders, but don't go over with it, mind. On the count of three, now. One, two, three ..."

The mattress toppled, tumbled, and finally landed. "Look at that!" Uncle Davy peered over with genuine pleasure. "Right in the bed of Daddy's truck. We couldn't have done that in a thousand years by trying. Well, that's the lot. Ready to go back? Hannah was talking about making a cake." He whistled for Rowdy, who came sniffing and snorting about being called back too soon.

"You'd think," I reported on *Unshaded Windows* that night, "the way people in Job's Corner act, that Clay Lamont's wedding is the only thing going on in the world. It's not, of course. Many of you are aware that President Truman is proposing that we build A-bomb shelters. Gilbert Mayhew, music teacher at Mount Vernon School, firmly believes shelters ought to be built immediately, but Stephen Whitfield remains unconvinced, so his family is unlikely to get one in time to do them any good.

"On the war front, the news seesaws up and down. We hear that the Chinese are battering our men; then we hear that Allied planes are killing two thousand Chinese soldiers a day. We hear that our boys may be home for Christmas, but the government is calling up more reserves. It seems to me that nobody in Washington can make up their minds whether we're having a war or not, but Mr. Stephen Whitfield says not to tell that to men freezing in Korea.

"Job's Corner is so small, we have no men young enough or boys old enough to be soldiers. Our whole end of Iredell County only has a few men in Korea. But three of their mothers are in our church. They walk around with faces that make my stomach hurt. Pray for our soldiers, as well as for a new school. This is Carley Marshall, signing off. Good night."

Chapter 23

Laura's sister had gotten married the Christmas before, and she was using the same bridesmaids' dresses: dark green taffeta, with a red poinsettia in each bouquet. Grace made Abby a long green velvet dress with a wide ruffle she would take off later to turn it into a Sunday dress. Laura asked Aunt Kate and me to wear red to sing.

"I look horrible in red with this hair," Aunt Kate protested to Uncle Stephen, "and we can't afford to buy a dress I'll only wear once."

"Could Grace make you something?"

"Not in the time we've got, she can't."

While Aunt Kate fumed and fretted, I did a far more sensible thing. I wrote Big Mama. The next week we got matching deep burgundy dresses with creamy collars. They looked wonderful with Aunt Kate's hair and made my cheeks look rosy. "It really brings out your coloring," she praised me as we stood in her bedroom deciding whether they'd need taking in.

I lifted one stand of hair and peered into the mirror. "If somebody was going to paint my portrait, they wouldn't have a color in the box for my hair. What color is that? It's not brown and it's not blond. It's just plain old nothing."

Uncle Stephen passed the open door. "I think it's called dishwater blond."

That made me feel so much prettier.

❧

Finally the day arrived. I got out of bed telling myself, "Anything can happen. Anything can happen. The wedding might not go on." But nothing happened and Miss Rilla began "*Liebestraum*" right on schedule.

Mr. Wash stood up as Clay's best man, Ruthie was a junior bridesmaid, and Jimmy was the ring bearer. Since Miss Rilla played the piano, the only people in the groom's pew were going to be Miss Nancy and Mr. Rob until Clay invited Aunt Kate and me to join them. "You'll be up front when it's time for you to sing, and Daddy won't be lonely."

"You can sit with them, too, Abby, if you get tired," Laura cooed.

"I won't get tired," Abby's eyes flashed and her lips puckered to frown.

"Of course not, but just in case you do," Aunt Kate soothed her.

Everybody came from miles around, of course. Except for going to the Air Force, Clay had lived in Job's Corner all his life, and Laura was from right up the road. The wedding party itself looked like a convention. Both her brothers and sisters were in it, plus some of their husbands and wives and all their daughters big enough to walk. She had a matron of honor, four bridesmaids, five junior bridesmaids, and two flower girls. He had Mr. Wash, four ushers, and a ring bearer.

One of Laura's brothers gave me his elbow—the first time I walked down an aisle with an usher instead of trailing behind a grown-up. I pretended I was going down on my daddy's arm to marry Clay. If that was wicked, I didn't care. It took all the charity I possessed just to be there.

It didn't feel funny sitting so close up front—I always did— but sitting on the right instead of the left made me feel like I was in a strange church. I was actually surprised when Mr. Hugh Fred and Miss Emily slid into the pew behind ours. Since homecoming night I'd managed to avoid him pretty well. As he sat down, he put one hand on my shoulder. "Hey, Carley,

Kate. How's it going?" I couldn't imagine those well-groomed fingers hitting Miss Emily, but she wore a broad-brimmed green felt hat to hide her still-crooked jaw.

Having them behind me made me so self-conscious, I didn't even enjoy Miss Rilla's music the way I'd have liked to. Hearing Miss Rilla play was the closest I got in those days to a real concert.

When the bridesmaids came in, all the others faced front like they were supposed to, but Freda kept turning and smiling at her parents. A rustle behind me gave me a chance to look around. Mrs. Raeburn slid down the pew from the side aisle to sit beside Miss Emily. She wore a smart black velvet suit and a velvet hat perched on top of her shining hair, and her eyes looked blue and mysterious behind a spotted veil. She gave me a little nod and a smile as she sat down.

I looked up to see if the roof showed any sign of falling. It looked fine, but how could I sing a duet in front of a wife beater, my teacher, and the man I loved who was marrying somebody else?

My thoughts were interrupted by a groan from Aunt Kate. "Oh no." At the back, after all her practicing, Abby stood frozen at the door. "Come on," Aunt Kate whispered. Abby didn't move. Finally Laura gave her a push. She came down the aisle at a dead run without strewing a single rose petal, until she got halfway down. Then she jerked to a stop, turned around, walked all the way back, turned again, and came back so slowly, you'd have thought all those people had come to Bethel Church that afternoon simply to watch her drop flowers. Now Aunt Kate was motioning her frantically with one hand to hurry up. Abby had her eyes focused on her daddy, like she'd been told, and he was so proud of her, he didn't make a move. Miss Rilla had to tack on several measures to get Abby up front.

Finally the loud notes sounded for us to stand and greet the bride. When I turned all the way around, I finally saw why Freda kept smiling at her daddy. Several rows behind him sat Charles, his face washed so hard that it looked like he'd polished it, and his shoulders almost bursting out of a dark blue suit. He saw me looking at him and blushed. I knew it wasn't his idea to sit behind Mr. Hugh Fred so Freda could smile at him and fool her daddy. Charles wasn't that smart.

Laura came down the aisle to the usual chorus of oohs and aahs. If she'd been marrying somebody else, I might have thought she looked pretty. As it was, I thought her piled-up hair too fancy, her lipstick too bright, and her dress too tight for her round figure. She walked almost as slow as Abby, in little mincing steps with a pause between each one. We had to stand up watching her forever. If I'd been marrying Clay, I'd have run down that aisle. Preston, standing a few pews back, asked Bonnie in hoarse whisper, "Why's she walk so slow? That's the slowest bride I ever saw." As far as I knew, he'd seen two.

Laura finally reached the front and we sank to our pews. It was all I could do, of course, not to jump to my feet when Uncle Stephen asked if anybody could show a reason why that man should not be married to that woman, but I restrained myself. Nobody else rose, either, to protest, "Because he's *Carley's!*"

Our duet, "O Perfect Love, All Human Thought Transcending," went well. Once the first notes sounded, I didn't think about anything except blending my voice with Aunt Kate's, until we reached the third line of the second verse.

Of patient hope, and quiet brave endurance . . .

I'd already promised myself I would look at Clay when I sang that, to see if he noticed how bravely I was enduring. He was so busy looking at Laura, we could have been singing the Howdy Doody song for all he cared.

After the wedding we all went down to the church fellowship hall in the basement to greet the wedding party, drink ginger ale with lime sherbet melting in it, and eat wedding cake, mints, and peanuts. I loved wedding cake, particularly the thick, sweet, greasy icing, followed by an occasional handful of salty nuts. And I had to admit that Laura's family had done a beautiful job of decorating that old fellowship hall. They'd even put up a big Christmas tree from her brother's farm and covered it with white velvet doves and silver bows.

I hated getting compliments, though. I didn't know what to say to people who said they didn't know I could sing so well, or said Aunt Kate and I sang together beautifully. I wished I could be as frank as Abby when people told her she looked beautiful. "Yes, I does."

I also hated it when women asked, "Isn't Laura a bee-*you*-ti-ful bride?" Not as far as I was concerned. I was still busy sneaking peeks at the groom and trying not to bawl.

All the high school kids made a big circle of chairs in one corner. As soon as she left the receiving line, Freda joined them, along with two other bridesmaids. She sat with her back to the room, and Charles sat beside her, their chairs barely six inches apart.

Mr. Hugh Fred finally noticed where she was.

"Excuse me," he said to the people he was talking to. He crossed the room and laid a hand on Freda's shoulder. "Honey? I need to talk to you a minute." As soon as they were out of the high school crowd's earshot (but within mine, because I'd sidled over to see what he wanted), he said, "Go talk to somebody your own age."

Freda pouted. "I want to talk to the other bridesmaids."

Mr. Hugh Fred didn't move but his hand tightened on her shoulder.

"Ow!" Freda jumped. "Okay, I'll go talk to Carley."

"You do that. And stay with her until we're ready to go."

Lucky me.

All Freda could babble about was how dumb her daddy was, how much she loved Charles, and what a beautiful bride Laura was. None of which was of any interest to me whatsoever. In a little while she said, "I need to go to the bathroom," held up her long skirt, and whisked upstairs. She was gone so long, I had time to eat a second piece of cake.

I wasn't thinking about Freda much. I was still waiting for that moment in the movie when the man looks across the room and realizes he's been in love with the heroine all the time. So far Clay hadn't looked my way, but when he did—

Instead I saw Mr. Hugh Fred looking at me with a frown. Maybe I'd better go see if Freda had gotten sick or something.

I found her with Charles in the adult Bible classroom, kissing like they were the ones who'd just gotten married. They didn't hear me coming, so I stood watching for a second, to see if I was practicing right. Then I backed down the hall, shut the door to the basement stairs as loudly as I dared, and tromped down the hall like I weighed as much as Charles's sister Mary. When I got to the door, they were standing, swinging hands between them. But her hair was mussed and her lipstick smeared.

"Your daddy's looking for you again."

Too late. In a gnat's second I felt his breath behind me.

When I turned and saw his face, I trembled. His eyes looked like fire would dart out any second to consume us all. Thank goodness they were fixed not on me but on poor Charles. Charles had tensed his shoulders like he was expecting a tackle—or another beating.

The silence stretched so long, I expected the sun to set. Mr. Hugh Fred's hands clenched and unclenched by his side. His nostrils looked like they were being pinched by an invisible hand. When he finally spoke, though, his voice was soft and still. It sent a shiver up my backbone. And although he was looking at Charles, he spoke to Freda.

"Honey, what you doing up here?"

Freda sidled over by me and took my hand, swinging it like she had Charles's. "Carley had to go to the bathroom, and you told me to stay with her."

Nobody noticed my face turn bright red. I didn't like all those people thinking about my bodily functions. No problem. They weren't thinking about me at all.

Her daddy felt in his pocket and handed her a clean white handkerchief. "Wipe your mouth. You've smeared it eating." She took the handkerchief and scrubbed her face. When she finished, she looked around for someplace to put it, but he held out his hand. She handed it to him, and he shoved it in his jacket pocket with one little white corner waving like a flag.

Nobody spoke for about three lifetimes. Then Mr. Hugh Fred went on in that soft, nice, terrifying voice. "Now you girls get on back downstairs. And Freda, don't leave the hall until your mother's ready to go. You understand me?"

She smiled at him like he was the most charming man in the world. "Yessir, Daddy. Come on Carley, Charles."

He put out one hand as Charles moved. "You stay here a minute, Son." I could have been the flagpole in the classroom corner for all he noticed me.

I looked from one man to the other, wondering who would win in a real fight. Mr. Hugh Fred was tall with broad, strong shoulders. Charles was shorter but very wide. For an instant I heard his classmates' cheers at homecoming game when Charles carried the ball for a touchdown. "The Unstoppable's got it. Go, Unstoppable! Go!"

Charles was young, too. Mr. Hugh Fred was old but he was also mad. His voice might have been soft but his eyes thundered, and one vein throbbed like something living was fighting in his neck to get out.

Freda's voice was a little girl's. "I'm going, Daddy." She dropped my hand and reached out to him. "Come with us. Please?"

He shook his head. "Not yet, honey. I'll be down in a minute. Now scoot."

She walked past him like a frozen princess, without waiting to see if I followed. I did—until I saw her disappear down the stairs. Then I stayed right by the basement door. If Mr. Hugh Fred murdered Charles, they might need a witness in court.

Mr. Hugh Fred didn't sound like he was going to kill anybody. If anything, his voice was milder, sympathetic. "You're a Beal, aren't you, boy? Brom's youngest?"

"Ye . . . yessir." Charles's voice was husky, like he hadn't planned on using it right then and had to fetch it from somewhere. I crept up and stood just outside the classroom door, peeping through the crack in the hinges.

Mr. Hugh Fred's back was to me, but he was leaning against a table like they were just two men talking. "I know your daddy raised you to respect your elders, didn't he?"

Charles gulped and had to try twice to get it out again. "Ye ... yessir."

"And I'm your elder. Isn't that right?" Mr. Hugh Fred's voice was milder than milk.

"Yes, sir."

Mr. Hugh Fred raised his head and cocked it a little.

"Yessir," Charles repeated, "you are." He sounded relieved.

I wasn't. Pop always said when the snake stopped rattling and reared back its head, it was gearing up to bite.

Mr. Hugh Fred's words hissed down the hall. "As your elder, boy, I'm telling you for the last time to stay away from my little girl. I can't whip you here in God's house, but you won't be in church forever. You hear me? I don't want you hanging around her at church or asking her out. She's still a child, not ready for that nonsense. Now you obey me, boy, or you will live to regret it."

If words were cannon balls, Charles was lying on the floor right now. He certainly wasn't answering.

"*Do you understand me, boy?*" A shower of chipped ice followed the cannon balls.

"Ye ... yessir. But—"

Charles Beal was never so brave in his life as when he uttered that *but*.

Hugh Fred's voice went softer. "Don't but me any buts, Charles Beal. If you don't stay away from my daughter, I will personally break every bone in your body. You will never play football again. Do you understand me now?"

I heard Charles gulp. "Yessir."

"That's good. Now. I want you to go right out to your car and wait for your folks there. They won't be long. I'll tell them you're out there. Go!"

Mr. Hugh Fred stepped back so fast that he'd have seen me if the door to which he was pointing wasn't in the other direction. I didn't wait to watch poor Charles slink out. I hurried downstairs and got another piece of cake.

After a while Mr. Hugh Fred came down, looking like he'd just run upstairs as clerk of session to check on something.

Freda was right beside me, chattering a blue streak about school. I had my mouth full of an icing rose sweet enough to make a bee gag.

She stopped mid-sentence and looked at her daddy. For an instant, before she got her face under control, I saw fear in her eyes. One little white flag still flew from his pocket.

Chapter 24

Aunt Sukie always said troubles come in threes. I counted Freda and Charles as one. Neither of them were at church Sunday. Mr. Hugh Fred said she had an upset stomach from too much wedding cake, and Mary Beal said Charles had homework.

The second trouble that week came on Tuesday afternoon. Aunt Kate was napping, Grace was sewing while the children finished their own naps, and Uncle Stephen was in the study. I was dawdling as long as possible over hot chocolate before changing my clothes and starting to study for a science test, when I heard somebody in the front hall fumbling with our telephone.

That wasn't unusual. When we first moved there, Job's Corner only had three phones: Aunt Hannah's, the Keenes', and the manse phone, which was used by everybody else. Then, the winter before, Statesville went to the dial system. Now that folks could dial their own numbers instead of going through an operator, telephones were sprouting like small black mushrooms in almost every home. Aunt Kate said dialing your own numbers made the telephone seem more personal. Uncle Stephen said people were just children, wanting to stick their fingers in a hole. For whatever reason, our three-number party line had expanded to five, and every one of the numbers rang in our house. We had to listen carefully to see if it was our ring before we picked up, and Aunt Kate said all that jingle jangle gave her headaches. Abby had to be spanked three times before she stopped picking up the phone whenever it rang to join in the conversation.

The manse phone, though, was still used by Mrs. Cameron and Miss Pauline, who couldn't afford phones, and Mr. Wash and Miss Nancy, who Uncle Stephen said probably didn't want to pay for their own phone when they already helped pay for ours. They didn't make too many calls, anyway, and Miss Nancy made them all.

So when I peeped out the dining room door, I was surprised to find it was Mr. Wash holding the receiver. I was especially surprised to find him there at that time of day. He carried a piece of paper and peered at it in the dim hall to dial. I went over and pushed the button to turn on the light. "Thanks," he said without bothering to look around.

I headed upstairs. Before I reached the top, I heard him say, "This is Washington Lamont and there's been some mistake."

When I came back down a few minutes later, he was sitting in the chair beside our phone, staring at nothing. His face, usually ruddy, was almost gray and his hands shook. I hurried up to the study for Uncle Stephen and clattered downstairs right behind him.

"I've been called up, Preacher." Mr. Wash's voice was husky and he looked about to cry. "Got a little brown envelope yesterday, no big deal. Had a letter in it, saying they're activating all the bomber crews who elected to go on reserve in forty-five. I wasn't worried. My time is up—they'd told us it was for five years, and mine ended December first. But I knocked off early today to call and tell them there's been a mistake. Now they say I didn't read the fine print, that what it really says is, 'the duration plus five years'"—the bushy black brows that nearly met over his nose wiggled with indignation—"and President Blankety-blank Truman claims the war didn't end until forty-seven."

While he was speaking, Abby and Aunt Kate came into the hall, still pink and drowsy from their naps. Abby lifted puzzled eyes to her mama. "What's thuderation?"

Uncle Stephen answered over one shoulder. "The duration was how long the war lasted."

"Is it all ober now?"

"No, this is another war."

"Oh." She stuck one thumb in her mouth and clutched her mother's skirt. I wished I could suck a thumb and clutch my mama's skirt, too. Mr. Wash was so upset, it scared me.

He pounded one fist into the other palm. "What it really means is, I've been messed with by the government. I'm going to Korea, Preacher. They don't care about my wife and two children; the feller said I knew this could happen when I took 'em up on the original offer. Heck, who thought we'd have another war so soon? I don't know what Nancy and the kids are gonna do." First his hands, then his whole body, started to shake.

Uncle Stephen put one hand on his shoulder and held it there until he grew still. "We'll watch out for Nancy and the children," he said gently. "When do you leave?"

"Two days after Christmas. Not even time to finish the house we're working on. We're way behind, with Clay gettin' married, and it's been hard to get materials—" He scratched at a scab on one finger like it was the most important thing in the world.

"Don't you worry about finishing that house. Rob and Clay will cover for you."

Aunt Kate went to put a hand on his other shoulder. "Why don't you and Nancy take a week and go somewhere together, just the two of you? We'll be glad to have the children."

Abby made a face at me and I made one back. But if putting up with Ruthie and Jimmy for a week was the sacrifice we had to make for our nation, we would manage.

Mr. Wash, however, relieved us both when he said, "Mama would take the children. That wouldn't be a problem. But I hate to spend the money. I just do."

Uncle Stephen stepped back and propped one folded hand on his hip. "How long's it been since you and Nancy went anywhere by yourselves, just for fun?"

He thought about it. "We went to Myrtle Beach once, back when I got home from the Pacific."

"That's been five years. I want you to do yourselves a favor. Go home, pack your suitcases, and aim your car at the beach again. Florida, maybe. Find some place you can just be together. Spend the money to make memories you can take with you and she can hold on to."

He looked up, fear in his eyes. "You think I'm not coming back, Preacher?"

"No, I think you could be gone awhile before you do come back."

Aunt Kate sounded almost cross but I knew she was just worried. "This isn't a time for saving money. What do you make it for, except to pay for things that matter?"

Uncle Stephen put his arm around her shoulders. "And what could matter more right now than time with your wife?"

Mr. Wash looked from one of them to the other and shook his head. "I don't know what Nancy will say—"

Uncle Stephen offered him a hand to help him up. "Don't ask her; tell her. Tell her you need to be with her. Tell her you need to get away and relax a little before you leave. And tell her we'll all watch out for her until you come home."

Mr. Wash walked to the door so stooped, he looked older than his daddy. "I still can't believe it." He shook his head as he went out the door. "I just can't believe it."

Aunt Kate watched him go heavily up the road. "What will Nancy do if he gets killed, Stephen? She's never worked a day in her life."

"Maybe one of our tasks while he's gone will be to help Nancy discover who she is and what she can be besides a wife and a mother."

❧

Our third trouble that week arrived Thursday afternoon as I was coming back from the store. Mrs. Raeburn's Cadillac passed me and stopped in front of our house. I was terrified I'd done something really wrong. Then, with relief, I saw Aunt Kate climb out.

"My battery died," she called cheerfully as I approached them, "so Mrs. Raeburn gave me a ride home. Won't you come in for a cup of coffee, Maddie?"

"Thanks. Do you think I could talk to Mr. Whitfield for a minute while you make it?"

"Sure. Come on in."

The two women headed up the front steps.

I cruised over and peered into the car. Amid all the shiny chrome and red leather, that lump of a faded doll sat smack in the middle of the wide front seat. Why would anybody keep something that ugly? The embroidery for one of her eyes was almost gone, so she looked like she had one eye open and one shut. Her nose only had one French knot nostril left. Her face was slick with age, and her body lumpy like she'd been washed so many times, the cotton stuffing had wadded up inside. Looked like Mrs. Raeburn could at least give her a new face and new stuffing.

I headed inside, glad my own dolls were pretty and neat. Softly I climbed the stairs to my room and hunkered down in my closet, mentally telling myself that Mrs. Raeburn might be telling Uncle Stephen something I needed to pray about.

At first I could only hear a few gasped words. " ... ever since that wedding ... haven't slept a wink ... don't know what's the matter ..." She seemed to be having trouble breathing.

I heard noises that meant he was lighting his pipe. He always lit his pipe before he talked seriously to people. Maybe it gave him time to think. "Could you sort of start at the beginning and fill me in a little? You said you went to Agnes Scott for college. Then you stayed in Atlanta?"

She raised her voice just enough. "Yes. Hugh Fred and Mama had a fit, but to tell you the truth, they nearly suffocated me between them. And I think I told you I'd been dating Taylor Hart? Well, when he up and left, there wasn't much I wanted around here anymore. I decided to try my wings in Atlanta." She laughed but didn't sound happy. "I tried them and Marcus clipped them."

"Where did you all meet?"

"At the Atlanta USO. I used to go down some evenings to dance and joke around with the soldiers, and one night he came in." She stopped abruptly, then gave a little rueful grunt. "People get married for the dumbest reasons, Mr. Whitfield—"

"Stephen," he interrupted, then sucked his pipe to get it going. "And your dumb reason?"

"I married Marcus simply because he made me tingle. Doesn't that take the cake for dumb when I'm actually a pretty smart lady?"

"In my experience, people *usually* get married for dumb reasons. Then they proceed to discover that marriage is a lot more than chemistry."

"Chemistry." She said it thoughtfully. "That's what we had, all right. It was pretty spectacular while it lasted. I probably oughtn't to be telling you this, you being a preacher—"

He chuckled. "I'm also a man. I understand chemistry."

I knew chemistry was something people took in high school, but I hadn't known before it was funny. It must be, because she laughed, too. "Well then, I'm not ashamed to admit that what we had was downright wonderful while the war lasted. I stayed in Atlanta teaching while he was stationed in the Pacific. When he got leave, I'd go meet him somewhere—anywhere. I didn't care how far. It was always incredible." She stopped.

"But?" He tapped his pipe lightly against the ashtray.

She gave a short, bitter laugh. "When he came home for good, I found out that Marcus's chemistry worked for any pretty girl within grabbing range. When I wasn't around, he'd settle for whoever was handy." She paused and I heard Uncle Stephen strike a match. "At first I blamed myself, until one of his friends' wives admitted that's how Marcus always was. She said I was real clever not to give in to him until he married me—nobody else had managed that."

She heaved a deep sigh that wrung my heart. "The last two years have been worse than I want to remember. I grew up in church, so I knew I ought to forgive him. And I didn't want to hurt his folks. They are decent people. But they won't face how

Marcus is. When I tried to tell them, they told me I ought to be a more loving wife. Loving?" She barked another short laugh. "I loved that man every way I knew how. I forgave him until I was well past seventy times seven. I tried to be home when he was there, so he wouldn't need to go out. I tried every trick I knew to keep him away from other women. But he was at Emory Law School by then, so he had a lot of free daytime hours. I couldn't stand coming home and wondering if somebody else had been using my sheets."

Her voice dropped on the last few words, and I heard Uncle Stephen fumbling around with his pipe. Maybe he didn't know quite what she was talking about any more than I did. I could understand the bit about her husband bringing women home but not about sheets. And how did a woman "give in" to a man?

I couldn't think of a single person I could ask.

Mrs. Raeburn's voice got even softer, like she was talking to herself. "I got to the point where I changed the bed every night before I got in it. Then one night last August I was making hospital corners in the top sheet when I stopped and asked myself, 'Maddie, why are you putting up with this?' I looked at him shaving in the bathroom—he always shaved before he went to bed—and the chemistry was gone. All I saw was a handsome man I neither knew nor wanted to know, standing in my bathroom in his underpants. I left the bed half made, got my suitcase out of the closet, and packed; then I went downstairs, got my pocketbook, and went to a hotel. I called the Iredell County school board the next morning on a whim. When they said they had a vacancy at Mount Vernon, it seemed like a sign from God." She gave a high, nervous little laugh. "You may wonder why I expected a sign from God when I'd stopped going to church—"

"God doesn't give up on people; we just give up on God."

"Well, I sure gave up on Marcus. I went back to the house while he was in class the next day and took my clothes and a few personal things. I figured if I left him all the rest, he wouldn't come after me—and he hasn't. When I got here, I filed for divorce. And I've never regretted leaving him for a minute. Right or wrong, I don't regret it."

I heard another match strike and sucking noises. He was having a time keeping that pipe lit. "I regret you didn't catch a bus home before you married the man. Didn't anybody warn you?"

Her chuckle was deep and throaty. "Have you ever tried to warn a twenty-three-year-old woman in love?"

"And you've been on your own since what, August?"

Again she laughed but again it wasn't funny. "I've been on my own since Marcus came home from the war. Well, not quite that long—he had the decency to be faithful for about a month. Then—" I heard her take a deep, shaky breath. "But at least he was around. Since August I've had nothing but a roomful of seventh-graders, four bare rooms to call my own, and an empty heart."

Her sigh was so sad, it gave me a stomach pain. "I took Marcus for better or for worse, and I don't feel really free—" She let the word dangle like a child too high on the monkey bars. Then she said softly, "But Clay and Laura's wedding stirred up some things I can't seem to deal with. Maybe in the eyes of God I'm still married, but I'm so lonely."

"In the eyes of God you are a beloved daughter. If I, as a new friend, can understand your pain and loneliness, don't you think God can?"

"The Bible says divorce is a sin."

"It also says God's in the sin-forgiving business. Have you prayed for forgiveness?"

"A million times. But even if God forgives me, I can't seem to forgive myself."

"Of course you can't. It's hogwash to think we can forgive ourselves. Worse, it's blasphemy—taking on ourselves the prerogative of God. God does the forgiving. Our part is to accept it. And then get on with living as forgiven people."

For a minute she didn't say anything. Then she sort of squeaked, "Really?"

"Really. Want to pray about that right now?"

I heard him set down the pipe, then the mumble of low voices. I hoped God could hear. I certainly couldn't. Finally he said, "Here" and she blew her nose.

Her voice was shaky as she asked, "You think the chemistry might still be there?" She sounded like Abby begging for a Golden Book at the grocery store.

He chuckled. "From the little chemistry I studied, elements don't change. Put one with the right catalyst, and you always get the same reaction."

She didn't say anything for a minute; then her own laugh was a bit trembly. "I'll let you know if I find a catalyst."

"You do that." I could tell from his voice that he was walking her to the door. "And you notice our church roof is still standing, if you want to come back some Sunday."

She laughed and it was her old happy laugh. "I might surprise you and do that."

I didn't bother to go out and say hello. I was wondering how I could look at her the next day in school without turning as red as one of Aunt Hannah's homegrown tomatoes.

Chapter 25

Decfor their honeymoon, and Mr. Wash and Miss Nancy, who went to Panama City. I kept wondering if Florida realized they had two families from Job's Corner down there at the very same time. If so, it never made our paper.

Bonnie and I were embroidering at recess again. She was embroidering dishtowels for Aunt Hannah's Christmas gift, and I was finishing the pillowcases I'd started for my hope chest. I'd decided to give them to Aunt Kate for Christmas. I wouldn't ever need them.

Miss Emily drove Freda to school every morning. She sat with us in the auditorium at recess, drooping like Rowdy when he got wet. All she could talk about was how wonderful Charles was and how mean her daddy was to them both.

"Was he really mad when you got home from the wedding?" I asked. She didn't have any bruises and her jaw wasn't wired.

"Yeah. He told me not to talk to Charles again or he'll send me away to school." She sat up straight and her face was pink. "Mama could make him change his mind but she won't do a thing! She's mean!" She got up and started out of the row. "I'm going to buy a Moon Pie."

Bonnie looked after her with worried eyes. "I don't like to hear her talk about her fine parents like that."

I could have told her a few things about Freda's fine parents but knew I mustn't. Sometimes living in the manse was almost more responsibility than my tongue could carry.

I didn't have much sympathy to waste on Freda, though. I still couldn't believe Clay had gotten in the car and gone on his honeymoon with Laura. I cried myself to sleep for four nights. The next day our family got a postcard with a palm tree against an impossible coral sunset.

> Having a terrific time. Don't wish you were here (ha ha). Back next week.

Aunt Kate tucked it in the kitchen mirror, but I dropped it in hot soapy water and we had to throw it away.

I transferred my yearnings toward Mrs. Raeburn in my first and only girlish crush. I did all the usual foolish things: hung around where she might pass, hoping we would exchange a couple of private words; memorized what she wore and what she ate; whispered elaborate stories to myself at bedtime in which she poured out her heart to me as she had to Uncle Stephen. Always as I drifted to sleep, she was saying, "You're the only person in the world who understands me."

I was thrilled when she chose me one day to greet a man from Sealtest Dairy who'd come all the way from Charlotte to show our class a film entitled *How Milk Gets to Your Table.* "Meet him on the front steps and show him where our room is. Ask questions to get to know him—his name, where he lives, what he does at Sealtest—and introduce him to the class."

I felt very important standing with him out in the hall. The other girls were jealous because he was handsome for an old man. His shoulders were wide, and he had curly black hair with a cute little bald patch at the crown, a square jaw, and glasses with thick black frames that made him look distinguished. He made everybody laugh, including me, when he started his talk, "Carley here is so charming, it's a shame she's too young for me. But I'll be forty-two my next birthday, and she doesn't look a day over thirty-five."

He told us that Iredell County was a major producer of milk, and many farmers sold milk to Sealtest Dairies down in Charlotte to be pasteurized and bottled or to Carnation's evaporation plant in town to be canned. "Some of you may know farmers who have a barrel out by the road full of cold water, where they keep the milk in metal cans until our truck picks it up each day."

"We do! We do!" Several kids waved their hands. That was the first time I'd realized what Uncle Davy's barrel was for.

His film on how milk got to our table was of little interest to me, however. Milk didn't come to us pasteurized, bottled, and taken to grocery stores. Milk got to our table in Uncle Davy's pickup, in quart canning jars he left on our porch each morning when he came for the mail. I was a lot more interested in what Mrs. Raeburn was doing.

She sat in the back with the man and talked softly to him all through the movie. She even walked out the door with him and didn't come back for so long that I finally took the bathroom pass and went looking for her. I didn't have to look far. She was standing just beyond our door talking and laughing like she'd known him all her life.

She looked startled to see me. "What do you want, Carley?"

I held the bathroom pass aloft and gave them a little smile. As I went downstairs, I heard her say, "Well, I guess I'd better get back to class." She didn't sound at all like she wanted to.

At the bottom of the steps I saw Mr. Donaldson standing just under the balcony, below them. When he saw me, he went to the nearest row of auditorium seats and shook one. "Checking on wobbly seats," he told me. I suspected he'd been checking on one of his teachers who was talking in the hall when she should have been in her room.

When I got back to class, Mrs. Raeburn was talking about cows and dairies like they were the most interesting things in the world. Her cheeks were pink and her eyes sparkling. She didn't even notice when a boy hit me with a spitball as I walked in the door.

"Your Aunt Maddie has a new boyfriend," I told Freda sourly at afternoon recess, jabbing my finger as I attempted to create a yellow daisy. "She was making eyes at the man who came to show our movie this morning."

Freda brightened. "Maybe they'll get married and I can be a bridesmaid again. Wasn't my dress dreamy for Clay's wedding?" She didn't expect an answer, which was just as well. Bonnie and I had said all we had to say about that blessed dress.

It was raining again, so the three of us were sitting in the back of the auditorium. That day Freda had finally brought a needle, red thread, and one of her mother's handkerchiefs. She was embroidering a red heart, an arrow, and the initials *F* and *C*. I don't think she'd ever embroidered before. Her stitches straggled and she never picked out a mistake, just went right on as if it didn't exist. "Charles is going to get me something real special for Christmas," she said in an offhand way, bending close to see her crooked stitches.

"You're making that up," I told her. "How can you know when you can't even talk to him?"

She giggled. "Yes, I can. He calls me every afternoon."

Bonnie neatly snipped her thread. "Does your daddy know he calls?"

Freda tossed her curls. "Of course not. He'd be furious. So Charles calls before Daddy gets home."

"Doesn't your Mama mind?" Bonnie's eyes were even darker with worry.

"She naps in the afternoon. Nobody knows but me."

"And Miranda," I pointed out.

"Miranda won't tell."

Bonnie folded up her dishtowel. "Well, I have to go back to the room early to finish studying for our arithmetic test. Don't you?"

Freda was notoriously bad in arithmetic, but she again shook her curls and continued embroidering her lopsided heart. "I brought my book down here." The fact that she hadn't yet opened it didn't seem to bother her.

❅

As December days slid by, I began to make presents and to worry. I didn't have much money saved, and there were only seven months until summer camp.

For Big Mama, of course, I had the tray I'd made back in August. Grace gave me scraps from her robe and helped me make Abby a flannel nightgown for her favorite doll, Maggie. Aunt Kate's pillowcases turned out so pretty, I'd spent thirty cents and bought a bib with a bear to embroider for John, and fifty cents for a dishtowel to embroider for Aunt Hannah. I wished Clay could see those pillowcases and know what he'd lost by not waiting for me.

"But I just don't know *what* to give Grace and Uncle Stephen," I confided to Aunt Hannah one afternoon when she finished talking to Aunt Kate about Christmas flowers for the church.

"You are sewing so well, why don't you make them each an apron? They like to cook."

"That's a good idea, but Grace would see me, and I'd need a pattern and material . . ." Patterns cost thirty-five cents, and material could be that much a yard. I could see my savings dwindling away.

"Come down to my place tomorrow afternoon and let's see what we can find."

When I walked down, she had already found blue-and-white striped material in her storeroom and had cut a brown-paper pattern from her own apron. After we'd cut out Uncle Stephen's apron on the kitchen table, she helped me cut the pattern smaller for Grace. Then she really surprised me. "I've had Davy bring down my machine to the dining room, and I've put on the heat in there." They mostly lived in their big kitchen during the winter to save heat. And the sewing machine usually sat in one of her unused upstairs bedrooms as a bedside table. "Do you know how to work a treadle?"

Under her machine was a fancy metal pedal. I eyed it dubiously. "No. Aunt Kate's machine is electric."

"It's easy. Let me show you." She sat down, placed both her large feet on the pedal, and sewed a perfect seam.

I slid into the seat she'd vacated and practiced on a scrap. It was harder than it looked, but once I got the hang of it, I loved it. There was a splendid sense that only I and the machine were sewing, without any help from outside.

"Why did you have Grace make your dress when you sew so well?"

She looked flustered. "Oh, I don't really like to sew, old dear. I just use this for mending. Now, while you hem those all around, let me go fix us both a glass of tea and some cake."

All afternoon I pedaled happily while the needle went up and down. By the time she ran me home at suppertime, I had made two blue-and-white striped bib aprons with almost straight seams. Not until years later would I realize Aunt Hannah had not only given me the fabric and made the pattern, she also gave me a whole afternoon as if she had nothing better to do. That's the kind of woman Hannah Anderson was.

Every evening I opened my bottom drawer and checked each gift with satisfaction. I also wondered what I would have given anybody that year if I hadn't learned to sew and embroider.

Even without buying Christmas presents, though, my music camp fund stood at three dollars and ten cents.

❄

As days grew shorter and the year ran down, Mount Vernon students spent most of our school hours preparing for the Christmas chapel program. This was the biggest event of the year. Every child had a part, so almost every parent would come. Aunt Kate's class and the third grade were acting a short Christmas play about animals in the forest. The fifth and sixth grades were giving a concert of carols—but, as I told Uncle Stephen, "Before you get excited about that, remember, Mr. Mayhew is letting Preston sing one of the Wise Men's verses in 'We Three Kings.'"

Mr. Mayhew insisted that students memorize words, but instead of giving them the words, he sang a line and let them sing it back. All the way to and from school on the bus Preston bellowed, "Murray's mind is bitter perfume. Breezes' life a gathering groom ..."

"It's not 'Murray's mind'; it's 'myrrh is mine: that bitter perfume, breathes a life of gathering gloom,'" I informed him. I'd looked it up in Aunt Kate's college hymnal.

"*Murr* isn't even a word," he informed me back, "and the rest doesn't make sense."

"Don't you know what myrrh is?" I was smug. "We learned that in Baptist Sunday school. It's perfume."

"Don't be dumb, Carley. Who'd give perfume to a baby? 'Specially a baby boy."

At church on Sunday I tried to show him the words, but the Presbyterian hymnal didn't have the song. "Come to our house and I'll show you," I promised.

"I don't want to know, if they're dumb," he said stubbornly.

So daily he bawled senseless words loud enough to startle people down in Charlotte into thinking husky-voiced angels were singing in the distance.

Our seventh-grade class was doing the Nativity story, with first- and second-graders as angels, sheep, cows, and donkeys. Mrs. Raeburn excused me, though, the day she handed out parts, saying right in front of everybody, "Carley won't have a part because she and Freda are playing a duet in the eighth-grade talent show."

"Yay, Carley," clapped one of the boys sarcastically.

"Hey, she's good," another chided him.

"She sure is," said one of the girls. "She plays almost as good as Mr. Mayhew."

I turned four colors of red. Those were the first nice things anybody in a Mount Vernon class had ever said about me.

The medley of carols Miss Rilla had chosen for our duet was beautiful but a little tricky, and as it turned out, Freda and

I were never able to practice together. The two days I went to meet her at Miss Rilla's, she didn't come, so I played the top and Miss Rilla played the bottom. I thought I played pretty good, but Miss Rilla's mouth was pinched up the whole time like something was wrong.

Freda said we could practice after church on Sundays, but one Sunday she forgot her music, and the next she forgot our practice session and went home. I asked her to come to the church basement some weekday, where we could roll two pianos close together, but she said she was busy.

I wasn't too worried. I'd memorized my part and practiced until I was note perfect, but I would have felt a lot better if we'd had time to run through it together at least once.

"Don't worry, " Freda insisted at recess the day before. "We'll be fine."

That morning I put on my burgundy wedding dress and brushed my thin hair until it stood out in a halo of electricity. When I got on the bus, Freda wailed, "We clash!" She was wearing a white angora sweater that was like a soft cloud, and a bright red plaid skirt.

When we got to school, she went right to Mr. Mayhew and asked him to move the piano to the other side of the stage, so she'd be on the side next to the audience. That meant the little kids would have to look the other way when they sang, but Mr. Mayhew would do anything for Freda. Almost anybody would. And I didn't mind being at the back. I was honored enough just to be playing with an eighth-grader.

Until we played.

To begin with, Freda accidentally took more than her share of the bench. I had so little to sit on, I was terrified the whole time I'd slide off. Then Miss Rilla had said I should cue us for four beats before we began, and I'd told Freda, but she forgot and just started playing when she got her skirt arranged to her satisfaction. I managed to come in on the second measure, but that must have made Freda nervous, because she sped up. Although I tried to keep up, she kept getting faster.

We also had a lot of discords. I thought at first Freda was missing notes, but she kept huffing hard in disgust and shaking her head, so everybody in the auditorium knew it was me—including me. She finished two measures ahead of me and sat disgusted until I was done. Then she stood up, took a bow completely alone, and flounced off the stage. I was so ashamed, I left without bowing.

At the bottom of the stage steps, Freda seethed. "I tried to get Aunt Rilla to give me the top part, but she wouldn't listen. I told her you couldn't play anything that hard." She swished her curls and stomped to her seat, where she whispered unimaginable things to eighth-grade girls. I went to the bathroom to cry.

When I came out, I could hear Preston singing on the stage. To my utter astonishment, he not only carried the tune, he sang every word perfectly. Uncle Stephen said later that was possibly the closest Preston Anderson would be to an angel until he died.

That night I locked my door and sat at my window. High overhead the sky was freckled with stars, but they seemed only cold, impersonal pinpricks in a dark loneliness. "Dear God," I whispered to the cold wavy glass, "if you've got a planet somewhere where people are happy, where nobody makes mistakes or hurts anybody else's feelings, please take me there. If you don't, I will never play or sing in public again."

Chapter 26

Saturday morning we went Christmas shopping. I bought Freda a beautiful gold cross at Rose's five-and-dime. The necklace cost ninety-four cents—nearly a third of my music camp fund—but it wasn't enough to make up for what I'd done. I just hoped we'd both live long enough for her to forgive me.

That afternoon I came down with the first and only cold I ever welcomed. I couldn't go to church to see Clay and Laura grinning after their honeymoon. I didn't have to watch Miss Nancy cry, which she was doing all the time right then. I didn't have to sit under Freda's glare from the piano bench or wonder which basement corner she and Charles were smooching in after church. I didn't have to avoid Miss Rilla, looking gently sad and disappointed about the mess I'd made of the duet. Freda was certain to have told her.

I stayed in bed through the first three days of Christmas vacation reading, embroidering a doll's skirt for Abby, and letting the hems down in my skirts. "We must have the water too hot in the washing machine," I complained to Aunt Kate. "Every one of my skirts has shrunk an inch."

She said she was too busy getting ready for Christmas to worry about that right then.

Thursday I finally felt well enough to run to the store. By this time the ground was freezing into tiny icy puddles at night. Even the days didn't warm up much. I found Mrs. Cameron in her coat, scarf, and gloves, wrapped in a ragged quilt. The store was so cold that I could see my breath, and she had a hacking cough.

I went home and told Uncle Stephen. He called Uncle Davy and asked him to bring up a load of firewood. Aunt Kate had Grace heat up some homemade chicken soup she'd made, and sent me over with it while the men unloaded the wood. That ungrateful old woman—she sat there spooning in soup and watching them unloading wood, and she complained the whole time she didn't need soup, didn't need a fire, didn't want people sitting by her stove.

"You remind me of a woman in a book I read," I told her. "If you don't stop grumbling, you're going to turn into a Grumble."

She gave me a sour look. "You're a fine one to talk, Missy. I'll do as I please."

But smoke rose from her chimney all day, and when I went back just before suppertime, the stove was still going. Uncle Stephen went over the next morning to light it again and said her cough was better. "You earned two stars for your heavenly crown"—he held out his hand—"and Mrs. Cameron sent you five Mary Janes."

Jay got home from college late that afternoon. As far as we knew, Grace hadn't written him a single letter since her trouble. Abby reminded her often that she needed to earn her "moneyfunt sum," but Grace only said, "I'll get around to it when I have the time." I couldn't figure why she had plenty of time to take care of Abby and John, sew for anybody who asked her, and keep our house but never had time to write a few simple lines and mail them. I wrote Jay twice some weeks, I felt so sorry for him.

The Greyhound bus stopped on the highway right in front of the manse. None of us were surprised when Jay showed up on our porch an hour after we'd seen him get off. I was shocked, however, when Grace refused to come down and say hello after he'd greeted the rest of us. He hung around nearly an hour, talking to Uncle Stephen about classes he was taking and letting Abby and John crawl all over him. He came back the next day, and the next, but Grace never so much as showed him her face.

Christmas came on Monday that year. The Sunday before, still mortified, I carefully wrapped the cross I'd bought and took it to church, hoping it would help Freda forgive me. She arrived wearing a silver bangle Charles gave her. "It's fourteen-carat silver," she told Bonnie, waving it around. I was standing right beside Bonnie but Freda pretended I didn't exist. "I never wear anything but real silver and gold, you know."

"When did he give it to you?" Bonnie asked. The Beals hadn't gotten to church yet.

Freda giggled. "We had all yesterday morning to ourselves. Aunt Maddie went up to the mountains this weekend and gave me her key to feed the cat. When I got there yesterday, I called Charles and Mary brought him over."

"You called a boy?" Bonnie sounded as scandalized as I felt. Girls didn't chase boys; boys chased girls. And calling was the worst kind of chasing.

"He wanted me to." Freda smoothed her green wool jumper.

Bonnie touched the collar of Freda's blouse, which was embroidered with holly leaves. "You'll never be able to wear that except at Christmas."

"I know, but it was so pretty, Mama said I could get it anyway. Do you want to hear about Charles or not?"

"Sure," Bonnie agreed.

I was trying to decide when I should give Freda her necklace. I hadn't bought anything for Bonnie, and I'd never get Freda by herself until she finished telling Bonnie about Charles.

"Mary went shopping and he got to stay all morning. It was real romantic—almost like being married in our very own house." She moved her arm so the bracelet shone in the light.

Bonnie watched it, mesmerized.

"Didn't your mother wonder where you were all that time?" I asked.

Freda didn't look at me but she answered. "No. I'd said I'd stay awhile to keep the cat from being lonely. Mama's allergic to cats, so I knew she wouldn't tell me to bring it home."

"What all did you do?" Bonnie asked. From the excited, curious look in her eyes, I suspected Miss Pauline had never told her the awful things Big Mama told me.

Freda shrugged. "Nothing much. Listened to music and drank Co-colas. Charles loves Co-colas. Then he gave me this." She was going to wear that bracelet out, wiggling it around.

Bonnie put out one fingertip and dared to touch it. "What did your daddy say about it?"

"He thinks it's pretty, but I told him it was from Aunt Maddie. When she gets home this afternoon, I'm going to ask her not to tell him it wasn't." She held it to her cheek. "Can you believe it? It's fourteen carats. I hate cheap jewelry."

I fingered the present in my pocket uncertainly. I didn't know if it was carrot gold or not.

I decided to take it home, put Bonnie's name on it, and carry it over to her later that day.

I was real glad I did. Bonnie gave me a dresser scarf she'd embroidered and hemmed for me, and she loved the cross. I didn't want to remind Freda of that awful duet anyway.

❧

Between them, Uncle Stephen and Aunt Kate made a miracle—they persuaded Mr. Donaldson to sing in a trio with Aunt Kate and Clay at the Christmas Morning service. A lot of choir members who lived on farms several miles away didn't want to come back on Christmas when they'd been at church the day before.

In order to get Miss Rilla to accompany them instead of Freda, Aunt Kate explained to everybody that it sure would be a lot easier for Miss Rilla to come to an evening practice than for Freda, if Clay would bring her. Only in the privacy of our own home did she admit she wanted to sing music that was too hard for Freda to play.

Aunt Kate invited Mr. Donaldson to come eat homemade vegetable soup and cornbread before Miss Rilla and Clay arrived. He ate three bowlfuls of soup and seemed regretful he couldn't hold a fourth. "I don't do much cooking," he admitted, wiping up the last of his molasses and peanut butter with his last bite of cornbread. "This was the perfect bribe to get me to sing with you, but don't ever expect a repeat performance."

"Not until Easter," Uncle Stephen assured him. "Or Groundhog Day."

When supper was over, the men went up to Uncle Stephen's study to smoke their pipes while Grace washed dishes and Aunt Kate put the children to bed. I followed her. "Aunt Kate, I have a problem. I made aprons for Uncle Stephen and Grace, but they are just alike, so I want to embroider their names on them so they can tell them apart. Should I put *Uncle Stephen* or just *Stephen*?"

"His weal name is Daddy," Abby reminded me severely.

Aunt Kate winked at me over her curls. "Why don't you put *World's Greatest Chef*? I think he'd really like that, if it's not too much embroidering."

"Perfect!" I scampered up the stairs to get started at once. Christmas was tomorrow!

As I pulled red thread through my needle, I heard Uncle Stephen and Mr. Donaldson in the study next door. With the crack under my closet door I could hear every word, but I wasn't really listening. They didn't sound like they were talking about anything private anyway, just books and how the war in Korea was going.

Then, just as I was trying to figure out how I could put the apostrophe in *World's* without having to knot my thread and cut it, Mr. Donaldson exploded bitterly. "More fine young men getting arms and legs blown off—and for what?"

"Do you still mind so much?"

"Only every minute of every day. You can't imagine what a difference it makes to everything I do. I'm generally adjusted to the little things, like how impossible it is to tie a tie or open a door while carrying a package. But when I realize I'll never again play the oboe or pitch a winning ball game or put my arms around a woman—"

"Hey," Uncle Stephen interrupted, "it just takes one arm to hold a woman."

"Sure—while she's wondering what horrors she'll see if I ever take off my shirt."

"Any decent woman wouldn't be thinking that. She'd be wondering when you'd stop thinking about a missing arm and start noticing how much she likes you."

Somebody tapped a pipe hard in his metal wastebasket.

"If you ever meet a woman like that, you can introduce us."

"What about Maddie Raeburn? She's a woman it would be worth getting to know."

Mr. Donaldson laughed but that was bitter, too. "Maddie Raeburn wouldn't have me on a platter. Not if I were the last man on earth."

"Have you asked her? Have you even tried to get to know her?"

"Know her? I was her twelfth-grade history teacher. Not that she learned much. She was too busy making eyes at the baseball pitcher behind her. She was a cheerleader, too, and I coached the baseball team, so I saw a lot of her one way or another. But in April 1940—" He stopped and didn't go on. I held my breath, afraid my bed would squeak.

Uncle Stephen sucked on his pipe, then asked mildly, "What happened?"

"The boy disappeared. Taylor Hart. Lived in the big house up the hill, where Maddie's brother lives now. Maddie thought I had something to do with his going away."

"Why should she think that?"

"I was apparently the last person to see him. We'd had a game in Albemarle and my old Packard was out of commission, so Taylor drove me down and back in his Pontiac. When he dropped me off, he acted perfectly normal. Never so much as hinted he was planning to light out. But that was the last anybody ever saw of him."

"Just rode off into the sunset?"

"He didn't exactly ride. When I got up the next morning, his car was parked in my driveway. It had been knocking on our way home, so I figured maybe it started giving him trouble before he got far down the road, and he'd brought it back to leave it at my place, then walked. It wasn't over three miles to his place from mine. I called to see what he planned to do about the car—it was blocking mine, which I needed to take to the shop—but his parents said he wasn't up yet. When they went to call him, he wasn't in bed and hadn't slept in it at all. By dinnertime they were frantic, as you can imagine. They had the police in all forty-eight states looking for him, but nobody ever found a trace."

"Never?" Uncle Stephen sounded as surprised as I felt. The first time I heard the story, from Mrs. Cameron, she hadn't let me know it was such a mystery. The old witch, she knew I loved mysteries, too. I wriggled to get more comfortable as Mr. Donaldson answered.

"Never. For a time the police made life pretty miserable for me, asking questions. If they'd found a body, I'd have been suspect number one. But eventually, after talking to his friends, they concluded he must have gone to Canada to join the war— which is the main reason Maddie blamed me. We weren't fighting yet, but I'd been talking a lot about how awful Hitler was and how we ought to be helping the British. Several of my students got hot to enlist, and Taylor was one of them. I signed up myself as soon as school was out. Couldn't take any more of the police's questions and Maddie's sad blue eyes. But as far as I know, his folks never heard from Taylor again. They finally gave up and moved away."

"What do you figure happened?"

"I figure he either joined up under another name and got killed before he got around to writing his folks—consideration wasn't one of Taylor's strong suits—or he started out and was worried his car wouldn't make it, so he ditched it at my place, hitched a ride with the wrong person, and wound up dead in a ditch with his identification stolen." He heaved a deep sigh. "In either case, now you know why Maddie Raeburn won't give me the time of day. Taylor Hart was the love of her life, I was the last person to see him alive, and if I didn't kill him myself, I inspired him to go to war and get himself killed. Maddie was furious with me at the time and she still is. She will blame me for Taylor's death as long as she lives."

Uncle Stephen sucked on his pipe, then said something that nearly made me fall off the bed. "You had a good motive, too."

"I swear to you I didn't."

"Sure you did. Maddie herself."

He gave a short, bitter laugh. "What makes you say that?"

"You say her name the same way I say Kate's. As if it is precious."

"You're just reading that into it. Sure, she was a cute student, batting those big blue eyes at Taylor in the back of my room, but—"

Uncle Stephen chuckled. "And driving you straight up a wall. You were how old then?"

"Twenty-three. I'd finished college and taught a year before."

"A real grandpa. Don't try to tell me you didn't feel a thing for her. She must have been one gorgeous co-ed."

"She was," Mr. Donaldson admitted grudgingly.

Outside I saw Clay's new car pull up in front of our house. Which did I want more, to avoid Miss Rilla or to see Clay? Clay won.

As soon as the doorbell rang, I slid off the bed to answer it. As I passed the study door, it opened. Uncle Stephen was saying, "She's a lot more than a cute co-ed now." He looked real startled to see me.

I opened the front door and stood in the chilly air looking at Clay anxiously for signs Laura had starved or mistreated

him. He looked tan, fit, and healthy. "Hello, Little Buddy." He
fished in his pocket. "I brought you something from Florida."
He laid a black triangle in my palm. "It's a shark's tooth I
found on the beach. Don't let it bite you!"

I took it and tried to hide my outrage. Did he think I was a
child, bringing me the sort of thing you'd bring to Abby? He
didn't think of me at all. He was already greeting Aunt Kate
and showing her some music he'd bought for later in the new
year.

My eyes met Miss Rilla's solemn gray ones. I could see
myself in her glasses and wondered if she could see herself in
mine. "I . . . the duet went awful," I blurted. "I played terrible."

She put her strong pianist's hand on my shoulder and
squeezed. "It was my fault, child. I should never have suggested it. I thought maybe competition would encourage more
practice, but I was very wrong."

"I *did* practice," I assured her. "And it didn't *seem* too hard.
I even came home and played it perfectly afterward. But on the
stage, with Freda . . ."

She squeezed my shoulder again. "I know. Freda told me
what happened. But I drew my own conclusions. I should have
remembered something a wise teacher once told me: duets are
never a good idea for friends."

Before I could ask why, Mr. Donaldson came downstairs.

"Well, look who's here!" Clay said, slugging him on the
shoulder. "You old renegade, you think you're good enough to
sing at Bethel just because you were a soloist in the U.N.C.
glee club?"

Mr. Donaldson cuffed him back. "I haven't told anybody
yet what a pest you were in high school, but if you start telling
tales, I have a few up my one good sleeve. How are you, Clay?
Haven't seen you in a hundred years."

"Hale, hearty, and newly married." Clay held up his new
ring and grinned. I was astonished to note that my heart didn't
feel a thing. Maybe shark's teeth had poison in them that made
you numb if you held them in a hot, sweaty hand.

Clay spoke to Aunt Kate, who had just come from the living room. "This man was not only a soloist, he was the pitcher of a champion baseball team. Folks around here were holding their breath about whether Jerry Donaldson was headed for opera or the New York Yankees." He reached out and grabbed Mr. Donaldson around the neck with his elbow. "Instead he decided to come home and become my baseball coach. How the heck are you, Coach Donaldson?"

Mr. Donaldson bent over so fast, I didn't know what was happening, and he flipped Clay right down the hall. Rowdy barked encouragement. Mr. Donaldson finished with one foot on Clay's chest. "Still able to toss a kid who gets too big for his britches."

I thought Clay would be furious, but he lay on the floor and laughed until tears ran down his cheeks. Aunt Kate shook her head at me. "Don't try to understand men, Carley. You never will. Would you two like to continue wrestling or shall we practice?"

They made beautiful music that night. They made beautiful music the next morning, too. Mrs. Raeburn was there to listen—since her talk with Uncle Stephen after the wedding, she'd come to almost every service if she was in town. I looked around a couple of times to see if she watched Mr. Donaldson while they sang, but each time I did, she was looking at her own lap.

I wonder if anybody else remembers that lovely trio now. It was the last beautiful thing in Job's Corner before one of its darkest secrets came to light.

Chapter 27

I'd have been a lot more excited about going to Aunt Hannah's for Christmas dinner if I hadn't known Preston would be there. We could see him all the way down the road, wearing his new Hopalong Cassidy cowboy hat. It looked a lot like his old one, except it was clean and had more fake silver on it. The hat looked real odd with the green windbreaker, red scarf, and mittens his mama made him wear, but it was below freezing outside.

He had tied a piece of old rope into a noose and was trying to lasso the mailbox. "He'd do better to aim for the milk barrel," I commented as we pulled in the drive. "At least he'd have a chance of grazing it."

"Don't be too hard on him," Uncle Stephen advised over his shoulder. "At least he's doing something besides sitting and watching TV."

As soon as we stopped, Aunt Kate clutched John so tightly that he squealed, and hurried in. I knew she wanted to get off her coat so she could preen in the new emerald twin sweater set Uncle Stephen had bought her for Christmas because "it exactly matches your eyes and I couldn't just give you a freezer. The first Christmas gift was delightful and unpredictable. Nobody ought to get just what she asks for." But he'd given her the freezer, too, and she had solemnly kissed it.

Grace climbed from the backseat carrying the bowl of cranberry relish Aunt Hannah had permitted us to bring. "I'm not going up to Janey Lou's for dinner," she declared to us one more time as she started up the walk. "I am not." She'd been saying that for the past two days, since Aunt Hannah called to say Grace should ride down with us to their house because she was invited to go with Janey Lou up to her house for Christmas dinner. Janey Lou's whole family would be there and wanted Grace to join them. Janey Lou's whole family included her sister Bess and Bess's son Jay.

"You don't have to talk to Jay," I told her. "Just let him look at you." She was gorgeous that day in a dress she'd remade from one of Miss Emily's castoffs: dark brown velvet trimmed in creamy lace.

"You better talk to Jay," Abby informed her as she followed Grace up the sidewalk, clutching her new doll. "He's your fwiend, but if you don't talk, he won't write you no more."

As Uncle Stephen headed to the house, he called, "Roped and tied anything yet, Preston?"

Preston pulled the rope back toward him and panted with exertion and determination. "Not yet but I will soon."

I moseyed out toward the road. "Don't expect to get hired as a cowboy this year," I warned as soon as Uncle Stephen was out of earshot.

"I figure it'll take me a week or two to get good." He threw the loop again, and again he missed. "What'd you get for Christmas?"

"Lots of stuff. Uncle Stephen and Aunt Kate gave me a pink clock radio to put by my bed. Abby gave me a headband with my name on it. But this was the best." I held out a new Madame Alexander doll. "Big Mama sent me and Abby each one. Abby's has red hair and mine has pure gold."

Without knowing a thing about Mrs. Raeburn, Big Mama had sent me a doll who looked just like her: big blue glass eyes, blond wavy hair, and a curvy figure just like I planned to have one day. The only difference was, the doll wore a red taffeta off-shoulder evening dress. I was already scheming how to get some black and white material to make her a wardrobe. Mrs. Raeburn never wore anything except black and white.

"Her name is Rae," I informed him, holding my breath. That was the first time I had said the name out loud, and I wanted to see if Preston would make the connection with *Raeburn*.

He just panted and heaved the silly rope again. "That's a boy's name."

"Not with an *e*, it's not. Big Mama sent me this outfit too." I held out my arms so he could see my first suit, cranberry and gray houndstooth wool with a short, straight jacket and an A-line skirt. She'd even sent a white long-sleeved blouse and gray socks that exactly matched the suit—and a note:

> Your last doll and your first suit, as you stand on the brink between childhood and adulthood.
>
> Love,
> Big Mama

I loved the suit so much, I'd refused to wear a coat for the few minutes we'd be outside. Which is why I now stood by the road shaking all over like I had some weird disease.

Preston wasn't any more impressed with my grown-up clothes than he'd been with the doll. He slung his rope again and fell about three feet short of the mailbox. I turned to go in before chattering chipped my teeth.

"Dolls are dumb." Preston threw his loop again and this time he caught a bush by the mailbox. "Look at that! Just where I was aiming."

"Like fun." I started up the drive. "I have to get Rae inside. She's cold." I warmed her in my arm and ran for the door. My feet crunched over frozen puddles in the drive.

We children had to eat in the kitchen while the grown-ups ate in the dining room, but Bonnie got to eat with the grown-ups. "Since I'm twelve, I really ought to eat with the grown-ups, too," I informed Aunt Hannah.

"My table only holds eight, old dear, and you'll have a lot more fun with the other children. Nobody's going to talk about a thing except that war and Wash's farewell reception." The Chinese had warned that very day that they were going to launch a big attack sometime soon. The whole nation was holding its breath. "Would you take in these beans?"

I set the hot bowl on the blue damask cloth, the table gleaming with her best china, crystal, and silver. "There aren't but five grown-ups and Bonnie. You've set too many places."

"Jerry's coming and bringing Mrs. Cameron. Here they are now." She bustled out to greet them.

Mrs. Cameron shuffled up the walk and climbed the three steps like they were Everest. "Yon's the one insisted I heat my store," she cawed, shaking her cane at me. "I suppose you insisted I make the trip all the way down here for Christmas dinner, too."

"Not me," I assured her. "I could have sat with the grown-ups if you hadn't come."

She cackled like a crow. "Gettin' big for your britches, ain't you?" She shuffled into the warm living room, shedding a black coat on the floor. "Hang that up for me."

It was limp with age and smelled of her seldom washed hair. I put it on a hanger but didn't put it in Aunt Hannah's tight downstairs closet, just hung it over the top of the door.

I kept Rae with me all during dinner, which for some reason annoyed Preston. Or maybe he was annoyed because I got to keep my doll and he'd had to hang up his hat.

"Put down that silly doll," he commanded, waving a turkey leg.

Instead I held Rae up to look at him, then turned her back to me. "What? Yes, he is rude but don't mind him. He's never learned any manners whatsoever. Well yes, he does eat like a pig but maybe he can't help it. No, he's not very tall but he says he's fixing to get a growth spurt. What? Oh. I hope he does, too, or he'll be five feet tall the rest of his life."

I kept my voice low, for Janey Lou and Grace were washing pots and pans at the sink. As soon as they finished, Janey Lou's husband, Meek, was coming to get her. I'd lived with Uncle Stephen long enough to be sorry they had to do most of the work for our dinner as well as the work for their own. But I had lived with Aunt Kate long enough to know I'd be elbow-deep in dishwater myself before the day was done.

Abby and Sue Mary giggled, wiggled down, and brought their own dolls to the table. Abby held hers up to look at Preston and said, "If you doesn't brush your hair, it will stand up like Preston's."

Even Sue Mary told her new Sparkle Plenty doll boldly, "Don't gulp your tea like Preston."

They both collapsed into giggles.

"What's going on over there?" Janey Lou asked.

Before any of us could respond, Preston snatched my doll and dashed out the back door without coat, mittens, or even his cowboy hat.

I hared after him, ignoring Grace yelling from the porch, "Carley Marshall, you come right back here. You hear me? You don't have a coat!"

Preston slogged through the yard, wriggled under the old rail fence that surrounded Uncle Davy's back pasture, and headed down the hill. I followed, running as fast as I could on the slick, frosty grass. I got leaves on the tail of my new skirt climbing through the fence and soon had a stitch in my side. Icy air cut a hole in my windpipe. "Come back! I didn't mean to make you mad. I was just teasing. Bring her back, Preston. Don't hurt her!"

A sob rose in my throat. He'd ruin that taffeta dress with his greasy hands. And her hair would be a mess from the wind. "Come back!"

He didn't slow down at all. Leaped through a stand of high brown grass like he was a fat rabbit. Darted around pines like a fleet, fat deer. Straight for the gully. At the edge he turned and waited. His face was so pink, I could hardly see the freckles, and his bristly hair stood up like a hedgehog's in the chilly wind. He waited until I got close enough to see clearly; then he turned and hurled my new doll into the abyss.

I fell to my knees on the frosty edge, crying so hard that my glasses blurred. "Where is she? How could you be so hateful? I told you I was teasing. I'm sorry I was mean. But that doll was from my Big Mama, and she said it's the last one I'll ever get. Ever! And I love her so much. . . ." I clutched my aching side and sobbed.

He shuffled his feet and clenched his jaw. "You shouldn't have made fun of my growth spurt."

"Nothing I said was that bad. Where is my doll?" I pulled off my glasses and wiped them on my new skirt, but the wool blurred them even worse. My teeth chattered from cold.

"Right there on that old piece of tin. She's got the world's biggest bed."

Everything blurred without my glasses. I tugged out my blouse tail and wiped them good, then peered over the edge again. By then I was shaking so much from cold, I was afraid I'd fall over.

But there was very good news. While the gully was deep and the top of the old Model A was far below us, Rae lay like a bright splash of red and gold on the rust-streaked piece of tin Uncle Davy had said was part of old Mr. Cameron's roof. The tin was balanced on boxes and branches on our side of the gully, not more than eight feet below, and Uncle Davy's rolls of baling wire made almost a staircase down to it.

"You go right down there and get her," I ordered.

"Go yourself. I ain't 'lowed in the gully."

"You're chicken."

"Chicken yourself."

"I'll show you who's chicken." I looked for a place to go over. Most of the bank was hard red clay, but a good many bushes and even small trees grew out of it here and there. I spotted one place where, if I was careful, I ought to be able to climb down and pick her off the roof.

"You can't go down there," Preston objected when I headed toward it. "They's snakes live in that gully."

"It's too cold for snakes."

"Not winter snakes."

I hesitated. Nobody had ever told me about winter snakes, but that didn't mean there weren't any. Every day or two somebody mentioned something I had never heard about before.

Maybe this was a part of my education that had just been, so far, overlooked.

But I had to have Rae....

"Then you're coming, too, to watch for them. You threw her over and you're gonna help me get her out." My teeth chattered so hard, I could hardly shape the words.

"In our Sunday clothes?" He was shivering, too, his hands bright pink. Drops of water hung from his red nose.

I hesitated again. If I tore or ruined that suit, Aunt Kate would kill me and I could never face Big Mama again. But if I left Rae lying there, anything might happen to her before I persuaded a grown-up to come get her. In fact, grown-ups would probably think I should let her go and "get a new one." They never understood that a new one isn't the same.

"Come on," I ordered.

"I'm not going down there. Mama'd skin me alive."

"I'll skin you alive right now if you don't help me get that doll. Come on!" I dragged him by one arm to the place I'd chosen, where the bank looked more solid and a network of bushes made for even safer footing. "We can climb down and back in a minute," I coaxed.

I went first so he couldn't look up my skirt. Carefully I lay on my stomach and slid over the edge, feeling for the first bush I'd chosen. "I ain't comin'," Preston said stubbornly.

"If you don't, I'll go right back in there and tell everybody what you did. Now come on!"

He hesitated just a second. "You won't tell if I come?"

"Not if you come."

With a mighty sigh he hunched his bulk to the ground and started slithering over the side, knocking cold clods of dirt onto my head.

The bushes held our feet as we slowly descended. When a bush gave way, we clutched another. Slowly, too keyed up and panting to say a word, we made our way down that bank. Finally I reached the first baling wire step. It gave a bit, then held firm. One by one I stepped down those airy stairs until finally I felt something solid beneath my toe.

"I've reached the roof," I told him, panting. At least I didn't feel cold anymore, except my hands. They were so stiff, I could hardly hold on to branches. "You stay where you are, and I'll see if I can reach her without going out on it." I clutched a branch and stretched as far as I could, but she was just beyond my grasp.

He came down one more step and leaned over. "Hold my hand. That'll give you a few more inches." He reached out a pudgy, warty paw. I shuddered but took it. Mothers risk much for their children. It still wasn't enough.

"Hold me tight. I'm going to step just on one corner of the roof." I stepped onto the tin and stretched toward the doll. As my fingers clutched her skirt, I felt the tin beneath me shift. "It's moving!" I screamed. "It's falling!"

Preston jerked my hand, and his bush held firm, but I was too overbalanced.

One second I was standing on the edge of a piece of roof, holding his hand—the next I was sliding down the gully on that sheet of tin. It jarred and stopped but I kept falling, falling, screaming. Then everything went black.

Chapter 28

I was having a dreadful dream. I lay wet and cold on my bed and hurt so bad, I wasn't sure I could open my eyes. *Have I wet the bed?* In the middle of my pain I was mortified. And where was my cover? I wanted to grope for it, but my right arm was tight against my body, with my fingers clutching something I knew I must not let go. Pain shot from my left arm, which was bent at a funny angle under me. I tried to pull it out but it hurt too much to move. One leg felt warm but numb. I shivered, chilled to the bone, and whimpered. Why couldn't I wake up?

I forced myself to open my eyes. To my surprise I saw cold blue sky and blurry pines, not my bedroom ceiling. I turned my head just the teensiest bit and found I was not in bed but lying in a jumble of junk with a big tin wall towering above me. Down below the wall, just on the edge of my vision, swam a blurry circle made up of an aqua Mason jar, an overturned wooden box, a skeleton head, and several of Uncle Davy's old oil cans, glinting in the sun.

"Help! Oh, help me!" The pines swam above me in a dizzying circle. I shut my eyes again.

Voices, faint and alarmed, were coming nearer. "Where is she?" That voice I knew but could not remember who he was.

"Over here." A boy's voice, trembling and hoarse. "Almost at the bottom. She just fell. I didn't push her or anything." He sounded like he was blubbering.

"We'll need a rope, then." Uncle Davy's was the first voice I recognized.

"Help!" I cried weakly. "Help me."

"Carley?" I opened my eyes and saw blurry faces far above me. Had I died? Was that old Mr. Cameron and his first wife, peering over heaven, awaiting my coming?

"Carley!" I couldn't see the face but I knew that voice and saw sunlight glinting on his glasses.

"Uncle Stephen!" Rivulets of tears left warm trails on my cheeks and tasted salty when they reached my lips. I licked them greedily, savoring the warmth even as their trail turned to ice on my cheeks. "I can't see you. I can't see you!" Sobs shook me and made me wince with pain.

"You've lost your glasses. Don't move. Jerry's coming down and Davy's gone for a rope. Just lie very still."

"It hurts."

"I know it hurts, honey. But be brave. Lie very still. Please don't move."

Later he would tell me what he could see. "You were lying on Hannah's old mattress in the back of a Model A truck, one leg streaming blood, with part of a rusty tin roof suspended right above you. It was caught between a refrigerator and a bale of wire, but it looked as if the least movement would send it straight down on you, and its edge was sharp as a knife. I wanted to come down myself, but Jerry said he'd done that sort of rescue in the army, and he'd need me up top to haul the rope. I never prayed so hard in my life. Never."

I didn't know any of that. I was finally getting warm and I was feeling drowsy. While they bustled and worried above me, I closed my eyes and sank into a deep, unconscious sleep.

The next thing I knew, Mr. Donaldson was towering above me, shouting up to somebody, "I've got it braced. Haul on the rope." He was shoving the metal wall with one shoulder, pushing so hard that I could see the muscles in his thighs through his pants.

"One, two, three!" Uncle Stephen shouted above me, and I saw the wall move away. In an instant I heard an enormous crash as it fell to the gully floor.

Mr. Donaldson knelt beside me. "Carley, can you hear me?"

"Ummm." I was still drowsy and felt far away. Then I screamed. He had touched my shoulder. "Don't! That hurts my arm!"

He stroked my hair. "Don't! It hurts my arm!" I sobbed with pain, turning my head from side to side, trying to get away from it. Wherever I went, it followed.

"Her arm's broken," he called up, "and I have to get a tourniquet on this leg; then we'll need to make a stretcher of some sort to get her up. And get a blanket. She's freezing."

"Would the hammock work?" I heard Aunt Hannah ask above.

"Good idea!" That was Uncle Stephen, though I couldn't see him. I wondered if they were going to cover me with the hammock, but then Aunt Kate's coat landed near me, and Mr. Donaldson tucked it over me. I was still soaked and cold underneath, worried that I had wet the bed, but the warmth on top was delicious.

Above me I saw a round green blob—Preston's jacket. He peered over the edge. A bigger blob must be Miss Pauline beside him, holding fast to his collar. "Don't you fall over, too, now."

Pain shot from my leg and my arm, a vortex of hurting that sucked me down, down, down. Mr. Donaldson had grabbed my leg and was tying a white cloth above my knee. He wrapped the rag around it, holding one end in his teeth. The rag looked a lot like Uncle Stephen's white shirt. I peered down, hoping my skirt hadn't come up so he could see my underpants. "I have to do this," he mumbled around a mouthful of rag when he saw me watching him, "so we can move you. I'll bet it's the first time you've been tied up by a one-armed man."

I smiled weakly, thinking it was the first time I'd heard Mr. Donaldson make a joke.

"I did a lot of this sort of thing in the war," he continued, tying my leg so tight that I cried out again. "We have to stop the bleeding until we can get you up. They've called for an ambulance and it ought to be here soon."

"Hello!" I heard another voice calling from the top. "I've had first aid. Shall I come down?" Jay stood at the lip of the gully. Without waiting for an answer, he nimbly leapt over the edge, scrabbled for a foothold. In another minute he stood beside me, concern in his dark eyes.

He gave me a smile. "Looks like your guardian angel was working overtime, landing you smack on that mattress—even if it is soaking wet. Next time pick one that hasn't been out in the rain."

"Hey, Jay." I smiled. It was good to know I hadn't wet the bed after all.

He turned to Mr. Donaldson. "Before we move her, think we'd better splint that arm?"

"We should, but I can't do it."

"You got any more of that shirt? Let me try." Jay looked around and ripped a board from an old orange crate. "Now, Carley, this is going to hurt, but I've got to immobilize that arm before we try to move you." He took my shoulder to lift me off my left arm.

Pain like fire ran through my whole body. I wanted desperately to be brave but couldn't help whimpering. Mr. Donaldson reached into his back pocket and shoved his wallet into my mouth. "Bite this. It will help." I chomped down on the leather as Jay took my shoulder again, sending a pain up my arm that made me gasp. I blacked out again, tasting leather.

Next thing I knew, Uncle Stephen was standing beside me, too, or at least the top half of him was, holding Aunt Hannah's hammock. "Watch out for snakes," I whispered.

"Snakes hibernate in winter."

"Not winter snakes."

"There aren't any winter snakes. We'll have you out of here in a jiffy."

Mr. Donaldson lifted my head, and Uncle Stephen slid part of Aunt Hannah's hammock under me. Together Jay and Uncle Stephen lifted me, and Mr. Donaldson awkwardly slid the hammock under me. "Now if we can tie ropes securely to each end ..."

Uncle Stephen took a step back. "Don't step on the man's head!" I tried to point with my good arm. Now I saw what I'd been holding so tight. Rae's skirt. She was a mess—cheeks cracked, one eye hanging from its socket, the other missing, her lovely red dress streaked with grease and torn.

Jay spoke softly to Mr. Donaldson. "She must be hallucinating."

"There's a man there," I insisted weakly. "I saw his head. Near a blue jar."

Uncle Stephen turned, then sucked in a whistle. "Jerry, Jay ..."

He moved to one side. Since I was now lying on my side, I could see better, too. Between a blurred aquamarine Mason jar and a weathered wooden box lay the head I'd seen. And just beyond it was a long, white bone partly covered in tattered blue.

Chapter 29

M r. Donaldson jumped down from beside me and gently fingered faded remnants of cloth. "That looks a lot like a Statesville High jacket. Could it be Taylor?" He squatted down beside the skull. "Remember the boy I was telling you about just last night? He was wearing a blue jacket the night he disappeared."

Uncle Stephen bent down for a closer look. "Whoever it is, he's been down here awhile." He straightened. "Let's get Carley up; then we'll call the police."

Mr. Donaldson looked up at him, his face white and his eyes wet. "If it's him, I didn't put him here. I swear before God I didn't. But do you think they'll believe me?"

Uncle Stephen put one hand on his shoulder. "Sure they will." I certainly hoped so.

They got me out of the gully by tying ropes to each end of the hammock and around its middle. Uncle Stephen, Jay, and Uncle Davy hauled while Mr. Donaldson climbed up alongside me to nudge the hammock off branches and debris. It felt a lot like Big Mama had said it felt to have a baby: I hurt so much that at times I wished I'd just die and get it over with, but I didn't. Whenever I see a modern rescue team on television, I think of the makeshift equipment they had to use to get me out of that abyss.

I didn't really see who all was up there waiting for me; I just saw Aunt Kate hovering by the edge of the gully watching every move and calling out sharp commands. "Don't let her hit that branch. Is her head lower than her feet?" I could tell she was worried. She was also pinched and pink with cold, because I still had her coat. But although she was shivering, she kept refusing the old brown coat Aunt Hannah kept holding out to her, the one she used to feed the hens and must have snatched up as she ran out the door.

"Take it; I'm not cold. I never feel the cold." Aunt Hannah bent down and peered over the edge of the gully, clucking like one of her own biddies. "We're so glad to see you, old dear. I just couldn't believe you fell down there. You'll be fine, just you wait and see. They'll get you out in just a second...." A mile a minute, as usual.

As soon as I was swung safely over the rim, Uncle Stephen dropped his rope and clasped me in his arms, hammock and all. I sobbed almost as much from happiness as from pain.

"You need your coat," I told Aunt Kate, trying to push it off me.

"Here's another one." Bonnie came breathlessly, having run from the house. She carried Aunt Hannah's best black coat. When Aunt Kate put it on, it nearly dragged the ground and the sleeves covered her hands. She didn't seem to care. She stood right by my head, stroking my hair with tears streaming down her cheeks.

Aunt Hannah put a large hand on her shoulder. "Don't cry. She's gonna be all right." She bent down and gave me a little pat. "You're going to be fine, Carley, do you hear me? Just fine—"

"Yeah," Miss Pauline interrupted. "Remember Preston last year this time?" The past Christmas Eve Preston had been hit by a car that broke his leg. "In a few months you'll be good as new, sugar."

Preston hadn't been very good when he was new, but I didn't say that, because I had just seen him, shivering and sniffing like he'd been crying already. Misery looked out of his piggy little blue eyes. "They think I pushed you." He wiped his nose on one sleeve. "Tell them I didn't, Carley. Tell them."

I was so glad right that minute that I felt charitable toward the whole living world. "He didn't push me," I muttered. "He even tried to save me. He just couldn't."

"He came and got help," Bonnie added loyally.

Uncle Stephen reached out and rumpled his bristly hair. "We're very grateful, Preston."

Preston stood a little taller. "Want me to help you carry her in, sir? I'm strong for my size. I'm almost ready for my growth spurt." He shot me a scared look in case I remembered that had started all this, but I didn't say anything.

"I think I can manage, thanks," Uncle Stephen told him. His arms were warm and solid beneath me, and he held me as close as if I'd been Abby or John. Once he even lightly kissed the top of my head.

"Let me have that doll," Aunt Kate commanded. "She doesn't need it. It's filthy now—"

"No!" I screamed, clutching Rae so hard that her sharp little fingers pricked my arm.

Aunt Kate stepped back like I'd slapped her. "All right. You can keep her. For now."

As we neared the house, we saw Janey Lou and Grace standing on the back porch holding Abby and Sue Mary back from joining the others. "Is Carley deaded?" Abby hollered across the lawn. She sounded more curious than grieving.

"No, I'm not dead," I tried to holler back. It came out a pitiful little croak.

"Pretty much alive," Uncle Stephen assured her. "And listen. Do you hear the ambulance up at the highway? Go meet them and tell them to come inside."

"But stay off the drive and out of their way," Aunt Kate added.

Delighted to be part of the action, Abby and Sue Mary scampered through the kitchen to the porch on the other side of the house.

Grace held the back door open, her eyes wide and worried. "I'm okay," I told her, trying to smile. "Just broke my arm. Can't sew for a while."

She smiled back. "Can't wash dishes, either. Some people will go to great lengths—" She broke off, for Jay was coming in after us.

"Jay splinted my arm so they could move me," I told her.

She looked at him with big, grateful eyes.

"Could someone get a pillow for the couch, and a warm blanket?" he asked, looking at her.

"I'll get it," Bonnie offered.

"No, let me." Grace headed toward Aunt Hannah's bedroom, and Bonnie stood off to one side of the room looking like she wanted to help but didn't know how.

Janey Lou stood by the table murmuring, "Sweet baby, oh, Jesus, take care of that sweet baby. Take care of that sweet baby." Lapped in prayer and love but still hurting too bad to talk much, I turned my cheek further into Uncle Stephen's chest so nobody could see the tears streaming down my cheeks.

Mrs. Cameron sat in a straight chair beside the couch. "Back again?" she cawed. "I knew you'd take more killin' than that."

"I saw Mr. and Mrs. Cameron," I told her drowsily as Uncle Stephen laid me on the couch. "Up in heaven waiting . . ."

"It's me they're waitin' for," she said tartly. "Took one look at you and sent you back."

"Here's the pillow and blanket." Grace handed them to Jay.

He made sure I was as comfortable as possible, then took both Grace's hands in his. "She's going to be fine. Stop trembling." Grace kept trembling but she didn't take away her hands.

"Did you get the head, too?" I asked.

Grace looked puzzled. "What's she talking about, the head?"

Jay drew her away, too far for me to hear.

I don't remember much about what happened after that. Men in white came and one of them gave me a shot. I dozed while they took me out and put me in what looked like a hearse. I was awake enough to want to wave at people on our way to Davis Hospital so they'd know I wasn't dead, but I didn't have the energy.

Very late that night, after everything was dark, a large shadow came into my hospital room and stood by my bed. More asleep than awake, I knew at once what it was: Big Mama's ghost. But it felt so friendly, I put out one hand. To my delight its arm was thick and warm. "You awake?" it asked.

"Yes, ma'am. What you doin' here?"

"Kate called to tell me what had happened and that you all wouldn't be coming to my place tomorrow, so I thought I'd come to you. You feeling all right?"

"Yes, ma'am."

"Then go back to sleep. I'll stay a little while and slip out but I'll be back in the morning."

She didn't say another word, just held my hand until I fell fast asleep.

The next morning Big Mama herself walked in with Aunt Kate, as early as they'd let them upstairs. "My arm feels better," I told them groggily, "but my leg is real sore."

"It's infected," Aunt Kate told me. "You aren't to walk on it, even to the bathroom, and they're coming in a few minutes to give you a penicillin shot."

"I already had a tetanus shot," I protested.

Big Mama patted my hand. "That was for lockjaw. The penicillin is for the infection."

"Lockjaw might or might not be a blessing," Aunt Kate teased from the foot of my bed.

"My arm's broken in three places, Big Mama." I held up the heavy cast that went from my shoulder to the tips of my fingers. "You can sign it if you want to." She dutifully added her name in handwriting as neat and round as she. "I had a minor concussion, too. Everything was real fuzzy until this morning. Was that you last night or your ghost?"

"I felt like a ghost." She sat heavily in my visitor's chair. "Don't ever scare me like that again. I practically flew getting here."

I giggled at the thought of my stout, round grandmother flying through the air. Then I remembered Rae. "I ruined my doll and my suit. I'm so sorry." I couldn't help crying.

"Dolls and suits are replaceable. You aren't." She sat patting my shoulder until I slept.

After Uncle Stephen took her home to rest awhile, though, I told Aunt Kate, "I think she's really mad at me for ruining the suit and Rae. She kept making her lips real tight."

"No, honey." She smoothed my blanket. "She was trying not to cry, too."

On her way back to the hospital, Big Mama had Uncle Stephen take her to buy a new doll that looked exactly the same to everybody else. I liked her and I named her Nancy for Nancy Drew, but she wasn't Rae. After Big Mama went back home, I had Aunt Kate put Nancy on my windowsill. Rae stayed by my pillow—no matter what Aunt Kate said about germs.

Some parts about being in the hospital were grim. The cast was heavy and soon started itching far down inside where I couldn't scratch. My leg was sore and had to stay propped up on pillows. I missed Mr. Wash's farewell party and was real sorry not to get to say good-bye. I kept telling myself he'd be back, but the Chinese communists were threatening a huge attack any day now, and I figured I might have seen him for my very last time on Christmas Morning. I hadn't even spoken to him then. That worried me so much that Uncle Stephen promised to get me an address where I could write him when I got better.

But being in the hospital wasn't all bad. I had a funny, jolly nurse who pretended to be gruff but wasn't. A lot of people came to bring candy, fruit, coloring books, books to read, and a couple of stuffed animals. A lot more called the manse to be sure I was doing all right. Aunt Kate said she was going to start answering calls, "Carley Marshall's Information Service." Uncle Stephen brought the paper each afternoon and read it with me. I couldn't hold it with the cast, and besides, I liked his company. Every day the top headline was news of the war. Were the Chinese really about to attack or not? I was real worried about that. "Looks like if we think they are going to attack, we could attack them first."

"We aren't at war with them. You can't attack somebody just because they threaten you. Now's here a funny story. They've found a still just south of Loray." Loray wasn't far from Job's Corner. "It was down by a creek, out of sight, and guess how they disguised it?" He didn't wait. "Under an old chicken house."

"What's a still?"

"A contraption for making liquor." He lit his pipe as he took his seat, and puffed clouds of cherry tobacco smoke to fill my room. "The man was making a hundred gallons a day."

I was scornful. "Nobody could drink that much."

"He was a bootlegger—somebody who makes liquor to sell."

"That's immoral!" All Big Mama's Baptist upbringing rose up within me in disgust.

"It's also illegal. In North Carolina folks are only supposed to buy liquor from state-run stores that collect taxes on it. People who make liquor—bootleggers—don't pay those taxes, so they sell it cheaper. The state doesn't like that. Iredell County has been having a big crackdown on local stills lately." He settled in his chair and riffled the pages. "Here. You want the funnies?"

Aunt Kate came each morning until school started again. She brought messages from the people who called. She also brought pictures from Abby to tape on my wall. Every picture, captioned in Grace's neat capitals, depicted the accident: *Carley falls down the gully. Carley on Uncle Davy's truck. Carley getting pulled up from the gully. Carley's broken arm. Carley riding in an ambulance. Carley's poor doll.* The last one had Rae in seven pieces scattered all over the page. One, a bent piece, was labeled, *Rae's broken arm, like Carley's.*

One afternoon when Uncle Stephen came, he had arranged a surprise. They let him put me in a wheelchair and take me downstairs to see Abby in the waiting room. "Dey won't lets me go up 'til I's twelve," she grumbled, lower lip stuck out.

"But I tell you what, Carley Cousin. When I's twelve, you fall down de gully again, and if you don't get deaded and come to de hospital, I'll come see you ebery day. What's dat on your arm?"

"It's a cast." I held it out for her inspection and invited her to knock it to see how hard it was. She was more interested in the names written on it. "*B-o-n-n-i-e,*" she spelled. "Dat's Bonnie. How come you got *Bonnie* on your cass?"

"People write their names on it to show they've been to see me."

"Can I write, too?"

"When she comes home, Abbikins," her daddy promised. "I don't have a pen with me. You want a ride in her wheelchair?"

She was so entranced with the wheelchair, she made him take her up the hall three times. Then she sat beside me and prattled on about new words John could say and what she and Sue Mary were learning in school. "Velma doesn't read, but Sue Mary says she is real good in 'rith-mo-nic.'" But when her daddy finally said, "I've got to take Carley upstairs so we can go home," she flung herself at my lap and burst into tears. "I misses you so much, I can't hardly stand it."

I stroked her red curls. "I'll be home before you know it, honey."

In the elevator, trying to keep from crying myself, I asked Uncle Stephen, "What about the head I found?"

"The police are investigating it. They've found more bones where they'd washed down the gully, and they're working on identifying it. That's all I know."

He was worried about it for some reason, though. I'd lived with him and Aunt Kate plenty long enough to be able to read their faces.

Part 4

In the Bleak Midwinter ...

January–February 1951

Chapter 30

I was worried, too, right then, but not about the skeleton in our gully. I was terrified because the Chinese kept threatening to attack South Korea, and if they did, a lot of people—including me—thought President Truman was sure to drop another atomic bomb. After all, that's what it had taken to end the last war. Why wouldn't he use it again? And we didn't even have a shelter.

January first, the day before Uncle Stephen came to take me home, the Chinese made good their threat and launched a savage attack. I tossed and turned all night, wondering if the bomb had already been dropped, if the Russians had dropped one on America, and if radiation was oozing in my hospital window. The instant Uncle Stephen came into my room the next morning, I demanded, "Did he drop it? Did the Russians bomb us, too?"

"Heavens no." He sounded so normal, I stopped worrying for about a minute.

"Between being worried about that bomb and excited about finally going home, she's going to make herself sick," my nurse warned him as she packed my things.

"She'd better be worried about how we're going to get all that stuff in my poor car. I didn't think about her having all those presents and flowers, so I didn't empty out my trunk. We may have to tie her on top. Do you have to take *both* dolls?"

I clutched Rae to me because I knew which one he would leave behind. "I need them both. I'll carry them."

The nurse considered my six vases of flowers. "If you don't need all these, I could give some to people who haven't gotten any." I chose two—Aunt Hannah's orchid in a basket and the pink roses Uncle Stephen and Aunt Kate had sent. She carried the others to the nurses' station.

The way those grown-ups joked and laughed packing up my stuff, you'd think they'd never heard of an atomic bomb. I pressed my lips together and decided I'd wait until I got Uncle Stephen alone in the car.

But we weren't going to be alone. The nurse came down to make sure we got everything in all right, and as soon as the elevator door opened, she exclaimed, "Isn't she just darlin'!" Abby perched on a chair across the waiting room, red curls glowing. Uncle Stephen must have told her not to leave her chair, because she was so close to the edge, she was about to fall off. Her lower lip, though, looked like a little pink shelf, and as soon as we stepped out of the elevator, she yelled, "You been a *bery* long time. You said dist a *minute*. My cwayon got melted." She held up a bent red crayon, soft from being held so long. "Now I can't wite on Carley's cass."

"It was a long minute," her daddy agreed. "We had a lot to pack."

"But I have a pencil in my pocket. Here." The nurse handed her a pencil. Little pink tongue sticking out one corner of her mouth, Abby carefully wrote *A-B-B-Y* on my forearm.

"Okay." Uncle Stephen looked at the boxes, flowers, and suitcase. "Let's see how all this stuff plus you two are going to fit in this car."

Abby climbed in back. "Come on, Carley. You can ride wif me."

"She can't get in the back, honey," the nurse told her. "She still has a very sore leg." Uncle Stephen's old Chevy only had two doors. When that lower lip shot out again, the nurse added quickly, "But can I put you in charge of her presents and these pretty flowers? Take good care of them, now." When she put the orchid basket on Abby's lap and packed the rest of my things around her, Abby sat holding the basket handle like she'd been appointed to guard a queen.

The nurse tucked me in the front seat with the roses between my feet. "Don't forget, the doctor says to stay home until you can walk without pain, and don't climb stairs for a week."

Uncle Stephen swung into his seat and lit his pipe before he started the engine. "Everybody ready?" The nurse waved as long as we could see her.

As we drove toward Front Street, I scanned the sky. So far it was mercifully clear of Russian bombers, but who knew how long that would last?

"Where's Mr. Truman going to drop the atomic bomb? If he drops it in Korea, he could hit our own men. And if he drops it in China, he won't hit Chinese soldiers; he'll just hit their wives and children."

"That's one of the problems with bombs." Uncle Stephen sucked hard on his pipe and blew out a small cloud of sweet blue smoke. "My guess is, he won't drop it at all."

"But will you finally dig us a bomb shelter? Please? Just because he doesn't drop a bomb this week doesn't mean the Russians won't drop one on us next week."

He puffed in exasperation. Abby called, "Dat's too much smoke in here, Daddy."

He ignored her to answer me. "You've seen a globe. Do you remember where Russia is?" I nodded but he told me anyway. "It's halfway around the world. And we're a good ways inland. How far do you think our soldiers would let a Russian plane carrying a bomb get from California? Or even from the Atlantic coast? Do you really think they'd ever get this far?"

I thought about that a second, then laid my head back and closed my eyes. Big round tears of relief rolled down my cheeks. I bowed my head over the two dolls in my lap, but I couldn't hide from Little Sharp Eyes in the backseat. "Tell her you're sorry," Abby commanded. "You made her mad, Daddy."

I shook my head. "I'm not mad. I'm glad. I've been so scared...."

Scared of bombs. Scared of my broken arm. Scared I would die of infection. Scared, scared, scared. And now everything was going to be all right. I was going home and we weren't going to get bombed. So why did that make me cry? I didn't know but I couldn't stop.

He reached out and laid one hand on my cast. "Let the grown-ups do the worrying. You'll be a grown-up yourself soon enough and can worry then for your own children."

I nodded but I couldn't speak. Even though I pressed my lips together so hard that I could feel my teeth, the tears fell like a stream whose dam has suddenly been lowered.

When Abby leaned up and patted my shoulder, I cried even harder. Finally Uncle Stephen warned, "If you flood the car, you'll kill your flowers. They don't like salt water."

That made me laugh. Laughing and crying at the same time got me so strangled, he had to thump me on the back, which made the car go all which way on the road.

"Watch out!" Abby shouted as we zigged toward the center line and a big truck.

Uncle Stephen straightened up. "Okay, can we get home without a flood or a wreck?"

I nodded and discovered I could smile at last. I felt so good, I almost didn't mind the heavy cast or the ache in my leg.

As soon as we got home and Uncle Stephen carried me inside, Abby jumped up and down. "Can we show her now, Daddy? Now?" He nodded and she clutched her hands under her chin and grinned. "We's got a secwet. Look!"

She flung open the door to the living room. It was a good thing Uncle Stephen was still holding me, or I might have sat flat on the floor. We had a brand-new sofa almost like Aunt Hannah's, except ours was gold and blue. "We gots it while you was in de hospital. It's Duncan Phyfe." Abby pronounced it so carefully, I knew she'd been practicing. "See de little fwuits carved on de back? Aunt Hannah's got woses, and carved fwuits and woses is Duncan Phyfe. Mama says," she added in case I didn't believe her.

"What else does Mama say?" Uncle Stephen asked.

"We're not to sit on it or eben touch it wifout a grown-up, but we can sit on de floor beside it and breave. It smells lovely. Look!" She plopped down beside the couch and sniffed the cushions. "Ummm."

"You want to stay down here awhile or go upstairs?" Uncle Stephen asked.

As much as I'd wanted to be home, I wanted my own bed. "Upstairs, please." As we left the room, I threw one look over his shoulder at the piano and wished I could sit there for an hour and play out everything I was feeling—happy to be home, relieved we lived too far for the Russians to bomb us, sadness about Rae, and heartbreak that I wasn't good enough to play in public. I used to get real nice compliments after piano recitals back at Big Mama's when I was a child, and when I played by myself I felt good enough for Carnegie Hall, but playing with Freda had showed me I had better play just for my own pleasure. It sure wasn't anybody else's.

I had thought one thing through while I was in the hospital, though. Even if I never intended to play in public again, I still wanted to go to music camp so bad, I could almost put out a hand and feel it. I figured even if I played worse than anybody there, I'd at least get to spend a week around other kids who didn't think it was weird to like music. And I'd never have to see them again if I messed up really bad.

Grace came from the kitchen to greet us, her face shining with gladness to see me. Little John toddled out behind her and shouted, "Leelee! Leelee!" He flung his arms around his daddy's legs and shouted, "Up!"

"Sorry, old man, I can't carry two of you." But Uncle Stephen bent down so John could give me a very wet kiss.

"Let me carry the dolls," Grace suggested. I handed her Nancy but kept Rae myself. She reached out one gentle hand and stroked Rae's scratched cheek. "Poor baby, she's had a rough time. Maybe we can fix her up a little." I gave her a grateful smile. She was the first person not to suggest just throwing her away. "Let's get you in bed now." She turned and hurried up ahead of us, calling over her shoulder, "I put my heater in your room and hot water bottles between your sheets. I think you'll be warm enough."

Big Mama's quilt and my own pillows. "Bed never looked so good," I told her.

Her gold tooth flashed as she smiled. "You can be a princess in your tower for a while."

"More like a knight in armor. This cast itches so bad, I can hardly stand it."

"Here." She reached into my closet for a hanger and straightened it out. "Reach down inside and scratch real gently."

That was the most practical medical advice I'd gotten all week.

As Uncle Stephen deposited me on the bed, he teased, "Boy, you weigh a ton. You've gotten fat lying around. I need to rest before I carry you down again."

"It's my cast," I protested. But somehow having him carry me made me feel funny in a way I couldn't name. "Can I just stay up here until I can climb stairs? Or is it too much trouble to bring up my meals?"

"No more trouble than his carrying you down," Grace told me. "But don't you think you'll get lonely?"

"I'll have my books and my new clock radio." While I was at the hospital, somebody had set a straight chair beside my bed and found an extension cord that would stretch all the way to the single plug in my room, beneath my desk. The radio—pink, gorgeous, and all mine—sat within easy reach. I leaned over and gave it a pat. I'd never imagined having a radio of my very own.

"And me," Abby added virtuously. "I'll take care of her. Do you need a dwink, Carley?" But before I could even answer, while Grace was heading back downstairs and Uncle Stephen to his study, she peered at the clock. "Oh!" She reached for the

radio button. "Dis is de time when dey has a funny show. Me'n
Sue Mary listens to it all de time wif Miss Pauline."

A woman's voice filled my room. "Oh, darling, I love you
so much. But my husband will be home any minute."

A man's deep voice answered, "Give me a kiss, then, and
I'll go." We heard a loud smack.

Abby giggled. "Isn't dey funny? Dey's all de time kissin'."
She pressed her ear closer to the speaker as a door slammed and
another man called, not so loudly, "Honey, I'm home."

Abby scrunched her head into her neck in delight. "Now
her daddy's comin' and he's gonna be *mad*."

Her own daddy came back instead. He crossed the room
and turned off the radio before we knew he was there. "That's
enough of that. Carley needs to rest." Carley wanted to hear
the show, but I could tell from his face it wasn't any good asking. I checked the clock so I could turn it on another day when
he wasn't around.

"I needs to west, too. I sat in dat waitin' room forty-leven
hours." Abby tugged off her shoes, climbed up beside me, and
slid under the covers. As anybody who knew her could have
predicted, her head was on the pillow about two seconds before
she sat straight up. Uncle Stephen hadn't even left the room.

"I gots six new liberry books we can wead. Dist a
minute. . . ." At the door she turned, propped one fist on her
hip, and commanded, "Wait wight dere, Daddy, so's you can
see how long a minute *is*."

All morning she and I read books and rested, looking over
the bare branches of the maples to the Keene house high on its
brown, wintry hill. Abby also asked a hundred questions about
"upstairs" in the hospital, like "But *how* does dey make de bed
go up and down? Could you touch de ceiling?" Years later I
could sympathize when astronauts tried to answer reporters'
questions about what it was really like on the moon.

Grace brought up a tray with two sandwiches and two
steaming bowls of soup. After Abby and I ate, we curled up in
my double bed and took a nap. When we woke, I found that

Rae's hair had been neatly brushed, her face rubbed with cream to take out some of the scratches, and her dress washed, ironed, and mended. Her left eye had been put back into its socket, although slightly askew. The other socket was empty, her nose was chipped, and she would never be beautiful, but I loved her better for that.

"The good fairy did it," Grace teased when I thanked her.

"Good Fairy Grace," I retorted.

❀

If I'd expected to lie around doing nothing, I had another think coming. Aunt Kate brought home all my books and assignments. "Stephen will check your work and give you your tests."

"I could go for Carley dis week," Abby wheedled. "I can wead."

"You can't even talk plain," I scoffed. "While I'm home, you are going to learn to talk right. It's *read*, not *wead*, and *this*, not *dis*."

Abby glowered. "I has to say *wead* and *dis*. Only people who go to real school say *read* and *this*." We stared at her in astonishment. Her grammar was perfect and both words came out clear as a bell. She put her little freckled nose in the air and stomped down the stairs.

Thursday Uncle Stephen came upstairs and dropped the newspaper on my bedspread. "Did you call the president? Says here he's got no plans to drop a bomb."

I heaved a sigh of relief. "I didn't call him but I'm glad." I picked up the paper and read the first paragraphs of another article. "Where's North Indochina? This says the French are launching their biggest offensive yet there."

"I'm not sure where it is. Near China, I believe. It has nothing to do with us." Twenty years later when John was slogging his way through Vietnamese jungles, we would remember that conversation.

I quickly moved on to the article about what the *Statesville Daily Record* was calling the Job's Corner Gully Mystery. "Hey! Did you read this? They know it's really Taylor Hart, who used to live in the Keenes' house. It says they used dental records and what was left of his jacket to positively identify him." I hurried to the next paragraph. "And it says they found most of his skeleton carried by all that rain down the gully...." As I read the next paragraph, I gasped. "And he has a hole in the back of his skull! He must have been murdered!"

"May have been," Uncle Stephen corrected me, reaching for the sports page and settling into the upholstered chair they'd brought up from their bedroom for my visitors. "It says 'may have been murdered.' I think he probably knocked a hole in his skull when he fell."

I shook my head. "Hunh-unh. This says that's what they thought at first, but a medical expert says if that were true, his head would have split like a cantaloupe, but because it was dented in, he got hit before he fell."

"Medical experts aren't always right."

"But—"

He rustled his paper like he always did when he'd rather be reading it than talking. "I think we should wait and see." That's what he said to everybody who came by that afternoon and wanted to talk about it, too.

I was almost relieved when Preston came by after *Western Theater* and settled himself on the side of my bed without being invited. If anybody knew anything, it would be Preston. But since it was the middle of the week, he smelled like he hadn't bathed since Saturday. He bounced happily on my springs, making my cast bounce on my hipbone. I'd be as bruised as Miss Emily if he kept that up. "Looks like we've got Job's Corner's second annual murder," he announced. "Last winter it was Ira Baines, and now everybody at the post office is talkin' about who killed the Hart boy and threw him in the gully."

I leaned forward and spoke soft so Uncle Stephen wouldn't hear in his study next door. "Do they *know* yet who did it?"

Preston bounced again and got so pink with excitement, his freckles stood out like orange dots. I shifted so my cast lay beside me instead of on top of me. "I can't say right now," he said importantly, "'cause he ain't been arrested."

"You don't even know."

"Do too. If you won't tell, I'll tell you."

"Who?"

"Mr. Donaldson, that's who! We're gonna have to get another new principal."

"You're crazy. He didn't do it."

"Just you wait, Smarty-pants. You'll see. Now, you want me to tell you about *Western Theater*? You missed a real good show. You oughta seen it—"

But before he could launch into his usual garbled version of a plot, we heard Miss Pauline bellowing down the road. "Supper must be ready. See you tomorrow." He slid off the bed and left, gone but not forgotten. He left a potent smell of dirty boy.

That evening Uncle Stephen brought up the checkerboard after supper. "Want a game?"

"Sure, but you need to know what Preston is saying. He says people think Mr. Donaldson—"

Uncle Stephen held up his hand. "All that happened before we got here, and we don't know a blessed thing about it, but you know as well as I do that Jerry Donaldson never killed anybody. Now, do you want me to beat you with reds or blacks?"

※

For days the war news was dreadful. The communists took cities with names I couldn't pronounce and cut off escape routes for our retreating soldiers. For a few days we feared they'd trap and destroy our entire eighth army. We prayed every night for Mr. Wash, and Abby reported, "When Miss Nancy comes to de post office, her eyes is red and watery all de time."

Aunt Kate and Uncle Stephen were pretty quiet. They still wouldn't talk about the murder with me, but I suspected that if I could creep downstairs at night, I'd hear them talking in their room. Mr. Donaldson hadn't been by the house since I got home.

Mrs. Raeburn came one sunny afternoon, though, bringing letters from every student in my class. She signed my cast and gave me a bar of rose-scented soap and *Little Women*, which I'd never read. She smelled like a fairy tale, mysterious and hopeful, and her yellow hair shone in the sunbeams streaming through my window. "What a wonderful room!" she exclaimed. "I love all those windows."

"I do, too. I love to watch the moon come up over there, and sometimes if I wake up real early"—I drew a rainbow in the air—"I see it go down over there."

"A room full of moonbeams! I've always wanted one of those." Then she noticed Rae. "Poor baby." She picked up the doll and stroked her ruined hair. "Did she fall with you?"

"No, ma'am. She fell first. I was trying to reach her when that old tin roof slid out from under me."

She touched Rae's empty eye socket. "You must love her very much. What's her name?"

"Rae—uh, Rachel," I lied. I couldn't bear for her to suspect whom I'd named Rae for.

"Well, Rachel"—she tucked the doll back beside my pillow—"I have a friend, Suzy, who looks a lot like you. And I keep her for the same reason Carley keeps you, I suspect. You get real attached to a doll who's been through a lot with you."

I glowed. I always knew Mrs. Raeburn and I could be friends. We thought exactly alike.

"Won't you stay for a cup of coffee?" Aunt Kate invited from the door. That was how she always got people to leave when she thought they were wearing me out.

Mrs. Raeburn turned to leave. "I really can't today. I have somewhere to go tonight and I need to dress." She was already dressed, as far as I was concerned. When I grew up, I was going to buy a smart black-and-white checked suit just like that one, and a black blouse with a big bow at the neck. I hadn't even known they made black blouses.

When she was gone, I lay quietly, holding my new rose soap close under my nose, lapped in happiness. Then I read the letters. Most students had written things like "Hope you get well soon" and "We're sorry you got hurt," but one girl wrote a long, newsy letter, concluding,

> Well, I'd better go. Excuse my writing. It's wobbly because it's dark in here. I'm writing during a movie— another one about Sealtest Dairy. This one is about Lewis Pasture, who first taught them to pasturize their milk. I guess he'd have to work on cows, with a name like that. The man who came to show the first movie is here again, and he and Mrs. Raeburn are holding hands in the back of the room. They think we can't see them but we can. I wonder how many movies he has?

Chapter 31

Poor Grace went around worried in those days. Her sister Pearl's girl, Geena, who was my age, was having bad stomach pains, and the doctor couldn't find out what was the matter. Every time they went for another test, Pearl went up to Big Mama's to tell her what the doctor said, and then Big Mama wrote Grace.

"Why doesn't Pearl just write you herself?" I asked.

Grace looked down at her hands. "Pearl never learned to read or write. Maybe someday Geena and I can teach her." I tried to imagine what it would be like not to be able to read, but I couldn't.

Thank goodness Jay was still home from college and could take Grace's mind off Geena for a while every day. He came over every evening, and they sat in the kitchen or up in the sewing room laughing and talking. A couple of times they went to a movie in his mama's old Plymouth. I heard her tell Aunt Kate one night after he'd gone whistling out our front door, "I'd forgotten how funny that man can be." I also heard her add under her breath as she went to her own room, "He deserves a lot better than me."

One night she was sewing when he came. I heard him go into the room and softly close the door. In a few minutes I limped to the bathroom in time to hear him say, like they were arguing, "You can't keep pushing me away forever, Grace. What's the matter with you?"

"I can't help it," she said angrily. "I can't ever feel that way about a man again. Not even you. I just can't!"

"That's not what you said last summer, honey," Jay protested. "What's changed?"

I heard Uncle Stephen hanging up the phone downstairs, so I hurried on down the hall in case he came up to his study. When I came back from the bathroom and passed the sewing center, I heard Grace's voice like a low moan. "So now you know. I am so ashamed, Jay. So very ashamed." She began to cry so softly, I could scarcely hear.

Jay shouted. "I could kill him! If he was here, I'd wring his fat neck."

"But it's made a difference, hasn't it?" she said bitterly. "You're looking at me different."

"I'm not looking at you any different."

"Yes, you are. You've got a . . . a sort of speculative look, like you're wondering if I wanted Ronnie to do that to me."

"You're crazy." His voice was so near the door, I had to practically run to get into my room before he stormed out. Grace sobbed softly in the sewing center.

I heard the front door slam, and in a second I heard Uncle Stephen going after Jay. I limped to my window and watched them stand in the road. Jay waved his arms. Uncle Stephen jabbed the air with his pipe to make a point. After a while Uncle Stephen came back in, but Jay stood under one of the maples, leaning on its trunk like he couldn't stand on his own.

I saw him look up, like he was praying, and I saw him kick the tree. I saw him rest his forehead against that thick trunk while his shoulders heaved. Then he turned and came back in the front door. I heard him climb the stairs like he was an old man and they were as high as Mount Everest. He tapped softly on the door. "Grace?" He went in without waiting for her to answer.

I tiptoed to the door and listened hard. I heard him say, " . . . doing some thinking. I'm sorry, honey. I'm sorry I stomped out of here and I'm sorry for you. But what I want to know is this: What you got to be ashamed about? If somebody hit you in the mouth, would you be ashamed? If they came in your house and stole something precious you had, would you be ashamed? Of course not. You'd be mad. I'm mad, too. What that man did was, he used violence against you and he stole something precious. You got no call to be ashamed. You take all the time you need to get over being mad and sad and scared, but I promise you one thing: I will never hurt you and I will never ask for more than you want to give. Just let me be there for you. Okay?"

Grace sniffled several times, and then her voice came out in a squeak. "Okay." Next thing I knew, he'd said something too soft for me to hear, but it made her giggle.

I suspected Freda was doing some giggling, too. Mr. Hugh Fred came by one evening right after supper to talk to Uncle Stephen about session business. When they were done, he brought me a fistful of Tootsie Rolls. "Hope you're feeling better. And I hope Freda's been able to help you keep up with your homework. She's stinted a bit on her own, riding down here every afternoon, but her horse needs the exercise, so we don't complain."

"Uh ... yeah," I stammered. "I don't think I'll be very far behind." What else *could* I say? I put my cast under the blanket until he left, though. I didn't want him reading the names and seeing that Freda hadn't signed it.

Thank goodness Uncle Stephen had gone back to his study for something and didn't hear us talking. As Mr. Hugh Fred left the room, he stopped at Uncle Stephen's door and said, "By the way, did you hear that Miranda's boy, Ronnie, is missing in action? Makes me real glad we weren't too hard on him about that other thing." He clomped off happily downstairs.

When Grace came upstairs later with a stack of clean clothes, I repeated, "Miranda's boy, Ronnie, is missing in action."

I expected her to shout, "Hooray!" Instead she exclaimed, "Oh no!" and clutched the clothes to her chest. "I wonder if

Janey Lou will take me by her place on Sunday after church to sit with her a little while?"

"You aren't glad?"

"Oh no, honey. I wouldn't wish that on any mother."

Uncle Stephen ran Grace up the very next day. I asked her how it was when they got back. "She's practically skin and bones with worrying. We'll need to all pray for his safety."

I had a hard time picturing Miranda down to skin and bones. She had so much skin, it must have wrinkled a good bit on the bones. I also had a hard time praying about Ronnie with the same charity Grace showed. In the simple, bloodthirsty creed of childhood, it seemed to me God was giving him precisely what he deserved.

But if God gave people what they deserved, why had he let Taylor Hart die? Mr. and Mrs. Hart drove up from Charlotte to talk to the police again; then they came out to the manse to ask Uncle Stephen to hold the funeral. Aunt Kate said she'd never seen two such sad people. "It's like he just died yesterday. I know they've grieved all these years, but his mama said she kept hoping he'd turn up. I truly don't know if she can survive definitely knowing he's gone. But since he grew up in Bethel Church, they said they want him buried in its earth."

Seemed to me they could have left him in the gully and achieved about the same thing. But I lay awake a long time that night wondering why good people don't live a long time and bad ones die young. Then I got to thinking I wasn't so good myself, so I was glad that wasn't the way things were. But I still couldn't pray for Ronnie, and I didn't know how to pray for Mr. and Mrs. Hart either. While I lay there thinking without coming to a single conclusion, all of a sudden my radio—which was on real low, so as not to bother Grace—started playing the national anthem. I shot straight up in bed and put my hand on my chest like we did for the flag salute, wondering if the war had ended or we were being bombed. I felt real silly when, as soon as they finished, my room filled with static. I had stayed awake so late, the station was signing off. I was so sleepy, I could scarcely drag my cast across the bed to turn off the radio.

The next afternoon they buried that little pile of bones. I looked across the highway to the cemetery thinking, *One more ghost to add to those I already see on foggy nights.* But Taylor had been in the gully so long, he'd probably been visiting them regular anyway.

❋

After a week I was able to hop down to our sunny dining room every morning. Sue Mary (and Velma) came each morning and we all played paper dolls. I couldn't figure out how to use scissors and cut with one hand, so Grace cut pictures from the old Sears and Roebuck catalog, and we made an enormous playhouse taped the length of the baseboard. She cut furniture and accessories for all the rooms, and a family with nine children to live in them. Nobody minded that some of the children were bigger than their parents.

Since I didn't have to get up early, I generally stayed downstairs pretty late reading. One night, though, I hopped up to bed early. Aunt Kate thought it was because I was tired, but actually it was so I could read *Wuthering Heights*. Uncle Stephen had brought it in a stack from the library, and from the first page I knew it was a book to be read under warm blankets in a chilly room with winter's wind whistling outside tower windows. Aunt Kate brought me up a cup of hot chocolate and settled me in bed with the cup beside my good arm, three hot water bottles around my legs and feet, and my bathrobe wrapped around my shoulders for extra warmth. A few minutes after she went downstairs, I had left Job's Corner for a windswept heath—whatever that was—somewhere in England.

At first I tried looking up all the words I didn't know, but soon I didn't notice them. I was suffering with Lockwood the indignities of the house of Heathcliff and—having already read *Jane Eyre*—wondering what awful things were going to happen there.

On opening the little door, two hairy monsters flew at my throat . . .

Something was coming softly up our stairs! I cringed beneath my covers, waiting for them to choose another door, but the quiet footsteps came straight for mine.

I heard a soft knock—to see if I was really there? I didn't say a word. Uncle Stephen, Aunt Kate, and Rowdy were in the dining room listening to Carnegie Hall. Grace had gone to the movies with Jay. John and Abby were asleep. Not one soul would know I'd been kidnapped or murdered.

. . . two hairy monsters . . .

"Hello? Are you awake?" The man's voice was muffled, one I didn't immediately recognize.

Still I didn't say a word. Then a cheery voice spoke behind him. "Sure she's awake, just got her nose in a book. Carley? Somebody's here to see you. Are you decent?"

I had to try my voice twice before I could reply. "I am now. I guess I dozed off." I dropped the book casually onto the pink chenille spread.

Uncle Stephen came in, followed by Mr. Donaldson.

"Thought I'd come see how you were feeling." Mr. Donaldson took his hand from behind him and brought out a Whitman Sampler of chocolates. "For the brave and valiant."

"Oh!" Lockwood and Heathcliff were forgotten. "Nobody ever gave me candy before and I love it!" I was already trying to tear the cellophane off but couldn't manage with only one hand. Uncle Stephen reached for it but Mr. Donaldson beat him to it.

"Use your chin." He picked up the box and wedged it firmly beneath his jaw while he ripped off the cellophane with his left arm. I looked down so he couldn't see my eyes. Just a week of living with one arm had showed me how hard it was, and at least I still had the one I used most. I understood better now the bitterness I'd heard in his voice that night in Uncle Stephen's study. There was no trace of it in his voice now, though, as he said, "Looks like we'll have two one-armers at Mount Vernon for a while."

"Yeah, looks that way. Sign my cast?" I held it out and he wrote his name while I burrowed with my other hand for a chocolate-covered cherry. I'd popped it into my mouth before I remembered. "Here, have one. Uncle Stephen, you want one?"

Uncle Stephen took a coconut cream (I was glad, for I hated them), and Mr. Donaldson considered them all, then took a caramel. I felt suddenly shy. "I never thanked you for getting me out of the gully. You could have been killed."

"It wasn't quite that big a risk. I grew up climbing in that gully. I spent my summers with Hannah and Davy when I was a boy. They used to call the upstairs back bedroom beside the kitchen stairs Jerry's room."

I looked at him in astonishment. "I had that room last summer when I stayed with them one week. Did you have to climb steps up into the bed at night?"

"I generally jumped up but it sounds like the same bed. Big high posts with a white ruffle around the top?"

"Yeah, and the room has wooden walls."

He nodded. "I loved waking up in the morning and seeing shadows of trees on those wide creamy boards. If I got up quietly and kneeled beside the windowsill, I could watch a mother bird feed her babies on a branch just beyond the porch gutter."

"There was a cardinal there last summer." We exchanged the long, satisfied look of people who'd shared a common experience of joy. It didn't matter that it had happened many years apart.

Uncle Stephen rumpled my hair. "Well, get back to your book, Miss Princess, and eat your bonbons. What a life! But don't eat all that candy tonight, and don't get used to this kind of treatment."

Since my closet door was open, I could hear them in the next room. Sounded like from the way chairs were scraping, they were settling in. "You think MacArthur's right, we'll have twenty-five more years of tension with the Reds?" I heard Uncle Stephen ask. Somebody moved the ashtray Aunt Kate bought him for Christmas—a big maroon glass one in a brass floor stand—so he'd probably set it between them. I doubted, though, that they'd be any better at hitting the ashtray with their matches than they'd been at hitting wastebaskets.

Mr. Donaldson didn't answer until I heard the little clickety-click that meant they had the train running around and around its track. "Hate to think it could go on that long. But if Truman declares war on China, anything's possible." If he didn't take that pipe out of his mouth, I'd be worn out trying to understand what he was saying.

"You think they'll vote to draft eighteen-year-olds?"

"If they do, they'll eventually have to give them the vote. And if they do that, they'll have to declare them adults."

"That would mean kids would be called adults without having any notion what adulthood is about."

"Do you think Congress stays up at night worrying about something like that?"

"I just don't think they'll go that far. I sure wasn't prepared to fight at eighteen."

Mr. Donaldson gave a bitter laugh. "I wasn't very well prepared at twenty-five. Should have stayed home and taught school."

"We've been missing you around here. You been real busy?"

He gave a sarcastic laugh. "Busy talking to the police. I figured I shouldn't tarnish you with my reputation until I get it cleared up."

"Any more news on that front?"

"Not much. They've had me in twice asking me to tell them again what I remember about that night. How do they expect me to remember precisely something that happened ten years ago? And I keep getting the feeling that if my story now doesn't match in every detail the one I told then, I'm in trouble. But I do know one thing. I never killed Taylor."

"They're probably just fishing. I doubt they can find anything now if they didn't then."

"Yeah, but I don't want to spend my life with people looking at me and wondering if I killed a student. Not to mention that it won't do me any good professionally. Would you send a child to a school with a principal who might have killed a student years ago?"

Uncle Stephen chuckled. "According to you, I already do—and Abby is rarin' to come. People have better sense than that around here, Jerry. They've known you all your life. But isn't there anybody who could prove you didn't do it? Or anything you remember him saying when you drove home?"

Mr. Donaldson didn't answer for a minute; then he said, "The only thing I remember him talking about, on and on, was plans he had to meet Maddie somewhere when he got home. He didn't say where. But he said it was one place they could go and be private without people interfering. If you want the truth, it made me want to strangle him. But I didn't. I truly didn't."

"I hope you didn't tell the police you felt like it."

"Don't worry; I didn't and won't."

"Have you told them about him and Maddie?"

"Why? She doesn't need to get involved. She obviously didn't know a thing about it. She went around the last few weeks of school looking like a ghost."

"How's she taking it since his body was found?"

"Hasn't said a word to me about it."

"Have you asked her about planning to meet him?"

Mr. Donaldson didn't say anything. He must have either shook his head or nodded.

"And I take it you haven't tried to stake a new claim."

"Come off it, Stephen. Why should she look twice at me?"

"Because she's been badly hurt. Unless I read you wrong, you're the kind of man to take care of a woman—and let her take care of you. Maddie could use some tenderness and kindness and a new interest in life. Offer them to her, and you may be surprised at the results—unless you aren't interested?"

Mr. Donaldson gave a short, barky laugh. "Interested? I could be real interested if I had two arms and didn't have Taylor Hart hanging around my neck. Almost every man at war has somebody who's his bright and happy thought. Maddie was mine. But you can't just walk up to a woman who despises you and say, 'Would you like to go out with me?' Believe it or not, there are limits to my masochism."

Uncle Stephen put his pipe back in his mouth, so I couldn't hear his reply.

❀

It didn't matter if Mr. Donaldson liked Mrs. Raeburn or not. She was frying other fish—as I learned the Sunday before I went back to school.

For Christmas the Keenes had given us a gift certificate to eat at the Vance Hotel, one of the fanciest restaurants in town. The weekend before I returned to school, Uncle Stephen decided, "We might as well use it Sunday to celebrate Carley getting better."

Aunt Kate and I spent all day Saturday going through my closet trying to decide what I could put on over my cast. "You'll outgrow all this by next year, so we might as well alter everything we can," she said with a sigh. "But it will ruin the dresses."

Grace looked at the cast and back at one of my favorite dresses. "I think if we pick out the left sleeve and I baste the armhole bigger, she can get it on and wear a sweater over it. When the cast comes off, we can just sew the sleeve back in."

That night Grace worked a miracle on three dresses, and I actually felt pretty when we walked into the Vance Hotel. Nobody would have known that my red plaid dress only had one sleeve under my cardigan.

Abby, proud to be included in a grown-up meal, was on her best behavior. When we went through the tall doors with silver mirrored panes, veined with gold to make them look like mica, she just pointed silently to be sure I noticed. She tiptoed behind her daddy across the carpet, which was thick as grass, and wiggled into the chair the waiter held for her like she'd had her chair held for her every meal of her life. But when she saw the big white napkins, she couldn't contain herself any longer. "Look, Mama, dey got diapers to wipe your mouf!"

After dinner, while Aunt Kate took Abby to the bathroom and Uncle Stephen took care of the bill, I went into the lobby to wait. I heard the thick door swoosh open; then Mrs. Raeburn came in, wearing a black fur coat, black high heels, a perky red and black hat, soft black kid gloves, and a big, happy smile. A gust of cold air came in with her, so she pulled the fur around her like a movie star would. "Hello, Carley! You feeling better?" She hadn't been in church but she didn't look at all embarrassed.

I was so embarrassed myself—imagine running into her like that!—I could hardly mumble, "I'll be back at school tomorrow."

"Are those new glasses?"

"Yes, ma'am. I, uh, lost my old ones."

"Very chic. The blue frames match your eyes."

I was flushed with pleasure and embarrassment when Uncle Stephen came out, putting his wallet back in his pocket. "Why, Maddie! You're mighty gussied up and beautiful."

She turned bright pink, but her eyes danced and she cocked her head to one side like Marilyn Monroe. "Why, thank you, Preacher."

"Haven't seen you at church recently. We're still open for business every Sunday."

She looked down and pulled off her gloves. "I've been real busy...."

He moved closer and spoke softly. "My experience is, when somebody stops coming to church, it's sometimes because they don't want to look the preacher in the eye."

She looked up quickly, then away, then turned back and grinned. "Let's just say that the laws of chemistry still apply. Can we leave it at that for now?"

He hesitated as if he'd like to say more. "Sure, Maddie. But I'm here if you need me. You know that, don't you? Carley, why don't you wait here until I bring the car, so you won't have to walk so far. Kate ought to be here in a minute." He headed out, jiggling his keys in his pocket.

Mrs. Raeburn went into the dining room, and the head-waiter acted like he wanted to put her in front of one of the big plate glass windows facing the street—just looking at her would make other people want to come in and eat. But she pointed to a table in the other direction and he led her that way. My sore leg had pretty much healed but it tired quickly. I went over and sat in a big wing chair in the lobby.

In just a minute a man came from the parking lot. He couldn't see me but I could see him. It was the handsome man from Sealtest Dairy.

When Uncle Stephen finally brought our car and I hobbled out, I peeked in the big window. I saw the man and Mrs. Rae-burn at a table back in the corner. His dark hair was near her perky hat and they were holding hands. She looked up and saw me and gave me a little wave. Then she said something to him and he turned and waved, too. I didn't know what else to do, so I waved back.

I wondered if she'd brought Suzy along and left her propped in the seat of his car.

Abby chattered all the way home about the fancy restaurant, the big white tablecloths, the thick rug, and Frank, our waiter. She was giggling about the napkins again when I heard Uncle Stephen ask Aunt Kate softly, "Is there a new man in Maddie Raeburn's life?"

"Not that I know of," she said softly back.

"You haven't seen her and Jerry Donaldson, for instance, lighting any fires?"

Aunt Kate laughed. "Jerry isn't the sort to light fires. He burns at a slow, steady simmer."

Uncle Stephen gave a deep, worried grunt. "Maddie strikes me as somebody who prefers bonfires."

Chapter 32

When I got back to school, Mrs. Raeburn didn't indicate by so much as a wink that we'd seen each other the day before or talked about dolls a couple of weeks before that. Seemed to me like we had been on the verge of being friends and now she had pulled back. At the end of the day, though, she came to my desk. "You look a little tired. Why don't you do homework up here until Mrs. Whitfield is ready to take you home? I'll send her a message to come get you when she's ready to leave."

As the other children streamed out, I imagined what good friends we were about to become and some of the conversation we would have. Instead Mrs. Raeburn worked quietly at her desk and I at mine. I was finishing my arithmetic when Aunt Kate finally arrived.

"Go to the back of the room for a few minutes and finish your work there. I need to talk to your teacher a minute."

My heart nearly stopped. "What have I done?"

"Nothing, that I know of. This is about something else."

Aunt Kate talked a long time but she whispered. I couldn't hear a word. Peeping up from my arithmetic book, I saw Mrs. Raeburn nod like she was answering a question. When Aunt Kate said something else, Mrs. Raeburn exclaimed, "But he never came!"

Aunt Kate's voice came softly to me. "Where were you supposed to meet? And when?"

"... creek ... between his property and ours ... old barn ... I went home first ..." For a minute her voice got loud enough for me to hear a whole sentence. "I meant to just pretend to go to bed but I fell asleep. I was real tired." Aunt Kate made a movement with her hand, and Mrs. Raeburn remembered I was in the back of the room. Again I could only hear a word now and then. "... nearly one o'clock ... ran the whole way ... late ... wasn't there ... dark ... pretty scary." Again her voice had risen as she talked. I heard the last sentence clearly. "I waited outside for about ten minutes; then I ran home every step of the way."

Aunt Kate murmured again. I thought I heard, "... bother to look inside?"

"... couldn't ... lock on the door."

Aunt Kate sighed and stood up. "I don't see how that could help. But Stephen thinks if you told the police, it might at least get them off Jerry's back."

"You don't think he had anything to do with it?"

Aunt Kate shook her head. "Do you?"

"Not anymore. I used to—I was certain, in fact, right up until I started teaching here, that he'd either sent Taylor off to war or knew exactly where he went. But now ..." She shook her head. "I truly don't think he had a thing to do with it. He had no reason to. But I doubt the little I can tell them will make any difference." She reached out and touched Aunt Kate's sleeve. "You won't tell anybody else, will you? I've never told a soul I was meeting Taylor."

"It's your secret," Aunt Kate assured her. "But if you would tell it to the police—"

She must have, because when we drove by the Keenes' house on our way home Wednesday afternoon, police cars were in their drive. I asked Freda about it Thursday at recess.

"A man who got murdered used to live in our house. The police went over every inch of our property, as far back as a creek way down in the old pasture. You know what they found? A still in an old barn down there! Somebody used to make liquor right in our backyard. But they stopped long before we moved there."

"Are you sure?" Seemed to me like almost every day all the past month the police had arrested somebody for making or transporting illegal liquor. You'd have thought Iredell County was the liquor-making capital of the United States.

"Yes, everything was covered with cobwebs. Daddy said they wouldn't dare operate a still with us riding horses all over those woods." She added in a voice very like her mother's, "One good thing. All this finally gives Miranda something to think about besides Ronnie."

Mr. Donaldson came by the house looking white and worried. Uncle Stephen brought him into the dining room, where I was doing history and Aunt Kate was grading papers. He threw himself into the big chair without seeming to notice us, and his hand shook as he struck a match against his shoe sole to light his pipe. "They're going to arrest me, Stephen. I've just spent time with Red Lamar and he says he's going to nail me in this case."

Aunt Kate put an anxious hand on her lips. "But why?"

I trembled. Red Lamar was the prosecutor in a trial Uncle Stephen and I attended the spring before. A big man with a shock of red hair, about as jolly as an angry bull.

"He doesn't have a shred of evidence," Uncle Stephen said reassuringly.

"Actually, he does. They found shreds of Taylor's jacket on a nail in a barn up on the Keenes' property—how it lasted all these years, I'll never know, but it was there under the dust and cobwebs. And they found blood on an upright, and an old high school medal of mine on the floor—a citizenship medal from the Daughters of the American Revolution, with my initials and the year engraved on the back. They're pretty sure that's where Taylor was killed. I told them until I was blue in the face that I was never in the barn and don't know how my medal got there, but—"

"Is that where Maddie was supposed to meet him?" Aunt Kate asked.

"Yes, but she says she never went inside, because it was padlocked." He gave a short, unfunny laugh. "Considering that one of the biggest stills in Iredell County was operating there at that time, I'll bet it was padlocked. I'm surprised they didn't have an armed guard in the bushes."

Uncle Stephen fished in his pocket for his pipe. "Obviously, it's a dreadful mistake. When did you first miss the medal?"

Mr. Donaldson shrugged. "I don't have the foggiest notion. I wore it on my key chain during college and a couple of years after that. Then I noticed one day it was gone. It probably dropped off but I don't know when or where." He added quickly, "But not in that barn."

The next afternoon I'd barely gotten home from school and Aunt Kate hadn't arrived yet when the phone rang. It was Aunt Hannah, talking faster than usual. "I need Stephen, Carley. Something's happened real bad."

Uncle Stephen looked his normal cheerful self when he took the receiver. But in a second his back stiffened. "Why?" He sounded like somebody was pulling his tie too tight. Her voice sounded like metallic little clicks. "Where is he now?" More metallic clicks. "Sure, I'll go. Shall I pick him up?" Another barrage of clicks. "I'll be on the porch." He hung up as slowly as I usually put my book away before a hard test. I started backing toward the bathroom door so I could pretend I'd been in there, but he didn't seem to care if I'd been listening. "Davy and I have to go somewhere. Tell Kate I don't know when I'll be back, so go ahead and eat if I'm not here."

"Where are you going?"

He hesitated and I knew he would rather not say. I hurried to get between him and the door. "You promised last summer not to keep secrets in this house. Not that you or Aunt Kate either one live up to that most of the time."

He took his gray felt winter hat from the rack by the door. "Some habits are hard to break and some secrets aren't ours to share. But you'd find this out soon enough, anyway. Jerry

Donaldson was just arrested for the murder of Taylor Hart. Davy and I are going down to post his bond."

"What's 'post his bond'?"

"Davy will give them the deed to his farm to demonstrate that he trusts Jerry not to run away before his trial."

"What if he does run away? Will they take Uncle Davy's farm?"

"Well, yes. But it won't come to that. Jerry's not going anywhere." We heard tires slide to a stop on the gravel outside the house. "I'm off. Tell Kate, okay?"

"Okay." Being included in grown-up secrets wasn't as special as I'd thought it would be. Some things were mighty heavy to know.

Mr. Donaldson wasn't at school the next day. Uncle Stephen did some checking and found out the school board had said he couldn't be principal while he was out on bond. That made Uncle Stephen so mad, he personally carried a petition to every family in our church who had kids at Mount Vernon, saying we believed in the American precept that a person is innocent until proven guilty and wanted Mr. Donaldson back at school until his trial.

Aunt Kate was real worried that Uncle Stephen was doing that. "Remember the trouble you got into last year over Jay? And we don't *know* Jerry didn't do it; we just *believe* he didn't. There's a difference."

He shoved back his hair, a sure sign he was upset. "Most people I've talked to were glad to sign. There's not a chance Jerry killed that boy."

"Sure there's a chance. I don't think he did it, but he liked Maddie and the boy liked Maddie. Maybe they got into an argument and Jerry just pushed him harder than he meant to."

"Then carried him to the gully and dropped him in? Let the parents grieve for years without knowing what had happened to their son? Swore years later he never did it?"

His eyes held hers for a long minute. Finally she looked down. "No. Jerry would never have done that." She held out her hand. "Give me the petition. I'll sign."

I signed, too. Abby wanted to, but Uncle Stephen said they might check signatures, and he didn't want to invalidate the whole petition because of zealousness within his own family. It took me half an hour to look up all those words and figure out what he was saying. "He meant you can't sign the petition because you don't go to school," I finally explained. Abby stuck out her lower lip and narrowed her eyes. "Let's read your new library book," I quickly suggested. If Abby started roaring, we might all join in.

The school board finally agreed to let Mr. Donaldson come back to school a week and a half after I got back, but that didn't matter right away. We had our third record cold wave of the winter, and they had to close schools anyway because so many of the bus routes were icy. Tired of staying home, I decided to limp down to the store and visit Mrs. Cameron. Fighting with her was better than being bored. Maybe she'd even let me rearrange her shelves a little.

Abby flat refused to put on her leggings, so she had to stay home. Aunt Kate made me put on a hat and gloves and such a thick sweater under my coat that I felt like a worm in a cocoon. But it was wonderful to be outdoors. The air was so cold, it hurt to breathe. The ground sparkled in the sunlight like somebody had sprinkled it with diamond dust. I walked slowly, enjoying the crunch when I stepped on an especially frosty bit, the song of one solitary bird, and the unusual sting of cold on my cheeks. The store would be warm enough. Uncle Stephen went over every morning now to light the stove.

Mrs. Cameron was sitting right beside it, leaning toward the warmth like she couldn't get enough. But when she saw it was me, she fanned her face. "Too hot in here to breathe. Leave that door open a minute to let some air in."

I closed it behind me anyway. "Got anything you need me to do?"

"You can shelve yon box of bread and clean off the lower shelf where I spilt some sugar. Don't want ants getting in."

"Ants are hibernating right now." I still cleaned the shelf, chatting with her about this and that. She was never a pleasant person, but that morning she seemed almost glad to see me. When I finished, she said, "What'll you take for pay?"

I resolutely ignored the jar of Mary Janes and pointed to paper doilies wrapped in cellophane. "Could I have those if nobody else buys them, to make paper lace edges for valentines? I'm making mine this year, to save my money for music camp."

"How much are they marked?"

"Thirty-five cents."

"Far more than the work is worth."

"But they've been there as long as I can remember."

She cackled. "Been there 'bout long as I can remember, too. I don't hold much with valentines, but you can have them if nobody buys them first. Come get them when you're ready to use 'em, and we'll see. For now take one Mary Jane. One, mind. Don't want you eatin' me out of house and home."

Sunday the worst spring blizzard in fifty years hit the whole South. School was still closed Monday, but Tuesday Uncle Stephen bundled up and braved the roads to attend the monthly school board meeting because they had promised to consider Mount Vernon's letter.

As soon as he got home and saw us all waiting expectantly at the dining room table, he shook his head and his shoulders slumped. "Troutman School and Cool Springs want new buildings, too, and the board says they just don't have funds for any of us at this time." He sighed as he hung up his hat. "I hate for Jerry to know how pitifully powerless concerned Christians can be."

"Nobody can get anything built with this war going on," Aunt Kate told him. "Jerry can't blame that on you, for heaven's sake."

Uncle Stephen grinned. "He can try." But he looked happier when he followed her to the kitchen to make hot chocolate. I found them in there smooching a few minutes later.

Saturday I woke to a stillness so deep, it seemed the whole world had been wrapped in cotton. A layer of cotton even lay on my windowsill.

Suddenly I realized what it was: real snow! Not driven sleet or howling wind but a deep gentle drift that covered the whole world. Across the highway the church and steeple wore thick white caps. The railroad track was one long white bed with two long humps.

I wrapped up in my bathrobe and the quilt from my bed and padded down to the front porch. Uncle Stephen was already standing there, his toes at the very edge of the snow, staring at the unmarked walk and steps and taking deep breaths of icy air. He turned when he heard me behind him. "I'm standing here thinking snow's a lot like grace—both cover a heap of dirt and make everything more beautiful. And I'm about to decide to forego my walk this morning. I don't want to be the first one to mess up that pristine world."

Rowdy pushed past me, waddled down the steps, and headed for the nearest bush. Uncle Stephen chuckled. "There's always somebody to volunteer."

As I headed up to my room to dress, I decided to make my valentines that morning. Valentine's Day wasn't until Thursday, but I'd need more time to paste and write with one arm in a cast. Besides, it would be just my luck for somebody to buy those doilies after they'd stayed on that shelf a hundred years. And I wanted to walk in the snow.

As soon as we finished breakfast, I asked Aunt Kate to help me put on my boots and button me into my coat. I struggled into my hat and gloves, took Rowdy, and set out.

The snow came almost over my boots, and Rowdy was stomach-deep in drifts. It took us a while to get there, but the store was still padlocked—probably the only door locked in Job's Corner. I stood waiting awhile on the porch, taking deep breaths of air so fresh, it had to have come straight from the North Pole. *Maybe,* I began to think, *Mrs. Cameron didn't want to come out in the snow. Maybe she'd like for me to open up for her today. She might even pay me.* I hurried across her yard and knocked on her back door. Rowdy put his nose to the bottom crack and whined.

Tentatively I turned the knob. The door opened. I stuck in my head. The house was cold and dark, the curtains still drawn. "Mrs. Cameron? Mrs. Cameron?" For a second I was terrified she'd died in the night. Instead I heard a weak voice.

"In here, girl. By the bed." Rowdy had already bounded through the door and stood waiting for me, whining.

She lay in a heap, wearing a gray flannel gown. Dry blood smeared her forehead. One foot stuck out, white and gnarled with giant yellow toenails. The room smelled like she'd wet her pants.

She shivered with cold, her face colorless and drawn, but her black eyes snapped. "Don't move me. I fell and think I broke my hip. Hand me a quilt and go call that uncle of yourn. Move smart, now!" I tugged the quilt off her bed, covered her awkwardly, then ran as well as I could through the thick snow. Rowdy wallowed just ahead of me.

Aunt Kate called the ambulance while Uncle Stephen went back with me. "I can't move you," he told Mrs. Cameron, "but I'll light the fire and make you some warm milk."

"Pap," she said, disgusted. "Make me some black coffee." I stood uneasily in the bedroom door, unable to think of a thing I could do but wishing I could. She muttered, "I'll be needing another nightgown. Look in that top drawer."

Thankful to be busy, I packed a brown grocery bag with two nightgowns, several pairs of long-legged underpants, a red toothbrush, a battered tube of Ipana toothpaste, and a hairbrush full of long gray hairs. The whole time I kept up a cheerful patter. "You're going to be all right. The ambulance will be here any minute. Just lie still. You're going to be fine." If I said it often enough, maybe both of us would believe it.

Finally she closed her eyes. "Hush, girl. You're driving me crazy."

Aunt Kate rode with Mrs. Cameron in the ambulance. I didn't care. I'd already had one ambulance ride too many. But I did resent not being allowed to go with Uncle Stephen in the Chevy. "I don't know how long we'll be. You stay home and help Grace."

I wandered back over to our house to find Grace drinking hot chocolate with Abby in the dining room. "That poor old woman," she said sadly, "but I guess she's had a good life."

"She's not *dying!*" I surprised even myself with my anger. "She just broke her hip."

"They usually go when they break a hip at that age."

"Well *she's* not going yet. She'll be home in a day or two. You wait and see!" Suddenly I started shaking and couldn't stop. When I tried to speak, I burst into tears and ran to my room. Behind my tears I kept seeing the flowers on Mama's casket.

All morning, awkwardly cutting and gluing pitifully plain valentines without paper lace edges, I felt crabby and close to tears. When Uncle Stephen and Aunt Kate hadn't gotten home by noon, Grace fed John and put him down for his nap, then made canned tomato soup and cheese sandwiches for the rest of us. I gave Abby my soup. It reminded me of the blood on Mrs. Cameron's forehead.

As soon as I heard Uncle Stephen and Aunt Kate coming in the door, I clattered into the cold hall. "Is she all right? When can she come"—the look on their faces made me pause mid-sentence—"home?" I finished in a squeak.

Aunt Kate put an arm around me. Uncle Stephen put a hand on my shoulder. They spoke like a congregational reading, side to side.

"We're not sure she will come home, honey."

"She'd been lying on that icy floor all night long."

"She has both a broken hip and a bad chill."

"If you hadn't found her when you did, she'd probably have died today."

I interrupted their litany. "They can warm her up and make her well." My voice was shrill in the cold hall. "They made me well."

"She's a lot older than you. We won't know anything for a few days."

"Will we keep the store open while she's gone?"

Uncle Stephen's hand tightened on my shoulder. "We're going to close the store. Even if she gets back home, she won't be able to work anymore."

I burst into tears. Ever since Mama died, life kept changing drastically on me from one day to the next. Yesterday I'd put bread on the shelves and Mrs. Cameron had fussed at me for missing a speck of paper when I swept. Today the store was shut forever.

"It can't close," I sobbed. "She just got a bread delivery. It will mold. Besides, where will I get Mary Janes? And where will you get tobacco? Where will Miss Pauline get Ex-Lax when she's irregular, or Miss Nancy get tissues when her allergies act up?"

Uncle Stephen chuckled. "You've learned a lot about the habits of Job's Corner from that store, haven't you?" I had such a lump in my throat, all I could do was nod. His hand was warm as it massaged my shoulder. "It's hard to give up things we're used to."

Aunt Kate leaned her forehead next to mine. She smelled clean, like Halo shampoo. "But Mrs. Cameron is old. You know what she said when they finally got her to bed?"

When I shook my head, tears spilled over. I brushed them away angrily.

Aunt Kate's voice roughened into a good imitation of Mrs. Cameron's. "'My birthday's the fifteenth. I'd like to be home by my birthday.'"

"See?" I demanded, sniffing away my tears. "She *is* coming home."

"No." She shook her head gently. "I said the same thing, but she said, 'I ain't talking about that poky house in Job's Corner. I got me a heavenly mansion I'm wanting to see. I 'speck Mr. Cameron's got it fixed up right smart.' Then she cackled like she does and added, 'And I 'speck old Mrs. Cameron's waitin' for me pretty eager, too. Just hope we don't have to share a kitchen.'"

※

"Mrs. Cameron's prayer was answered," Uncle Stephen said at her funeral the next Saturday morning. "Quietly, on the eve of her birthday, she went home."

I sat in my usual second pew next to the center aisle, with Aunt Kate and Abby beside me. Aunt Kate hadn't wanted to take Abby, but she'd wanted to come, and Uncle Stephen always felt strongly that children ought to know that death is a part of life. She mostly drew cats and bunnies during the service and sat on her mother's lap.

Mrs. Cameron lay in a steel gray casket, so close that I could have reached out and touched it. As was the custom, the top half of the casket was open. She lay on pale blue velvet in her best black dress. Her eyes were closed, as if she were taking a Sunday afternoon nap, and her face was blank and completely unwrinkled. She looked almost as beautiful as she'd boasted she used to be.

At Mama's funeral the church had been full and smelled of flowers. But Mama was loved. When I went to mail a letter the afternoon after Mrs. Cameron died, I had to go to Miss Pauline's living room for a stamp. She and Miss Nancy were sitting there gossiping. As I left, I said, "I'll see you at the funeral, I 'spect."

"I'm not getting dressed up for that old bat," Miss Pauline declared. "Charged near twice what her stuff was worth."

"Too cheap to heat the place, too, until recently," Miss Nancy seconded her. "I doubt Mr. Whitfield will have anybody there but you and your aunt and Hannah and Davy."

Sure enough, there were only a handful of people at the funeral—including Mr. Rob and Miss Rilla, Aunt Hannah and Uncle Davy, and a short, stout old woman Aunt Hannah whispered to Aunt Kate was "Nora's stepdaughter, hoping for a little inheritance." The only flowers were Miss Hannah's purple and white cattleya orchid and a blanket of yellow and white chrysanthemums Uncle Stephen had ordered from the church. "I'll pay for it out of my own pocket if the elders object," he'd told Aunt Kate.

I tried not to cry but I couldn't help it. I kept wishing she'd open her eyes and say sharply, "Come on, girl, hurry up! I haven't got all day." I scrubbed tears off my cheeks with a tissue and wished I'd been nicer to her.

About halfway through the service Abby leaned over and whispered loud enough for the whole church to hear, "She's cold, Carley. She doesn't got a coat." We were *all* cold. The weather had warmed up some, but the building still held the previous week's cold, and Uncle Stephen had forgotten to go over and turn on the heat until just before the service. We shivered even in our coats. I looked at Abby's leggings and wished I had some. My knees were blue and my legs blotched red and white.

I remembered how cold Mrs. Cameron had been when I found her, and what Uncle Stephen had said. *"If you hadn't found her when you did, she'd probably have died today."*

He'd said that to comfort me, but I wept harder to think how miserable she'd been all night in that cold, cold house. It wasn't fair to put her in a chilly hole of red clay wearing only a dress. They could have at least wrapped her in a quilt.

"Hand me a quilt." That was practically the last thing she'd ever said to me. I hadn't gone to see her in the hospital, because I'd believed that if I didn't go, she'd have to come home. It hadn't worked. I tried to remember something nice she'd ever said, but I couldn't think of one. I couldn't remember a single nice thing I'd ever said back, either.

As if reading my thoughts, Uncle Stephen looked down and seemed to speak just to me. "Sometimes Mrs. Cameron was a curmudgeon. But there was always humor in her life, and honor in her relationships. Her store might be ramshackle, but it stood as a monument to her integrity and determination to be self-supporting. And she told me last week that she's left almost everything she possessed—her house, her store, and most of her money—to this church, to use as we see fit."

The stout woman sat up straighter and sniffed. But Uncle Stephen went right on. "We shall miss her. But she will remain part of us as long as we live." I broke down and sobbed.

As soon as we left the cemetery, Uncle Davy and Mr. Rob went to load their trucks with all the usable food and stuff from the store.

"They're stealing it!" I stormed in to tell Uncle Stephen. He came out onto the porch and looked across the cotton field.

"They aren't stealing it. She and I agreed we should take all the stuff on the shelves up to Rock of Hope for them to give to people who need it."

"You could have at least waited to see if somebody else wants to buy the store."

"That old store is like Mrs. Cameron; it's seen its day." He fumbled in his pocket for his pipe. "Why don't we go over and see if we can give them a hand?"

Inside the store, Uncle Davy pointed to a bottle of fountain pen ink and the glass jar holding Mary Janes. "I set that aside for you, Carley. I think she'd have wanted you to have them. She used to say you liked Mary Janes more than any other young'un she knew."

I could almost hear her saying it, and I felt if I turned my head real quick, I'd catch her standing behind me. My eyes smarted with tears. "Can I have the shoe buttons up on the top shelf, too?"

The men laughed. "I don't think anybody else would object," Mr. Rob told me.

I didn't care a bit if they laughed. If button shoes ever came back in style, I'd be glad to have them.

After the men left, I dusted all the shelves and tore down the flypaper. Then I swept the floor. Aunt Hannah came in as I was hanging up the dustpan. "This looks lovely," she said, "but why—" She stopped, not wanting to add what I knew she meant: *bother.*

I couldn't tell even Aunt Hannah that I felt like I was saying good-bye. Instead I said, "Uncle Stephen says the new owners of the house will decide whether to have a store or tear it down. I figure if it's clean, they'll be more likely to open it again. Do you know who the owners will be?"

She shook her head. "Her lawyer's in Statesville. That's all I know. I came to see if you'd like to come down tonight and help me try out a new chicken recipe. You'll have to stay for supper, of course. We can't make Davy eat it all. If you're not too busy?"

I sighed. "I'm never going to be busy again."

As we left, I pulled the old wood doors closed behind us and stuck the padlock in its loop. I didn't click it shut, though. That was too final.

I was almost asleep that night when Aunt Kate tapped on my door. "Get up and put on your robe and slippers. Stephen wants to show you something."

When I limped downstairs, he was holding Abby, wrapped in a quilt. She was rosy with sleep, burrowing her head into his neck. Grace, wearing her coat, stood by the front door. "Get your coat," Aunt Kate told me. "It's freezing outside."

It was a crisp, clear night. I had never seen so many stars. Uncle Stephen pointed to a little line of three. "That's the belt of Orion," he told us. "He was a mighty hunter. And see those up there?" He traced the pattern with the arm that wasn't holding Abby. "That's the Big Dipper. See how it looks like a dipper?"

"I doesn't know what a dipper is," Abby complained softly into his shoulder.

"It's like a big spoon to drink out of. See the handle, and the cup to hold the water?"

"I sees it!" In an instant she was awake and her usual ebullient self.

"I wanted you all to see the stars tonight, girls, because I wanted to tell you something special about them. Who made those stars?"

"God." Even Abby knew that.

"Do you know when God made them?"

"Tonight."

"No, Abbikins, he made them long before there were people, animals, even an earth. Some of those stars are so far away, their light has been traveling many, many years. In fact, some of the stars we see tonight may have already burned out, but their light is just now getting here. Nobody knows how old they are, except God. And nobody knows how long they will last except God, either. That's true of people too. Nobody knows how long any of us will last, but God knows, and God has that under control. God has everything under control. What do you think of that?"

"I tink it's nice," Abby obligingly replied, snuggling down in her quilt. Suddenly she jerked her head up. "Look!" She jumped in his arms, pointing. "One dropped."

Grace pulled her coat closer around her. "Mama always said when you see a falling star, somebody's died."

"O' *torse* somebody died," Abby said impatiently. "Mrs. Cam'ron died. Good-bye, Mrs. Cam'ron!" She waved at the sky where the star had fallen.

I stepped back behind the grown-ups so they couldn't see me, and I waved, too. "Good-bye, Mrs. Cameron," I whispered.

I'm sure I heard a whisper on the breeze. "Good-bye, girl."

Chapter 33

The next morning Uncle Stephen swapped pulpits with the preacher of the Mooresville Presbyterian Church, up near Charlotte. At breakfast Aunt Kate suggested, "Why don't you take Carley with you? I think she needs a trip out of town."

I looked at her gratefully. I'd been wondering how I could bear to sit in church with that new mound in the cemetery just beyond the window. I'd woken up several times thinking about Mrs. Cameron and Mama and how you never knew to appreciate people until you lost them.

Abby bounced in her chair. "Me, too! Me, too! I needs a twip out of town."

Uncle Stephen shook his head and sighed. "So much for a peaceful, contemplative journey." But he didn't really mind. His eyes were twinkling behind his glasses.

Abby and I sat up front at church of course, like always, so I didn't see who was in the congregation until the service was done. Then we went back and stood next to Uncle Stephen while he shook hands. A skinny, dark-haired woman took his hand in both of hers and gushed, "You are such a fine preacher, Mr. Whitfield. If you ever think of leaving Job's Corner, you let us know." She had a trilling, brittle laugh. "I am Marsha Taylor, and this"—she turned slightly—"is my husband Jake."

It was Mrs. Raeburn's handsome man. I knew him and he knew me.

We both pretended we didn't, of course. We shook hands and said, "How do you do?" like perfect strangers. But at the foot of the church steps he turned and looked at me over his shoulder like a dog who's just been whipped.

All the way home I wondered whether to say anything to Uncle Stephen—and what. Thank goodness Abby chattered so much, he didn't notice how quiet I was.

The next morning was warm and foggy, a sad day to match my sad mood. I was scared to death Red Lamar would convict Mr. Donaldson, and I couldn't meet Mrs. Raeburn's eye. My stomach ached so much by lunchtime that I kept my head on my desk the rest of the day.

It was not until after supper, when I was finishing spelling homework and Aunt Kate was grading papers, that I finally dared to ask, "Isn't it wrong to go out with somebody who's married to somebody else?"

"It certainly is," she agreed, looking up curiously. "Why?"

"I just wondered. It was in a book I've been reading."

For a second her face looked just like Big Mama's. The next second, I knew she'd decided not to say what she'd been fixing to. Instead she murmured, "Maybe you'd better not read that book anymore" and reached for another paper to grade.

Tuesday the world cried in little showers. Mrs. Raeburn was absent. She returned on Wednesday, a beautiful day, but she looked like she was about to cry little showers herself. It nearly broke my heart to look at her. She wore a lot of rouge and lipstick, but her full black skirt didn't swirl and her eyes didn't sparkle. She also didn't look me straight in the eye. I wondered if the man had told her he'd seen me. What was the punishment for finding out your teacher's boyfriend was married? Would I have to repeat seventh grade?

I kept telling myself, though, that whatever happened to me wouldn't be as bad as if poor Mr. Donaldson went to jail. Uncle Stephen had asked him over and over again to try and remember just one time when he'd been in that old barn behind Keenes'. He flat-out insisted he'd never been there.

"You must have once. Your medal was there," Uncle Stephen pointed out one evening as they sat in the dining room puffing away. "Maybe when you were at Hannah's as a child?"

"I didn't get the medal until senior awards night in high school. And I told you, I can't explain how it got into that barn. I don't even remember when I lost it. It was on my key ring; then it wasn't. That's all I know."

"You didn't try to think then where you could have lost it?"

"Not that I recall. By then it wasn't the end of the world to lose a high school award."

"It may be the end of your world if you can't explain its being in that barn."

❋

My own world tilted slightly one night at supper when Uncle Stephen announced, "You'll never guess what's happened to Mrs. Cameron's house." We all waited expectantly. "Clay and Laura have bought it. He said the lawyer was delighted for them to get it. Saved him advertising it."

I was so shocked and excited, I could hardly breathe. *Clay right next door!*

Aunt Kate frowned. "I hate for them to leave Nancy right now."

Uncle Stephen shook his head. "Clay said she's driving them crazy. Comes up there every evening until bedtime. They never have privacy."

Good for her, I thought.

But Aunt Kate nodded. "Then they need to move. That house is a perfect size for two, with plenty of yard space to add on when they have children. I've always wondered why anybody ever built such a little house on that big lot, anyway."

"They used to have as big a house as we do, but it burned down." When they all stared, I added, "Mrs. Cameron told me. She said she wasn't sorry, either—she preferred her own little house. She said every woman needs to have one house just her own size."

Aunt Kate looked at dust balls under the Philco. "I could vote for that."

Clay and Mr. Rob spent every evening that week painting and putting down new rugs and linoleum in the kitchen. Miss Nancy surprised everybody by helping Laura measure and make curtains and by spending Friday with her hanging the curtains and putting new shelf paper in the cabinets and drawers. Uncle Stephen said she was almost her old perky self.

They moved Saturday. Uncle Stephen and I went to help load trucks, and it took both Uncle Davy's and Mr. Rob's to carry everything. Clay saw me looking at the second truck and grinned. "Before I married Laura, everything I owned fit into one suitcase. Now look at me. A bloomin' plutocrat with two truckloads of stuff."

A few days later Preston came over just when it was turning dark. "Wanna see something?" He whispered hoarsely. "Over at Clay's?"

I hesitated but the temptation was great. I hadn't seen Clay since they'd moved in. Maybe we could drop in and have a glass of tea with them or something. Going with Preston wouldn't look as funny as going on my own.

"Come on." Preston beckoned with his arm. When Rowdy climbed to his feet and started with us, though, he ordered, "Leave the dog here." And outside he started toward the back of our lot instead of the road.

"Where are you going?"

"The back way."

He bent nearly double and crept along the pasture edge of the cotton field, now bare and bleak, past the back of the abandoned store, behind the empty henhouse and the back edge of Mrs. Cameron's derelict garden. It was dusk, the day collapsing with a gray weariness. I saw that there was a worn path along the fence and wondered if Preston went that way a lot.

Clay's new Mercury convertible stood in the drive. My heart began to pound. I couldn't think of any good excuse we could give for coming to their house from the back.

I didn't know that fat little boy could be so quiet. Still bent nearly double, he crept past the kitchen window with only a glance inside, then to the far back window. He rose to peer into the bedroom window, which had one soft light on. His hand gave a quick, excited jerk.

I had a hundred questions and protestations. Listening at doors in your own house was one thing. Peering in somebody else's windows was another. I couldn't have told you how it was different; I just felt it was. Besides, why were we going to the bedroom window instead of to the kitchen? Why didn't we just knock on the door?

Preston's piggy eyes glittered with an expression I had never seen before. I wanted to go back home and read. I wanted to be anywhere except where we were. Yet I was drawn to that window like a child to a bubble gum machine.

Awkward with my cast, I glided to Preston's side. The window was open an inch—probably to let out the smell from the oil heater—and the new shade pulled down to it. The one-inch slit was just level with Preston's eye, but I had to scrunch down a little. His dirty boy smell almost made me gag. I shifted away so I wouldn't have to feel him trembling against my side, but he didn't notice. He was too busy watching what was going on inside.

The room was dim. Clay lay on the bed, covered with a sheet. Laura came walking from the bathroom and she was naked. She was shaped almost exactly like Ruth had drawn the naked lady, except Laura was beautiful. I had never known women looked so nice.

My knees were so stiff from scrunching, I shifted my foot to get more comfortable. I hit a bottle, which rolled and hit a rock. Maybe it didn't sound like Gabriel's trumpet, but it did to me. Clay heard it, too. He lifted his head and looked around. "Who's there?"

Years later, backpacking in the Colorado mountains, I would climb halfway up a cliff and have a sudden moment of panic. I could not climb higher but was equally sure I could not climb down. The feeling was familiar. That's how I felt that evening under Clay and Laura's window. How on earth could I get away without being seen? Eyes seemed to stare from Davy Anderson's open pasture at our back and from all the manse windows to our side. Maybe the ghosts of Mr. Cameron and both his wives. Inside, Clay climbed to his hands and knees.

Preston dropped to all fours and started to crawl back the way we had come. Numb with shame and fear, I bent to follow him, but my sore leg wasn't yet swift and I couldn't crawl well in the cast. To make matters worse, my foot hit that bottle again. With a crash, I sprawled on my face.

"Who's there?" Clay bellowed. "Who's out there?"

I jumped to my feet and hobbled away, straight for the road. Before I got past the cotton field, my shadow leaped ahead of me as their front porch light came on. Never had I loathed Preston Anderson so much. Almost as much as I loathed myself.

Preston waited just past the cotton field, behind one of our maples. He gave a snigger. "You get caught?"

I gave him what I hoped was a withering look and swept up our steps without a word. He scuttled home, pink and disgusting, wheezing with glee.

I huddled in my dark room fully expecting Clay to get dressed and come straight to tell Uncle Stephen. He didn't. But I crept down to supper scared to death he'd arrive any minute. I was so quiet that Aunt Kate asked, "Are you getting sick, honey?"

"No, ma'am. But I've been thinking. I don't think it's fair for Bonnie to miss church every Sunday. Besides, it hurts my leg to sit so long. I can read to the children and still move around, so why don't I help Grace keep the nursery awhile and let Bonnie go to church?"

Uncle Stephen said I was real thoughtful. I tiptoed around waiting for the wrath of God.

I also examined my body after my bath to see if it looked anything like Laura's. We must have come from different species.

A week passed and still nobody had mentioned what Preston and I had done. Then one day when I got home from school, Uncle Stephen leaned over the upstairs rail and called down, "Carley, I need to talk to you. Can you come up here a minute?"

My hands got clammy and my heart beat like a drum. Nothing in my whole life had equipped me to face the lecture I was about to get.

We sat down and faced each other. He didn't look mad, just bewildered. "Carley—" He stopped. Then he picked up a piece of paper. Was it a letter to Big Mama—or even an orphanage—saying he couldn't keep me any longer?

He held it like he wasn't sure whether to give it to me or read it out loud. Finally he shoved it at me.

It had three men's names in fancy printing at the top, and the first sentences were so complicated, I shoved it back. "Tell me what it means."

He laid it carefully on his desk. "It means that Mrs. Cameron liked you very much."

"Mrs. Cameron? I thought—" I nearly said, "I thought you wanted to talk about Clay" but changed it quickly to "I thought she hated me. She sure fooled me."

The deep down knowing that I had loved and truly grieved that ornery old woman was a secret I wasn't ready to share.

"She didn't show it much, that's true. But I think she liked having someone around with as much mettle as she."

"What kind of metal?"

"Mettle. Look it up." He reached for his dictionary and spelled it. *"M-e-t-t-l-e."*

I thumbed the pages, wishing just once Uncle Stephen would tell me something without making a lesson out of it. After I'd read the definition, I looked up suspiciously. "Are you saying I'm as ornery as she was?"

"Let's just say you gave her back as good as you got. She told me once she liked talking to you because you treated her like a person instead of an old woman. Said you made her feel almost young again. So now she's giving you something you can't give back." He tapped the paper. "This says that since the house has been sold, you are to have one thousand dollars. Part is to send you to summer music camp, and the rest is to help with your college education."

I fell back in his chair with my mouth wide open. How many cans of pork and beans and packages of shoelaces had Mrs. Cameron had to sell to earn one thousand dollars?

He burst out laughing. "Bless her heart, that old woman's done something nobody else has ever done. She's left you speechless."

Part 5

Through Thorny Ways

Spring 1951

"I [...] Kae to me because I know which and he would [...] behind. I need them both. I'll save them."

The nurse considered my armload of flowers. If you don't need all these I could give some to people who haven't gotten any. I chose two—Aunt Hannah's orchid in a basket, and the pink rose Lily to Stephen and Aunt Kate had [...] the [...] [...] the nurses' station.

[...]

Chapter 34

Since my accident Freda had been avoiding me. Maybe it was because of our dreadful duet, or maybe it had something to do with not wanting me to mention to her daddy that she hadn't ever come riding over on her black charger to save me from failing arithmetic. But while I was gone, she'd made new friends to sit with at recess. She avoided me at church, too—not that her daddy gave her much time to talk to anybody. He'd volunteered to teach our Sunday school class, took her straight home after church, and still brought her to school every morning.

One evening while we sewed, Bonnie listened to make sure Grace wasn't coming up yet with the hot chocolate she'd gone to make, then leaned closer and whispered, "Freda told me she's sneaking out to meet Charles when her parents go to Charlotte and have Miranda spend the night. She brags about it! I don't know what Mr. Hugh Fred will do to her if he finds out."

"He wouldn't hurt *her*," I whispered back, "but he might kill Charles. And Miranda."

"You think so?" Bonnie's eyes were wide and brown. "But it's not their fault."

"It sure isn't. Charles would never be doing any of this if Freda didn't make him."

"What you girls whispering about in here?" Grace came gracefully through the door, her new yellow skirt swishing about her calves. Since Christmas Grace had made herself a lot of new clothes, all of them cheerful. She was writing Jay, too. Between writing him and writing Pearl about how Geena was doing, she was mailing so many letters that Abby was asking for a real piggy bank. Her pennies overflowed two baby food jars.

As Grace set a tray of three cups and a plate of cookies on the cutting table, Bonnie looked up from the skirt she was pinning together. "Do you think girls ought to sneak out to meet boyfriends, Grace?"

Grace gave her a stern look. "Who you thinking about sneaking out to meet?"

"Not me," Bonnie said quickly.

"Not me either," I hastened to add.

Grace dismissed me with twist of her mouth. "You need to grow a few more inches before I start worrying about you." She turned back to Bonnie. "But if you really want to know what I think, a young girl is a lot safer in a crowd than with just one person."

Bonnie sighed. "That's what I think, too. But what if her daddy won't let her go out with the boy she likes?"

Grace looked relieved that Bonnie was talking about daddies. "Chances are, her daddy's got the right idea. Now, why are you pinning the inside of the front of that skirt to the outside of the back?"

❋

A few mornings later I stood on our porch, pretend microphone at my lips, swinging my light left arm and explaining the new activity in our side yard. "This is Carley Marshall with *Unshaded Windows*. Prisoners from the county jail have come to dig a drainage ditch between our soggy yard and Miss Pauline's. I had to go down and get my cast off early this morning, so I didn't go to school today. Now I'm on our porch watching Abby and John."

Hearing his name, John let go of the porch banister and attached himself to my leg. "Up."

I bent and picked him up awkwardly with my right arm, switching the pretend microphone to my left. Abby clambered up on one of the rockers and pretended to speak into it.

"I doesn't need watching. I's watching the chain gang."

"They aren't a chain gang," I corrected her. "They don't have a chain."

"Dey's just a jail gang," she said into the microphone. "See dem over dere? Hello, jail gang." She shouted and waved across the yard. "We sure is glad you came. My name is Abigail Marshall Whitfield and I live right here."

"Now the men are waving back," I reported. "The man on the overturned bucket has a shotgun to shoot them if they try to kidnap us."

We watched a while longer, but I had a hard time keeping John from going out to help and an even harder time trying to think of something interesting to say about men digging a ditch. I wondered if real reporters ever had trouble making their stories interesting. Even Abby got bored after a while, so I took them to Grace and went to play the piano with both hands at last.

I sat on the stool trying to figure out what to play. I didn't want to play anything loud enough for the prisoners to hear, so I finally settled for Strauss waltzes played real soft. At first my fingers stumbled awkwardly, but gradually they remembered what they were supposed to do. I played brilliantly until Grace called me to eat. It was a shame I couldn't play that well in front of other people.

After we ate, Uncle Stephen asked Abby if she wanted to ride along to the hospital. "I's had enuf of dat waitin' room to las' me a lifetime," she informed me. "'Sides, I forgot to get the mail."

"Bring it right back and take your nap," Uncle Stephen commanded. "Don't you stay over at Miss Pauline's and watch television."

She gave a huff as she went for her coat. "You nebber lets me watch *Guidin' Light*." We heard the door slam behind her.

"You think she'll be all right on the road by herself?" Grace asked with a worried frown. "If one of those men—"

"They're down at the back by now." Uncle Stephen went for his own coat. "I have to do some errands after the hospital, so I won't be back for a while."

I went up to my room to read a new Nancy Drew book while Abby and John napped. Aunt Kate had left the nice chair from her bedroom in mine, and it was a wonderful place to read. I scarcely noticed when Aunt Kate came home and went for her nap, like she often did. What finally got my attention was the sound of muffled sobs. I tiptoed down the hall and listened at Grace's door. Finally I knocked and opened her door.

All I could see was the top of her head, for she was sitting on the side of her bed, holding her face in her hands. "Has something happened to Jay?" I asked quickly.

She wiped her cheeks as she lifted her head, and tried to smile, but it wobbled. "He's fine, honey. But Geena's sicker and they can't figure out what it is." She held out a postcard covered with a script as round and solid as Big Mama herself.

"It says the doctor was going to try a few more tests," I pointed out. "Maybe soon they'll find out what's the matter."

Grace shook her head. "They've been testing her for nearly three months."

"Let's pray," I said daringly. I'd never suggested praying with a grown-up before. "Let's pray right now that they'll know exactly the right test to give her and it will show what they need to do to make her well."

It was such a serious prayer that I got down on my knees and clasped her strong brown hands. We each prayed, and then I squeezed Grace's hands and climbed to my feet. "Thanks," she said softly. Then she looked around as if she'd just noticed something. "Where's Abby? Did you all already finish your picnic?"

"Not me. I've been up here since we finished eating. I thought she was napping."

Her thin eyebrows drew down in puzzlement. "She's been up a long time. She came to the kitchen and said you all were having a picnic and needed Kool-Aid and cookies. 'Lotsa Kool-Aid,' she said. I made her a gallon in a bucket and gave her a stack of paper cups. She carried them out to the yard, then came back and wanted all my molasses cookies. She said you all were having a *big* picnic."

I shook my head. "Not with me, she isn't."

Grace and I had the same thought at the same time. She jumped up and dashed downstairs with me on her heels. "Lawsamercy," she breathed, "with Miss Kate napping and Mr. Stephen off visiting hospitals!"

As we got to the porch, Mrs. Raeburn's Cadillac cruised up our road, but I didn't have time to worry about what she was doing there. I was too busy looking at Abby perched on the lap of the man with the gun. He held her in the crook of one arm and his gun in the other, and she was feeding him a cookie while she chattered happily.

The prisoners sat in a circle nearby, eating the last of Grace's molasses cookies and draining the last of the Kool-Aid. "Abby, come here a minute," Grace called sharply. Her hands were curved into tight fists by her side, and her voice was a little wobbly.

Mrs. Raeburn parked under our maples and opened her door. Miss Emily got out the other side just as the prisoners called in a chorus of voices: "Sure was good." "Bes' cookies I mos' ever ate." "Juice was fine, too." "Thanky, ma'am. Thanky."

Abby wriggled down and ran to the porch calling happily, "De jail gang mens are weal nice. And dat man has a gwand-daughter who's five, dist like me. Her name's Betty Lou. Isn't dat nice?" She ran to the banister and waved to her new friends. They all waved back with wide smiles, then went back to work.

"Hello, Mrs. Raeburn, Miss Emily." I greeted the two women coming up our walk and tried to make it sound like we entertained prisoners in our yard every day.

Behind me Grace was warning Abby softly, "Don't you tell your mama and daddy you had that picnic. You could have been killed!"

"Dey wouldn't kill me," Abby disagreed with serene confidence. "Dey is my friends."

"Is your uncle in?" In spite of all the rouge and lipstick Miss Emily wore, her face looked bonier and whiter than

usual, like a cemetery skeleton risen from the dead. Mrs. Raeburn was white, too, and she didn't look at me.

"He's at the hospital." They both looked startled. I kept forgetting that other people don't talk the way manse people do.
Uncle Stephen going to the hospital or marrying other women
was part of our normal life. I quickly added, "To visit people. But
Aunt Kate's here—" I almost said "napping," but I didn't want
them thinking she was as lazy as Miss Pauline. "I'll call her."

They looked at one another without a word. Mrs. Raeburn
turned like she was fixing to leave, but Miss Emily put a hand
on her arm. "Mrs. Whitfield has a lot of common sense."

Mrs. Raeburn fingered a black choker she wore at the neck
of her black-and-white polka-dot dress and seemed about to
say no. Then she changed her mind. "Yes—maybe Kate would
be even better."

"I'll get her." I hurried inside, too flustered to remember to
invite them in.

As soon as Aunt Kate came to the front door, Mrs. Raeburn's eyes filled with tears. "Oh, Kate!" She pressed a lacy
white handkerchief to her eyes. It was already a damp wad.

Aunt Kate darted me a quick look, then took Mrs. Raeburn's hand. "Let's go up to Stephen's study." The three of
them went upstairs and I ambled back out to the porch.

I hightailed it after them as soon as I safely could and crept
into my closet. I felt so guilty about being there, though, that
I quickly grabbed my pretend microphone. "Carley Marshall,
Unshaded Windows," I whispered, pressing the microphone
to the wall. Journalists had to go all sorts of places other people
couldn't go, I reminded myself.

I heard Aunt Kate ask, "How far along are you?"

And Mrs. Raeburn answer, "Six weeks."

"Surely you can't be sure in six weeks. You ought to see a
doctor—"

"I've seen a doctor. I'd been feeling puny, and Mama died of
women's cancer, so I went to somebody in Charlotte this morning. He said I'm going to have a baby." She stopped; then her
voice was high and squeaky. "What on earth am I going to do?"

This was worse than anything I had imagined. Big Mama's scary stories flitted around my closet. Poor Mrs. Raeburn! But Big Mama said you didn't have babies until you got married. She'd been very firm on that. "When you are married ..." She had said it a lot of times. So how could Mrs. Raeburn—I pressed my ear closer to the wall and forgot the microphone.

I heard Aunt Kate get up and close the window. Maybe she knew more about Preston's habits than she let on. "It's not Jerry Donaldson's, is it?"

"Mr. *Donaldson?* He doesn't even speak to me unless he has to. Why would you think it was his?"

"Stephen has a crazy idea he may be in love with you." Aunt Kate sounded flustered.

"Stephen's crazy, all right, if that's what he thinks. The man doesn't come within twenty feet of me unless it's absolutely necessary." She sniffed. "Besides, you know principals aren't allowed to date teachers. We'd both get fired."

"Not to mention that Mr. Donaldson may be a murderer," Miss Emily added.

She and Mr. Hugh Fred hadn't signed Uncle Stephen's petition. I'd heard Mr. Hugh Fred tell Uncle Stephen in the back hall of the church, "I'd like to, but Emily put her foot down for once. She says she won't prevent Freda going to school if Mr. Donaldson is reinstated, but she doesn't want us putting our names on a petition to send a possible murderer back to all those children. I've got to refuse to sign, Stephen, on the grounds of domestic tranquillity."

Aunt Kate spoke in the tone Big Mama used at the Women's Missionary Society, trying to get the women back on the subject. "Will the daddy of the baby marry you?"

"I wouldn't have him if he could. But he can't. He's already married. I didn't know—I swear I didn't—when we started ..."

"But later?" Aunt Kate still sounded a lot like Big Mama.

Mrs. Raeburn didn't answer right away. Then she sniffed and her voice was so thick, I knew she was crying again. "I didn't find out until it was too late. I've been such a fool!" The way she was blowing her nose and crying in there, Uncle Stephen was going to need a new box of tissues by the time she left.

Aunt Kate sounded like herself again. "Honey, that isn't the issue now. You've got to decide what you're going to do."

"I can't think of anything *to* do. I won't, you know, get rid of it, so I guess I'll have to go somewhere and have it, then give it up for adoption. But where can I go? How can I afford to live without working? And I don't think I *can* give up my baby!" She started gasping and crying so hard, I was afraid she'd throw up. Aunt Kate and Miss Emily made the little sympathy sounds women use when another woman's heart is breaking. Finally they all got real quiet. The only noise was Mrs. Raeburn sniffing and blowing her nose.

Poor Mrs. Raeburn. I wished I had a tissue, too. Warm tears were trickling down my cheeks and my nose was dripping, but I didn't dare sniff. I picked up my skirt and wiped my nose on the hem, then used another piece of hem to polish my tear-streaked glasses and dry my eyes.

"Let me go get us all something warm to drink," Aunt Kate suggested. "Coffee or hot chocolate?"

My bottom was numb and I was getting cold in the closet. I'd have loved a cup of hot chocolate, but I didn't dare get up and go down to make some. I was terrified the floor would creak and they'd hear me. Besides, I might not be able to sneak back up. Abby was a notorious tagalong. As I carefully shifted to get more comfortable, I wondered how often television reporters had to suffer that much to get a story.

After Aunt Kate left, Miss Emily said, "If all this wasn't hanging over Jerry Donaldson's head, he'd have been a real good answer to your problem. Don't I remember you had a big crush on him in high school?"

My jaw dropped in surprise when Mrs. Raeburn give a little chokey laugh and said, "I thought he hung the moon and polished it." Her voice grew soft, like she was talking more to herself than to Miss Emily. I had to press my ear right against the wall to hear her. "He was the gentlest, kindest, smartest, funniest teacher I ever had. At the beginning of the year I used to go out of my way changing classes so I could pass his door and wave. I finally came to my senses of course and started dating Taylor."

Mrs. Raeburn once loved Mr. Donaldson the same way I had loved Clay? While I thought that over, I took off my glasses again and rubbed behind my ear where the earpiece had pressed a trench practically clear to the bone as I listened.

"He may have killed that boy," Miss Emily reminded her.

"He never killed anybody," she said angrily.

"You thought he did, at the time."

"I blamed him because I thought he'd inspired Taylor to leave and join the army, that's all. Taylor admired him so much, he wanted to be just like him. But Mr. Donaldson isn't a killer. He goes out of his way to *help* people. As mean as I was to him after Taylor left and as little as I studied then, he could have flunked me. Instead he said, 'I know the kind of work you can do and the strain you are under. Don't bother writing my last paper.' That's the kind of teacher he was. And remember? He was the one who kept insisting I go to Agnes Scott. 'You can be somebody, Maddie,' he used to say. 'You can get a scholarship and you can become anything you—" She broke off with another chokey sound but this one was more like a sob. "Now look what I've done! If he ever found out, I'd be mortified." Her last word was a groan.

Faraway I heard the clink of spoons and cups as Aunt Kate started up the stairs. Mrs. Raeburn added, "Of course, if I told him I'm in trouble, he might marry me. He's always had a soft spot for an underdog."

"Don't tell him!" Miss Emily's voice was shrill. "He'd spend the rest of his life feeling like he rescued you from a fate worse than death, and you'd spend the rest of *your* life beholden to him. But if you could, you know, flirt with him, go out with him, and marry him quick, at least your baby would be legitimate. Jerry will probably go to jail before the baby is born, so you could tell him it came early."

"I couldn't lie!" Mrs. Raeburn sounded as shocked as I felt.

"You certainly wouldn't have to tell him the whole truth. And don't stare at me like I'm suggesting something wicked. Sometimes it's better if men don't know everything. But you'd have to carry the secret to your grave," Miss Emily warned. "You could never tell Jerry. Not even if he ever gets out of jail."

"Three coffees," Aunt Kate said, pushing open the door. "Are you still talking about Jerry Donaldson? I sure hope something turns up soon to clear him. It just has to."

"You said it might help if I told them I'd planned to meet Taylor that night down by the old barn," Mrs. Raeburn said indignantly, "but after I'd steeled myself to admit I hadn't told them everything back when it first happened, and after I answered all the questions their nasty minds could come up with, it didn't make a bit of difference. The very next thing I knew, they'd arrested him."

"May I have milk and sugar?" Miss Emily interrupted as if they were discussing last spring's dresses.

They all got down to spooning and stirring then. I heard the click of metal on wood as Aunt Kate set the tray down on Uncle Stephen's desk, so she must have used the tray she'd made the first day Mrs. Raeburn came to town. I took advantage of the rustles next door and the creak of the desk chair as Aunt Kate sat down to carefully climb onto my knees. My seat was dead.

To my surprise they didn't talk about either Mr. Donaldson or Mrs. Raeburn's baby while they drank their coffee. Miss Emily said Freda had a new piano piece that was real pretty, and Aunt Kate said she and Uncle Stephen really appreciated Miss Rilla teaching me, too. Mrs. Raeburn said she needed to tell Mr. Hugh Fred that her roof was leaking, and Miss Emily said she'd let him know. Finally Aunt Kate said, "I don't exactly know how to help you with this other thing, Maddie, but I'll do anything I can. And Stephen might be able to help you find a couple to take your baby. We knew some people up in West Virginia who would make fine parents . . ."

"Don't tell Stephen yet. Please?" Mrs. Raeburn sounded very sad. "I can't bear for him to think badly of me."

They didn't bother with the usual chirpy things women say when some of them are leaving: "Do you have to go so soon?" "Yes, I simply must." Mrs. Raeburn just said, "I need to do some serious thinking," and the next thing I knew, they were gone. I crept from the closet and wondered how old you had to be before they handed out the rules for being a grown-up.

❦

At supper Aunt Kate, Grace, and I were all three real quiet, but Abby talked a blue streak. Grace and I held our breath, afraid she'd talk about the prisoners, but she'd seen Miss Pauline in the meantime and was full of other news.

"Miss Pauline says all de dogs in Taylorsville got reebees and has to be killed, and maybe Rowdy's got it and needs to be killed, too, but I tole her no matter how sick Rowdy gets, we isn't *neber* killing him. But she said dey will come from town and do it, so we better hide him. Mama? Mama, are you listenin' to me? We got to hide Rowdy wight now!"

Aunt Kate shook her head like she needed to clear it. "What did you say, Abby?"

She repeated it almost verbatim, adding, "Wight now before de mens get here."

"Nobody is going to hurt Rowdy," Uncle Stephen promised.

Aunt Kate looked worried. "Is it true about the rabies, though?"

"Yes, but it's only strays and unvaccinated dogs they are destroying. Rowdy's shots are up to date."

Grace chimed in softly. "I heard a cow developed rabies in Alexander County, too. It bellowed and bellowed, then just fell forward onto its knees and died."

"Oh, great." I waved my half-buttered biscuit for emphasis. "All we need is for all Uncle Davy's cows to get rabies, get out of their pasture, and start biting everybody. Big Mama knew a person who got bitten by a mad dog, and they had to have over twenty shots in their stomach!"

Abby clutched her stomach. "I doesn't want *any* shots."

"Nobody is going to get shots." Uncle Stephen frowned at me. "Have you ever heard of a cow actually biting somebody?"

"Not exactly, but—"

"When you do, we will continue this conversation. Now who wants to get a bath early so they can listen to *Father Knows Best*?"

"Me, me!" Abby jumped in her chair. John bounced in his, too. Rowdy gave an encouraging bark—safe in the knowledge that he never got a bath at night. As Abby climbed down from her chair, she reminded us, "But we better find a place to hide Rowdy if de mens come." She padded off to the bathroom.

Uncle Stephen rocked back his chair on two legs. "Between Carley being sure we need a bomb shelter and Abby wanting a safe place to hide the dog, we don't need a manse, Kate—we need a fortress."

"You laugh now," I warned him darkly, "but if the Russians do ever get this far, they'll be the ones laughing."

❧

The next weeks I anxiously watched to see if Mrs. Raeburn's tummy was poking out and if she and Mr. Donaldson showed any signs of getting married. It was a perfect time to be falling in love. Spring had really come, with flowers and fruit trees blossoming all over the place.

But her tummy stayed the same as far as I could see, and the two of them only ate lunch together one day. Mr. Donaldson smiled three times—I counted. When I put up my tray, she was leaning over the table teasing him about something. As I went out the door, I actually heard him laugh out loud.

But a few days after that they stopped talking.

They didn't even seem to want to be in the same room. If she came into the cafeteria, he went out. If he came in, she found a reason to leave. One day she bumped into him going out as he came in. "Oh, pardon *you!*" she said rudely.

He replied curtly, "You should have been looking where you were going."

I had given the matter a lot of thought and decided she ought to marry him before he went to jail. He wouldn't know when she had the baby, and she could surprise him with it. But the way things were going, Cupid needed a shove.

The next morning I went up to our room as soon as I got to school. Mrs. Raeburn looked prettier than ever, it seemed to me. That day her hair was freshly washed and waved, and she had a bright red silk flower pinned to the neck of her black and white gingham dress. Her shoes were red, too, and exactly matched her nails and lips. She looked up from the *Ladies Home Journal*. "Mr. Donaldson likes to read," I informed her. "Did you know that?"

"You aren't supposed to be in the room this early," she said coolly. "But since you've come all the way up the stairs, go to your desk and wait for the bell."

That afternoon while I waited for Aunt Kate to take me home, I sidled into the office where Mr. Donaldson was standing at his front window looking out. As I came in, he was singing softly a song from a new musical, *Guys and Dolls*.

I went over and stood by him. Mrs. Raeburn had bus duty that afternoon and was just sending off the last big orange bus. "Don't you think Mrs. Raeburn is the dreamiest teacher in the whole school?"

He looked down with a frown. "Is she napping when she should be doing her work?"

"Oh no, sir. I don't mean she is dreaming; I mean she's beautiful. Don't you think so?"

"Is she a decent teacher?"

"Oh, yes, sir."

"That's all that matters to me. Did you want something?"

"No, sir." I backed out of the office. Grown-ups were so *dumb*.

✳

Easter was the last Sunday in March. "Doesn't really matter when it comes," Aunt Kate lamented, "we're never ready." For most families getting ready for Easter just meant dying eggs for their own children and shopping for new outfits. Thank goodness Big Mama sent our outfits. We'd never have had time to shop. We were too busy helping Aunt Hannah decorate the church with lilies, dying eggs for the church's egg hunt in the cemetery, mimeographing and folding twice as many bulletins as usual for the extra people who would come to church, and getting music ready for the service. Clay had decided that year we'd introduce the children's choir on Easter Sunday, so Abby and I had almost as many rehearsals as Aunt Kate.

I had the added burden of trying to follow a choir director when I couldn't meet his eye.

In the middle of that confusing week, Mr. Donaldson showed up one evening around eight while I was learning a new Chopin prelude. I went to the door and turned on the porch light. Through the big glass pane he'd looked like he was whistling and doing a wiggly dance, but as soon as the light went on, he froze. "Good evening, Carley," he said when I opened the door, and pressed his lips together like he didn't want to say anything else.

"Uncle Stephen's in the dining room," I told him, "listening to the radio as usual."

He cleared his throat a couple of times, then seemed to take a deep breath before he headed to the dining room door. As he stuck his head in the door, I heard Uncle Stephen turn the dial down low and call out a greeting. Mr. Donaldson asked, "Mind if we go up to your study tonight?"

I went back and quickly dashed off Chopin's shortest, easiest prelude, then went to the dining room and told Aunt Kate with a yawn, "I'm so sleepy, I think I'll go on to bed."

"Don't forget to brush your teeth," she reminded me without looking up from her lesson plans.

When I got to my closet, the two men were talking baseball. Mr. Donaldson was a Brooklyn Dodgers fan, like me. Uncle Stephen was dumb enough to like the Yankees. I kept telling him no southerner ought to like a ball team with that name, but he said he could forgive anybody's name if they could play ball like the Yankees.

I sat on my closet floor until my bottom started to ache, and they still hadn't said one blessed thing they couldn't have said down in front of Aunt Kate and me. At last Uncle Stephen asked, "Okay, what's going on? You're gonna bust if you don't tell me."

Mr. Donaldson laughed. "Am I that obvious? I was trying to play Mr. Cool." He cleared his throat again. "I came to ask you to marry me."

I gasped so loudly, I was terrified they'd heard me.

"I'm already married," Uncle Stephen objected calmly.

Mr. Donaldson gave another shout of laughter. "Congratulate me, you old reprobate. I did it! I asked Maddie and she said yes!"

"Wow!" Uncle Stephen knocked his pipe against his shoe. "That happened fast."

"Sure did. Of course, we've known each other for years. But we have you to thank for this new development."

"Me?"

"Sure. You pushed me to get to know her better. A few weeks ago I was eating alone and she joined me and smiled. We talked and I gathered my courage and asked her out. Since then we've seen a lot of each other." Even sucking on his pipe, he sounded happy. "But the school board has a fit if a principal dates a teacher, so we've had to be extremely discreet."

For years afterward I would think *discreet* meant "hateful to one another."

"You work pretty fast once you get started. When did you have in mind to get married?"

"Saturday. I've got a license. We'd like to do it here in your living room, if you'll let us."

"Whoa! For one thing, you heathen, that's Easter Saturday. The rest of us will be up to our ears in an egg hunt over in the cemetery. For another thing, in case you've forgotten, you've got a trial hanging over your head. Have you told her how serious this could be?"

"She knows I'm out on bail, if that's what you mean."

"Have you told her they found your medal in the barn?"

"No. I don't want to worry her."

"You don't think it will worry her if you go to jail?"

"Hey, man, you're the one who's supposed to believe in miracles."

"Miracles, Jerry, not magic. We don't know how that thing is going to go. Why not wait until the trial's over and school's out?"

Mr. Donaldson sucked his pipe a time or two. "We'd like to go ahead and do it. The trial's been delayed again, until June. Anything can happen by then. Maybe they'll find out who really killed Taylor. And even if they don't, if I have to go to trial and even to prison, Maddie will have my house and the savings I've got to live on." He stopped, then said real softly, "I think I could stand to go to jail if I knew she'd be waiting when I got out. But we won't tell the school board until June—if you and Kate can keep a secret. They'd want one of us to transfer to another school, and it's not worth it for the little time left."

"We can keep a secret, but what's your hurry?" When Mr. Donaldson didn't reply, he added, "June's just a couple of months."

I hugged myself. I knew what the hurry was. I wondered if Mr. Donaldson did. He was certainly being stubborn about having the wedding right away. "No point in waiting, now that we know our minds."

Uncle Stephen sucked his pipe and didn't say anything for a minute. "Are you sure about this, Jerry? I know you've carried a torch a long time, but it may be a new idea for Maddie. Don't you want to give her a while to get used to your ornery ways?"

"No. I want to marry her now before she can change her mind. She'll have the rest of our lives to get used to my ways. Will the following Saturday suit you?"

Uncle Stephen hesitated, then agreed. "The following Saturday it is." He added, in a voice like he was trying to be excited even if he wasn't, "Congratulations! Let's go tell Kate." He was trying even harder when they both clattered downstairs a minute later and he called, "Hold on to your hat, Kate. Jerry's got a surprise for you!"

I climbed stiffly from my closet and spoke into the microphone that even I was beginning to know was just a way of speaking my thoughts aloud. "Lots of people have surprises coming. I used to think a surprise was the nicest thing in the world. When did that change? Stay tuned for further developments. This is Carley Marshall with *Unshaded Windows*."

I went to bed and shut my eyes against the pallid sliver of moon crossing the sky. I pretended I was lying all alone on a white planet covered in moondust. A cold, beautiful planet where love was romantic and kind, where hurting was not allowed. It did occur to me that if I was alone, there would be nobody to love, but maybe being alone wasn't so bad. People were too complicated to bear.

Outside I heard Mr. Donaldson's car door slam. "Poor man, he thinks he's so happy and really everything is very sad," I muttered to my viewers, huddling further under the covers. Seemed like I just couldn't get warm that night. "I wish somebody would warn him that he is marrying a woman who loves somebody else. I wish somebody would tell her he is too nice to get fooled into marrying her so her baby can have a daddy. I wish somebody would tell the police he never murdered her old boyfriend. But if I do any of that, everybody I know will kill me. If you have any ideas, please send them to me on a postcard. This is Carley Marshall for *Unshaded Windows*."

But I couldn't just let him leave with nobody to watch or care. When I heard his motor start, I jumped out of bed, ran to my window, and watched him pull away. I stared after him until his taillights, like little eyes red from crying, disappeared.

Chapter 35

Thursday afternoon Mrs. Raeburn and Mr. Donaldson came to talk to Uncle Stephen, but Abby, Aunt Kate, and I had children's choir practice in the church basement. As we were finishing and heading to the fellowship hall for juice and cookies, Clay called from over near the piano, "Carley, could I talk to you a minute?"

Not if I could help it.

I tried not to squirm. "Uh, sorry, but I gotta get home and do my chores." It was all I could do to look him in the face. Practicing every week like we'd been doing, I knew I didn't love him anymore—not like I used to. I wondered why I'd thought his little fox's face handsome. But I still liked him and was sorry we'd never again laugh and joke like we used to.

"What chores haven't you done?" Aunt Kate was busy gathering up the music, but trust her to overhear me.

"I haven't mopped or swept yet and I'll be busy Saturday with the egg hunt."

Abby, who'd been helping her mother, propped one fist on her hip. "Is dat arm good enough to mop *fin'lly?*" You'd think she'd been doing the mopping since I went to the hospital.

Aunt Kate waved away my excuse. "You can do it later. Go ahead and talk with Clay right now. He has something real important he wants to talk about."

Sure he did. That was precisely the problem. I just hoped she didn't know that *what* he wanted to talk about was me looking in his bedroom window.

"Okay, Abby, let's go talk to Clay." I took her by the shoulder and started pushing her ahead of me toward the piano.

The next minute we heard Laura's gurgling voice at the door. "Hey, Kate. How you doin', Carley?" She had on a blue sweater that hugged her curves and matched her eyes, and a straight black skirt, but no matter what she wore, every time I saw her I remembered what she looked like underneath. "We got some thirsty kids today. You all better come get some juice before it's gone."

Abby yelped, "Oh no!" and abandoned me without a backward look.

"My stomach aches," I muttered truthfully. "I think we better talk later."

"It won't take but a minute. Go on, now." When Aunt Kate jerked her head that way, it was easy to tell she was related to Big Mama.

I sidled over toward the piano. Clay sat at the bench playing chords. He kept his red head bent over the keys and spoke too soft for her to hear. "Hey, Little Buddy, you mad at me?"

I looked at the keyboard, too. His fingers could reach far more than an octave without even trying. He played D minor, D major, then D minor again. "You think I'm mad at you?"

I bit my lip and still didn't answer. He reached out his left hand and gently tilted my face toward his. I tried to keep my eyes down but finally I looked at him. Stupid tears filled my eyes, even when I bit my lips to make them stop. I sure was glad I had my back to Aunt Kate.

He shook his head, then bent his head and started playing softly again. "Well, I'm not. Maybe I ought to be but I'm not. I guess all of us have done some things in life we wish we hadn't done. Don't you think?" He looked up and I nodded before I thought. "Just don't do that again. Next time you come to our front door and ring the bell, all right?" I nodded again.

He grinned. "Good. We'd like to have you." He reached up and rumpled the top of my hair. "I've missed you, Little Singing Buddy." He raised his voice loud enough for Aunt Kate to hear easily. "Now here's what I want to talk about. This piece we're doing for Easter sounds a little tame, don't you think?"

My knees turned to rubber from relief. I sat down beside him on the bench to keep from falling and once there found I could say sassily, "More than a little. It's a baby piece."

"I know. Kate and I thought we ought to start out easy, since most of these kids haven't sung in a choir before, but I've been wondering if you and I couldn't spice it up a little by adding harmony to the second verse. We'd have to make it up, because the composer didn't write it that way. Think we could?" He played three chords, then swung into the melody. Aunt Kate drifted over and started singing the regular children's part. Clay came in a third higher, like tenors often do. I picked up on the lower third, then moved the notes around a little.

It took us three run-throughs before we were satisfied, but we all liked what we came out with. "That's going to make all the difference," he told Aunt Kate.

She nodded. "Thanks, Carley. Now go see if there's any juice left before you go home to your chores."

It took me over an hour to sweep and mop that house. Consciences are dreadfully inconvenient sometimes. But it went a lot faster than it could have. I found myself singing as I worked, all the songs we used to sing out on the porch.

❊

After the children went to bed that night, Uncle Stephen and Aunt Kate sat Grace and me down in front of hot chocolate, and Uncle Stephen lifted his cup. "A toast. On the Saturday after Easter, at four o'clock, Madeleine Louise Raeburn and Jeremiah Tait Donaldson will be secretly married in our living room. Let's wish them happiness." I pretended to be real surprised and we all clinked our cups and drank deeply. Madeleine Louise was the prettiest name I'd ever heard. I decided I would rename my new doll *Nancy Louise.*

"We'll have to do a lot of cleaning," Aunt Kate warned.

I held out my poor, red, still-wrinkled fingers. "I just finished cleaning. And it's secret."

"Yes, but this is for next week, and 'secret' doesn't mean nobody is coming; it means nobody is telling the school board or anybody who could tell the school board. You must absolutely promise, Carley, not to tell *anybody* at school that they are getting married. Or that they *are* married, until school is out. If I had anywhere to send Abby away, I would. As it is, we aren't telling her until the morning of the wedding."

"Her connection to the Iredell County school board is minimal," Uncle Stephen added.

"But Pauline's brother is a teacher, and you know how he likes to make trouble ..."

"We'll make Abby promise not to tell anybody, even Sue Mary or Miss Pauline. She'll keep her word," Grace assured us.

"You haven't known her as long as we have," I warned.

"Well, if Pauline gets wind of this, we can kiss secrecy good-bye." Uncle Stephen didn't have to say that. We all knew Miss Pauline as well as he did.

I ran my finger around my cup to get the last of the foam. "Who all's coming?"

Uncle Stephen listed them. "Only family, and they are sworn to keep it a secret. Miss Rilla will play and Clay sing, since he and Maddie are cousins. They're asking Hugh Fred to be best man, Emily to be matron of honor, and Freda to be one bridesmaid. They want you to be the other one."

"Me? I'm not in their family."

"They both said they'd like you to be in the wedding."

"Do I need a new dress?" I hated to ask Big Mama for another one so close to Easter.

"Maddie said to wear your Easter dress."

When Uncle Stephen had gone upstairs, Aunt Kate said, "For the reception, Carley, I'd like to sing them a special song. Will you play for me?"

"No, *ma'am*." Aunt Kate's memory was pretty short if she couldn't remember the mess I'd made the last time I played in public. My stomach flinched just thinking about it. But she just sat there looking at me like I needed to say something else. "I'm still not playing right," I mumbled. "My arm and fingers are a little stiff."

"Would you sing? I'll ask Miss Rilla to play piano and I'll play cello. Would you do that?"

"No, ma'am. Let Miss Rilla play and you sing. I don't wanna."

She gave me an odd look but she didn't insist.

Easter came and went. Our children's choir sounded pretty good, and Clay and I sounded great on the harmony, but it wouldn't have mattered if we hadn't. People were so busy waving at their children and telling each other how cute the little ones were, I don't think they'd have noticed if we'd sung "My Darlin' Clementine."

As soon as Easter was over, Aunt Kate started working us all like dogs—except Rowdy. He just lay around in everybody's way. On Friday evening I went early to my room, raised the shades, and spoke to my television audience. "Everybody ought to have at least one wedding in their house just to see how much work it is. First you have to dust, mop, and polish every single room in the house, in case somebody wanders where they aren't supposed to. I suggested putting satin ribbon across doors we didn't want opened, but Aunt Kate said that would be tacky. Then you have to make lots and lots of sandwiches, cut off the crusts for the family to eat, and cut each little sandwich into four squares or triangles. You have to polish silver trays until you can see your face in them, and small silver dishes to hold nuts and mints. You have to iron a white tablecloth without a single crease or fold. Then you have to iron your best clothes, and on the morning of the wedding you have to take a bath, then tidy your bedroom to look like nobody ever sleeps there. You have to get all that done before the first guest arrives, and if they say, 'Doesn't everything look gorgeous?' you say in an offhand manner, 'Thank you very much. It wasn't really much trouble.' At least that's what you do if you live in a house with my Aunt Kate. This is a very exhausted Carley Marshall for *Unshaded Windows*. Good night."

Saturday morning we still had to make the sandwiches so they'd be fresh, and polish the silver forks and spoons. That was supposed to be Abby's job but she mostly hugged herself and giggled. Uncle Stephen told her he'd go for the mail after everything was over. He told the rest of us there was no point in testing a child beyond her strength.

I was elbow-deep in kitchen mop water when Uncle Stephen answered the phone and came to get me. "There's a call for you."

I hadn't ever gotten a call of my own before.

It was Freda. She sounded breathless, like she'd been running. "Listen, I have to talk fast, before Mama and Daddy catch me. Can I spend the night with you?"

"Uh, I guess so. I'll have to ask...." I hurried across the hall to the dining room. "Can Freda spend the night tonight after the wedding?"

Aunt Kate was busy giving the room one final dusting. "I don't see why not."

I did a little dance on my way back to the phone. I hadn't had a friend spend the night since I'd moved to Job's Corner—except Bonnie when Preston had his accident. That was an emergency, so it didn't count. "She says yes." I sounded almost as breathless as Freda. "Bring your things when you come to the wedding."

"I will. And listen. What time do you go to bed?"

"Around nine, why?"

"Because I want us to go real early tonight. I'll tell you why later." She hung up. I hated going to bed early, but if Freda wanted to—we'd probably talk and giggle all night anyway.

After the house was spotless, we all put on our very best clothes. Aunt Kate and I wore our Easter dresses—hers yellow and mine white dotted Swiss with tiny red polka dots and a wide red satin sash. Abby insisted on wearing her green velvet flower girl's dress.

"You'll be awfully hot. And you aren't a flower girl," Aunt Kate warned her.

"I can be. I knows how."

"This is Carley's time to be a bridesmaid, honey."

"I doesn't want to be a *maid;* I wants to be a *flower* girl." She stood in the hall with one hand on her hip. Sunlight streamed through the big glass pane in the front door and lit her hair like burnished copper as she opened her mouth to roar.

I grabbed her hand. "Let's go see if anybody's coming." She closed her mouth, thank goodness, and willingly followed me out into the yard. It was a glorious day. The sky was blue and gold, the ground spongy and fresh underfoot. And something soft in the air made me think winter had finally remembered spring. But then something red caught my eye—Sue Mary in her little red windbreaker, riding her tricycle up and down their front walk, obviously hoping Abby would come over. I tugged Abby's hand to go back in. All we needed was Abby yelling to Sue Mary that nobody would let her be a flower girl.

All the guests arrived before the bride and groom. Mr. Hugh Fred, in a black suit, looked like a handsome executioner. Miss Emily wore a pale blue silk dress as matron of honor. Freda's dress was my favorite shade of pink, with a wide ruffle on the hem. I suspected they'd bought them especially for the wedding.

"Where's Maddie?" Aunt Kate asked.

Miss Emily looked so upset, I was afraid at first the bride had died. "She called and said Jerry would bring her. I tried to tell her it's bad luck for him to see her before the wedding, but she wouldn't listen. She's always known her own mind."

Freda hoisted a white suitcase big enough for her to stay a week. "Where can I put this? It's heavy."

"Here." I lugged it up to my room and she followed. I was glad the house was so clean. I had even remembered to hide her ruined tray in a drawer under my summer shorts.

She practically danced over to my mirror and smiled at her reflection. Her eyes were shining. "Guess what. Charles and I are going to the Villa Heights drive-in!"

"When?"

"Tonight! They're showing an Abbot and Costello film and I adore them. So he's going to park in front of the old store at six-forty-five, and I'll meet him there. That's why I want us to come up at six-thirty. Then I'll go down the back stairs—"

"We don't have a back stairs. Besides, you can't go sneaking out when you're supposed to be here."

"Why not? Nobody will ever know. Now let's go down and have a wedding. Don't you just love weddings? Aren't they the most romantic things?" She held out her arm so Charles's bangle could catch the light. Then she really noticed me for the first time. "You can't wear red; we'll look tacky together. And you ought to have a long dress." She hurried over and pawed through my closet. "Don't you have any *nice* dresses?"

"No long ones."

She pulled out a navy dress I always hated. "This will do. At least we won't clash."

I was reaching behind me for my buttons when Aunt Kate came to the top step and peered through the banister. "I need you, Carley. What are you doing?"

"Changing clothes."

"You don't have time to change. I need you down here."

Miss Emily was standing at the bottom of the stairs when we got down, almost exactly where we had left her. She held out a green and gold tin. "Here are some of Miranda's butter mints. They melt in your mouth."

"Thank you so much. Carley, put these in the silver shell on the dining room table." Not by one flicker of her eyelid did Aunt Kate imply the Keenes should have brought more, although I'd heard her say softly to Uncle Stephen in the kitchen just that morning, while he washed dishes and she finished making deviled ham sandwiches, "Wouldn't you think Emily and Hugh Fred would have provided *some* of the food? Maddie is his sister, after all, and they've got Miranda."

Freda followed me to the dining room with a swish of her long skirt and watched me put the little pink, green, and yellow

mints in the silver shell. "They really do melt in your mouth."
She chose a pink one. "Try one and see."

I put a yellow mint in my mouth and it melted like fresh,
sweet butter. But it wasn't sweet enough to take the taste out
of my mouth from learning Freda was using me to see Charles.

Before I could mention that again, though, the four Lamonts arrived. I glimpsed them through the dining room door:
Miss Rilla in her best gray dress, Mr. Rob in his only suit and
tie, with his cheeks bright red and his gray hair slicked back
with Brill Creme. Clay looked real handsome in his wedding
suit, and Laura almost pretty in a light blue dress with her hair
piled on her head and her cheeks bright pink. "I fixed Maddie's
hair this mornin'," she was telling Aunt Kate. "She looks just
darlin'."

I waved at Clay as he and Aunt Kate went with Miss Rilla
to practice their music. Mr. Rob went to listen. Uncle Stephen
went upstairs for his white wedding Bible and to put on his
robe. Laura came back to the dining room, where Grace was
putting sandwiches on the trays. "What pretty trays. Are they
real silver?" She turned one over to see if it had a hallmark.

"Of course," I told her. "I polished them."

"Silver is such a lot of work." Freda sounded like she spent
her life polishing it.

Laura looked around. "Where are the bride and groom?"

Before I could tell her I had no idea, Freda picked up a sandwich and took a bite, then gagged. "Ugh! I hate pimento
cheese! Why didn't you make cream cheese with olives?" She
looked for somewhere to throw away her sandwich.

"Because dat costs more money," Abby told her.

Grace frowned. "That's not how you speak to guests." She
added to Freda, "We have deviled ham and chicken salad, if
you like those better. They're still in the kitchen."

Freda headed to the kitchen and came back a minute later
munching one of the chicken salad sandwiches. Abby opened
her mouth again but I pushed her toward the kitchen. "Bring
those little white napkins and silver paper plates." Aunt Kate

had asked Abby and me to hold back on the chicken salad sandwiches because they were more expensive and we had fewer of them, but Abby didn't need to tell the world. I brought the rest of the sandwiches from the kitchen, and Laura and Freda started putting them out like they'd spent all morning making them.

"Laws a mercy, look at that pretty table." Aunt Hannah carried in one of Janey Lou's famous cakes, decorated in white icing roses. Uncle Davy followed with their punchbowl full of little glass cups. "We've still got all the flowers and the tray for under the punchbowl to bring in," she told us. "Can you help us carry things?"

"I has to make the punch," Abby told her importantly.

"You don't need to make the punch until after the ceremony," I informed her.

Abby's lower lip trembled and her eyes clouded. "Come out to the car, old dear," Aunt Hannah said quickly. "I've got something especially for you."

"I want to bring in the bride's bouquet," Freda told her. She carried it low in front of her all the way up the walk, like she was getting married. I saw Preston standing on his porch watching everything.

Aunt Hannah handed Uncle Davy a big arrangement of white flowers. "Put them on the piano for the ceremony; then we'll move them to the dining room for the reception. Here, Carley, can you carry all of these?" She handed me three identical bridesmaid's bouquets. It was the first time I'd ever gotten flowers of my own. I felt like a bride myself. Next Aunt Hannah took out a pink basket with a white satin bow. "Abby, this is for you."

Abby looked at the basket and glowered. "I doesn't get to be the flower girl. And it's not fair, 'cause I already knows how."

"They didn't ask you." I repeated what Aunt Kate had already explained many times.

"This is very important," Aunt Hannah told her. "We're going to fill it up with rice, and before the bride and groom leave, you are to pass it to everybody."

Abby wrinkled her nose. "Wice? We got cake. Who's gonna want wice?"

"Silly!" Freda turned at the top porch step and her curls bounced with delight. "We get to throw it at them as they run down the walk."

"Goody!" Seeing her daddy come onto the porch, Abby called, "You gonna frow some wice, Daddy?"

Uncle Stephen stepped back to hold the door for Freda. "Heavens no. If Pauline saw that, the word would be all over the county in two days."

"Preston's already watching us carrying stuff in," I informed him.

He glanced that way and gave a little grunt of dismay. "If Maddie and Jerry really hoped for a secret wedding, they should have gone to South Carolina."

"What's Souf Car'lina?" Abby demanded as we all hurried inside.

"It's where people run away to get married," Aunt Hannah told her with a chuckle. "But don't get any ideas, old dear. You have to be at least fourteen."

Uncle Stephen looked at his watch. "Well, we're all here except the bride and groom. Reckon they changed their minds?"

We milled around the house. Aunt Kate and Clay practiced some more. Miss Emily, Laura, and Aunt Hannah kept rearranging things on the dining room table. Freda and I went back to the kitchen and sneaked mints from those remaining in the tin.

"When I get married, I'm going to have mint icing on my cake," she informed me. "I like mint better than anything."

"Me, too," I agreed.

"You can't. It was my idea." She popped in another mint and asked thoughtfully, "I wonder if Charles likes mint icing? Oh, well. He'll learn." She reached for yet another mint.

"You'll make yourselves sick," Grace warned us.

Finally we heard a noise at the door and everybody hurried to the hall. Mrs. Raeburn came in first, wearing a pink silk suit, pink pillbox hat, and dyed-to-match taffeta shoes. Mr. Donaldson came behind her like a porcupine in a black suit and tie. His face looked chiseled out of stone, and her eyes were as pink as her suit.

"We're not—," she began.

Mr. Donaldson tightened his lips and glared at her and she stopped. "Let's get this show on the road," he said woodenly.

Uncle Stephen looked from one to the other. "Could I speak with you upstairs?"

"I've got to go to the bathroom," I whispered to Aunt Kate. I hurried to the upstairs bathroom, peeked out to make sure nobody was looking up the steps, and tiptoed to my room. On my way, outside the study door, I heard voices. Uncle Stephen's sounded tentative, probing. Mr. Donaldson's sounded raw and bleeding. Mrs. Raeburn was crying.

I arranged myself carefully on my closet floor, glad I'd swept it and wouldn't get dust on my nice skirt. Uncle Stephen was saying, " . . . isn't a funeral. I don't marry brides in tears and grooms who look like they are being hung."

"It's none of your business how we look," Mr. Donaldson said angrily. "Just do it and get it over with. For God's sake, man!"

"For God's sake I ought to refuse to marry you at all. Now, what's going on? Let's talk—"

"It's past talking. My *bride*"—he made it sound like a dirty word—"has a cake in the oven."

"Jerry!" Mrs. Raeburn burst out.

Mr. Donaldson gave a short laugh. "You can't hide it forever. Every week is going to make it more obvious. The problem is, Stephen, that until an hour and a half ago, I presumed it was my cake. Then Maddie called and said she had to talk to me; she couldn't go through with this after all. When I got to her place, she informed me the baby belongs to somebody else. A man who is already married, so can't do the honors. I'm a stand-in at my own wedding."

"I told you I can't go through with it," she said hotly.

"Why didn't you tell him before?" Uncle Stephen asked sternly.

"I thought ... I thought I could live without telling him for the rest of my life. But I couldn't. He's ... he's too fine to lie to."

"You lied to me already." His words broke in sharp, jagged edges.

"So why are you marrying her, Jerry?"

"Because I said I would. I don't go back on my word."

"Really? That's the real reason?" I could almost see Uncle Stephen's raised brows.

"Yes, really. I won't make her have that baby without giving it a name. After it comes, she'll be free to go."

"Not if I marry you, she won't!" I jumped. Now I knew where Abby got her roar. I'd never heard Uncle Stephen so angry. "I won't stand before God and those people downstairs and perform a farce. Either you both mean to try with all your hearts to make this marriage work or it's off. Go to the courthouse. Go to Hades, if you choose. But I'm not marrying anybody unless you really mean it."

"I'm not, either," Mrs. Raeburn said in a small, wet voice. "I'm not marrying you, Jerry. I told you before and I'm telling you again. You deserve better than this, and I deserve more than somebody I'll owe a favor to for the rest of my life." High heels clicked across the study floor. The door slammed and I heard her running down the stairs. In another minute I heard a car start outside and drive away.

The whole house held its breath while both men breathed hard. Then Uncle Stephen said softly, "Did you tell her about them finding the medal?"

"Not yet. The trial may never happen."

"Right. Like her baby may never happen. Jerry, what's the matter with you two? You're *both* too fine to start this marriage with lies between you."

He gave a bitter laugh. "We aren't starting any marriage. Or did you forget?" His sigh seemed to come from the toes of his polished black shoes. "I love her, Stephen. I wanted her more than life itself. But I can't live with a liar."

"Neither can she. When the two of you get that straight, come back and we'll talk about a wedding. Meanwhile you stay here while I go down and announce that we're having a party today instead. Read a couple of books. I'll come get you when the coast is clear."

In a minute I heard Uncle Stephen clump downstairs. I waited another minute, then tiptoed to the bathroom and flushed. When I started downstairs, Uncle Stephen and Mr. Hugh Fred were standing in the hall. Uncle Stephen was right in front of the stairs, like he was blocking them.

"I think I ought to talk to him," Mr. Hugh Fred insisted. "Nobody jilts my little sister without telling me why."

I saw Freda come to the dining room door. She saw me and motioned me to be still.

"He didn't jilt her; they both agreed to call it off," Uncle Stephen said in the tone of somebody repeating something for the third or fourth time. "They're adults, Hugh Fred. When she got married the first time, she was a legal adult. She can do as she pleases."

"But we all got dressed up, wasted a perfectly good Saturday afternoon—"

"Is that all you can think about?" Freda blazed from the door. "Your wasted afternoon? Aunt Maddie has a broken heart. I saw her face as they left. She's just brokenhearted."

Mr. Hugh Fred went over and put his arm around her. "Don't you worry about Maddie Lou, honey. She's tougher than she looks. Besides, what do you know about broken hearts? You don't have to worry your pretty little head about that for years yet." He looked up and noticed me. "Isn't that right, Carley?"

I shrugged. "I guess so."

I went into the dining room and found Abby standing on a chair, carefully ladling ginger ale and lime sherbet into punch cups. After each cup she stirred it with such a serious face, you'd have thought she was mixing a love potion. Maybe she *should* have made the punch before the wedding. When we'd cut Janey Lou's cake and everybody had eaten more than any of us normally ate at four on a Saturday afternoon, Clay jiggled Laura's elbow.

"We gotta go get out of these fancy clothes and get some supper before the movie starts." He grinned. "We're gonna try the Villa Heights drive-in as old married folks."

I choked on my punch. Freda quickly asked Aunt Hannah, "Could I have the bride's bouquet? She left it."

"Sure, old dear. Take it home and put it in water. It won't last long, though."

Freda lifted it to her nose, then thrust it at her mother. "Take it home and put it in water." While the rest of us carried dishes back to the kitchen and Aunt Kate filled the dishpan with hot water, she developed a little headache and had to go lie down.

I had wondered how Uncle Stephen would get Mr. Donaldson out of the house without seeing anybody, but Uncle Davy did that while the rest of us were eating cake and drinking punch. Uncle Davy was so quiet, nobody missed him until Aunt Hannah looked around and said, "Why lands, Davy's gone and left without me. That man gets more absentminded every day."

"He took Jerry down to your place," Uncle Stephen told her. "I promised to run you home when you get ready to go."

After everybody else had left, Abby and I went to sit in the swing. It seemed a shame to take our dresses off, we felt so pretty.

Preston bicycled from his house to ours and right up the walk. "Saw you had a wedding over here today," he said with a certainty that would have done Miss Pauline proud.

"No, we didn't," Abby corrected him glumly. "Ev'ybody got dwessed up in weddin' clo'es but we dist had a party." She heaved a most adult sigh and said with perfect diction, "No bride, no groom, no rice."

That about summed up our day.

Chapter 36

One good thing came out of that dreadful day. Once I finally changed my clothes, I remembered we hadn't gotten our mail. I figured I might as well go over to Miss Pauline's for the key and see if Abby's latest Cheerios comics had arrived. In those days you could get three little comic books for a dime and box tops, and since I didn't need my money anymore for music camp, I'd sent away for some to surprise her. They might make her feel better.

Miss Pauline and Miss Nancy were sitting on the porch talking while Bonnie let down one of Sue Mary's hems. "You don't have mail," Miss Pauline informed me helpfully. "But sit down and rest a spell. Looked like you were having quite a to-do over there this afternoon."

"Not really, just a few friends in for cake and punch." I felt terrible, since none of them had been invited. "It was, ah, Grace's birthday." I didn't know when Grace's birthday was, but it was unlikely they did, either. "It was just, ah, people she's sewed for."

"You girls are getting to be regular little seamstresses, aren't you?" Miss Nancy asked. "I've seen some of Bonnie's work and she's learned a lot."

"But it's hard to get material," Bonnie complained gently. Miss Pauline almost never took her to town.

"It sure is," Miss Nancy agreed. "I wish there was a fabric store closer."

"Why don't you start one?" Miss Pauline suggested. "You could get you some remnants from the mills up near Hickory and probably do pretty well."

Miss Nancy shook her head. "I could never do anything like that." But she didn't sound real sure she couldn't.

"You could use Mrs. Cameron's old store," I contributed. "It's clean and I'll bet Clay and Laura wouldn't mind."

"Clay's fixin' to bulldoze it in the next few weeks," Miss Pauline informed me. "He wants to put up a garage where he can work on other people's cars and store his own."

Miss Nancy had a thoughtful look on her little bird's face. "I could use our big front room. We never go in there and it already has shelves. Wash built them thinking he'd fill them with books, but we're neither one of us much for reading. And he built me a real long sewing table upstairs. I could have Clay and Daddy Rob bring it down to cut on."

"Rob could put you in a door where one of the windows is, so folks don't have to come into your house." Miss Pauline was always real good at thinking up work for other people. But that was actually a good idea.

Miss Nancy shook her head like she wished she could do it but couldn't. "How would I manage when the children are home from school?"

"I could help you in the shop some afternoons," Bonnie offered.

"Me, too," I added. "You could pay us in fabric."

The seed planted that day bore fruit within just a few weeks. Nancy's Nook opened with punch, cookies, and balloons, and women came from miles around to buy material and patterns for themselves and their daughters.

❦

Freda came down to supper that night in a darling plaid skirt, bright blue sweater, and blue socks to match. I could tell Aunt Kate thought she was mighty dressed up for Saturday night at the manse (I'd put on my after-school play clothes), but she didn't say anything. I kept thinking I ought to tell Aunt

Kate or Uncle Stephen what Freda was planning, but I never got a chance. She was a perfect guest, acting like eating left-over sandwiches and drinking punch was what the Keenes did every Saturday night. But we had scarcely finished what Abby called our "no-wedding cake" when Freda gave a huge yawn. "I don't know what's the matter with me. This wedding seems to have worn me out. Aren't you exhausted, Carley?"

Actually, I was. But it was my night to help clean up. "I'll be ready for bed as soon as I wash the dishes."

"Why don't you all run on upstairs?" Aunt Kate suggested. "You've already done enough today."

That should have made me jig with joy. Instead I went heavily up the stairs feeling like Benedict Arnold. In my room I started getting out my pajamas. Freda brushed curls around her fingers as she peered out my window. "How can I get down-stairs, Carley? I can't climb off that roof. I wouldn't have come if I'd known you didn't have a back stairs. Everybody else does."

"Just you."

"And Aunt Hannah. And Miss Nancy and Mr. Wash—everybody except you."

It was a deprivation I'd never felt before.

She went to the mirror and checked to be sure her lipstick hadn't smeared when she'd pressed her face to the window. "Think of something. You're smart."

I wasn't really but I did know she could easily leave. "You can just walk downstairs and go out, if you want. Everybody else will be in the dining room or the kitchen for a while yet, and they'll have the radio on. Not one soul will hear you if you tiptoe. Just don't bang the door."

"How do I get back in?"

"Just walk. We don't usually lock our door. But you'll have to come up the stairs in almost dark. We just have a little night-light in each bathroom. And Uncle Stephen doesn't go to bed until eleven."

"I'll wait until after eleven, then." She reached into her suitcase and brought out Charles's football jacket. No wonder she had needed such a big suitcase.

I sat at the window and watched our walk. In a minute I saw her hurry down it and disappear into the shadows of the maples. I raised my window and heard Charles's pickup start.

I wished I could go down and listen to the radio with Uncle Stephen and Aunt Kate, but I didn't dare. I didn't even dare go next door to help Grace sew. Freda's deceit had jailed me in my own room.

I read until eight-thirty, then turned off my light. But tired though I was, I couldn't get to sleep. I knew what I'd been waiting for when, about nine, the telephone rang. Uncle Stephen came upstairs and tapped lightly on my door. "Freda? Your daddy's on the phone."

I froze.

As moonlight streamed over my pink chenille spread, I considered my options. I could creep to the door, turn the key, and pretend we were sleeping too hard to hear. But he'd only knock louder.

My stomach ached.

I could tiptoe to the door and tell Uncle Stephen Freda was so fast asleep, I'd go talk to Mr. Hugh Fred myself. But what could I say? Even Big Mama would be hard put to come up with a socially acceptable lie for this situation.

I felt like I wanted to throw up.

I could go down and tell Mr. Hugh Fred the truth. He'd go to the drive-in and drag Freda from Charles's truck, kill Charles, then come back to beat me up for helping Freda deceive him.

At the thought of the pain when he broke my arm again, my stomach rebelled.

I flung off the covers, hurtled past a startled Uncle Stephen, and barely made it to the toilet before I threw up butter mints, "no-wedding cake," and fear.

"Honey, are you all right?" He wet a wash rag and held it to the back of my neck while I rinsed out my mouth.

I nodded. "I am now. Must have eaten too many butter mints."

"Or something. Did you hear me say Mr. Hugh Fred's on the phone?"

"My knees are wobbly." I perched on the side of the tub. "I don't feel like talking to him right now."

"He wants to talk to Freda."

I looked at the wide, bare floorboards, noticing that the tub's claw feet just looked like big balls without my glasses. I didn't say a word.

Uncle Stephen left the bathroom and went back to my room. Then, instead of coming back to me, he went down the stairs. "Hugh Fred, Carley's got an upset stomach right now. Yeah, throwing up and everything. Possibly too much wedding cake. Let me call you back in a minute or two."

We weren't solving the problem, just postponing it. I was going to die before morning no matter what we did.

Uncle Stephen tiptoed back upstairs and leaned against the bathroom door. "Where is she?"

I shrugged.

"That's a lie even if you don't say a word," he warned.

I shot him a baleful glance. "At the movies."

"With whom?"

"Charles Beal."

"From the church?"

I nodded.

"Which movie?"

"Villa Heights drive-in."

"Good heavens!" He sank to the side of the tub beside me. "We're in the soup."

I nodded again. "Mr. Hugh Fred's gonna kill me."

"I doubt it will get that serious—"

"It will!" I interrupted with a wail. "You didn't see him hit Charles the night of the dance. And he almost killed him after Clay's wedding. I heard what he said. He said if Charles didn't leave Freda alone, he'd break every bone in his body and he'd never play football again. He meant it, Uncle Stephen. He did!" By then I was sobbing tears of terror. "And that's what he'll do to me when he finds out I knew where she was going."

"Not to mention what he'll do to Freda."

"He won't do anything to her. She's his princess. He'll just lock her up some more and she'll keep sneaking out when he's not there. They've been doing that since Christmas."

He shoved back his hair. "That long, huh?"

I nodded. "And Charles calls her every afternoon while her mama naps, and—"

"I'd never have credited Charles Beal with so much romantic zeal." Uncle Stephen sounded dazed.

"It's Freda. She thinks up what they'll do, and then he does it. He's crazy about her."

"He is crazy. I'll give you that." Uncle Stephen sat on the side of the tub with his hands dangling between his legs. He studied the tips of his worn brown shoes for so long, I had time to separate out the smells of Swan soap, Dutch cleanser, and Pepsodent toothpaste. Then he sighed. "Any good ideas what we ought to do?"

My bottom was growing numb, so I shifted a little. "We could go get her, I guess. Bring her home."

"I don't like to come between parents and their daughter or help her lie to them. At the same time, I do feel Hugh Fred may be a tad unreasonable ... " He took off his glasses, pulled out his shirttail, and polished them, as if that would help him see his way clear.

"If we could get ahold of Clay, he could tell her to come home. He and Laura went to Villa Heights."

"They sure did." Uncle Stephen looked at me like he'd suddenly discovered I was brilliant. He stood up. "Go get your robe on. You're freezing."

That was the first time I realized I didn't have it on or that my teeth were chattering. My heart was beating so hard, I hadn't heard them.

I got down and found him at the dining room table looking up the number. "Where's everybody else?" I asked.

"Kate went to bed, exhausted, and Grace has gone over to see Bess, Jay's mother, for the evening. Let's see if we can rustle up Clay." While he called the drive-in and asked them to page Clay Lamont, I stood right beside him and burned with shame to remember the night Clay paged *him*. In a few minutes I could hear Clay clear as anything, and even as awful as things were, I liked hearing his voice. "I'll cruise around and find them, then call you back."

We stood in the hall like extra coatracks until Clay called back. "I have Freda here with me. You want her brought back there or taken to Hugh Fred's?"

"Bring her home!" another voice thundered through the receiver. We'd plumb forgotten the Keenes were on our party line and could hear our phone when it rang.

"Hugh Fred," Uncle Stephen said quickly, "it turns out Carley was throwing up because she was scared you were going to find out that Freda's gone to the movies."

"She never said a thing to us about going to a movie."

"Yeah, well, she didn't say anything to us either, but she's with Clay and Laura. Isn't that right, Clay?"

"Yessir, she's with Laura in our new convertible. I'll have to give you a ride sometime, Hugh Fred. Runs like a dream."

"I don't care how it runs; when I send my child to spend the night somewhere, I expect her to stay there."

"I agree," Uncle Stephen chimed in. "When a child is at my house, I expect her to stay put, too. We'll talk about that as soon as she gets back here."

"She doesn't need to keep you folks up. Clay, bring her on home. You hear me?"

"That okay with you, Preacher?"

Uncle Stephen hesitated, then said, "Sure, Clay. We'll bring her suitcase to church in the morning."

"That will be fine. We'll see you then. Good night." That was Mr. Hugh Fred.

"Good night." That was Clay.

"Good night." Uncle Stephen hung up, put one hand on my shoulder, and steered me to the dining room. "I think we both need a drink." He gently pressed me to the couch and went to the kitchen. In a minute he came back with two small glasses of cold ginger ale. "I've heard this is good for stomach upsets. I don't know if it's true, but since we've got it handy, you might as well give it a try."

He drained his glass in three swallows, but I sipped the cold, fizzy liquid and felt my nose tingle. The slower I drank, the longer I could postpone the rest of our conversation. But a small glass of ginger ale can't last forever. As soon as I set it down, Uncle Stephen leaned his elbows on the table across from me. "That's the closest I have come in years to telling an outright lie."

"But you didn't," I pointed out admiringly. "You didn't tell a single one."

"No, but I came too close for comfort. And you could have prevented this whole thing, couldn't you? If you'd told us what she was planning to do?"

"But wouldn't that be tattling?"

"Not if someone else's health or well-being is endangered."

"You think he'll hit Miss Emily again?"

"Did Miss Emily know where she was going?"

"I don't think so."

"Then let's hope not. But if Emily isn't at church, I'll go straight up there right afterward to make sure she is all right." He ran a hand over his face and shoved back his hair. "I can't believe I am saying these things to you, particularly about a member of my session. But Kate told me you and Abby were real troopers while I was out looking for Freda before."

"What makes him hit people? He's so nice most of the time. Or is he just pretending?"

"No, honey, people are seldom all bad or all good. But some people's bad parts hurt themselves, while other people's hurt others."

"Can you make him stop?"

"I hope so. But if you've got an extra prayer before you go to bed, pray for Freda and her family, okay?"

I sighed. "I thought their family had everything in the world."

He grunted. "I've had the same illusion a few times myself. But the closest thing we have to somebody with everything in our church is Hannah Anderson, and even she's got a few warts. The incredible thing is, God loves us, warts and all." He stood up. "Now go on back up to bed. Stomach feel better?"

"Yessir. I'm fine."

As I climbed into bed, the huge full moon stood right over the Keenes' high roof. I thought about Mrs. Raeburn and wondered if she was crying in her little house down behind the big house. I wondered what Mr. Donaldson was doing. I wondered if Freda was home yet and what would happen to Charles.

Rays of moonlight streamed into my room and filled it with silver. I'd read in a story once that if you could hold a handful of moondust, you could have any wish you wanted. But no matter how I cupped my hand, I couldn't catch a single grain to keep anybody safe.

Chapter 37

Uncle Stephen didn't have to go to the Keenes' after church. They came for him at dawn.

I woke when I heard a car door slam. Feet ran lightly up our walk and somebody turned our doorbell again and again. We still had one of those big round ones you had to turn. When I opened my eyes, the sky was that pearly color when it has put off gray but hasn't yet decided to wear blue. I was climbing sleepily out of bed to see whose car it was when I heard another car drive up and another door slam.

"Emily! Come back here!"

Our doorbell rang more frantically. Miss Emily must not have known we never locked our door.

I ran to the window. Both Keene cars were parked crookedly under our maples, and Mr. Hugh Fred was hurrying up our walk in a long maroon bathrobe. Even in pajamas he was the handsomest man I ever saw, but he was also one of the angriest.

I heard Uncle Stephen open the door as I reached the top step. By the time I slid down the banister to the bottom, Miss Emily had practically fallen into the hall. She had on a pink chenille bathrobe with her hair in a net and her face shiny with cold cream.

"Freda!" she cried urgently, waving a pink piece of paper.

"I told you to let me see that." Mr. Hugh Fred crossed our porch in two strides and shoved Uncle Stephen aside like he was little John. He snatched the paper from Miss Emily and read it real fast. Then he threw back his head and gave a roar that would have done Abby proud. "You knew about this!" He lunged for Miss Emily but she darted behind Uncle Stephen. Mr. Hugh Fred's palm hit his shoulder instead of her face, sending Uncle Stephen back a step or two.

"Calm down." Uncle Stephen waved both hands. "Calm down."

Hugh Fred drew back his fist like he would hit him again on purpose, but Uncle Stephen grabbed his arm and twisted it behind him so fast, none of us knew it was coming. Mr. Hugh Fred yelped in pain. "Are you going to sit down and shut up?" Uncle Stephen demanded.

Mr. Hugh Fred panted hard but he nodded. Uncle Stephen let him go and pointed to the living room. "In there. Although you've probably awakened our whole family, there's no need for them to hear the rest."

Mr. Hugh Fred marched into the living room but Miss Emily hung back. Uncle Stephen stepped in front of her. "This is one time when I think a gentleman ought to go first." She crept in after him. Not one of them acted like they had seen me at all.

I tiptoed to the door, but both the Keenes were talking at once, so I couldn't tell what anybody was saying. Uncle Stephen must have had the same problem, because he said, "One at a time. Emily, what was in the note?"

I could tell Miss Emily was reading, because her voice was all on one level. "I am going to marry the man I love. After this, you will not be able to tell me what to do. Love, Freda." Miss Emily's voice went up nearly an octave. "Stephen! The child's fourteen!"

"So help me, I'll take him apart limb from limb!" If Charles Beal was anywhere in North Carolina, he could hear Mr. Hugh Fred's roar.

"The first thing to do is to find them," said Uncle Stephen. "Maybe Carley can help."

"Did she know this was going on?"

I sure was glad I wasn't in Mr. Hugh Fred's hitting range right then. But when I heard footsteps heading for the door, I darted to the foot of the stairs like I'd been waiting there all the time. Uncle Stephen stuck his head out and motioned me to join them. "We need to talk to you."

Mr. Hugh Fred perched on the very edge of Aunt Kate's new sofa as if he were ready to leap to his feet any second. Miss Emily had the chair farthest away from him, and she pressed back into it like she wanted to be invisible. If I looked like that in the morning, I'd want to be invisible, too. But I knew she was just afraid Mr. Hugh Fred would hurt her again.

I stood on one foot, then the other, while Uncle Stephen explained to me what I already knew. "Freda's run away, maybe to get married. Do you know anything about it?"

"No, sir," I answered truthfully.

"You have no idea where she might be?"

I started to shake my head again; then I remembered something. "Maybe she went to South Carolina."

Mr. Hugh Fred started to his feet but Uncle Stephen waved him back. "Why would you think that?"

"You said yesterday that if Mrs. Raeburn wanted a secret wedding, she should have gone to South Carolina. And when Abby asked what was in South Carolina, Aunt Hannah said she'd have to wait awhile; you can't get married there until you are fourteen."

Now Mr. Hugh Fred did leap to his feet. "Freda heard that? You are sure?" A vein pounded in his temple and his fists were clenched.

I backed farther away from those fists. "Yessir. She was carrying in the bride's bouquet."

"Did Hannah happen to mention any specific place in South Carolina?" Uncle Stephen had sweat on his forehead and he had shoved his hair all askew.

"No, sir. I guess we could call Mary Beal and ask if she knows where they were going."

Mr. Hugh Fred was already at the door. "Where's your phone book, Stephen?"

Uncle Stephen went after him. "I think you'd better let me do the talking." I sidled to the door and watched as he dialed.

"Good morning, Mrs. Beal. This is Stephen Whitfield. I hate to bother you this early, but I badly need to talk to Mary. Is she up? Oh." He laughed. "That's where I'd have been at her age, too. Could you get her for me? It's real important."

He covered the mouthpiece. "She's milking." Nobody said another word until we heard a little scratch on the line. "Mary? This is Mr. Whitfield from the church. How are you? Listen, Mr. and Mrs. Keene are here, and they think Freda may have gone somewhere with Charles, either late last night or early this morning. Do you know anything about that?"

We heard a few little scratches while Mary replied.

"I appreciate your wanting to keep your promise, but Charles and Freda aren't thinking real straight right now. You don't want them to get in trouble, do you?"

One small scratch.

"I didn't think so. Sometimes people ask us to make unwise promises, and this is one of them. If you'll tell me where they went, I will do all I can to assure that neither is unduly punished." Mr. Hugh Fred snorted but Uncle Stephen ignored him. "Will you trust me?"

Mary still seemed reluctant.

"Yes, but she's just fourteen, Mary, and not as smart as you are." Mr. Hugh Fred's hand shot out like he wanted to disagree, but Uncle Stephen went right on. "Would you have been ready to take on a whole house on your own at fourteen? No, I didn't think so. It's a big responsibility, and I don't think Freda's ready for it, either. And Charles will be giving up any chance he has of getting a football scholarship. You and I both know how important that can be with a lot of children in a family. So I need you to tell me where they went, for their own sakes. I'll bring them back and nobody need ever know a thing." He listened intently. "Thank you so much. Good-bye."

He hung up and turned to Mr. Hugh Fred. "Dumb kids. Went to Rock Hill. Who they expect to find to marry them without a license, I don't know, and offices are closed Sundays. I have a seminary friend down there. Want me to rouse him and let him do some looking for us?"

Mr. Hugh Fred started for the door. "I'm going down to do some looking myself."

Uncle Stephen grabbed his shoulder. "If you go down there, you are going to lose your daughter. You know that, don't you?"

Mr. Hugh Fred whirled. "What are you talking about?"

"There's a verse in the Bible that says things we hold on to, we lose, and things we give up, we get to keep. That certainly applies in this case. You're holding that child too tight. Charles Beal isn't a bad boy. He's actually one of the best we have around here. He just wants to go out with your daughter. He doesn't really want to carry her away to some cave. He's probably only been persuaded to do this dumb thing because he thinks he's protecting Freda from you."

"Whoever gave him that idea? And what makes her think I'd let her stay with him?"

"Uncle Stephen said—," I blurted, then stopped. They both turned to stare at me like they had forgotten I was there.

"Uncle Stephen said . . . ," Uncle Stephen reminded me.

"You said yesterday that Miss Maddie doesn't have to do anything Mr. Hugh Fred says, because when she got married the first time, she was a legal adult and could do what she pleased. I'll bet Freda thinks that if she gets married, she won't have to do what her daddy says, either."

Uncle Stephen shoved back his hair. "I don't remember saying any such thing."

Mr. Hugh Fred nodded. "You did, standing right there." He pointed to the spot. "But what I took you to mean was, Maddie was already a legal adult before she got married the first time. Dang it!" He pounded one fist into another. "Do these children do nothing but hang around listening and misinterpreting everything we say?"

"Not much," Uncle Stephen agreed wryly.

"I love her, Stephen. I don't want her hurt. And I don't want her growing up too fast. Can you understand that?"

"Perfectly. But somebody once said a child grows up a couple of years after they think they do and a couple of years before we parents think they do. Freda's in the gray area right now, and you all are going to have to walk the tightrope between what she thinks she can do, what you think she can do, and what she really is ready to do. We can talk about that later. Right now I think maybe I ought to call my friend in Rock Hill. Carley, go make some coffee, would you?"

I hurried to the kitchen feeling a little like a grown-up, but it wasn't all that much fun.

Over coffee Uncle Stephen reported what his friend told him. "He said he'll go to places couples usually go and see if he can find them. He also said he has daddies in his church who work with him on this sort of thing. They are used to getting calls like mine from North Carolina preachers." He sipped his coffee. "He told me, 'Tell her daddy not to worry; we'll find her.'"

Mr. Hugh Fred's mouth flickered in a rueful grin. "I'm not the only crazy daddy?"

Miss Emily leaned over and patted his hand. "You aren't crazy, honey; you just love her too much. I keep telling you, we've got to let her grow up."

Uncle Stephen rubbed his face. "Right now you need to let me go bathe and shave, if I'm going to preach."

Miss Emily's hands fluttered. "We both have to teach Sunday school and Hugh Fred has a solo in the anthem."

Uncle Stephen walked them to the door. "Don't worry. I'll leave Carley to take a call if they find her, and tell her exactly what to say."

Thank goodness he wrote it down. I thought at the time that was utterly silly, but when the phone rang and a man said, "Ma'am? I have Freda Keene right here and she wants to speak to you," my mind went blank.

"Hey, Freda. This is Carley" was all I could think to say.

"Carley? I thought it was Mama on the line."

"No." I reached for the paper and struggled to read Uncle Stephen's scrawl. "Uncle Stephen thought we ought to talk to you first and assure you that you will not be punished if you come on back home. He's going to meet with you, Charles, and your folks to see if you all can't work out a compromise everybody can agree on."

"I don't want to talk to you; I want my mama. Where's my mama? I want her right now!"

My script had run out. "She's over at church. I can run get her, but you'll have to wait, and it's long distance. Why don't you all just come on home?"

"I won't ride one more mile with Charles in that filthy truck. It smells of cows and pigs, and the springs are all broken, and he ... he ..." She broke down and sobbed.

The man's voice came back on the line. "The little lady is pretty upset, ma'am. We've sent the boy on home but she refused to go. Says she wants you to come get her yourself."

I started to tell him I was too young to drive but it seemed like a lot to explain. Besides, I'd just deciphered Uncle Stephen's last line. "Tell me exactly where she is and we'll come get her." I carefully wrote down the address and directions to get there.

"She'll be fine until you arrive. I've got two girls of my own and she's welcome to stay right here with us. We'll feed her dinner and let her get some rest. I figure it'll take you three hours at the very least."

It would take more than that. First I had to go to the church and figure out how to tell Miss Emily without Mr. Hugh Fred seeing me from the choir. No matter what Uncle Stephen told him, if he knew I'd found Freda, he'd be hightailing it to Rock Hill.

I stretched up on tiptoe and peered through the little window in the swinging doors between the narthex and the sanctuary. She was sitting real near the back. I couldn't see Mr. Hugh Fred, which meant he was behind Uncle Stephen. If I went down the middle aisle, he shouldn't see me.

Have you ever had to walk down the aisle during a sermon? I felt myself growing ten feet tall and nine feet wide and knew every head in that congregation would swivel to watch me instead of listening to Uncle Stephen. Then I remembered something I'd read once: if you want to be invisible, just act like you know exactly what you are doing. *I am going to get*

Miss Emily, I told myself. *I am going to walk down that aisle like I do it every week.* Without looking at a single person, I hurried in and tapped Miss Emily on the shoulder. I put one finger on my lips and motioned her to follow me. Then I turned and walked out. It was over in ten seconds. Uncle Stephen hadn't paused for breath. Mr. Hugh Fred hadn't seen a thing.

Miss Emily needed to take a breath, though, or she was going to pass out. "Did she call?" she hissed as soon as the sanctuary doors swung shut behind us.

"Yes, ma'am. Here's the address. She wants you to come get her yourself. She said she wouldn't ride home with Charles."

"I can't go all that way by myself. I'd be scared to death. You'll have to come with me." She clutched my arm. "I'll be so grateful."

Which is how I got to Rock Hill, South Carolina, for the very first time. I'd heard of Rock Hill all my life. Big Mama went to Winthrop College and even took Mama back to a reunion when she was just a little girl. I knew they had a train station and the college was beautiful. But somehow I suspected I wasn't about to get a tour of town.

I was right. Miss Emily had one thing on her mind, and she talked about it all the way down: Freda, Freda, Freda. If I'd ever thought it was a pretty name, I changed my mind about the time we got to Huntersville, and we still had two hours to go.

I also wished Miss Emily wasn't such an awful driver. She perched right on the edge of her seat and clutched that wheel like it was running away with her instead of her turning it. She went sixty miles an hour right up to the rear of other cars, then slammed on her brakes. She wouldn't pass for ages but kept swinging out into the other lane and then back, saying, "I don't know if I can make it; do you think I can?" as if I knew a thing about it. When we finally got around a slow driver, she'd speed up again, saying over and over, "I can't believe I'm driving this fast. It makes me nervous to drive this fast." But she didn't slow down, except to put on her brakes at every curve and, when we went through towns, at every stoplight whether they were red or green. And when she had to turn right, she pulled to the middle of the road, came to a dead halt, then turned. I wanted to say what Uncle Stephen always said under his breath when he followed somebody like that: "You aren't driving a tractor and pulling a hay wagon, lady."

I didn't, though. I was too busy trying to keep one eye on the road and one ear listening to what she was saying so I'd know when to say, "Yes, ma'am," "no, ma'am," and "I'm sure she'll be all right, ma'am." That's all I had to say the entire trip. She poured out Freda's whole life story since she was little bitty girl: how Mr. Hugh Fred had doted on her since she was born; how he wasn't an unnatural father, just one who loved too much; how she had tried and tried to tell him he needed to loosen the reins a bit; how he never listened to a word she said.

If she talked that much to him, I could see why he'd stopped listening. I was scarcely listening to her, either. I was listening to my stomach growl. We were missing dinner, and the chances were good she wasn't going to want to eat after we found Freda (who would have already eaten with that nice family). She probably wouldn't even stop on the way home. I'd only had one bowl of Cheerios for breakfast. It was very possible I would give my life getting Freda back home from her elopement.

Thank goodness, it didn't turn out quite that bad. The Blantons, the folks who found Freda, offered us a bite to eat as soon as we got there. Before Miss Emily could turn them down, I said loudly, "That would be wonderful! Thank you so much."

We had to wait awhile for Freda anyway. She was napping when we got there, having been up most of the night. So while Miss Emily went up to wake her and talk to her alone, I shoveled in a plateful of cold fried chicken, cold green beans, hot mashed potatoes with gravy, and two warm biscuits. I finished up with a slice of the best peach pie I ever tasted. "Big Mama always said no peaches are as good as those grown in South

Carolina's iodine soil," I informed Mrs. Blanton. She beamed and gave me a second piece, just like I hoped she would.

Freda came down yawning prettily, with every curl in place, wearing the dress she'd worn to be in the no-wedding and carrying the bride's bouquet. Her dress was wrinkled and had smears of dirt on it, but Miss Emily didn't seem to mind. She kept hugging and kissing her and crying. Then Freda started crying, too, and between them they sogged up the Blanton's living room pretty good.

Meanwhile I ate my way through that second slice of pie and hoped I could doze in the backseat on the way home. I had done my best by Miss Emily on the way down. It was Freda's turn to listen.

She certainly wasn't listening to me. The way she acted, you'd have thought I was Miss Raeburn's filthy doll in the backseat. She didn't say one word to me from the time she came down until Miss Emily pulled up in front of our house. That was fine with me. I wasn't sure what I had to say to her, either. So far she'd consumed the better part of my weekend without one word of thanks or apology.

I thought of some of the books I'd read in which heroines got into all sorts of scrapes. From now on I was going to pay more attention to the people who brought their tea in the morning, mended the dresses they tore, and rescued them from distress. Looked like those were the roles I was destined to play.

Speaking of princesses, instead of getting out of her car when we got home, Miss Emily asked me to tell Uncle Stephen to come out, please. She said it was getting late and they couldn't stay to visit, but I think she didn't want to have to see Aunt Kate. The whole family was in the dining room listening to the radio. Uncle Stephen put his shoes on and went out to talk to them. For the first time in my life I didn't even try to hear what anybody said. I was too exhausted from my first full day of being a grown-up.

Chapter 38

Mrs. Raeburn and Mr. Donaldson were both at school on Monday, but they were definitely not all right. They weren't talking to one another. Weren't talking to anybody much. She spoke sharply to our class, then apologized. "Sorry, I'm not feeling well today." It seemed to me her tummy did poke out just a little.

Mr. Donaldson walked stonily through the building speaking in the clipped, curt voice he brought with him in the beginning. When I called, "Hey, Mr. Donaldson" at lunchtime, his "Hello" could have been spoken to a perfect stranger. You'd never have guessed I'd fed the man chocolate cake on Aunt Kate's wedding china, been saved by him from a rusty tin roof, or shared with him the early morning sweetness of Aunt Hannah's special guest room.

By the time I got home, I felt like my body was made of lead. It took more strength than I had to keep my eyelids up. Aunt Kate had stayed after school to redo her bulletin boards, and Grace said John was napping, Abby was over at Sue Mary's and Uncle Stephen was visiting people in the hospital. "I think I'll stretch out awhile," I told Grace. I climbed slowly up to my room and fell asleep with my clothes on. When I woke, I discovered somebody had taken off my shoes and covered me up. It felt real good to be a child again. Unfortunately, I soon discovered that life is a one-way journey.

Did I hear the telephone ring? I don't remember. What I first consciously heard was Grace running swiftly up the stairs and closing the door to her room. I drowsily grabbed my glasses and stumbled toward the bathroom. I heard her in her room next door sobbing but trying not to make a sound. Fuddled with sleep, my first thought was that Ronnie had come back and hurt her again. But Ronnie was missing. Had he been found and come home?

I tiptoed to her door and pushed it open. "Grace? What's the matter?"

She was lying facedown on her bed, but she lifted a tear-drenched face to mine. "Geena's got a bad gall bladder. Pearl says she's got to have an operation this week or she could die. But Pearl doesn't have anywhere near enough money."

I was too sleepy to feel more than a vague sadness. "Won't her insurance pay it?"

"What insurance? Poor folks don't have insurance. And the county hospital says it's already done all the charity operations they can afford this year—come back next year."

It would take fifty years for the horror of too-expensive health care and inadequate health coverage to seep around my own feet, securely planted in America's middle class. Then I would realize, as incredible as it sounds, that only public hospitals are required to treat people who cannot pay. Ambulances continue to pass private hospitals carrying desperately ill persons without insurance, and persons continue to suffer and even die because they are too rich for welfare and too poor to pay insurance premiums. When I eventually found myself caught in that crack for a time in my life, that moment with Grace came back to mind.

Grace sat up on her bed and straightened her clothes. "I've got nearly seven hundred dollars saved." She grabbed a tissue and scrubbed her face. "I can send her that. But she'll still have to borrow three hundred. God only knows how she'll pay it back in this lifetime."

"Has Pearl asked Big Mama for money? Maybe she—"

Grace pressed one hand to her mouth. "Oh! I shouldn't have told you about this. Pearl doesn't want Mrs. Marshall to know. She already feels beholden to her for giving her a house and finding her work all these years. Don't you say a thing about it, you hear? We'll work it out some way. It's not your problem."

She went to the dresser and started powdering her nose. "Don't look so worried. Geena's gonna be all right. I didn't mean to scare you."

I hadn't spent a second yet worrying about Geena. What was worrying me was the burden of wealth. I went back to my room and sat by my window, caught in the vise of all who would do good. I wanted to help but I didn't want to suffer.

But Geena was suffering and Geena was my friend.

Grace was my friend, too, and she'd worked hard more than a year to save seven hundred dollars for college. *If she gives that money to Pearl, she'll have to wait another year for college.* I heard that as clear in my head as if somebody had said it. *Or not go at all.*

The words echoed in my brain. Grace's money stretched beyond my windowpane in a shadowy row of coin piles, each an exchange for an hour of work. I saw my own college fund in Big Mama's bank, stacks of bonds for which she had exchanged hours of her own. Accustomed to being handed a casual allowance and handing it over just as casually for candy or gum, I'd never realized before that our true currency is not coin but life.

Uncle Stephen's old black Chevy came down the dusty road and pulled in under the maples in front of the house, but I scarcely noticed. I was remembering a verse I'd learned in third grade back in Baptist Sunday school: *"Present your bodies a living sacrifice ..."* It hadn't meant a thing to me when I'd parroted it for points. Now I knew we present our bodies as a sacrifice, knowingly or unknowingly, every time we approach a cash register. Spending money is spending somebody's life.

How many hours did Mrs. Cameron spend making the money she gave me? Sitting in that store with no heat, little light. Putting a few coins a day in her old cigar box. *"A living sacrifice ..."*

Could I make one, too? My feet didn't think so. They almost refused to move. It took all the energy I had to force myself down the stairs, looking for Uncle Stephen. He was smoking a solitary pipe out on the front porch swing. "Can I talk to you?"

"Sure." He gestured toward a rocker.

"Can we go somewhere more private?"

He looked around. "I don't see a soul for a mile in any direction."

I shifted nervously from one foot to the other. "But somebody might hear us."

He puffed a couple of times and regarded me gravely. I looked right back, desperate. Any second I might change my mind. With relief I heard him offer, "Want to stroll down to Davy's?"

That was perfect. The only house between ours and theirs was Clay and Laura's, and they were both at work. If old Job Watt was still hovering around his ruins, he was welcome to anything I had to say.

It was hard to begin, though. We walked in companionable silence, enjoying the fresh spring air, the songs of courting birds, sweet pipe smoke, and company without demand. He didn't press me until I finally blurted, "Grace was crying in her room. Geena's real sick and has to have an operation this very week. But it costs a thousand dollars. A lot more money than Pearl has. Grace says if she gives her all her savings, Pearl will still have to borrow some, and only God knows how she'll pay it back in her lifetime."

Uncle Stephen kicked a clod of dirt, sent it spinning ahead of us. "It's dreadful being poor."

"It's hard being rich, too." I didn't mean to sound sullen, but I was already beginning to resent how difficult this was for me.

"I wouldn't know. But after this weekend"—he nodded slightly toward the Keenes'—"I think we're both a bit less enamored of wealth than we used to be."

I'd completely forgotten the Keenes. "What happened?"

"Emily took Freda home and I went up to talk with them a little. I'm not sure what they are going to do yet, but at least they're talking to one another. It's a beginning."

"Are they going to let Freda date Charles?"

He chuckled. "Freda says she never wants to see Charles again as long as she lives."

"What did he do?" I didn't really expect him to tell me but I might as well ask.

"His major sins seem to be that he stopped at a filthy filling station when she needed to go to the bathroom, and he took her to a drive-in for dinner. That was all he could afford, poor boy, but Finicky Freda was not impressed. He was also planning to bring her back to his daddy's house as soon as the wedding was over."

"Sounds like a poor excuse for a wedding."

"May it discourage you from trying the same thing. Take my advice. Don't get married until you can support yourselves." He puffed a couple of times on his pipe. "Was it Freda you wanted to talk about or Geena?"

I sighed. "Neither one. It's Grace. I don't think she ought to have to give up her college money when I have Mrs. Cameron's legacy. I know she meant me to use it for music camp, but do I have to?"

He opened his mouth like he was going to say something, then clamped his lips around his pipe again and began to puff furiously. One hand shoved back his hair. Finally he spoke. "Whew. That's a biggie. You know that there's no way you are going to music camp if you give Grace that money."

He didn't make it a question. He was just stating a plain fact. But I answered anyway to reassure him. "Yessir." I wished I could say it loud and strong but all I could manage was a whisper.

"You don't mind giving that up?"

I kicked a large granite rock, which hurt my toe more than it did the rock. "Of course I mind! I mind a lot. I wish Geena hadn't gotten sick or that Jesus was here and could just put his hands on her and make her well. But what good does wishing do, I ask you that?"

"You sound a lot like your Big Mama right now."

"If I was Big Mama, I'd have enough money to pay her bills. But Grace says Pearl doesn't want Big Mama to know, because she's already beholden to Big Mama for her house and finding her work. That's silly, of course. Big Mama wouldn't look at it that way."

"That's one of the reasons it is more blessed to give than to receive. A receiver is likely to feel a lot more beholden than the giver wants or even deserves. If you give Grace your money, she's going to feel beholden to you. Have you thought about that?"

I hadn't. "I don't want her to feel beholden. Besides, if she feels beholden to anybody, it ought to be to Mrs. Cameron. She's the one who sat in that poky little store day after day selling a couple of dollars' worth of stuff. I didn't do a thing to earn it myself!"

He put a warm hand on my shoulder. "If all the people who inherit wealth had that attitude, the world would be a far better place."

I flushed, glad that Uncle Stephen was proud of me, but it was sort of like Mama being proud when I went to get my first cavity filled. People being proud of you didn't keep the thing from hurting. I wanted this over as soon as possible. I turned my head so he couldn't see I had tears in my eyes. "Can I give it to Grace in secret? Leave it on her pillow or something, so she doesn't know where it came from?"

"If Grace found a thousand dollars lying on her pillow—" He laughed instead of finishing the sentence.

I laughed, too, even if was a bit weak. "So what can I do so she doesn't know where the money came from?"

He sighed. "You are sure about this?"

I had to take a deep breath before I nodded. This felt as solemn as a wedding. "I do. I mean, I am."

"Then we need to have the lawyer write up a document transferring the money from you to the church, designated for Grace."

"Won't that take too long? Geena needs the operation this week."

He nodded toward Aunt Hannah's drive, which was now just a few steps away. "Davy's treasurer of the church, and Hannah has a cousin who's a lawyer. I think we can have a check to Grace by tomorrow afternoon."

Aunt Hannah called from her side porch door. "Do I see two pilgrims, come from afar for a piece of my new chocolate cake?"

"Come in, come in," Uncle Davy beckoned from where he'd been tinkering with his old truck.

As we got to the porch, Aunt Hannah said, "Do you think they'll be all right?"

So much had happened that weekend, I had to think a minute before I realized she meant Mr. Donaldson and Mrs. Raeburn. That no-wedding seemed like two lifetimes away.

"They'll be fine," Uncle Stephen assured her, knocking out his pipe on the side of the porch. He was a far better preacher than prophet.

Chapter 39

I got home the next afternoon to find Grace packing. "Where you going?" I asked, pretending I didn't know.

"Home." She slid a pile of underwear into one of Aunt Kate's suitcases.

"Dis is home," Abby reminded her, bouncing on her bed and toppling a pile of clothes.

I picked up the clothes and still pretended I didn't know a thing. "Is Geena worse?"

"Oh, honey!" She squeezed me so hard, I could hardly breathe. "Who'd you tell about Geena?"

"Just Uncle Stephen," I answered truthfully. "Why?"

"The most wonderful thing has happened. Somebody at Bethel Church heard about that operation she needs, and they've given the money to pay for it. Mr. Whitfield brought me a check and a ticket on the late afternoon bus. Geena's going to get that operation. She's going to be all right!" Her gold tooth flashed and her eyes glowed. I hugged her tightly, making sure she couldn't see my face. Abby sat glumly on her bed repeating, "But dis is home, Grace. 'Member? Dis is home."

Grace gave her a hug, too. "Oh, honey, I'll remember. I'll hurry back fast as I can."

For two weeks Jay's sister Cecile and her little girl, Maggie, came down to stay with Abby and John while Aunt Kate and I were at school. Then Grace was back, bringing us each a new outfit from Big Mama and the good news that Geena was home from the hospital and feeling much better.

All that time Mr. Donaldson and Mrs. Raeburn weren't speaking to one another.

Whenever Aunt Kate saw one of them, she gave a sad little sigh. I expect I did, too, because Bonnie asked me at recess one day as we sat on a grassy bank sewing, "What's the matter? You seem so sad. Is it because Freda's so sick?"

Freda wasn't sick; she was just staying home until her parents could agree on what to do with her. Besides, Freda couldn't bother me anymore. I no longer found her special, merely silly—and silliness, I had discovered, has little power to inflict pain.

Nor does generosity guarantee happiness. I was delighted that Geena was doing so well, but every time I played the piano, I still wished I could have gone to music camp. When Miss Rilla put her arm around me after one piano lesson and said, "Your uncle told me what you did and I think it was wonderful," I could hardly wait for my lesson to be over so I could run to the cemetery and burst into tears.

I couldn't explain any of those things to Bonnie. So there I sat, miserable during a fine spring recess—the time of day when for a blissful half hour morning and afternoon, teachers sat on the steps talking to one another while children played baseball or tag or did whatever their hearts desired. Bonnie and I had brought the hand stitching from our latest sewing projects. She was blind stitching the collar of her first blouse, and I was awkwardly hemming my first skirt. But when I saw Bonnie expected some explanation for my sighs, I said, "I just don't think this skirt is going be nice enough for me to wear in public, after all the work and money I put in it."

Then I felt guilty for letting somebody as saintly as Bonnie think I was upset over something as dumb as a skirt. I wished I was as little as Abby and secrets lasted only until you found somebody to share them.

Who would have guessed it would be Preston to bring things to a head?

But then, I'd been warning them about him for months.

✻

Preston's class had the chapel program that coming Friday, and they were doing a play about famous Revolutionary War patriots. Preston had been chosen for Paul Revere and had been galloping around the neighborhood for days yelling, "The Redcoats are coming! The Redcoats are coming!" Both Abby and Sue Mary were begging for red coats.

On Thursday afternoon I had to go to the bathroom while the class was having its final rehearsal. As I started back up the stairs, I dawdled a little to watch.

Betsy Ross proudly unfurled her flag at one side of the stage while Patrick Henry began his famous speech on the other. Near the back of the stage I saw Preston and the boy who was to swing a lamp from the Old South Church tower waiting their turn. The way I remembered it, the lamp was hung, not swung, but Aunt Kate said they probably needed more parts for the play.

The lamp was a real one, with a real candle in it, but their teacher had glued a big yellow paper flame to the wick. The puny way that boy was swinging it, Paul would never have been inspired to ride across the street, much less across town. Preston must have thought so, too, because as I watched, he snatched the lamp and, quick as a blink, whipped a match from his pocket, scratched it on his corduroy leg, lit the paper wick, and swung the lantern high. Most matches lit on anything in those days.

That candle flew like a rocket out of the lantern and straight into the old cloth curtains at the back of the stage. Just as Patrick Henry shouted loud enough for the back rows to hear, "Give me liberty or give me death!" the dusty curtains erupted in flames.

"Fire!" yelled the boy with Preston.

Young Patrick turned around. Faced with the real possibil-
ity of death, he led the race for the front door as fast as his
skinny legs could carry him—followed by the rest of his
screaming class. Their teacher hurried after them faster than
I knew that old woman could run. She stopped only long
enough to pull down the red handle of the fire alarm. I knew I
should follow them but stood mesmerized by those red and
purple flames. Smoke and years of dust rose to choke me. Only
when I coughed was the spell broken.

"Fire!" I yelled, racing up the stairs and along the balcony.
"FIRE!" A crackle overhead and the smell of burning wood let
me know the fire had moved beyond the stage's old hangings
to the building itself.

Doors opened upstairs and down. "Line up," startled
teachers commanded. "Go at once to our assigned area out
front. Hurry!" We'd practiced fire drills often enough for students to march out of their rooms in an orderly process, but
as children reached the doors and saw flames leaping across the
stage, I saw each child give a little hitch like they wanted to
run. Fortunately, practice made perfect. Out they streamed in
perfect lines.

Mr. Donaldson stood nearby shouting, "Keep calm and go
to assigned places. Keep calm and go to assigned places."

Shoved against the balcony rail by huge eighth-graders
rushing past, I watched Aunt Kate shepherd the last of her
class out the door. I wondered if that would be my last glimpse
of her. Finally the balcony crowd thinned and I could start
down, too. By now the flames were crackling merrily at the
front of the auditorium and along the side with windows. They
had not yet reached our side but the smoke made us cough.

Mrs. Raeburn was just ahead of me as I hurried down the
steps. We burst out the front door like peas from a pod, gasping for air. I'd been holding my breath for a couple of eternities.
Mrs. Raeburn ran to our area of the parking lot and frantically
counted, then counted again.

"I'm here," I called.

She turned with obvious relief. "Why were you so long getting here?"

I didn't see any point in telling her I had been right behind her. Instead I looked around the front yard and felt proud. Every single class was in its assigned place, teacher at its head, watching the building. From outside we looked like we were just having another fire drill. None of the cars going up and down the highway had any idea of the raging maelstrom within. But not too far away I heard a faint whine that gradually became the noise of not one but two sirens. In the distance I heard a third.

I turned back to the school and gasped. Mrs. Raeburn was running up the steps!

I dashed across the parking lot to where Mr. Donaldson stood counting classes. I jerked his elbow. "Mrs. Raeburn went back in there! She's gone back in!"

He gave me a frantic look, then turned and dashed up the steps. I am no conscious hero, but I didn't think with my mind; I thought with my heart. I raced after them as fast as I could.

The swinging double doors between the auditorium and the front hall still stirred gently on their hinges. Gasping and panting for breath, I pushed through, then stopped in horror. The high old auditorium was full of smoke, billowing thick near the ceiling and drifting in wisps down toward the floor. Fire raged in the back roof, danced onstage, leaped along the wall with the high windows, and sent licking tongues along the floor just in front of the stage. Only the side with the classrooms had been spared so far.

The heat was so intense, I felt sweat break out on my forehead and bead my upper lip. My arms got slick and wet. My hair stuck to my forehead. Where were they? I peered through the haze and saw them at the bottom of the stairs, arguing. She was trying to go up; he was tugging her back. Finally she broke away from him and dashed up the stairs. He followed her and caught her halfway up. Again he spoke urgently and tried to tug her down. Gasping and crying, she held on to the rail and wouldn't come. He threw a desperate look toward the advancing flames and smoke, then pushed past her and sprinted up the remaining stairs. I heard him cough furiously just before our classroom door slammed.

Mrs. Raeburn waited anxiously on the stairs, covering her nose with one hand. She went up a step, backed down, went back up, backed down. Wisps of smoke floated toward her, and I found myself muttering, "Smoke follows beauty."

"Come down!" I yelled. "Please come down." The fire roared too loud for her to hear. What was I doing there? A strong urge rose up inside me to turn and run back to safety. I had pivoted on one toe when a ball of fire fell from above onto a row of auditorium seats just beyond me. The old wooden seats blazed up like well-dried kindling. Flames flowed like lava in all directions. Smoke billowed around me like a fog and I bent double, coughing.

Over the hack of my coughs I heard Mrs. Raeburn shout. "Carley! What are you doing here? Get out!" I could see her only in fits and starts, for a wall of fire rose between us.

I found myself murmuring a one-sentence prayer: "PleaseGodpleaseGodpleaseGodplease!" My brain couldn't seem to think of any other words.

She turned back to the classroom. "Jerry!" she screamed. "Come back! Forget her. Come back! Come back!" She climbed up two more steps, still breathing into her hand. One tongue of fire licked its way toward the classroom wall, climbed like a vine, and twined itself around the upstairs banister. I could not see Mr. Donaldson but I heard him slam the door above me.

Coughing. Gasping. Running along the balcony. Mrs. Raeburn turned and ran in front of him as he came thundering down the stairs.

A ball of fire fell directly where he was.

I heard a cry, a crash, and Mrs. Raeburn's scream. "Jerry! Oh, help. Help us! Help us!"

Stay low.

In the midst of the roar and heat, I felt a moment of beautiful calm. Clear as anything, I heard the voice of a fireman who came to chapel once to discuss fire safety.

Breathe through something wet, if possible.

I had nothing wet, so I fell to the floor and spat in my hand. Breathing as little as possible, I inched my way toward them, feeling my clothes slick with sweat beneath me. There was a clear corridor along the classroom wall except for that one short fence of fire. Could I leap it?

I didn't give myself time to think. I stood to a crouch and hurtled over.

Beyond me Mr. Donaldson lay where he had fallen, on his stomach in a crumpled heap. The back of his shirt was on fire. Mrs. Raeburn knelt in the smoke, beating the fire with her bare hands. "Don't die," she sobbed, coughing and beating out flames. "I love you! Don't die!"

In his one arm he clutched that filthy old doll, Suzy.

I slid to my knees beside her, wincing as one knee got a splinter. She looked up, startled, but didn't object as I helped slap out the fire. Blisters rose on his back as I watched. I could scarcely breathe and my lungs felt like the fire was inside them. I tasted it on my tongue, felt it burn my throat as I swallowed. As she beat out the last spark in his shirt, I grasped one of his legs, but I couldn't budge him.

"Chair!" she cried, grabbing one of the wooden folding chairs lining the auditorium wall. She flattened it and together we shoved it under him. I turned my back to him and picked up his legs, pulling him like a wheelbarrow. She bent at his head, pushing the chair across the floor. Desperately we moved our burden toward swinging doors that seemed a mile away.

My left arm, still weak from its break, didn't want to bear his weight. I stiffened my jaw and ordered it to work. When we reached that narrow fence of fire, we didn't even pause, just doubled our effort and with strength neither of us knew we had, slid across it and on toward the double doors. Breathing as seldom as possible. Gasping. Coughing. Me feeling like my arm would break again in three more places.

Tears streamed down our cheeks. The knees of her nylons were now large holes from where she'd crawled, shoving that chair. Her lovely face and dress were streaked with soot, and mine probably were, too. I felt like I wanted to throw up, but knew I had nothing inside but smoky air. I pushed one swinging door with my shoulder, then gasped. The library to my left was in flames. A dense black cloud billowed from it toward us, a dreadful seeking thing blocking the front door.

"Office," she gasped. "Try ... office!" Sobbing and coughing, we more jerked than dragged Mr. Donaldson through that cloud to the closed door of his secretary's office. Jerked him through quickly and slammed the door behind us. Suddenly the air seemed sweet and fresh, barely tinged with the odor of smoke. That was probably us. When I turned my head and my hair swung toward my cheek, I coughed at the reek.

How long were we in the auditorium? Maybe five minutes. Far less time than it takes to tell it. But enough to make me feel I'd been hung like bacon and smoked. I gulped air and pointed at gray wisps curling under the door.

"Block the crack," she commanded. "Then break the window and shout for help." She still knelt over Mr. Donaldson, stroking his cheek with her hands. "Jerry, honey, don't give up. I love you."

His eyes flickered but did not open.

I seized the secretary's sweater from the back of her chair and stuffed it under the door. Raced to the window. Grabbed a heavy book and hit the glass. It did not break. Outside I saw two fire trucks standing by the steps and busy firemen, no longer the friendly helpers who came to talk but professionals about a serious business. Grimly they uncoiled hoses and hooked them to hydrants that were usually nothing more than tests of little boys' jumping skills.

"The pole! Use the pole!" Mrs. Raeburn raced to a corner and grabbed the long pole used to open transoms on hot days. "Stand back!" Like a knight of old, she flung herself at the window with the pole before her like a lance. It shattered the glass and clattered to the floor. "Help!" she screamed. "There are three of us in here. Help!"

I met a fireman's startled eyes and waved frantically, adding my shouts to hers. "Help us!" He shouted something to the others and one ran to a truck.

Mrs. Raeburn ran back to Mr. Donaldson. "Jerry, they've seen us. They're coming!"

He didn't move.

Across the parking lot I saw Aunt Kate still shepherding her students. She wasn't worrying about me at all. She had no idea where I was. Desolation swept over me. Dying was bad enough, but dying when those I loved didn't know I was in danger seemed infinitely worse.

Our class stood in an anxious clump, talking excitedly and waving arms as if wanting somebody to take responsibility. I watched the third fire truck skid to a stop on the gravel by the steps and more firemen leap out.

When I dared a look over my shoulder and through the large glass pane of the door, the smoke was so dense in the hall, it looked like night. The office was beginning to get warmer, too. I thrust my nose to the break in the windowpane, seeking air. Then I held my breath and darted to Mr. Donaldson's office. The air was still fresh there. "Can we get him in here? It's easier to breathe."

"We'd never be able to move him again."

Without thinking I snatched his jacket from the back of his chair and clutched it to me as I returned to them.

"Look out there! Ladder coming up!" someone called from below. I saw the top of a ladder rise and come to a rest just beyond our sill. I peered out and saw one of my classmates break from the herd and dash to Aunt Kate. He pointed to the building, talking and gesturing. Aunt Kate looked toward the window and swayed as if she would faint. Then she abandoned her classroom and dashed to one of the firemen. When he shoved back his hat, I recognized him. He went to our church. She spoke frantically, pointing to the window. He pointed to the ladder.

Meanwhile on the school steps a hose bucked and leaped like a living thing, then steadied as several men aimed it straight at Mount Vernon's front door. A hissing rose in the front hall, a thousand snakes of steam.

Was it cold water hitting hot glass that shattered it?

I don't know. But a second later the door window exploded and black smoke poured into the office. "The floor!" Mrs. Raeburn gasped. "Get down!" I pitched to the dirty gray linoleum beside her and Mr. Donaldson as that black cloud rolled in toward us.

PleaseGodpleaseGodpleaseGod! As the hot smoke rolled over me, I crouched with Mr. Donaldson's jacket covering my head, breathing the comforting smell of his pipe.

"Stand back!" someone yelled.

I heard glass shatter and felt shards sting my arms, my legs, knew they must have lodged in my hair. But in another instant I felt strong arms lift me up and hand me over the windowsill to arms waiting there. I floated down like a small child against a broad chest. I couldn't stop sobbing. "Don't let them die. Don't let them die."

I was set on the grass and struggled to stand up. "Relax," someone urged me, pressing me back by one shoulder. "Just rest a minute."

I rolled to one arm and looked toward the building. Flames shot into the air from the roof and smoke billowed from the library window. Against the wall I saw, like toy figures in a book, a fireman carrying Mr. Donaldson down. Mrs. Raeburn stood in the window, watching like Juliet on her balcony, except the brightness breaking behind her was not the sun but fire.

"She's going to die!" Tears streamed down my face and I coughed so hard, I couldn't catch my breath.

Aunt Kate caught me in her arms and her salt tears stung my hot, blistered face. "No, she's not. They're going to get her. See?" Another fireman lumbered up the ladder and helped Mrs. Raeburn down. As soon as she reached the ground, I buried my face in Aunt Kate's blouse. She pressed her face close to my hair and moaned, "Oh, honey! Honey!" over and over again.

I coughed so hard that I retched, had to squirm away, and throw back my head for deep breaths of precious air. How could I have ever taken breathing for granted?

One of the firemen carried Mr. Donaldson to the grass, laid him near me, and bent over him. His back was to me, so I couldn't tell what he was doing. But as soon as Mrs. Raeburn was helped across the parking lot, she crumpled onto the grass beside them, begging, "Is he going to be all right? Is he?"

"Can't tell," the fireman said laconically.

You couldn't tell by looking if either would ever be all right again. Mr. Donaldson's eyebrows and most of his hair were singed off. Mrs. Raeburn's golden hair was scorched, her beautiful clothes ruined with fire and smoke. Both their faces were black with soot and pink like they'd stayed on the beach too long. Her pretty hands were curled and blistered. One of his pant legs was burned off to the knee. She fell to her knees beside him and began to stroke his leg, white and bony, as if it were very dear. Then she took Suzy from him, clutched her to her chest, and began to weep long trails of tears that snailed down her blackened cheeks.

Tears streamed down my own face. I buried my face in Aunt Kate's shoulder and felt her tears landing on my head. We knelt there holding one another and crying like nobody else existed in the world.

Suddenly something happened that terrified me as much as the fire. One minute Mrs. Raeburn was kneeling on the grass holding Suzy; the next she was clutching her stomach, bent double, making high little sounds of pain. Seeing Aunt Kate nearby, she begged, "Kate, help me. Help me!" She struggled to her feet, still clutching her middle. Suzy lay forgotten on the grass.

Aunt Kate hurried over to hold her like she'd held me. Blood trickled down Mrs. Raeburn's leg. I watched, appalled. Had she swallowed too much smoke after all? Had it burned up her insides? Were she and Mr. Donaldson both going to die?

I doubled over coughing and still felt much too healthy, guilty for not being equally overcome. I also found I was still

holding Mr. Donaldson's jacket and didn't know what to do
with it. I sidled over and picked up Suzy and put her under it.
I knew what anybody except Mrs. Raeburn or I would do with
her: throw her back in the fire.

Mrs. Raeburn acted like she'd gone crazy. She bucked and
rocked while Aunt Kate held her and looked frantically around
for help. One of the other teachers came over and asked a question, but before Aunt Kate could answer, two long Cadillacs
roared up the school's drive, sirens blaring. Expert men bundled Mrs. Raeburn into one and Mr. Donaldson into another.
I coughed a couple of times to clear my throat so I could ask
and be sure, "Are they ambulances or hearses?"

"Ambulances, dummy," a nearby boy assured me. "Hearses
don't use sirens."

As they wailed away and Aunt Kate rejoined me, she whispered, "Dear God, don't let them be too late."

Chapter 40

The ambulances were barely out of earshot when Uncle Stephen's old Chevy screeched to a stop at the bottom of the hill. He came tearing up the drive faster than most people think a preacher can run, and when he reached the parking lot and saw Aunt Kate and me, his whole body sagged in relief. "Good. You're all right."

Aunt Kate held on to him for a minute; then I guess she remembered she was a teacher and supposed to be setting a good example, because she stepped quickly away. "We're fine but as you can see, the school isn't."

Uncle Stephen turned for his first good look and whistled. The firemen had put out most of the front blaze and moved to the back, but anybody could see Mount Vernon's days were over. Sooty, roofless, streaked with black water, still licked by flames, it hung its head in defeat. He put both hands in his pockets and leaned back to peer up at the skeletal beams of the roof. "Whew! How'd it start? Does anybody know?"

"Preston lit a match. I've been telling you for months he'd burn us all up," I reminded him.

He reached out to clasp my shoulder. "Carley the prophet."

"Ow!" I flinched and pulled away.

For the first time he really looked at me. "You didn't get caught inside, did you? How come yours is the only dirty face among all these kids?"

"She ran back in." I could tell from Aunt Kate's voice that we'd gotten beyond the "Oh, honey!" stage and were fast approaching "How could you do a dumb thing like that?"

"Mr. Donaldson and Mrs. Raeburn were in there. I helped save them," I bragged. "I even saved his jacket." I held it up.

"Yes, but—," Aunt Kate began.

"Ma'am?" A fireman touched her arm. "I think she ought to run by the hospital so they can check her for smoke inhalation and burns and maybe glass fragments." I could have kissed him. Aunt Kate got worried again and forgot to fuss.

I didn't want to go to the hospital, though; I wanted to go home. But the next thing I knew, Uncle Stephen and I were headed to town. Aunt Kate had to stay to be sure her class—and mine—got on the school buses. Besides, her car was still blocked by fire trucks. Just before we left, I pulled Suzy from under the coat I was still clutching. "Take her home, and don't you dare—"

Aunt Kate gave a huff of disgust but she nodded. "I know. Don't dare throw her away. I'll put her with yours and we'll call them the Disaster Dolls."

The emergency room doctor put salve on my blisters and iodine on four cuts, pounded my back to make me cough, and took a long splinter from my knee. Meanwhile Uncle Stephen moseyed to the desk to ask about Mr. Donaldson and Mrs. Raeburn. "No word on their condition as of yet," he informed me. "They're both being admitted."

Over my stout objections the doctors decided I ought to spend one night at the hospital, too, to let them tend my burns and observe me. I was put on the same floor I'd been on right after Christmas. My nurse was even the same.

"You're getting to be a regular." She sounded grumpy but her eyes twinkled.

"Yeah. They say you can't come upstairs in a hospital until you are twelve. They don't tell you you'll spend half your life there after that."

"Only some people, honey. Just you lucky ones." She thrust a thermometer between my blistered lips.

While I was putting on that awful johnny gown, I sent Uncle Stephen to check on Mrs. Raeburn and Mr. Donaldson again and take him his coat. As soon as he walked back in my door, I demanded, "How are they? Do you know?"

Preachers were privileged people in hospitals in those days. Perhaps they still are. He'd seen Mr. Donaldson and talked to Mrs. Raeburn's nurse. He shoved back his hair.

"Her burns aren't too bad and he's conscious and as ornery as ever. Of course, his back is pretty raw and he breathed a lot of smoke, so he'll be here a few days."

"But she was bleeding. I saw it, Uncle Stephen. Did she burn up her insides?"

"No, honey, she—" He stopped and shoved back his hair. "She has to have a little operation. They've taken her in already."

"Will she be all right?"

"We hope she'll be fine. But she's going to need to rest awhile." He came over and sat in the chair by my bed. "Do you want to tell me what happened?"

"It was awful!" Unbidden, tears spilled over my eyelids. Seemed like I cried every time somebody looked at me lately. I swallowed hard, trying to make them stop, but my voice was still thick. "I looked over at the school and saw her running up the stairs. I told him and he dashed right in after her. I couldn't let them burn up. I just couldn't!"

He reached over and caught a tear on one finger. "Loyalty is one of your dearest attributes but sometimes you take it too far." He leaned back in the chair. "So what happened? Did you fly through the air like Superman and scoop them to safety?"

I laughed. "No, I crawled on my belly like a snake." With a little prodding I remembered the whole thing. He sat in the visitor's chair and listened while I poured out every detail. Gradually the fire became not so much a dreadful thing that happened as a story to be told. When I got old enough to learn the word *catharsis*, I would remember what happened to me as I told Uncle Stephen about the Mount Vernon fire.

❉

He came to get me the next morning, but I couldn't leave without seeing Mr. Donaldson and Mrs. Raeburn. "I'm twelve," I reminded Uncle Stephen. "I'm allowed to visit them."

But I stopped in shock at Mr. Donaldson's door. He lay like a log in bed, his arm and chest covered in bandages. When he saw us, he raised his arm. "Behold the one-armed mummy. Do you like the no-eyebrow look?" His voice was a hoarse croak.

"Extremely chic," Uncle Stephen agreed easily. He pointed me to one of the visitor's chairs. "Why don't you all visit while I check on Maddie?" Without waiting for an answer, he headed down the hall.

I perched uneasily on my chair and looked at all the hideous dead skin where my hands had blistered. This was the first time I'd visited anybody in the hospital, and to save my life I couldn't think of a thing to say.

"Were any other children burned?" he asked anxiously.

I realized he didn't know what happened. "No, sir. Just me."

"How did that happen?"

"I, uh, I went back in."

His forehead wrinkled. His eyebrows would have met if he'd had any left. "After us?" I nodded. "That was real dumb."

"Yessir, but I'm fine. I'm going home." Then I squirmed. Maybe I shouldn't have said that. Would it make him sad that he had to stay? Being a good hospital visitor was trickier than I'd supposed. "How are you?" Should I have even asked that?

He didn't seem to mind. "Better than could have been expected a few hours ago. I still don't remember a lot of what happened, though. I remember running downstairs, then—blank."

"Some of the ceiling fell on you. It gave you a mild concussion and caught your shirt on fire. Mrs. Raeburn saved you, though. She laid you on a chair and pushed it like a sled."

"She couldn't. Not all by herself."

"I helped a little." I didn't mind taking some praise, but if he thought she'd saved his life, he might not mind so much that she'd lied to him about the baby.

He stared in astonishment. "Just you two? What about your arm?"

I rubbed it because it hurt more today than it had during the fire. "It's okay. And Mrs. Raeburn did most of the work. She's a lot stronger than you might think. Is your back terribly sore?"

He didn't exactly answer my question. "It'll heal. But Maddie saved me, huh?" He turned his face away. "After what I'd done to her, I wouldn't have blamed her if she'd let me burn up."

"Have you seen her?" I knew I sounded too eager.

He still didn't look back at me. "I don't imagine she'll want me to inflict myself on her."

"And you think *I'm* dumb!" I spoke before I thought, and once my mouth opened, it seemed to have a will of its own. "You ran up into all that smoke to save her doll, so you must love her. And all the time you were lying on the floor and we were about to burn up, she knelt there saying, 'I love you, Jerry. I love you. Don't die! I love you' like we were in some stupid movie. And now today you won't even go see how she is." I stopped and held my breath, horrified at how my tongue had sped ahead of my manners.

He reached his hand across the space between us and gripped mine. "She said that? You're sure?"

"You don't make a mistake about a thing like that when you think you are going to die."

"Hmmm." He seemed to go into a faraway place that made his lips twitch now and then. I think he was out of the smiling habit and it was hard.

Meanwhile, embarrassed at having said so much—and thinking of all the awful things that could happen to somebody who was rude to her principal—I started babbling about how well the students had done on the fire drill, except it wasn't a drill, and how brave the firemen were, and didn't God work in mysterious ways—

"God?" Finally he spoke.

"Yessir. Uncle Stephen's had us praying about getting a new school, and now we'll get one. But if Preston hadn't lit a match and slung the lit candle into the curtains, we wouldn't."

Now his mouth did twist into a grin. "Even if I believed in God, I'd have a hard time thinking his plans are so mysterious that they include Preston Anderson as a major player."

"It is a lowering thought."

I was wondering what else to talk about when Uncle Stephen appeared in the door with a wheelchair. "You up to traveling, Jerry? I think you ought to visit Maddie. She's asking about you and won't believe me that you're too mean to die. Why don't you and Carley go down while I finish signing Carley out?" To my surprise Mr. Donaldson seemed willing to go. Even made us wait while he brushed what hair he had left.

Uncle Stephen just wheeled him to the door, then told me he'd be back in a little while and left. I pushed him the rest of the way in. "It isn't as hard as I thought to push a grown man," I told him. "It's a lot easier than pulling you by the legs."

I wheeled him close to the bed, where Mrs. Raeburn lay pale and sad on her pillow. Her face was peeling, both her hands were bandaged, and the room smelled not of perfume but of singed skin and hair and medicines. The whites of her eyes were bright pink, like she'd been crying all night. You'd never have guessed she'd been beautiful just one day before. But Mr. Donaldson didn't seem to notice. He leaned close and said hoarsely, "Hey, we match. No eyebrows. It's the latest look."

She gave him a wan smile. "Are you going to be all right? Truly?"

"Truly. I may be a bass for a while instead of a baritone, and my hair's as thin in front as Stephen's . . ." Now that I thought about it, Uncle Stephen's hair was a little thinner in front than it used to be.

I was standing over near the door and I think Mr. Donaldson forgot I was there. He covered one of her bandaged paws with his. "Maddie, will you marry me? Here? Today? I had the license in my coat pocket, and somehow it got out of the building unscathed. If you will, I'll be the happiest—"

To my astonishment she gave a yelp of utter pain and turned her head away. Without looking toward him, she flailed the air with one bandaged hand as if to drive him away. All the time she kept making little high sounds that scared me to death. One of Pop's bird dogs got hit by a car once and sounded exactly like that until it died. Was she dying?

Mr. Donaldson used both feet to shove himself away from the bed and looked up at me like he expected me to do something. I didn't know what to do. Dying teachers weren't my specialty. But I hurried around the bed and saw tears rolling from between her eyelids and down her cheeks. Maybe it was salty tears on her burned cheeks that were driving her crazy. I grabbed a tissue from the box on her nightstand and dabbed her cheeks gently.

She opened her eyes and stopped waving her arms. Slowly she lowered them to lie beside her on the sheet. "Thank you," she whispered. "Is he gone?" When I shook my head, she painfully turned over so her back was to where he sat. Then she closed her eyes as if shutting us both out.

But still tears oozed in a steady stream from beneath her closed eyelids, down her sore and blistered cheeks. I didn't know what else to do except keep wiping them away. Where was Uncle Stephen? I'd never visit anybody in the hospital again as long as I lived.

Mr. Donaldson awkwardly walked his wheelchair closer, since his arm was no use. His voice was soft, tentative. "Maddie? I didn't mean to hurt you. What did I say wrong?"

She took a deep, ragged breath. At first I thought she wasn't going to answer, but finally she spoke over her shoulder, her voice raw with pain. "You come in here asking me to marry you just as soon as my baby's gone? How could you? How dare you?" She drew her legs up toward her chest and cried out, "Oh, baby. My poor little baby! You didn't deserve to die." She covered her blistered cheeks with her bandaged paws and sobbed.

"Oh, honey!" The words—Aunt Kate's words, Big Mama's words—burst from me before I expected them. I bent down and held her like Aunt Kate held me the day before. Awkwardly, perhaps. I had little experience as consoler. But my skinny arms shaped themselves around her poor shaking shoulders, and all she seemed to need was my flat chest to cry on.

Across the bed I heard Mr. Donaldson say in a shocked voice, "You lost the baby? I didn't know. Stephen didn't tell me."

"I thought she'd want to tell you herself." Uncle Stephen had just come in the door, and he sounded as miserable as the rest of us felt.

Mrs. Raeburn sobbed so hard, I was afraid she'd make herself sicker. "Call her nurse." I motioned with my head to Uncle Stephen. The button was across the bed, too far for me to reach. "She needs something to calm her." I remembered somebody saying exactly those words the first night I was in the hospital, tortured by pain.

Only later would I realize that he obeyed me without a word.

A large woman in white bustled in with a needle on a tray. "What's going on here? You don't need to get upset, honey. Let me give you something to help you sleep."

I didn't want to watch the needle going into her arm, but she wouldn't let go of me. I closed my eyes and hoped she didn't notice.

Uncle Stephen laid one hand on Mr. Donaldson's shoulder, then removed it quickly as he winced with pain. "Why don't we let her rest for now?"

"Not yet." Mr. Donaldson's voice sounded funny, like it was still choked by smoke. "I'll go in a minute, but I have something to say to Maddie first. Push me over to the bed again." He laid his arm on her legs. "Maddie, before you go to sleep, I have to tell you this. I did not know about the baby. I asked you to marry me because I realize I was a fool. I love you. I've loved you a very long time. And I would have loved that baby, too." She didn't move but we could all tell she was listening. His voice wobbled and tears filled his eyes. "I came in here to ask you both to marry me—you and the baby. I swear it. Look at me, Maddie. I'm crying for the baby, too. And for you." The tears spilled over and he didn't lift his hand to wipe them away.

I felt something tickle my own cheek. A bug? When I swiped at it, my fingers came away wet. Even Uncle Stephen's eyes were glistening behind his glasses.

I looked away, uneasy. Men didn't cry. But when I sneaked another quick look, big fat tears were streaming down Mr. Donaldson's sore cheeks. He laid his head beside her on the bed. "Oh, honey, I am so sorry. So very sorry." His shoulders heaved with sobs.

Finally she turned. Her eyes opened and she looked at him. Then she laid one hand gently on his head and stroked it as best she could. They lay there and cried and cried. The whole bed shook with their grief.

Uncle Stephen motioned for me to come tiptoe out, but I couldn't get past Mr. Donaldson's chair without asking him to move. I wondered if I could crawl under but was afraid I'd scrape a sore place. Looked like we'd be right there until all our sore places healed.

Finally Mr. Donaldson asked, his voice still full of tears, "Someday, whenever you say, will you marry me?"

"Of course I will," she said. "Whenever you like."

Uncle Stephen stepped closer and laid one hand on Mr. Donaldson's shoulder again. "Aren't you forgetting one thing?" Seemed to me Uncle Stephen kept forgetting something, too—burns hurt.

Mr. Donaldson winced and Uncle Stephen took away his hand. But the memory of Uncle Stephen's hand has a way of staying on your shoulder even after he takes it away, until you do what is right. Mr. Donaldson took a deep breath and sat up straighter. "Yeah. Before you answer so quick, Maddie, you need to know why they think I killed Taylor. Red Lamar is working hard to find more evidence, but he's already got one piece he thinks will nail me. If he does, I'll go to jail."

She sniffed. I held a tissue to her nose just like she was Abby or John, and she obediently blew, then said, "That's silly. What could he possibly have?"

"An old medal of mine. One I got in high school. It used to be on my key ring, but they found it in the old barn, and—"

He stopped because she'd put one bandaged paw to her mouth. Her eyes were wide and horrified. "A silver one? From the D.A.R.?"

He nodded.

"Oh, Jerry, I took it. I had an awful crush on you in high school, and one day I was in the room and you'd left your keys on your desk. I picked them up to see what that silver disk was . . ." She looked at Uncle Stephen in dismay. "I'm not normally a thief. It's just that I liked him so much. . . . And after I took it, I couldn't figure out how to give it back."

I understood completely. Maybe I'd better empty my Clay Lamont box. I wouldn't want any of those gum wrappers and bulletins convicting him of murder.

Uncle Stephen came closer to the bed. "But how did it get in the barn? Did you leave it there?"

"I was never in the barn. And I don't know what happened to the medal. I used to carry it in my wallet; then one day it wasn't there. I was real upset, but I figured I must have spent it, thinking it was a half dollar. It was about the same size."

"Maybe Taylor took it from your wallet, like you took it from Jerry's key ring." Uncle Stephen's face was bright. "That's certainly worth pointing out to your lawyer, Jerry."

"Good idea." But Mr. Donaldson had a one-track mind. "Will you still marry me when we get this cleared up? Unless I have to go to jail?"

Mrs. Raeburn blinked her wet lashes and smiled at him. "I'll marry you before the trial. If you go to jail, I'll wait for you. I'd even be proud to marry you right now, looking like this."

"Wahoo!" They probably heard his yelp of happiness all the way in Job's Corner. "You look beautiful to me." He reached his arm and gently touched her burned cheeks.

If women knew how little men actually notice about us, we wouldn't spend so much time primping and powdering.

She looked up at Uncle Stephen. "Could we do it today, right now?"

Before Uncle Stephen had decided how to answer, Mr. Hugh Fred spoke at the door. "Maddie?" He came in, his hat in his hand, looking so handsome, clean, and normal in a dark navy suit and a red silk tie, he didn't belong in the room with the rest of us. Even Uncle Stephen was rumpled from shoving back his hair, and his eyes hadn't quite dried.

Mrs. Raeburn pulled back from Mr. Donaldson and blinked like she was coming from another world. Tears still stood like diamonds on her lashes. "Hello, Bud."

"You're looking better than I expected." He held out a bouquet of red roses and a box of candy. "Brought you a few things. How're you feeling?" He looked around the room and added, "All of you?"

Mr. Donaldson wheeled his chair away from the bed. "I'm doing pretty well, considering, and Carley here's a marvel. Perky and talky as ever."

Mr. Hugh Fred stood by Mrs. Raeburn's bed and shifted from one foot to another. "I talked to your doctor," he said softly. "He told me about your, ah, other problem." He leaned forward and put one hand on her shoulder. "Sounds like one good thing came from that fire, at least. You doin' all right?"

She jerked away. "It wasn't a good thing, no matter what you think. But I'm doin' about as well as could be expected. They say I'll have to stay a few days, though."

Mr. Donaldson wheeled back near the bed. "And I'm asking her to marry me today, right now. Since you're here, you can be best man."

"That right?" Mr. Hugh Fred looked from him to Uncle Stephen and back again. "Seems a little sudden to me but I guess you know your business. Before you do, though, could I leave you two lovebirds for just a few minutes and talk with Stephen here? Got something private to discuss."

Mr. Donaldson hesitated but Mrs. Raeburn waved him away. "You need to go get the license anyway. Why don't you all push him that far and have your talk after you get him there?"

"Sure." Mr. Hugh Fred took the handles of his chair and pushed him out.

"Kicked out already," Mr. Donaldson grumbled. But his cheeks weren't pink just from being burned. He sparkled almost like our other principal, Mr. White, had after hearing his boy play. Maybe principals just naturally got all pink and shiny with happiness.

As they headed to the door, Uncle Stephen turned to me. "You want to come or stay?"

"Stay," Mrs. Raeburn said softly. "I want to talk to you a minute."

I perched happily on the visitor's chair. "I'll stay."

"We'll be right back." As they rolled off down the hall, Uncle Stephen's voice floated back. "We'll need to get one more witness. Carley's not old enough."

"I've been old enough to witness a powerful lot of other things. What dumb law doesn't think I'm old enough to say I've seen a wedding?"

Mrs. Raeburn gave me a smile so happy, the whole room seemed to light up. "You're plenty old enough to be my maid of honor. Will you do that?"

I nearly flew to the ceiling with joy.

I even dared to tease her. "You're lucky Mr. Hugh Fred is letting you get married. He won't let Freda even near a boy."

She gurgled happily. "He wouldn't let me near a boy at that age, either. Taylor and I never did a thing wrong but we had to sneak around like burglars. Hugh Fred would have killed me if he knew I was sneaking out to meet anybody, so don't tell him about Taylor and the barn, okay?"

By then I would have promised her the moon. But all she wanted was some pretty nightgowns.

For some reason, though, she'd stopped talking in full sentences. " ... up in my little house ... Emily has a key." I nodded to show I understood. "Tell Kate ... first long drawer of my chest ... red, maybe blue. And some makeup ..." Her eyes closed; then she opened them and said with drowsy sadness, "After all that trouble, we lost Suzy."

"No, ma'am, we didn't. She's at our house. I sent her home with Aunt Kate."

Her lips curved into a smile; then the next thing I knew, her eyes were closed and she was gently snoring.

Our doorbell rang quite frantically. Miss Finley must not have known we never locked our door.

I ran to the window. Both Keeneys were parked crookedly under our maples, and Mr. Hugh Fred was hurrying up our walk in a long maroon bathrobe. Even in pajamas he was the handsomest man I ever saw, but he was also one of the hungriest.

I heard Uncle Stephen open the door as I reached the top of the stairs. I slid down the banister to the bottom. Miss

Our Heart's True Home

Late Spring 1951

Chapter 41

I went searching for the men and found Uncle Stephen and Mr. Hugh Fred just coming from Mr. Donaldson's room. "We forgot about her shot," I said. "She's gone to sleep."

Uncle Stephen leaned in Mr. Donaldson's door. "Carley says your bride is fast asleep."

"Not to sound unromantic, but I could use a snooze, too. Could you come back this evening, when we're awake enough to know what we're doing?" My chances of being maid of honor went up in wisps of smoke. Miss Emily and Freda were sure to be there then.

Uncle Stephen disappeared back into the room. "You need help getting back to bed?" We heard grunts, a yelp, a groan, and the sound of sheets rustling.

Mr. Hugh Fred and I stood awkwardly in the hall trying to pretend we couldn't hear the yelp and groan. When he leaned against the wall and crossed one ankle over the other, I saw he was wearing the finest brand of silk socks Marshall's store sold, the kind Pop only wore on Sundays. I tried hard to think of something to say. "How's Freda taking the fire?"

"She was pretty scared at the time. You could have all been killed."

"Well, actually—" I was about to brag on how well everybody followed our fire drill rules, and let him know Freda was never in a speck of danger, but he didn't give me a chance.

"She says she'll never go back to school again, but we think she'll be fine after a little coddling to help her get over the fright. Emily's fixed her a bed on my den couch, and we're letting her lie there and watch television while she recovers."

For just a second I felt a twinge of jealousy. But I was finally smart enough to know that if I had to be Freda in order to have what she had, it wouldn't be worth it.

When Uncle Stephen finally came out, Mr. Hugh Fred said, "Do you have time for a quick bite downstairs before you go?"

Uncle Stephen shoved up his watch. "Is it noon already? Kate's home, of course, since she can't go to school ..." He hesitated, and I wondered if he was having a hard time choosing between going to eat with his family and getting taken out by Mr. Hugh Fred. He decided to leave it up to me. "Okay with you, Carley?"

Looked like I wasn't getting home anytime soon, but what could I say? Sitting down would feel good. I was a little shaky on my legs from all that standing around and the scene in Mrs. Raeburn's room.

Mr. Hugh Fred ushered us into the hospital coffee shop like it was the Vance Hotel. I grabbed a paper napkin and put it in my lap to be polite, while he motioned a waitress to bring us menus. "What would you like, Carley? Maybe a cheeseburger and a milk shake?"

I looked at Uncle Stephen to see if he thought that was too expensive, but he was reading his menu. "Yessir, that would be nice. Chocolate," I told the waitress.

"With whipped cream and a cherry," he added. "She's been through a fire and deserves a little something special."

"You poor thing." She was real country. Said *thang* for *thing*. But she brought me two cherries and lots of whipped cream and even brought the extra part of the shake from the blender. That was the first milk shake I'd ever had all to myself. Back home Mama gave me part of hers, and since I'd come to live with Aunt Kate, Abby and I always shared.

I felt a little guilty at not saving her any—and a lot more guilty for being happy we couldn't get it home without it melting. I bent over my straw with the serious intent of proving I could drink every drop.

Until our food came, the men talked about baseball and how long it might take the school board to build a new school. But I could tell Mr. Hugh Fred was working up to something. He sat uneasily in his chair, like a man with something on his mind. Finally he heaved a sigh. "I want you to stall this wedding a bit, Stephen. Just until this trial is over. We all hope they aren't going to have enough evidence to convict him, but ... well, Maddie's always been headstrong and tends to rush into things. I hate to see her dragged through all that. You know what I mean?"

Uncle Stephen spooned some ice from his water into his coffee to cool it—he hated drinking it hot and constantly had to guard it in restaurants so the waitresses wouldn't heat it up just as he got it cool enough to drink. "I know what you mean. But she sounds like she wants to stand by Jerry through this. I just wish we could come up with some hard evidence to prove he didn't kill Taylor."

Mr. Hugh Fred had a mouthful of club sandwich, so all he could do was nod agreement until he swallowed. Then he asked, "You got any ideas about what they think they've got?"

"Some of it. Jerry said they found threads from Taylor's jacket and blood to indicate he was killed in your old barn—"

Mr. Hugh Fred flapped one hand. "It wasn't my barn then. It was the Harts' barn."

"Right. But whoever owned it, that's apparently where he was killed. And the most damaging piece of evidence against Jerry is a little medal Maddie took from his key ring in the throes of a high school crush. They found it near the other things, and Red Lamar thinks that proves Jerry was there and did it."

"A medal? How'd it get there?"

"Who knows? Jerry and Maddie both swear they weren't ever in the barn."

Mr. Hugh Fred chewed thoughtfully. "Stands to reason one of them must've left it there, though. Unless maybe she gave it to Taylor and it fell out of his pocket."

"I thought of that. Or that maybe Taylor took it from her wallet like she took it from Jerry. You know what kids are like—any little talisman of the person they love."

I looked down into my milk shake so he couldn't look into my eyes and see my box of Clay treasures.

Uncle Stephen waved away the waitress's coffeepot. "I told Jerry to at least suggest that to his lawyer. It ought to instill reasonable doubt in a jury's mind. But dang it! We don't just want reasonable doubt. We want Jerry completely cleared so they can get on with their lives."

Mr. Hugh Fred sipped his reheated coffee and didn't seem to mind that it was steaming. "That medal makes it tougher, though—especially if they get married now. They're bound to say maybe Jerry liked her even way back then and knew she was planning to meet Taylor down at the old barn late that night. They'll say he hid out down there, waiting for them to come, and when Taylor got there first, he hit him hard and killed him by accident." He scratched one side of his forehead with his forefinger. "You think any jury would send him to jail after all these years?"

"Who knows what they might do? There's no statute of limitations on murder." Seeing my puzzled look, Uncle Stephen explained, "That means no matter how long it is after one is committed, they can still try you for it." He turned back to Mr. Hugh Fred. "The thing is, Jerry swears he didn't kill Taylor. I for one believe him."

Mr. Hugh Fred signaled for another cup of coffee. "I believe him, too. Wouldn't consider letting Maddie marry him otherwise. But he'd better have a good reason for that medal being there." He waited until the waitress refilled his cup, then stirred in a little sugar. "I only allow myself sugar in my very last cup." He set down his spoon with a clink on the saucer. "My main point, though, is this: I don't want Maddie hurt again. She's all the family I've got, except Emily and Freda. My women. I work my fingers to the bone for them, and I'm proud to do it." He pulled out his wallet and took out a thick wad of pictures. I glimpsed a wad of money, too, and stopped worrying that my cheeseburger and milk shake would cost too much.

He shuffled through the pictures and held one out. "Look. Here's what Maddie was like at six. She had curls then, and those same big blue eyes. Wasn't she a cutie? And at eight— look at those Bugs Bunny teeth. And here's her high school graduation picture—no, that's Emily. Here's Maddie—wasn't she the prettiest thing you ever saw? Except Freda." He held up a picture of Freda in the dress she wore on the float in the Christmas parade. "She's even prettier than Maddie. I've got some gorgeous women."

I'm sure he didn't intentionally mean to hurt my feelings. It wasn't his fault that I was sitting there peeling and pink, with singed hair and no eyebrows. I looked down at my blistered hands and wondered if any man would ever sound that proud to have me in his family.

Uncle Stephen seemed to know what I was thinking, because he reached out and put a hand on my shoulder. I had to shrug it away, because it hurt too much to leave it there, but I gave him a smile of thanks as Mr. Hugh Fred shoved the wallet back in his pocket. He rested his elbows on the table in a way that would have made Big Mama cringe, no matter how much money he had. "Maybe you don't know the story, but Maddie married a real loser the first time. I beg you, don't help her rush into something else she'll regret. I'd like for us all to be sure—" He half rose from his chair. "Why, that's Emily. I didn't know she was coming to town."

He hurried out the door and greeted Miss Emily with obvious pleasure. They looked so happy to run into each other, you'd never have known he'd beaten her up a few months before. In just a minute he ushered her in, and I knew that Miss Emily might not be as pretty as Mrs. Raeburn or Freda, but she had what Pop used to call class. He said it came from having nice things all your life and coming to take it for granted that the best is worth whatever it costs. "I always like to see a woman of class come into the store," he'd say. "She won't buy every time, but she'll never quibble about the price of good, quality merchandise."

He'd have approved the soft linen dress she wore today, the camel-and-white checked jacket, and the little brown silk hat over one eye. Her shoes were brown and shiny but looked rough.

She caught my eye and her bright mouth curved into a wide smile. She headed toward us while Mr. Hugh Fred went to speak to the waitress. Before she came into earshot, I leaned over and said real quickly to Uncle Stephen, "Are her shoes and pocketbook made from lizard skin?"

"Alligator," he murmured back. "Probably cost more than everything we've got on put together."

"Oh, honey, are you all right?" She slipped into the fourth chair at our table. As always, she had on a lot of rouge and lipstick, but it couldn't hide her colorless skin, which stretched so tight across her bones that you could actually see their shape.

"I'm fine."

"Freda said it was dreadful—the smell of smoke, the crackle of the flames. I don't know how you all stood it." She pulled off her gloves and noticed my hands. That made her look up and notice the rest of me. "You must have gotten even closer to the fire than she did."

"Yes, ma'am. A little."

"I'm so glad I ran into you all before I went upstairs. I've been to a D.A.R. meeting and thought I'd stop by to see Maddie on my way home. But Hugh Fred says she's sleeping."

He came back right then with another cup of coffee, in time to hear her. "One of Emily's ancestors came over on the Mayflower. Can you imagine that? I almost didn't ask her out the first time, I thought she was so much better than me."

"Silly." She smacked him lightly on the hand. "Did you order me chocolate pie?"

"Here it is." The waitress set it before her. It had sugar beads on the meringue, just the way I liked it.

Seeing me looking at it, he asked, "You want some, too?"

"Oh, no, sir. Thank you. I've still got half a milk shake to finish." I bent over my straw.

"Maybe next time."

I didn't plan for there to be a next time. I'd had about as much of hanging around that hospital as I wanted for a while. I sucked on my straw while Mr. Hugh Fred explained to Miss Emily about how Mrs. Raeburn fell asleep instead of getting married. He made such a funny story out of it that we all had a good laugh. But then he got solemn again right away. "I just hope somebody can figure out how Jerry's medal got in that barn. That's pretty serious evidence. I was telling Stephen here I don't want Maddie to think about marrying him until Jerry explains it."

Miss Emily had picked up her fork to start eating her pie, pointed end first, but her hand started shaking so hard that she set the fork down and put both hands in her lap.

Uncle Stephen noticed that, too. He had taken his pipe from his jacket pocket to have an after-snack smoke. People who didn't smoke were not yet brave enough to ask smokers not to light up in a restaurant. He reached into his pocket and brought out his tobacco pouch. As he filled the bowl and tamped it down, he said, "*Somebody* had sure better explain how that medal got there, or Red will use the blasted thing to convict him. Jerry's likely to spend the rest of his life in jail, and from what I've seen today, that would break Maddie's heart."

Miss Emily slumped face-forward into her pie.

❅

The waitress frantically summoned a man from another table. He rose and hurried over. "I'm a doctor." He felt for her pulse and gently lifted her head. Chocolate and meringue stuck in globs all over her face. "Cold water," he called to the waitress.

I wet a handful of napkins in my water glass and held them out. "Here."

As he wiped her face, the napkins smeared chocolate, rouge, and makeup base all together, then began to fall apart, leaving little white blobs stuck all over her forehead and cheeks. She lolled in her chair and her head slipped to one side. "What happened?" the doctor asked, holding her in place.

We all shook our heads, baffled. "She was eating her pie—," Mr. Hugh Fred started.

I interrupted. "No, she'd put her hands in her lap. She was just sitting there when suddenly she went *wham!* right into the pie."

"That pretty much covers it," Uncle Stephen agreed. He looked down and seemed surprised to find his pipe in his hand. He shoved it back in his pocket.

"Does she have a history of fainting?"

"Never did before, to my knowledge. I'm her husband," Mr. Hugh Fred added.

Miss Emily fluttered her eyelids. "Where ... What ..." She saw Uncle Stephen, shuddered, and closed her eyes again.

The doctor gave him a strange look. Mr. Hugh Fred said, "This is our pastor, Stephen Whitfield, and his daughter, Carley."

It didn't seem worth pointing out I was a niece, not a daughter. The doctor wasn't the least bit interested in me.

Not until he asked, "And you don't know what brought on this attack?"

"Nobody attacked her," I assured him. "We were just sitting here talking about how we hope a friend of ours can clear himself of a murder charge, and—"

Now it was me the doctor was giving the strange look. Uncle Stephen motioned for me to hush.

"I think we ought to take her into the emergency room and at least check her out. I'll call an orderly." The doctor left the coffee shop.

Miss Emily opened her eyes again. "Hugh Fred?"

"I'm right here, honey. Don't worry. They're going to take you to the emergency room just to check you out. Maybe you're anemic or something."

She shook her head. "I'm not anemic. I ... Don't let them put Jerry in jail because of the medal. It was ... I ..." Her head slid to the side again. She would have fallen from her chair if Uncle Stephen hadn't caught her.

Mr. Hugh Fred jerked his chair close to her and held her in his arms. "She doesn't know what she's saying."

Orderlies arrived with a stretcher. Miss Emily was lifted onto it and covered with a sheet. Her poor smeared face and yellow hair looked too bright above all that whiteness.

Mr. Hugh Fred followed them out, then hurried back. "Almost forgot to pay. Here." He handed Uncle Stephen a ten-dollar bill. "Give that to the girl."

"You want us to stay with you?"

He shook his head. "We'll be fine. Get Carley home. She looks like she could use a nap."

Until he mentioned it, I hadn't known I was tired.

I stumbled to the car practically walking in my sleep. But I had to ask Uncle Stephen one question in private, so I waited until we were in the car. "Did Miss Emily say she killed Taylor Hart?"

"Not that I heard. But honey? Let's don't mention this to anybody right yet. Not even to Kate. Not until I can talk to Emily again. Okay?"

"Okay," I agreed drowsily. I didn't mind not having a rich daddy. I'd rather have an uncle who could talk to people and make everything all right.

I fell asleep almost before we pulled out of the parking lot, and slept all the way home.

I woke as the car came to a stop. Before I could get out, Abby came barreling down the front steps, yelling, "Carley's home! Carley's home!"

She held up her arms like she used to a year before. In spite of my burns I picked her up and let her wrap her legs around me, surprised to feel how long they were growing. She squeezed my neck so hard, I could scarcely breathe. "I do love you, Carley Cousin! I's so glad you didn't get bunned up. But you wasn't 'posed to go to de hospital again yet. Nex' time"— she shook her small finger in my face—"you wait 'til I is twelve."

Chapter 42

Abby went back over to Sue Mary's. I stayed on the porch, rocking and trying to remember if Miss Emily had actually confessed that she'd killed Taylor Hart. I couldn't figure out why she would decide to confess in a hospital coffee shop after all those years. Or why she'd gotten so upset all of a sudden. Looked to me like she'd have gotten upset around the time they'd started searching her barn.

I shifted to get more comfortable and tried to remember what Uncle Stephen had been saying just before she fell in her pie. Something about how if Mr. Donaldson went to jail, it would break Mrs. Raeburn's heart.

I decided that must be what made Miss Emily decide to confess. She was a peculiar woman where people in her family were concerned. Look how she went home with Mr. Hugh Fred the night he beat the tar out of her. And look how she drove like a madwoman down to Rock Hill to pick up Freda. She hadn't cared before if Mr. Donaldson went to jail for her murder, but now that he was about to become one of the family ...

When I was in sixth grade, I'd visited a big jail with Uncle Stephen. It was the dreariest, saddest place I'd ever been. I hated to think of Miss Emily locked up there. Her bright hair would fade, and I doubted they'd let her have her rouge and lipstick. Pretty soon she'd look like a ghost in all that grayness. I just hoped Freda would deign to visit her.

I'd gotten to that point in my thinking when I saw Mr. Keene's Hudson raising dust up the road toward their house. "They're home," I called to Aunt Kate.

She called to see how Miss Emily was and to ask if she could come get the key to fetch Mrs. Raeburn's things. Miranda said Miss Emily was "a bit shook up by life but all right, considering."

When Aunt Kate repeated her words, Uncle Stephen said, "That's not a bad description of a lot of folks most of the time. How about if we drive up together? And Carley, I'd like you to come visit Freda while I'm there."

I didn't want to go up there to be with a possible murderess. What if she decided to kill us all so we couldn't tell? But I couldn't say that, so I said instead, "Freda doesn't want me visiting her. She's watching television."

"Then come along and watch television."

I couldn't believe he'd said that, but it was an invitation that might never come again in our household. And surely Uncle Stephen and Mr. Hugh Fred between them could restrain Miss Emily if she got murderous again. "Should I call Abby to come, too?"

"Not this time." His voice was real serious. I figured he was going to see if Miss Emily would talk about what she'd said.

Aunt Kate dropped us off. Miranda came out with the key, her apron off. "Miss Emily said for me to go with you to help you find things." Uncle Stephen and I got out of the car and she climbed into the backseat. She didn't know maids rode in the front in our family.

I was both nervous and excited about going to the Keenes', since I'd never been inside. Uncle Stephen went into the kitchen and called softly, "Yoo-hoo. Hugh Fred? You around?"

"We're in the living room."

I stayed behind him for safety as we crossed a pale gold dining room carpet so thick, I was afraid I'd trip. The Keenes' living room was elegant, with the same thick, pale carpet as their dining room and all new mahogany furniture. The couch sat out from the wall and was pale cream with light celery and dark green pillows. The drapes were the same celery green with dark green tassels hung from the valance. One chair was dark green and one dark gold. Fancy china knickknacks sat on the creamy mantelpiece and on the mahogany tables. But nothing looked warm or friendly or even like it got used much.

Miss Emily was lying on the couch. I peered around and didn't see a gun, knife, or anything else she could use to kill us. Mr. Hugh Fred was sitting beside her holding her hand, though, and he looked real serious. I wondered if she'd made a full confession to him.

His eyebrows drew together as we came in. "Kate didn't say you were coming, too."

"She didn't know." Uncle Stephen bravely walked over to the couch. "You feeling better, Emily?"

She gave him a nod as pale as her living room. Maybe she wouldn't mind living in a gray jail after all. She might feel right at home.

"Where's Freda?" I asked when their gaze shifted to me.

He answered for them both. "In the back den watching television."

I headed that way feeling like an explorer on an expedition. I had no idea what a den was, how far back it might be, or what rooms I might blunder into on the way.

First I opened a closet door, then one into a tiny little bathroom under the stairs that made me wonder if the Keenes were as rich as everybody thought they were. Their bathroom didn't even have a tub, just a toilet and a lavatory for washing your hands.

Finally I found what must be the den. The biggest television I'd ever seen sat in one corner with a show going, but Freda was nowhere to be seen. Should I go looking for her or just wait for her to come back?

I decided to stay, because the room was so nice to be in. The walls were paneled wood and the dark red curtains looked like pure linen. A bookshelf filled one wall, but I was sorry to see that all the books were in sets. Big Mama said you could tell when people didn't read. They bought their books by the yard. The lower shelves were crowded with what looked like school notebooks and stacks of magazines. I walked over and saw they all had to do with lumber and furniture. Over in the corner was a large, fancy desk with a big brown leather chair on casters. More big leather chairs and a red Oriental rug made the room much nicer than the poky little office up at the chair factory.

A telephone sat right on the desk. Boy, Uncle Stephen sure could use one of those. He always had to go downstairs to use ours. But I didn't know anybody ever had two telephones.

Since I knew nobody was using the phone in the hall, I tip-toed over and picked up the receiver to see if it really worked or was just for show. I heard Freda giggle. "Oh, Frank, don't be silly."

"I do," a boy's voice replied. "I think you are simply beautiful."

I put my finger on the button as quietly as I knew how. Frank was the handsomest boy in her classroom. It looked like Charles Beal had been replaced. And it looked like the Keenes had not two but three telephones. One must be upstairs. No running down to answer and nearly breaking their necks in this house.

In the window over the desk I saw my own faint reflection. My glasses hid my eyes, which Mama used to say were my best feature. My face was peeling and all my hair in front was singed off. Nobody would be calling me beautiful anytime soon.

If ever.

With that cheerful thought, I sat down to watch TV. The show got pretty boring after a while—a lot of grown-ups complicating their lives and then complaining about them. I started to think about our own lives right then and about how far back I was in that big house, away from everybody. What if Miss Emily left the others and came looking for me?

Mr. Hugh Fred had no key in his door. I would have felt odd locking somebody else's door anyway, so I decided I'd just go check to be sure Uncle Stephen was all right.

I tiptoed down the hall and back to the living room in time to hear him say, "Emily, if you know something, you need to tell Jerry's lawyer. You can't let an innocent man go to jail."

I pressed my back to the wall beside the wide door between the two rooms. They couldn't see me and I could hear real well.

Except there wasn't anything *to* hear. Nobody was saying a word. If people on television stayed quiet that long, nobody would ever watch.

"Emily?" Uncle Stephen prodded.

"Don't bother her!" Mr. Hugh Fred lashed out. "She's had a shock. She needs to rest."

"She needs to clear her conscience."

Miss Emily whimpered.

"She doesn't know a thing, I tell you. She just came all over strange. Maybe there was something in the pie."

"She hadn't touched the pie."

"Well, maybe she had some refreshments at that D.A.R. meeting. Did you, Emily? Did you eat something there that disagreed with you?"

Miss Emily whimpered again, a pitiful little sound.

"Just leave her alone. I tell you, Stephen, if you keep sticking your nose in where it doesn't belong, you may have to find yourself another church. People won't stand for it much longer."

"Even if it costs me my job, I'm going to tell Jerry's lawyer that Emily knows something about that medal." Uncle Stephen sounded very sad.

"She'll deny it."

"Will you, Emily? Will you let Jerry go to jail for something he didn't do?"

She burst into tears.

Mr. Hugh Fred shouted, "I thought you'd have learned your lesson by now. So help me, Stephen—" I heard an enormous crash. "Remember where meddling got you last year? Remember?" His voice came in short gasps. I heard another thud and Uncle Stephen groaned.

I peered around the door. Uncle Stephen sprawled across his chair, which had fallen on its back. He was rubbing his face and his glasses hung crooked from his nose. Above him Mr. Hugh Fred stood panting like a furious bull.

As Uncle Stephen struggled to get up, Mr. Hugh Fred pulled back his foot and kicked him on the shoulder. "Go on home! Stop bothering Emily. I told you, she doesn't know a thing."

I flew into the room, shouting too. "But *you* know something. Something you aren't supposed to know. How did you know Mrs. Raeburn was meeting Taylor down at the barn that night? How did you find out? She told me this morning she and Taylor sneaked around like burglars, because they were afraid you'd kill 'em if—" I stopped, mortified.

Mr. Hugh Fred and Uncle Stephen couldn't have looked more astonished if Freda's horse had galloped into the living room. But I doubted Mr. Hugh Fred would glare that way at a horse. I wished I could call back my words and swallow them. Especially since Miss Emily had stopped crying and started to moan.

Uncle Stephen had to pull up his legs and roll over to get up. He rubbed his shoulder with one hand and reset his twisted glasses on his nose with the other. "Well, Hugh Fred?"

Mr. Hugh Fred gave a short, unfunny laugh, backed toward the other chair, and sat down. "What makes her think I knew they were meeting down there? And if I had, I wouldn't have followed them. I'd have locked Maddie up." He turned to Uncle Stephen and lowered his voice. "You know as well as I do that any man's going to naturally try to get what he can from a woman. It's up to the woman to set the limits, so it's your womenfolk you have to watch."

"I thought you were watching television with Freda," Uncle Stephen said mildly to me. But he couldn't fool me that they'd just been having a chat. He was still rubbing his shoulder.

"Freda isn't there. She's upstairs talking on the phone. Everybody in this blessed house has secrets. And I got, uh, nervous back there. But he did know they were going to meet. Remember? In the coffee shop this morning, he said maybe Mr. Donaldson found out they were going to meet down there and went early. You heard him."

Uncle Stephen stopped rubbing his shoulder and shoved back his hair. "That's right. I did." He wasn't looking at me. He was looking at Mr. Hugh Fred.

Miss Emily reached toward him. "No, honey. Please!" She sounded like he was about to leave her forever.

Mr. Hugh Fred made a little movement with his hand to show that what we were talking about wasn't very important. "I knew a lot of things Maddie didn't know I knew. Mama and I kept pretty close tabs on her."

Uncle Stephen turned his chair right side up and sat gingerly on the edge of it. He fumbled for his tobacco pouch and his pipe. "I've had some interesting discussions with Carley here about truth. We've talked about truth that's slanted to infer a lie, and truth that deliberately is less than the whole truth, which is another kind of lie. We've touched on God's truth, which takes in all there is to know but which we aren't given many glimpses of in this lifetime. But I don't think we've ever mentioned the kind of truth which looks like God's truth but has actually just been made to look that way."

As he filled the pipe with tobacco and tamped it down, I pressed my back against the wall and tried not to sneeze at the smell of something Miss Emily had in a bowl to make her room smell good. I didn't want them to remember I was there. But I was determined not to leave Uncle Stephen again until Aunt Kate got back. Slowly I slid down, and when nobody was looking, I scooted along the floor to where they couldn't see me over the back of the couch, unless they stood up and peered over.

"I wonder," Uncle Stephen said, almost as if he were talking to himself, "what the real truth is in this situation? Jerry says he was never in that barn. That's a truth I for one believe. Now, you say, Hugh Fred, that you didn't go down to the barn to warn young Taylor away from Maddie. That sounds like truth to me, too." He struck a match and sucked the pipe to get it going. "Emily here faints when I mention that a certain medal might convict Jerry and break Maddie's heart. I suspect there's a truth there somewhere, too."

I peeked between the legs of a nest of tables at one end of the couch and could see Mr. Hugh Fred real good and most of Uncle Stephen. Miss Emily, of course, I couldn't see, since she was on the other side of the couch.

Mr. Hugh Fred didn't move a muscle. Just watched Uncle Stephen lighting that pipe like it was a spectacle he'd never observed before. Uncle Stephen looked around for an ashtray but didn't see one. I'd never seen Mr. Hugh Fred smoke—not a pipe, not a cigarette, not a cigar. I couldn't think of another man in our whole church except Clay and Uncle Davy who didn't.

Uncle Stephen pinched the match and dropped it into his pocket, took several puffs, and filled the room with sweet blue smoke. "But I wonder if there's still another truth, one we haven't considered yet." Mr. Hugh Fred started cleaning the nails of one hand with the nails of the other.

"It must have taken a good bit of money to buy out that chair factory and bring it up to its current level of production, then buy this house."

Miss Emily whimpered. Mr. Hugh Fred nodded. "The war was good to us." His voice was hoarse. He stopped to clear his throat, then went on. "I had to work hard, of course, but the war orders helped."

"I understand you bought the factory practically at the beginning of the war. I called somebody this afternoon and checked on that. They said the old owner sold out in late forty or early forty-one. Before we even got into the war. Want to tell me where you got that kind of money working as a factory foreman?"

Miss Emily made a sharp little sound of pain. Mr. Hugh Fred was as charming as ever. "That's private, Stephen. Sorry."

"Not if it has anything to do with Taylor Hart's death. You're going to have to tell somebody eventually."

"What's he talking about, Daddy?" Nobody had seen Freda come to the door. I decided that when I grew up, I would never have thick carpet in my house. It made it too easy for people to sneak up on you.

"Nothing, honey," her mother said in a weak voice. "Go on back upstairs."

"No, I want to know. Why does he think Daddy knew about that boy's death?"

"He doesn't. Go on upstairs, Freda."

When she didn't move, Mr. Hugh Fred said sternly, "Honey, this is a grown-up talk." I scrunched farther behind the couch so nobody would suspect I was there. "Stephen here just wanted to know how I got the money to buy the factory."

"Oh." She went from interested to bored in nothing flat. "So tell him." When nobody spoke, she gave a little huff of disgust and decided to do it herself. "He made juice, Mr. Whitfield. My daddy was a juice maker."

Still none of the adults spoke but somebody shifted uneasily. Freda sounded more uncertain as she asked, "Isn't that right, Mama? Remember when I was real little and used to ask where Daddy was going at night? You said he was going to make juice."

The room grew so still, I had the feeling that everybody had left except Freda and me. Then I heard Miss Emily start sobbing softly.

"Why would you have said that?" her husband demanded angrily.

Miss Emily didn't answer; Freda did. She still sounded puzzled. "I begged to go with you, and she said you were going to make juice, but I must never go or I'd get burned."

Miss Emily's sobs grew louder. "Oh, honey! Don't! Don't!" Through the couch I felt her thrash back and forth. I hoped she couldn't feel the solid lump behind her that was me.

"Don't what?" Freda snapped. "I'm not doing anything! What's the matter?" When nobody answered, she gave a big huff. "Grown-ups are so silly." She turned and marched out of the room.

I crept back to where I could keep an eye on Mr. Hugh Fred and Uncle Stephen. Mr. Hugh Fred bent his head and swiped a hand across his face as if it needed cleaning. Then he spoke in a low voice. "Okay, Emily, I'm going to tell him." She moaned and whimpered the whole time he talked. "We had a still—Daddy and me. Daddy was a pharmacist and knew enough chemistry to make real good liquor. He sure didn't know enough about farming to feed and clothe us. And that old barn was standing there like it had been built especially for us. Clean water nearby. Private. And the Harts never went down there. They didn't even farm. So Daddy and I built a little still when I was about fifteen. He ran it nights, when Mama was asleep. It kept food on our table and put by a little bit for Maddie's education. Even as a little thing, she was already more interested in books than I was. But some two years later Daddy died." He looked at his hands as if he could see that day in his palm. "I was seventeen and dirt poor. When I looked down life's long road, I saw no future at all except working for Uncle Rob all my life. I wanted more than that. I wanted Emily, for one thing." Miss Emily moaned louder. "And nice things. I wanted nice things. So I decided to heed the Bible's wisdom that God helps those who help themselves."

"Actually, that's Ben Franklin," Uncle Stephen interrupted apologetically. "God's far more likely to help those who can't help themselves. But go on."

"I enlarged that still—tripled its size. And I made a good product. For ten years I sold hooch all over this part of the state and even down in South Carolina. Until I made enough money to buy the factory and send Maddie to college."

"And then you quit?" Uncle Stephen didn't sound like he believed that.

"Sure. I'm not greedy. And I always knew moonshining was wrong. I just figured on keeping at it 'til I didn't need it anymore."

"Same way any of us justify our sins. Go on."

"That's all. Now you know. You gonna turn me in?"

Uncle Stephen sighed. "Is that all, Emily?"

She whimpered and thrashed on the couch.

Mr. Hugh Fred gave an exasperated huff. "Okay, Emily, tell him about the medal." Without giving her a chance, he went right on. "I didn't know this until this afternoon, but one night Emily found that medal in Maddie's jewelry box. Maddie had borrowed one of her necklaces—"

"Earrings," Miss Emily said in a voice full of tears. "The pearls Daddy gave me."

"Earrings, then. So Emily went looking for them and found that medal. She thought maybe Maddie and Jerry—he was a teacher, for heaven's sake. He oughtn't be fooling around with a student. She went down to the barn looking for me to talk about what we should do. I wasn't there, so she came on back up here, then she realized she'd dropped the thing. She didn't want to go back for it, so she left it there. That's all there was to it. That's how it got there. But if we explain that to a lawyer, he's going to want to know how our family got into that locked barn when it was on Hart property."

Uncle Stephen scratched his jaw. "Maddie didn't say the medal was in a jewelry box."

"It wasn't." Miss Emily's voice was a scratchy whisper. "It was in the coin part of her wallet. That's where she often put earrings if she took them off while she was out, so after she came in and went to bed that night, that's where I went looking for them. She'd left her purse on the kitchen table."

"Emily sure wasn't stealing money from Maddie." Mr. Hugh Fred sounded exasperated, although Uncle Stephen hadn't spoken. "I gave Maddie every penny she had in those days. Supported Mama, Maddie, Emily, and Freda at that point. Emily went without a lot of things she was used to, just so Maddie and Mama could eat."

Uncle Stephen puffed at his pipe. "I suspected that barn had more to do with this than just being a good meeting place." He sat back in the chair, stretched his longs legs out before him, and smoked away. Mr. Hugh Fred watched him. Miss Emily moved fretfully on the couch.

Mr. Hugh Fred stood up. "Well, I hate to ask somebody to leave, Stephen, but I need to get back to the office. Think you and Carley—where's Carley?" He looked around. I scooted farther behind the couch again to be sure I was invisible. How on earth would I ever get out from there without being seen?

"Went back to watch TV, I expect." Uncle Stephen sucked on his pipe. "She's always begging me to get one of those things."

"You want one? I'll get it for you. Be pleased to do it. But Emily needs to rest, and I need—"

"You need to finish that story. The story of the night Emily went down looking for you and didn't find you."

That room grew so still, you'd have thought everybody had vanished like smoke. I heard a chair creak but nobody spoke. I was terrified to breathe.

Then Miss Emily hissed, "Don't tell him, Hugh Fred. He can't prove anything. He can't!"

The coffee table crashed to the floor and his voice lashed her, practically over my head. "You fool!"

She gasped and I felt her cringe hard against the couch cushions. "It was an accident! You said it was an accident."

"But I can't prove that, can I? Did you stop to think about that before you opened your mouth? Did you?"

"Don't hit her!" I heard a thump, then Uncle Stephen's voice, too, was almost over me. "Don't hit her," he repeated.

"I oughta beat her to a pulp." Mr. Hugh Fred took one huge breath, then slumped to the couch as if all the air had suddenly gone out of him. "Oh, honey, why did you have to tell him? Why did you have to tell him?" I heard great, racking sobs.

"Maddie?" Uncle Stephen asked. It sounded to me like he was righting the coffee table. "He wanted Maddie?"

"It wasn't Maddie. It was the still." Mr. Hugh Fred spoke in short, jerky sentences with gasps in between. "He showed up at the barn door. Demanded to know what I was doing there. Figured it out in a second. Came at me like a fury. Said it wasn't my property, I'd get his daddy in trouble. Said he'd call the cops. He shouted so loud, they could probably hear him up in the big house. Said I was ruining his daddy's good name and not fit for my sister to be related to. That's when I knew why he'd come down there in the first place—he must be meeting Maddie. I told him I'd make him a deal. He could leave her alone and I'd break up the still." He stopped to cough, a deep hacking sound that went on and on. Finally he took another deep and rasping breath.

"I would have, too. I never meant to kill him, Stephen. I didn't. I put out my hand to shake. He took a swing at me instead. Socked me in the jaw and sent me reeling back against a hot pipe. I came back hotter than that pipe. I hit him hard, he slammed against the edge of a two-by-four, and the next thing I knew, he was sliding to the ground. He was dead. I knew it before I even felt his pulse. And there I was, standing on his daddy's property wondering how the dickens I was going to get out of that fix." He gave a bark of a laugh that wasn't funny at all. "I was done with hitting for a while. Didn't hit a single person between then and just a few months ago." I heard a rustle and then he said softly, "I'm so sorry, honey." His hand practically grazed my hair as he reached over to stroke hers.

I ducked and inched back toward the end tables in time to see Uncle Stephen shoving back his hair. "So you loaded him on your truck and took him to the gully?"

"No, I put him in his own car and took him, then drove the car down the road and left it in a driveway. I didn't know it was Donaldson's driveway. It just seemed far enough away and handy. That was a dreadful coincidence."

Uncle Stephen didn't believe in coincidence. He often said everything was part of some pattern. I sure couldn't see the pattern right now, though.

"Was that the same night you went down with the medal, Emily?" he asked gently.

She nodded. "I had the windows open and I heard the shouts. I had it in my hand and forgot about it. I just grabbed up Hugh Fred's gun and headed down to the barn. I thought somebody was hurting him. When I got there, he wasn't there, but Taylor Hart was lying on the floor dead."

"I must have gone for the car." Hugh Fred sounded like he was hearing this for the first time, too.

"I was very wicked, Stephen. I knew it was Jerry's medal. But I couldn't let them take Hugh Fred. I couldn't! So I put it behind some old farm equipment near where Taylor was lying. I figured that would at least give them somebody to chase. Then I went home and got in bed. Hugh Fred came back much later. I didn't ask where he'd been or what he'd done, and I didn't tell him where I'd been or what I'd done. Some things are best left unsaid."

Some things are best unheard too. I huddled against that couch and wished I had gone to watch TV. Miss Emily wept on one end of the couch; Mr. Hugh Fred sobbed on the other. And Uncle Stephen stood over them looking like he wished the angel Gabriel would fly down and tell him what he ought to do next.

What he ought to do next was put out that fire!

That thump I'd heard a while back was him dropping his pipe. Now I watched in horror as a wisp of smoke, then a little flame, curled from where the pipe had landed. I tried to call out but my voice wouldn't work. All I could think of was the Mount Vernon auditorium and the roar of flames.

Before I knew I was going to move, I had jumped from behind the couch and was stomping the coals again and again. "Fire! Fire!" I yelled hoarsely.

I couldn't believe it went out so easily. I must have stomped it ten times after it was gone.

"Okay, Carley. Okay." Uncle Stephen held my shoulder.

I winced and squirmed away. "Ouch! That still hurts."

As he bent to pick up the pipe, we heard Aunt Kate toot outside. "Go on home," he said to me. "I'll be here a little while longer; then I'll walk on back. The exercise will do me good."

❃

I didn't tell Aunt Kate a thing about what had happened. When she asked about Uncle Stephen, I said he and Mr. Hugh Fred had to talk over church business. They did, in a way.

I sat on the porch watching. In a while I saw the sheriff climb the hill to the Keenes', trailing dust. He didn't have his siren on. He didn't have it on when he left, either. I looked hard but couldn't see how many people were in the car.

I was still rocking when Uncle Stephen got home. He looked a lot older than he had that morning. "Did they take them away?"

"Him. He begged me to leave Emily out of it and I agreed. She did what she did trying to protect him. And Freda will need her. So he told them what happened with the medal, except he said he took it from Maddie's wallet." He sank to the top step and spoke almost to himself. "I never saw a sadder sight than Hugh Fred's back as the sheriff led him away. His shoulders slumped and his feet just shuffled down the steps. If I hadn't known him back when he was the richest and most important person in town, I'd have sworn he was nothing but a big, overgrown boy." He sighed heavily, like he was carrying the world on his shoulders, uphill all the way.

"Pop used to say we're all like little children to God. That when people act big and important, it makes God chuckle like we chuckle at Abby trying to act big. And when we are most helpless, we most touch God's big heart."

"Your Pop was a very wise man."

"But Mr. Hugh Fred did dreadful things. Will God forgive him?"

"Would I forgive Abby, no matter what she did? Would I love her anyway?"

I remembered the squeeze of her arms around my neck that afternoon and how as soon as she put out her arms, I picked her up, no matter how much it hurt.

But before I could do any more thinking, Uncle Stephen pulled himself wearily to his feet. "We need to wash our hands and eat supper. I've still got to talk to Maddie and Jerry."

"Will we have the wedding tonight?"

"Not tonight. Hugh Fred's her brother, remember." He murmured as he went through the screened door, "She's already having the hardest day of her life, and I've got to go make it worse."

Chapter 43

They waited a week to have the wedding. By then Mr. Donaldson's burns were healing nicely and Mrs. Raeburn was up and walking around. They would both be going home the next day and wanted to go home together.

Uncle Stephen went down early, but he asked Clay and Laura to bring Aunt Kate and me. I was more excited about riding in the convertible than I was about riding with Clay, and was real sorry he wouldn't put the top down on the way. "When we come back," he promised, "and these ladies don't have to worry about their hair."

We left Abby pouting because she wasn't twelve and couldn't hold the rice basket. Grace told her to be good and she'd tell her a secret nobody else knew. That quieted her down, but she still glowered at us as we drove away.

Aunt Kate took along her cello so they'd have at least some music.

When we got there, we found Aunt Hannah, Uncle Davy, Miss Rilla, and Mr. Rob. "I called Emily," Aunt Hannah said in her breathless way, "but she's gone to her sister's down in Charlotte. Without Hugh Fred, who's gonna be best man?"

"I think Davy is the best man in Job's Corner," Mr. Donaldson said. "Will you do the honors?"

Uncle Davy straightened his shoulders in his blue Sunday suit. "I'd be honored."

Aunt Hannah had made two beautiful bouquets of orchids: white for the bride and pink for the maid of honor. I wondered whether it would be Aunt Kate or Laura who got to hold it, and couldn't believe it when Mrs. Raeburn said, "I have asked Carley to be my maid of honor."

We closed the door and Uncle Stephen read the service just like we were in church. When Clay and Aunt Kate sang their duet, Mrs. Raeburn—almost Mrs. Donaldson—got real teared up. But when they got to the place where they needed rings, Mr. Donaldson looked disgusted with himself. "I didn't think about that. I bought one but it's back at my house."

I unclasped the chain around my neck. "Here. It was my mama's, but you can borrow it until you get your own."

Never in my wildest dreams had I imagined Miss Maddie kissing me, but she held up her arm for me to bend down, and she did.

Finally Uncle Stephen finished with the questions and answers and got to the part we'd all been waiting for. "You may kiss your bride."

Mr. Donaldson bent over and gently touched her lips. Then they started to kiss like they couldn't stop. I could see that I hadn't practiced half enough for that kind of kissing.

"Well, old dears," Aunt Hannah said briskly. "Looks like it's time for the cake."

We passed around slices of cake on little silver paper plates we'd bought for the no-wedding, and punch in paper cups. I wondered if it was Sealtest lime sherbet, then was ashamed of myself and hoped Miss Maddie couldn't read my thoughts.

I got a whole rose of icing with my cake and was just licking the last bit from the corner of my mouth when Aunt Kate asked, "Carley, if I play it, will you sing the song I'd planned to sing at the reception?"

I looked around anxiously. "I'm not—" I'd vowed never to make music in public again.

Mrs. Raeburn—I mean, Mrs. Donaldson—gave me a little hopeful smile.

"I don't—I can't—" I sputtered like little John blowing bubbles.

Aunt Kate had her bow already on the cello.

In despair, I looked around the room. My eyes met Uncle Stephen's. He put a hand on my shoulder. "Just give us what you've got."

I guess that's all any of us can do. Know we aren't good enough, wish we had something better to offer, but step up and give the best we've got, warts and all. I swallowed my pride and sang.

God of our life, through all our circling years,
We trust in thee.
In all the past, through all our hopes and fears,
Thy hand we see.
With each new day, when morning lifts the veil,
We own thy mercies, Lord, which never fail.
God of the coming years, through paths unknown,
We follow thee.
When we are strong, Lord, leave us not alone;
Our refuge be.
Be thou for us in life our daily bread,
Our heart's true home when all our years have sped.

While I sang, I thought of Mr. Hugh Fred and all his hopes and fears. I thought of the mercy that Mr. Donaldson and Mrs. Raeburn had finally found now that they were in love. I thought of how much Miss Emily and Freda were going to need a refuge in coming months. And I thought how all of us would go home from the wedding to our own hearts' true homes.

When I finished, I darted a quick look at Mr. Donaldson. I wasn't sure how he'd take having a prayer sung at his wedding reception, but he was still smiling. Maybe it was the light, but it looked to me like he had tears in his eyes.

I was smiling and had tears in my eyes, too, by the time we got home. Laura had insisted that I sit in the front seat, and Clay put the top down. It was a glorious ride.

And when we got home, Abby came running to meet us, up well past her bedtime. "Did you have your weddin'?"

"We sure did."

"Did you t'row wice?"

"No, no rice. They'd have had to sweep the hospital."

"Did you bring me'n Grace some cake?"

"Yep." I handed her the pieces we'd brought back.

She gave us a smile like a cat who's overturned a milk can. "We's gonna haf anuffer weddin' in a few years. Jay asked Grace and she said yes. And she told me *first*." With a proud toss of her curls, she carried their cake to the dining room table.

Aunt Kate looked at Grace. "Is that right?"

Grace glowed with happiness. "Yes, ma'am."

"When did this happen?"

"He came over home when Geena had her operation, and we kind of fixed it up then. But we're gonna wait until I finish college, so I gotta sew faster and save more. I talked to Miss Nancy, and if you don't mind, she's gonna get me some sewing jobs from her customers, to do in the evenings."

Aunt Kate was so happy, she said she'd put both children to bed so Grace could go finish a dress for Laura.

Uncle Stephen came home to find Aunt Kate and me sitting in the dining room, drinking strong sweet iced tea and still talking about the wedding. He slumped into another chair. "Well, that's one more week in the life of Bethel Church. I can't remember many that have been this draining. I feel like I've been rode hard and put up wet."

Aunt Kate brought him some tea. He took a long swallow, then set down his glass and wiped his mouth. "Before I forget, how set were you on that music camp, Carley?"

I shrugged, then winced as the muscles tugged the sore skin on my back. "It would have been fun but maybe I can do it another year. When I learn to play better."

"What do you mean?" Aunt Kate had gotten up to take our glasses to the sink, but she came back and sat down again.

I traced the wet circle my glass had left on the table. "You know, when I get as good as Freda, maybe."

She reached out and put one hand over mine. I wished my nails were oval and polished like hers instead of square and short. "Mama has always believed you shouldn't brag on a child to its face, but I want you to hear me say this and know I mean it. You play beautifully. Far better than Freda ever will."

"Huh. Have you forgotten what a mess I made of the Christmas duet?"

"It wasn't you that messed that up. I know that and Miss Rilla knows it. She thinks you are exceptionally good, or she wouldn't have recommended you for the music camp."

"Really?" It felt like some big heavy bubble around my heart had just split wide open. I held on to the edge of the table to keep from floating to the ceiling like a balloon.

Uncle Stephen reached into his pocket and pulled out a piece of paper. "And it seems like there's another anonymous donor at Bethel who thinks you ought to go to camp. Davy gave me the check this evening."

It sat on the table between us, too precious to touch. Too precious to talk about. Too precious to hardly believe.

Then Aunt Kate started humming the song I'd sung earlier. I picked up the tune and started humming the harmony. Finally Uncle Stephen came in, a little off-key as usual.

> *. . . through paths unknown,*
> *We follow thee.*
> *When we are strong, Lord, leave us not alone;*
> *Our refuge be.*
> *Be thou for us in life our daily bread,*
> *Our heart's true home . . .*

He grinned and changed the last line:

> *. . . as we fall into bed.*

Postlude

Dear Abby,

Here are the stories I promised you. The reason you probably don't remember the Keenes is because they moved away that spring and the wonderful family who still lives there bought the house soon afterward. Mr. Hugh Fred didn't have to go to jail—the judge believed him when he said it was self-defense. I heard Uncle Stephen tell Aunt Kate that all the money Mr. Hugh Fred had given to politicians over the years didn't hurt any. But he sold the chair factory and bought a pickle company down near the coast. Freda actually turned out rather well. Married a small-town doctor, I believe.

I almost didn't tell you the complete story of the Donaldsons, since our John married their Louise. I wonder if they have ever told her about their wedding?

Mr. Donaldson remained principal of the new Mount Vernon school until he was promoted to Statesville High. But you know that. He was your principal after he was mine.

Mr. Wash got back from the war in one piece, except his hair had turned completely gray. By then Clay and Laura already had two of their four children and had

437

built their new brick house and his garage in the yard where Mrs. Cameron's store used to be.

I'm sure you remember Nancy's Nook. By the time Mr. Wash got home, it was such a successful business, he told Uncle Stephen, "I couldn't shut her down if I tried. Nancy's a born businesswoman and simply loves what she's doing."

"She's also making money," Uncle Stephen told Aunt Kate later. "Wash never turned down a dollar in his life."

Geena, of course, was all right after her surgery, and Grace went to college the year Jay graduated. They were married when he finished medical school, and Uncle Stephen and Aunt Kate drove back to Job's Corner so Uncle Stephen could help officiate at the wedding. Uncle Stephen told me once he was almost prouder at that wedding than he was at yours and mine.

As for Unshaded Windows, it went the way of any other failed television show. What Uncle Stephen said about truth made me do some serious thinking. I realized that you and I left our shades up for very different reasons. You wanted to offer hope and help; I merely wanted to pry. Since I went through the hard school of experience in the spring of fifty-one, I have never needed to know more about anybody else's life than they wanted to share. I went home from the Donaldsons' wedding and pulled down my shades.

If your children read this story, you can tell them that as soon as you started school the following fall, you stopped talking funny. Not that it's entirely true, but I think Big Mama would call that a socially acceptable lie. It's at least a family myth.

Enjoy.

With love,
Carley

PATRICIA SPRINKLE draws on her deep Southern roots to write three Southern mystery series. For a complete list of titles, see www.patriciasprinkle.com. She lives in Smyrna, Georgia, with her husband, and when she's not writing, likes to read, swim, work with children, and do nothing.

"...at life," Donaldson asked. He ... removed it quickly as he squinted with pain. "Why don't ... let her rest for now?"

"Not yet." Mr. Donaldson's voice sounded funny, like it was still choked by smoke. "I'll go in a minute, but I have something to say to Maddie first. Push me over to the bed again." He said

She could look in ... could tell from Kate's voice that ...

Breinigsville, PA USA
28 July 2010
242594BV00001B/123/P